SUN, MOON & SHADOW

Sun, Moon & Shadow

LORIN COFFLER

Copyedited by Briana Ozor with Ozor Edits (@ozoredits)

Cover Design by Rena Violet with Covers by Violet (@violet.book.design)

Map Illustration by @shepengul

Formatted by Lorin Coffler with Atticus

First Edition 2025

ISBN 979-8-9988357-2-8 (Hardcover)

ISBN 979-8-9988357-1-1 (Paperback)

ISBN 979-8-9988357-0-4 (eBook)

For those who have fought for the peace they have,

and for those still fighting to find it.

AUTHOR'S NOTE

Sun, Moon & Shadow is a romantasy novel with dark themes and is intended for readers who are age 18+. It contains material that some readers may find upsetting, including the following:

Some explicit language

Explicit sexual content

Death (including magical creatures)

Violence

Gore

Abduction

Attempted SA (unsuccessful)

Strangulation

Murder

Domestic violence/abuse

Reference to depressive episodes

Mention of suicide (off page)

Mention of death in childbirth (off page)

Loss of a parent

Animal attacks

Sleep paralysis

Bullying

Please don't hesitate to reach out to the author if you feel anything should be added to this content warning.

CYRAELIAN

RAVEN'S ISLE

SCHADWEN
MOUNTAIN

SILVERGARD

DIRE WOODS

ISLE OF ILLORA

NEPHARI
MOUNTAINS

TUNDARA

THE GRAY
MOUNTAINS

ICE FIELDS

NIVALI

LOTUS
LAKE

MAP OF AEMORIA
THE FAE REALM

TERRITORIES OF AEMORIA

Pyralis – Autumn Court
Patron Goddess – Embra | Hunt & Harvest
Noble Magic – Fire Wielding

Nivali – Winter Court
Patron God – Brumal | Transformation
Noble Magic – Snow & Ice Wielding

Silvergard – Lunar Court
Patron Goddess – Orika | Change & Influence
Noble Magic – Mind Reading, Mind Control

Tundara – Summer Court
Patron God – Brakos | Sea & Storms
Noble Magic – Water Wielding, Storm Conjuring

Maedwen – Spring Court
Patron Goddess – Elowen | Birth & Growth
Noble Magic – Shapeshifting

Sonnend – Solar Court
Patron Goddess – Aurore | Life & Light
Noble Magic – Healing, Conjuring Sunlight

Raven's Isle – Shadow Court
Patron God – Unknown
Noble Magic – Unknown

Independent Lands

Isle of Illora – Temple of Illora
Patron Goddess – Illora | Protection & Guidance

PRONUNCIATION GUIDE

Character Names

Nova – NO-vuh
Callan – CAL-inn

Agnes – AG-niss
Anders – ANN-derz
Anson – ANN-sin
Arik – ARE-ick
Bronna – BRAWN-uh
Clara – CLAIR-uh
Daví – dah-VEE
Eir – AIR
Elena – ell-AY-nuh
Estrid – ESS-trid
Evander – eh-VAN-der
Fawn – FONN
Idrian – IDGE-ree-inn
Iris – EYE-riss
Isla – EYE-luh
Ithan Greylock – EE-thin GRAY-lock
Karlsen – CARL-sin
Lilith – LILL-ith
Liv – LIV
Lucan – LOO-kin
Luna – LOO-nuh
Nox – NOX

Omen – OH-min

Onyx – ON-icks

Oren – OR-inn

Rowan – ROW-inn

Ryker – RYE-ker

Sable – SAY-bull

Thorn – THORN

Zara – ZAR-uh

Family Names

Greenmore – GREEN-more

Nyhauslen – NYE-hows-linn

Elsever – ELL-sev-er

Place Names

Timberfell – TIM-ber-fell

Aemoria – eh-MORE-ee-uh

Pyralis – puh-RALL-iss

Nivali – nih-VAHL-ee

Silvergard – SIL-ver-gard

Sonnend – SONN-ind

Maedwen – MED-when

Tundara – tun-DAH-ruh

Raven's Isle – RAY-vins isle

Schadwen – SHAD-when

Nephari – neh-FAR-ee

Deities

Embra – EM-bruh
Brumal – BRUM-all
Orika – OR-ick-uh
Aurore – uh-ROAR-uh
Elowen – EH-loh-when
Brakos – BRACK-ose
Illora – ih-LORE-uh

Creatures

Lycane – LIE-cane
Yaesira – yeh-ZEER-uh

Celebrations

Hayer – HIGH-er

ONE

NOVA GREENMORE STOOD HIDDEN away in a prison of her own making: her two-story limestone cottage, located on the outskirts of Timberfell.

"Go away. Go away," she murmured as she spied on her unwanted visitor through a narrow slit in the curtains.

She watched as Ryker glanced toward his carriage parked on the street at the end of the walkway, its door emblazoned with the Ramdon family crest. But he didn't go away. Much to her dismay, he resumed his insistent knocking, rapping his gloved knuckles against the solid oak of her front door with renewed enthusiasm.

Nova pressed herself flat against the wall beside the second-story window, holding her breath as she continued watching him through the gap in the pleated fabric. Thank the gods Agnes was tending to the garden, too far away to hear.

Several agonizing minutes later, Ryker's chest rose and fell in a visible huff. He spun on the heels of his shiny leather boots, his short cape twirling around his shoulders as he stormed down the stone walkway and disappeared into his waiting carriage. Nova released a hushed sigh of relief when the coach rounded the corner, finally out of sight.

She exited her chamber, rushing down the hallway, the sound of her low-heeled boots jarring in the quiet of the empty house. Stopping short, she paused before the door leading to her father's chamber and reached her hand out slowly. The ornate metal knob felt cool against her palm. She hesitated for a breath before easing the door open a crack.

The heavy drapes were drawn, leaving the space dark and surprisingly cold for late summer. *Like a tomb*, she thought. Apart from a thick layer of dust coating every flat surface, the room was immaculate. Nova's gaze fell upon the bed, and she flinched, tugging the door closed and hastening her steps toward the back staircase.

Nova reached the base of the stairs just as Agnes entered the kitchen. Her housekeeper smiled warmly, swiping a hand over wisps of golden hair hanging loose from her high bun. Ten years her senior, Agnes had come to work for the Greenmores when Nova was only six. She was the closest thing to family Nova had left in the world.

"Did I hear knocking?" Agnes asked, turning out the potatoes and onions she carried in her apron onto the wooden worktop. She wiped her hands on the smock clinging to the swell of her pregnant belly, her cheeks flushed a healthy pink from the exertion of digging in the soil.

"It was only Ryker Ramdon," Nova replied blandly, leaning against the sideboard.

"And what did he have to say for himself?" Agnes raised an eyebrow.

"Nothing." Nova looked down at her boots. "I didn't answer the door."

Agnes shook her head, clicking her tongue as she set to work rinsing the vegetables in a basin of water.

"I imagine he was hoping for an answer to his proposal."

"Most likely," Nova said, lazily dragging her forefinger through the thin layer of flour that dusted the worktop. "But it's far too early in the day to entertain visitors."

"Nova." Agnes twisted to face her, a nagging finger held out in the space between them. "You could do a lot worse than Ryker Ramdon."

Agnes turned back to the basin, resuming her task. Nova rolled her eyes.

If she were at all inclined to join her life with another's—and she definitely was not—Nova knew she could do much better than Ryker Ramdon. He came from a well-to-do Timberfell family, but there was already an heir ahead of him set to inherit the family fortune. A union with Nova would give him control of her land and properties, which had passed to Nova upon her father's death two years earlier.

"To him, I'm no different than those rare horses of his. I'd be nothing more than a broodmare to trot out whenever he feels like showing off."

Nova had no desire to be possessed by such a man, kept as a unusual addition to his collection.

Agnes sprinkled some more flour on the worktop and began rolling out a ball of dough to form the crust of a savory meat pie. Taking up her wicker basket, Nova crossed to the door.

"It's just not right. You living all alone in this big, empty house with nothing but ghosts and bad memories to keep you company." Agnes shook her head with an exasperated sigh. "Where are you headed?"

"The Wood. I'm running low on supplies."

"Watch yourself, and see that you return home in one piece—and on time! The babe is already hungry." Agnes ran a hand over her stomach, resting the other on her lower back. "I can't promise I won't eat your supper as well as my own."

Several hours later, Nova emerged from the Wood, the dense forest stretching along the western edge of the city. She'd lost herself foraging, wandering happily through the thick undergrowth. The late-afternoon sun beat down on her back, and her basket swung on her elbow, heavy with fresh cuts of willow bark and bundles of chamomile.

Like all children of Timberfell, Nova had grown up hearing cautionary tales about the ravenous, wild beasts and supernatural creatures believed to inhabit the Wood. Unlike other children, though, she'd spent the better part of her childhood exploring it without ever encountering any danger, and she considered the stories to be just that—stories.

As a child, she had been fixated on faerie tales, legends, and folklore. Her father indulged her interest, filling his library with collections of such tales, all of which Nova read countless times.

As she grew older, she took an interest in the books her mother had left behind, books on the medicinal uses of plants. Nova's dedicated study of that topic led to her profession as a healer of sorts, which supplemented the rents she collected from her tenants. The women in town might gossip about her, but they still knocked on her back door for teas and tonics to ease the pain of their cycles or prevent them from falling pregnant.

Nova sifted through her haul with soil-coated fingers, suddenly halting her steps beside the crumbling rock wall that crept along the edge of the dirt cart road. She shot a glance over her shoulder, brushing loose strands of long black hair out of her face.

Nothing.

Narrowing her eyes, she peered into the thick forest beyond the rock wall, listening intently. No sound apart from the trill of the swallows and warblers. She started up again and continued down the road, unable to escape the sensation of eyes upon her back.

Before long, her footsteps met the gray stone streets of downtown Timberfell. The main thoroughfare was alive with the sounds of customers bartering with street vendors for the last deals of the day. Nova paused for a moment beside the florist's cart, admiring the vibrant pinks and purples of the freshly cut dahlias and chrysanthemums.

"What have I told you about begging in front of my shop?" a gruff voice shouted nearby, drawing Nova's attention.

She turned just in time to see the butcher yanking a boy, one of the many urchins that roamed the streets begging, up by his elbow. The butcher, a disagreeable, red-faced man, shoved the boy off the curb, sending him careening into the street. He came to rest in a crumpled pile of slender limbs and soiled clothing at Nova's feet.

She crouched down, took the boy gently under the arms, and hoisted him onto his bare feet. Without speaking, she turned her gaze on the butcher, staring at him until he took several backward steps toward the door of his shop.

"Don't let me catch you out here again," he warned the child with a menacing look, jabbing a finger in the boy's direction. He briefly met Nova's eyes again, muttering "witch" under his breath, before passing swiftly into his shop and slamming the door.

Nova faced the boy. He appeared largely unharmed, though he stood unmoving, staring at her with sunken eyes as wide as an owl's. Nova opened her purse and pressed two silver coins into the boy's grimy hand, dirt caked under his unkempt fingernails. He glanced down briefly then scampered off into the crowd without a word of thanks or a backward glance. Nova sighed quietly and returned the pouch to a pocket hidden in the folds of her skirt.

The streets grew crowded as she reached the Temple in the town square. The faithful pushed past her, making their way inside to secure a seat for the evening ritual. Nova's eyes traveled from the polished silver collection vessel beside the entrance to the intricate carving in the gray granite above it: the Two-Faced God, a symbol of balance in all things. Life and death. Order and chaos. Good and evil.

Nova preferred the Forgotten Gods, the ancient ones, so human in their spite and passion. But they'd been replaced, lost to time. All she knew of them had been gleaned from a single aged book of folklore.

She turned her back on the towering structure of cold stone and the deity keeping careful watch over the city. The faithful veered around her, a stubborn stone in a riverbed, refusing to yield to the current. The remaining coins in her purse clinked against one another as she began to make her way home. The Two-Faced God had taken more from her than it had ever given; she'd keep her money for herself.

The familiar sound of hushed voices carried from the farm stand across the way. Two young women about her age stood casting sideways glances at her and whispering to one another. Nova kept her expression neutral but fixed her pale gray eyes on the gossips, staring unblinkingly at them until they hooked arms and rushed off, weaving a path through the bustling crowd.

Once the women were out of sight, she looked up to the sky, sensing a hum of energy in the air. A storm was coming. She pointed her mud-caked boots toward home as the sky began to darken with thunderheads rolling in from the west.

Stares and whispers from the townsfolk were nothing new. Nova's mother had been an outsider, and folk often whispered that she was a faerie from the Wood. That she bewitched poor, unsuspecting Anson Greenmore, saddling him with a strange half-breed daughter when she died in childbirth less than a year after they wed.

As a child, Nova's eyes had been large, set on her pale face below a cascade of raven hair—a stark contrast to the fair-haired and ruddy residents of Timberfell. It was her eyes that seemed to inspire the most distrust, the pale gray color giving her a somewhat otherworldly appearance. The other children were generous with their taunts. *Half-breed. Changeling.* Now, on the eve of her twenty-fifth birthday, Nova's armor against such abuse was damn near impenetrable.

The wind gusted as she turned onto the narrow drive that ran alongside her home, billowing the fabric of her charcoal day dress. Clasping her basket close to her chest, she gathered her skirts in her free hand, preparing to outrun the rain.

She spotted it an instant too late. A carriage sat parked nearly around the corner, hidden by an overgrown bush bursting with pale pink hydrangeas. A cloaked figure emerged from behind a nearby elm, catching her off guard. She sidestepped, bumping against the corner of the house just out of view of the street.

Looking up, Nova found herself face-to-face with Ryker Ramdon, a man she had unfortunately known since childhood. He had been one of her most enthusiastic tormentors, though she'd obviously captured his attention for other reasons once she'd come of age.

"Miss Greenmore." He addressed her formally, as if there was anything proper about his unannounced and unwelcome visit. He lowered the hood of his cloak, his hair, the color of cornsilk, blowing in the breeze.

"Mister Ramdon," she replied flatly, pulling her head as far back from him as her position against the house would allow. "How . . . unexpected."

"I was under the impression that all women enjoyed surprises." He smirked, icy blue eyes glinting.

"I suppose it depends on the surprise," she said, glancing briefly at the empty road. No one walking or riding by. She was on her own.

"I expected an answer by now." He took a step toward her, his body now uncomfortably close to hers. "I think you'll agree I've been more than patient."

Nova restrained the grimace threatening to spread across her face.

"My answer is no," she said matter-of-factly. "I have no interest in marrying."

Placing a palm firmly on his chest, she attempted to push past him. He took her by the shoulders and pressed her against the wall, the corner of a limestone brick digging into the space between her shoulder blades.

Still a bully, desperate for a reaction, after all these years.

Anger tinged with fear swirled in her chest, but she maintained an outward mask of calm, refusing to give him the satisfaction. The wind was picking up speed, and loose strands of her hair lashed her across the face.

"My proposal was perfectly respectable, Nova." His tenor voice hissed past his teeth, a sneer stretched across his thin lips. "Any woman can see what I have to offer."

"Then, by all means, go pursue any other woman," Nova replied, disinterested. Inwardly, she seethed at his use of her first name.

"As if you're some prize," he spat. "Surely you know what everyone says about you."

She clenched her jaw at his arrogance. As if she needed him. Or anyone else for that matter.

"I'd be doing you a favor, you know." He pressed the length of his body against hers. A high-pitched warning tone rang out in her mind.

"You should be on your knees . . . thanking me," he rasped against her ear.

Nova shoved him, knocking him off balance. He released her, stumbling back a few steps before falling on his ass in the dirt. She spun away, her long strides carrying her to the rear door of the house as the sky opened up and fat raindrops pelted down from above.

"I'll be seeing you again soon, Nova," Ryker called out after her, his voice bordering on a snarl. "I always get what I want eventually."

Nova slammed the door behind her, the click of the lock falling into place a balm for the panic churning in her chest. She rested her forehead against the smooth wood, willing her breaths to slow.

Hasty footsteps approached the kitchen from the hall, stopping just inside the doorway.

"Nova?" Agnes's reedy voice was laced with concern. "Is something the matter?"

"Nothing at all, Agnes," Nova sighed, crossing to the window in the far corner of the room, pausing to pat Agnes's arm reassuringly.

Nova peeked discreetly through the gap in the pale blue curtains. A heavy rain was falling, the wind shaking the limbs of the trees lining the road. Ryker had disappeared, likely gone to lick his wounds at the tavern nearby. Nova turned to face her housekeeper and leaned back casually against the windowsill.

"Shall I draw you a bath before I leave for the night?"

"Yes, Agnes. That would be lovely."

TWO

Night fell, and the rain continued to come down in sheets, falling at an angle and pinging against the windowpanes. Agnes had returned to the cottage she shared with her husband outside the city limits. Nova draped a damp washcloth over her face, wondering what she would do once Agnes's baby was born and Agnes left to begin her new role as a mother.

Perhaps she would travel. Seek out some far-off destination and start fresh as she'd so often dreamt of doing when she was younger. Ryker's increasingly aggressive pursuit of her certainly made the idea of disappearing all together an appealing one. In all likelihood, though, Nova would refuse to hire a replacement, fully submerging herself into her life as a social outcast.

Every night, Agnes made a fuss before she left, going on about how she hated leaving Nova alone at the end of the day. But Nova considered herself a night owl and secretly treasured the time alone, cocooned in the quiet safety of her home, free to spend the dark hours however she pleased. All too often, memories blew in on the evening breeze, wrapping around her thoughts like coiling snakes and hindering her sleep.

Rising out of the bath once it started to go lukewarm, Nova toweled off her long limbs and walked from the bathing chamber into her adjoining bedroom. She stood before the mirror, turning her face from side to side to inspect her reflection. Ryker insisted she was nothing special, but surely judgments made on the basis of looks were subjective.

Nova regarded herself in the antique glass. Her pale cheeks were still pinked from the steaming bath. Glossy black hair hung to her mid-back; it fell in loose waves when dry. Her gray eyes, admittedly piercing, were crowned by fine, dark brows. One brow arched a touch higher than the other, giving her a somewhat prim, inquisitive expression. Her nose sloped delicately, the end slightly upturned over her mouth with a full bottom lip. Wide cheekbones tapered down to a pointed chin.

Nova rose on her tiptoes, glancing down at her body. Her breasts weren't large, but they were perky. Her torso narrowed at her waist before spreading out at her wide hips and round bottom. Long, shapely legs, strong from regular horseback riding, extended down to slender ankles.

Nova huffed and turned her back on the mirror. Honestly, who cared what that pompous prick thought anyway?

She pulled a white sleeveless shift over her head, the airy fabric gliding over her warm skin. Taking the candlestick from atop her chest of drawers, she padded barefoot past the gallery wall lining the hallway to the den, which had once been her father's study.

A low fire crackled amiably in the fireplace. Agnes had kindled it before she left, knowing Nova spent most nights curled up in a chair reading. Nova fed another log to the flames, her eye catching on the lifelike oil painting of her parents hanging above the mantel when she stood. As she studied it, her mind wandered to an evening many years before.

She'd been thirteen, sitting on the carpet, resting her chin on the worn-leather arm of her father's chair, and staring up at the canvas.

"Will you tell me the story of how you met?" she asked. Normally, she didn't press her father for information about her mother, wary of dredging up painful memories and setting off one of his moods. But she'd heard the story so many times it could have been one of the tales in her anthology of faerie stories tucked away on the nearby shelf.

Her father smiled faintly, taking a deep breath before he began.

"It was a fine autumn day," he said, looking up at the portrait of his late wife. "The sky was a wide-open field of blue. Not a cloud in sight. I'd been out surveying property lines at the far end of the fields near the Wood all morning. Around midday, I found myself with an empty stomach, so I settled onto the bench of the wagon and signaled for my horse to head home."

He always acted out this part of the story, clicking his tongue on the roof of his mouth and jiggling a set of imaginary reins.

"She didn't move. I tried again and gave her a little tap with the switch, but she stayed put. Just turned her head and looked at me. I hopped down and checked all four hooves, legs, and . . . nothing. But still the horse wouldn't budge, just stood there twitching her tail without a care in the world. I was scratching my head like a fool when suddenly I saw her—Elena—standing at the edge of the Wood."

He paused, and Nova knew he was seeing her mother in his mind, as clearly as if it had been only the day before.

"I couldn't breathe the entire time she walked toward me. Her hair was long and dark, flowing down her back, and she had the most striking eyes I'd ever seen. Green and gold, shining from within."

Nova had often heard folk speak of her mother's beauty. Had any other man happened upon her at the edge of the Wood, they would have cast the strange woman out of town. But her father had always treated everyone he met with respect regardless of their rank, earning him a place as a trusted member of the community despite his lack of nobility.

"We were joined at the temple two weeks after we first laid eyes on each other. Folk wished us well, but most kept their distance. Elena was as kind and gracious as any noble lady, but there was an energy about her, a hum like an approaching storm. It was partly what drew me to her, but many found it unsettling.

"We lived together happily until the following summer when Elena left this world giving me the greatest gift imaginable—you. Our time together was so short, I awoke many mornings convinced she'd been only a dream. But there you were, my living, breathing reminder of Elena and the love we shared, however brief it was."

He cupped her cheek tenderly and smiled down at her, though he couldn't hide the immense grief she knew he still felt. Guilt gnawed at Nova's stomach, knowing she didn't share his pain. It was difficult to mourn someone she'd never known.

A sudden pop from the logs drew Nova back to the present moment, eyes once again scanning the smooth lines of the painting. The artist had captured her father's likeness perfectly, from the golden swirls of his hair and his wide, proud smile to the playful gleam in his warm brown eyes.

Another image of her father's face flashed in her mind, unbidden. Ashen skin and a fixed gaze, as he'd looked the day she found him in his bed two years earlier, dead from an attack the physician said had stopped his heart. Prone to bouts of profound sadness, her father had often relied on Nova as a caretaker. His episodes kept him bedridden, refusing to eat or bathe, often for weeks at a time. Nova stifled a shudder, refocusing her attention on the painting. She preferred to remember him that way.

It was the only likeness she had ever seen of her mother, her wavy hair a dark mahogany complementing her olive skin. With their vastly different coloring, Nova could see no resemblance between herself and the beautiful woman in the painting.

Her mother stared down at her from her perch on the wall, head bowed slightly, green eyes gazing up from under thick lashes. Her demure smile conveyed genuine happiness, but she seemed to be shrinking back slightly, her arms wrapped protectively around the swell of her belly in the foreground. Adorning her hand was a unique ring: a simple silver band set with a large oval stone the color of fresh milk.

Nova had spent countless nights analyzing her mother's expression. Her eyes held a hint of something Nova could never quite put her finger on, as if she knew something Nova didn't.

Nova set the candlestick on the wide desk on the right-hand side of the room and approached the bookshelves lining the wall directly behind it. The knotted-pine walls glowed warmly in the firelight, giving the den the feel of a secluded mountain cabin, cloistered away from the outside world. She ran her fingertips along the leather-bound spines of the books, her most prized possessions and, somewhat pathetically, she thought, her dearest friends.

Settling on a collection of legends about the creatures of the Fae Realm, she flopped down onto the armchair, hooking her legs over the side. Soon, she was transported to the exciting and dangerous world of the Fae, teeming with mythical creatures like lycane, massive bloodthirsty wolves, and large reptilian cats called yaesira.

As the clock in the hall chimed ten, a sudden surge of energy flooded Nova's body, an intense sense of awareness settling over her like a shroud. She sprang to her feet and crept to the nearby window, parting the heavy drapes slightly to survey the garden below.

The rain had stopped. The moon, nearly full, bathed the yard in pale light. A flicker of movement at the edge of her vision drew her attention to the narrow laneway at the side of the house. Immediately, she thought of Ryker. Perhaps he'd returned to avenge his wounded pride. She swatted the thought away. Perhaps it was someone in need of a tonic. But no one ever visited her home so late.

A few moments passed in silence. She had nearly convinced herself the flicker had been nothing more than a trick of her eyes when a firm string of knocks sounded against the door at the rear of the house. Her heart leapt into her throat, her breath coming out in a startled choke. She waited for a beat, and the visitor knocked again.

Nova crossed to the desk and threw open a shallow drawer, searching blindly for the letter opener stowed there, her eyes trained on the darkness beyond the study door, which stood slightly ajar. Finally locating the makeshift blade, she grasped it tightly, curling her fingers around its tiny hilt. She took the candlestick in her free hand, the taper melted down to a waxy stump, and entered the darkened hallway, holding both the candle and the letter opener out in front of her.

Nova slipped through the house quickly even in the dim light, skipping over the one step that always groaned in protest as she descended the back staircase to the kitchen. Peeking her head through the archway at the bottom of the stairs, she scanned the room before entering. Nothing appeared out of place.

She crept into the kitchen and set the candle on the sideboard before approaching the door, her back hugging the wall and furniture as she went. Holding her breath, she rose up on her toes and peeked through the pane of decorative stained glass on the upper portion of the door.

She saw no one.

Confused, she flipped the lock and grasped the knob, pulling the heavy door open slightly, her shoulder braced against it as a precaution. She stuck her head through the opening and craned her neck from one side to the other. Suddenly, a towering figure draped in a cloak stepped out of the shadows and into a shaft of moonlight falling upon her doorstep.

Definitely not Ryker.

"Nova Greenmore?" the stranger asked, the voice low and unfamiliar.

With the moon at his back, his face was hidden in shadow below his hood.

Nova gathered all the composure she could muster in spite of the alarm twisting in her stomach.

"Yes. Who are you?" she demanded, silently thanking the gods for keeping her voice from trembling.

"My name is Callan Nyhauslen. I've been sent on behalf of your mother."

"My mother?"

Disarmed by the unexpected and unbelievable statement, Nova stepped back and waved the stranger into her kitchen before she could think better of it.

THREE

THE ABSURDITY OF WHAT she'd done struck her like an arrow as soon as she heard the latch fall into place, and she turned to face the imposing figure standing in her kitchen. Water dripped from his charcoal cloak and brown boots, a puddle forming on the slate tile beneath him. Nova took several backward steps before bumping against the wooden worktop in the center of the room. She glanced down at her flimsy shift and the letter opener still clutched in her hand.

Nova slapped the paper knife down on the worktop and spun around, searching the room for anything to serve as a robe. The best option was Agnes's apron hanging on a hook by the hearth. Nova snatched the flour-dusted smock, slipping it over her head and tugging the strings tight behind her back. Finally, she turned to face the stranger who stood motionless, observing her.

She could see him more clearly in the candlelight, though his hood still obscured his face. Beneath his cloak, he wore a gray tunic and black breeches, his leather boots reaching just below his knees. His clothing was well-made but rumpled, the soles of his boots caked with mud. Brown leather bracers covered each wrist, and a dagger sat sheathed at his right thigh. His broad shoulders spanned the doorway, and, while Nova was taller than most women she encountered, this man's chin could rest comfortably atop her h ead.

She cleared her throat, ridding her voice of any emotion before she spoke.

"What do you know of my mother?" she asked, motioning for him to sit.

He crossed to the small table and lowered himself onto a dining chair, the seat looking decidedly dainty beneath his large frame.

"Her name was Elena," he began, his voice low and smooth. He laid his right hand flat on the tabletop and rested his left on top of a long, muscled thigh. "She arrived in Timberfell roughly twenty-six years ago."

Nova regarded him with interest as he spoke but kept her expression blank, her arms folded across her aproned chest.

"She was a healer," he continued.

Nova blinked. She hadn't realized her mother's interest in plants was anything more than a hobby. She crossed to the sideboard where the candle-flame flickered lower and lower, the wick nearly spent. Keeping a watchful eye on her visitor, she rifled through the top drawer for a new taper, lighting it on the old one's flame just before it extinguished. The small kitchen was bathed in warm light. She placed the candlestick in the center of the table where her visitor sat, taking the chair opposite him.

The light illuminated Callan's face below his hood. He appeared to be roughly her age. He had the look of a hunter or a tracker. Someone often on the road and accustomed to sleeping under the stars. Damp strands of dark hair fell across his forehead. Stubble covered his strong jaw and edged his full lips. His eyes in the candlelight captivated her. Brown with vibrant gold striations, they glinted against his warm brown skin, reminding her of the tiger's-eye gemstones from the southern shores she'd once seen for sale in the market.

Nova closed her eyes briefly, reining in her racing thoughts. "Did you know her?" The question felt silly even as she asked it. He could have been no more than a few years old when her mother died.

"No. But I know someone who did." He leaned forward, placing both hands flat on the table in front of him, as if bracing himself. "Someone who wishes to see her again."

"I'm afraid that's impossible," Nova said flatly. "My mother died bringing me into the world."

"It's true no one has seen your mother in many years, but she didn't die the night you were born."

"I don't understand. What do you mean?" Fighting the impulse to laugh at the absurdity of the conversation, she leaned in closer, eyes narrowed.

"Your mother didn't die," he repeated, his voice dipping lower. "She returned to her home in Aemoria. The Fae Realm."

Nova stared at him dumbly for a beat, unable to form coherent thoughts, let alone speak.

"Your mother was Fae," he clarified, his eyes locking with hers.

Nova's chest seized as if her breath had been stolen, whether by the revelation or the effect of his gaze, she couldn't be certain.

"And how would you know that?" she whispered, an almost imperceptible tremble in her voice, born of equal parts disbelief and hope.

"Because I've traveled from the Fae Realm to find you." He shifted in his seat and lowered his hood.

A bright light filled the room, seeming to shine from within him. The ends of his dark hair brushed his shoulders, the strands damp and slightly wavy. Silver flecks glistened on his cheekbones, standing out against his rich complexion and drawing her attention to the fine points of his ears. For an instant, gone was the road-weary tracker, and in his place sat a regal Fae male.

The sight of him left her breathless.

Nova sat stone-faced as a shield fell back into place, putting a damper on Callan's light. Her heart thundered in her chest, so forcefully she was certain it must be visible through her thin gown. She rose from her seat, battling the urge to start pacing before the hearth.

"If my mother is Fae," she asked, "what does that make me?"

Callan stood, taking a tentative step toward her. She did not shrink away from him.

"It makes you Fae, as well."

"But my father was a mortal man. He died only two years past." Her words spilled out of her. The unsettling image of her father's pale face flashed in her mind once again, but she shoved it aside.

Her grip on her composure was beginning to slip. Suddenly, the room was spinning.

"Nova, sit," Callan said firmly. He took her hand in his, and an unmistakable rush of energy shot through her at his touch. She stifled a gasp, nearly yanking her hand away. He guided her back to her seat, and she fell into it.

"I'll tell you a story." He crouched before her, speaking in a low, lilting voice, as if soothing a skittish horse.

"There once was a Fae female who fled to the Human Realm. There, she wed a human male and gave birth to a Fae child. A daughter she shielded with a glamour set to expire on the twenty-fifth anniversary of her birth. Once the glamour faded, her true nature would no longer be hidden in the mortal lands." He paused. "That child was you."

Nova felt as if she'd sunk underwater, her movements slowed, Callan's words muffled and almost unintelligible. She stared at his hand loosely holding her own, unable to decide if she was offended by him speaking to her as if she were an upset child, or grateful he'd sought to find a way to soften the blow.

"Your mother left this for you," he said, releasing her hand and reaching into a small leather pouch at his hip. He produced a folded parcel of yellowed parchment. Nova peeled open the package and tipped it, something solid scratching along the aged paper as it slid out then landed in her palm.

A ring.

Nova pinched her brows together. A simple silver band set with a white oval stone. She turned the treasure over in her hands, holding it up to the light and examining it closely. It certainly looked like the ring from her mother's portrait.

Nova slid the ring onto her finger, calling to mind a dream she often had as a girl. In it, she would see her mother calling out to her from the Wood, glowing faintly like an apparition, her voice a distorted, faraway echo. Each time Nova neared, her mother would vanish, reappearing a short distance away and calling her name once again. A wisp luring Nova deeper and deeper into the forest.

Looking back, Nova always considered the dream a manifestation of the childish wish she'd kept hidden in her heart: that her mother was *not* dead. That one day they would be reunited, far from her lonely existence in Timberfell. Now, she wondered if perhaps the dream was a vision planted by her mother. An invitation extended all those years ago.

"What part do you play in all of this?" Nova murmured, slowly spinning the band around her knuckle.

"I've been sent to collect you."

An image flashed in her mind: Callan slinging her over his broad shoulder and carrying her back to the Fae Realm. The thought sent an unexpected thrill along her spine.

"Time is short," he said, pulling her from her thoughts. "We have only hours before the glamour expires. You can't be in the Human Realm when that happens. You won't be able to hide your true form, and I suspect the townsfolk won't take kindly to a Fae living among them."

Callan held her gaze, still kneeling on one knee before her. Nova clasped her hands tightly in her lap, mind reeling. Superstition would have her believe that one should never trust a faerie. She searched his eyes, finding nothing but sincerity there. Deep within her, smoldering like an ember, was an inexplicable but overwhelming sense that she could trust *him*.

"I suppose I ought to get dressed first," she said as she stood and tugged at the apron strings.

Nova braved the chill of her father's chamber for the second time that day, seeking some of his old clothes, still neatly folded in the armoire. Though baggy, the brown breeches were the right length thanks to her height. The gauzy, cream-colored shirt hung loose about her shoulders but concealed her stays underneath. She pulled on a pair of her own brown leather riding boots and a hooded cloak of forest green.

As an afterthought, she lifted the lid of the decorative box atop her father's chest of drawers, gingerly removing a dagger from within. The narrow blade extended from the base of her hand to just beyond the tip of her middle finger. It was a simple, practical weapon, the blade a bit tarnished and a strip of brown leather wrapped tightly around the hilt. It slid nicely into place inside the makeshift sheath of her boot.

As she turned to leave, Nova's eyes fell upon the bed. Her chest tightened with the weight of finally bidding her father the farewell she'd been unable to utter in the two years since his death. Her cheeks heated with the shame of how often she'd wished to escape her life. To escape *him* and the gloomy pall of his melancholy, so oppressive she often feared it might consume her as well. How she, so absorbed with her own self-pity, had dreamt of disappearing and starting fresh somewhere new.

Nova shook her head, as if the motion could erase the terrible memories, and opened the door. She inhaled sharply, startled to see Callan waiting on the other side, his form nearly filling the entire doorway. His face was partially in shadow, lit only by the low flame of a candle. She cleared her throat, unsettled by how silently he moved and the way he observed her. As someone accustomed to being viewed with disdain, she found his benign interest unnerving.

Nova pushed past him, quickly descending the front stairs and heading for the writing desk in the parlor. Once she sat, her pen hung poised in the air over a piece of blank parchment for several minutes. How could she possibly explain to Agnes what had happened? Where she'd gone? Still, she couldn't bear the thought of her friend finding an even emptier house and no explanation. No, she had to leave a note.

She hastily penned some nonsense about a last-minute journey to visit relations far from Timberfell. She asked Agnes and her husband to look after her affairs in her absence, weighing the paper down with a small leather pouch full of coins. There was no other family, as far as she knew. The previous winter, Nova had paid a magistrate to draw up documents naming Agnes as the beneficiary of her estate. If she never returned, her land and property would legally pass to her dear friend. The knowledge that Agnes and her family would be provided for eased the sting of leaving a bit.

Pressing her lips together, she scanned the familiar room, taking it in for what was likely the last time. The fading floral wallpaper. The small throw pillow on the sofa she had embroidered as a girl.

A faint knock sounded on the doorframe, and she looked up to find Callan waiting there.

"We should be going," he said quietly, urgency clinging to the edge of his voice.

Nova signed her name to the message and laid the pen flat on the desk.

She joined Callan at the parlor door. Biting back sentimental tears, she looked up at him with a resolute nod.

"I'm ready. Let's go," she said and blew out the candle.

FOUR

CALLAN LED THE WAY through the darkened house with Nova close on his heels. He regretted there hadn't been more time to ease her into the reality of the situation, but it had taken him much longer than expected to track her down.

Humans with the family name of Greenmore lived in nearly every city he'd stopped in along the border with Aemoria. Most were squat and stout, their sanguine complexions clashing with cornsilk hair. He'd known she was the female he sought the moment he laid eyes upon her as she walked along the cart road earlier in the day. An unmistakable energy surrounded her, invisible and crackling. It set her apart from everyone else. Marked her as different. If the interactions he'd observed were any indication, the humans could sense it as well, though they likely didn't understand what they were feeling.

Callan had trailed her through the city center, keeping close to the storefronts and observing her from beneath his hood. The townsfolk avoided her much as one avoids a root in one's path, weaving and sidestepping, wary of making contact. Her stony countenance had broken only once, when she'd helped the boy off the ground, and Callan had smiled to himself at her

25

kindness.

When he followed her home, he'd sensed the male hiding behind the elm tree from a distance, but could do nothing to warn her. Callan had nearly revealed himself when the swine laid his hands on her, his intentions clearly written in the sneer cutting across his ruddy face. But before he could act, she'd knocked the bastard flat on his ass and made it safely into the house.

The male had taken his carriage to a nearby tavern, where he proceeded to down mug after mug of ale. Callan watched him like a hawk from a shadowy corner, forcing down bites of stale bread and dry cheese. Hours passed before the fair-haired male finally stumbled out of the pub and into his waiting coach, which carted him off in the opposite direction of Nova's residence. Only then was Callan satisfied she was safe.

He met Frost in front of the tavern, his horse's hooves clacking rhythmically on the wet stones. Mounting the steed, Callan rode back to Nova's cottage. The street had been sleepy in the daylight; under the light of the moon, it was dead. Dismounting quickly, he sent Frost trotting around the back of the house with a slap on the rear. The horse liked to wander but never strayed too far. Hiding himself behind the same elm along the laneway as the male had earlier, Callan waited. For what, he wasn't certain. He sensed her within. Knew she was alone. Even so, he found himself gathering his courage to approach the quiet house. To approach her.

After all he'd observed, he understood why she so readily accepted what he told her. Considering the significance of the revelation, he was impressed by how calm she was. Her only outward reaction was the slight quickening in her pulse fluttering at her throat, a change imperceptible to humans but obvious to him.

The hinges creaked slightly as he eased the rear door open and peered out into the quiet night. He whistled sharply, and Frost trotted out from the shadows. Callan jogged over to the brilliant white stallion and patted the side of his long neck. He detached his sword sheath from the saddle and slipped it over his head so the blade lay across his back.

Nova appeared opposite him, slowly approaching Frost with an out-stretched hand. Laying her palm flat on his muzzle, she murmured softly, and Frost snorted a friendly greeting.

"Let's be going." Callan held the stirrup steady and motioned with a tilt of his head for her to mount.

"I'm perfectly capable of riding my own horse. I can fetch her from the stables." She pointed to a small barn a short distance behind the house.

"I have no doubt. But she won't be able to cross the Boundary into the Fae Realm. I'm afraid you'll have to leave her behind. And you'll have to ride with me."

Nova stared at him for a beat, then crossed in front of the horse to where Callan stood waiting.

"Very well," she said, grabbing the pommel as she stepped into the stirrup and swung her long leg over the horse's back with ease. She adjusted her cloak as he mounted behind her. Taking hold of the reins, he nudged Frost into a canter toward the dense forest west of the city.

They reached the edge of the Wood a short time later. The full moon had illuminated the expanse of open field as they neared the forest, but it was dark under the thick canopy. Frost moved deftly through the shadows, his hooves navigating nimbly over rocks and roots.

Callan attempted to focus on the overgrown path, but time and again, his attention drifted to the female in front of him. The act of sharing a saddle was unavoidably intimate. The warmth of her body nestled close to his chest distracted him. As did the feeling of her ass seated firmly between his thighs. Her hair, still damp at the ends, hung in a long braid down her back, and a pleasing scent wafted off the inky-black strands. Closing his eyes for an instant, Callan inhaled discreetly.

"Where is this Boundary?" Nova's hushed whisper startled him. "I've explored these woods since I was a child, and I've never seen anything."

"It's invisible," he said, grateful for the diversion from his thoughts. "Thousands of years ago, some benevolent Fae rulers decided humans were ill-suited for the Fae Realm. The Boundary was formed to prevent mortals from entering. Approach the Boundary by sea, and it appears as a great, impassable rock face rising out of the water. By land, it appears as treacherous mountain ranges, or dense, pathless forests."

"Have you ever entered the Human Realm before?"

"No. Fae generally take little interest in the lives of mortals."

She asked no further questions.

After nearly an hour of riding in silence, Callan sensed the Boundary ahead and pulled back on the reins, bringing Frost to a halt. Nova straightened in the saddle as he swung his leg over the horse's rear and dropped to the forest floor.

"Why have we stopped?"

"We should cross on foot." He reached out a hand to help her down, but she dismounted on her own, sliding down from the saddle and standing toe to toe with him. Callan felt the urge to lean in and pull away in the same instant. "Once you pass to the other side, the glamour will vanish, revealing your Fae form."

He grasped Frost's reins in one hand and took Nova's hand in the other, starting toward the invisible wall separating the human lands from Aemoria. Nova tugged her hand out of his grasp. Her expression was neutral, but he spied the telltale flutter at her throat.

"When I change, will it hurt?" she asked, her tone not fearful but pragmatic.

"No," he said. "No doubt it will feel strange, but, if anything, you should feel energy coursing through you, not pain."

Nova gave a determined nod and followed close behind as he continued on. A familiar sensation greeted Callan as he crossed the Boundary: All sound faded, and time seemed to slow to a crawl. A great pressure pushed against his body, like swimming into a strong current.

He glanced at Nova, who trailed him by a few steps, her eyes shut tightly. Taking her hand, he pulled her the rest of the way through. The pressure lifted when they reached the other side, and he could once again hear the wind rustling through the trees.

Nova opened her eyes and took a couple of steps toward Frost before stopping short and bringing her hands to her chest, clutching at the loose fabric of her shirt. Beneath her hands, a ball of pale light bloomed, slowly spreading along her limbs and up her neck toward her face. Nova's eyes grew wide, and her body trembled faintly. She fell to her knees and hunched forward, digging her fingers into the moss carpeting the forest floor. Her cloak enveloped her body entirely, the hood falling over her head. A sudden burst of white light appeared, emanating from within her and vanishing just as quickly into the surrounding darkness.

Nova crouched on the wet ground, motionless. Callan approached her slowly, placing a hand lightly on her shoulder. She bolted upright at his touch, stretching her arms out in front of her. A faint glow radiated from beneath her milky skin, like pale moonlight. She brought her hands to her face and lowered her hood, peering up at him.

Callan's breath caught at the sight of her. In her human form, she had been lovely; without the glamour to dim her true essence, she was stunning. Her features were sharper, from her pointed nose and her high cheekbones to her ears tapering into delicate points. Her hair was a shade so black it seemed to absorb all light.

But the most extraordinary change was to her eyes. Only moments before, they had been a steel gray, bold and striking. The eyes looking up at him now were the palest shade of gray with a glinting ring of silver around the iris.

Callan shook his head, breaking her hold on him, and knelt down in front of her.

"Are you injured?" he asked. She appeared stunned but unharmed. He reached out for her hand, but, again, she pulled it away. "Can you stand?"

She nodded and shot up onto her feet, wobbling a bit. He braced her by the elbow as they walked toward his horse.

"It will take some time to adjust," he explained. "You'll be faster and stronger. All of your senses will be heightened. It'll be overwhelming at first."

He placed her foot in the stirrup and hoisted her up into the saddle.

An eerie howl rang out through the trees, and Callan's spine straightened to attention. A lycane was nearby. Nova was no match for one of the beasts in her current condition, even with her newfound strength. He shoved the reins into her trembling hands and unsheathed his sword.

"Nova, listen to me."

She was obviously dazed and overwhelmed by the world around her. Her eyes didn't meet his, but she cocked her head in his direction, a vague indication that she could hear him.

"Stay with Frost. I'll lead the lycane away. Do not get off the horse."

She still couldn't meet his gaze, but she nodded jerkily, her eyes flitting rapidly from one random spot to the next.

Callan cursed under his breath as he sprinted off through the trees in the direction of the howl, his sword ready.

FIVE

NOVA'S SENSES WERE AMPLIFIED, and she took notice of every tiny detail in the forest around her.

The forked veins on the leaves.

The faint whistling of the wind blowing through the limbs of the ancient trees.

The loamy scent of fallen leaves decomposing in the soil beneath Frost's great hooves.

She was aware of everything, but incapable of focusing on anything.

Her eyes darted around the forest illuminated by the pale moonlight filtering through the treetops. She twisted in the saddle at the sharp snap of a twig cutting through the quiet from behind her. Her breath came in short, rapid bursts through her nose as she stared into the night. At first there was nothing—no sound, no movement.

Then, two glowing eyes appeared, glinting like gold coins against the darkness. Nova instantly recognized the creature stalking toward her.

A lycane.

The dark fur of the beast's coat split from the surrounding shadows as it drew closer, looking exactly as described in her faerie books. It emitted a low growl, and Frost shook his head, snorting nervously. The lycane lunged forward, snapping at the horse's hind legs. Frost released a startled whinny before tearing off at a gallop and heading deeper into the woods. It was all Nova could do to keep hold of the reins, pressing her thighs together as hard as she could to remain seated atop the panic-stricken animal.

Without warning, the lycane shot out in front of Frost from the flank, cutting him off, and the mighty stallion ground to a halt. Nova pulled hard on the reins, sending Frost rearing up on his hind legs. She tried to hold on, but the horse threw his head back, launching her through the air. Her temple struck something hard as she landed on the ground, and pain tore through the side of her skull.

Nova rolled onto her hands and knees and attempted to stand. A sharp, searing agony in her head sent her right back to the ground. The world spun around her, and she braced herself, tunneling her fingers into the damp soil. She vomited on the ground, intensifying the throbbing pressure in her skull. Disoriented, she vaguely registered the lycane slinking in a wide circle around her.

The beast approached unhurriedly. As it closed the distance between them, nearly coming within striking distance, a wave of fresh terror washed over her. Its fur was coal black, the moonlight reflecting off it like armor as it stalked through the trees. If she were standing, the creature's snout would nearly reach her shoulder. It lifted its head in her direction and sniffed at the air, its lip curling back to reveal long, curved teeth as it dipped its head low to the ground, yellowed eyes narrowed on her.

With a snarl, the beast lunged.

Nova was on her feet in a heartbeat, turning and sprinting for her life. Outrunning the lycane was impossible. She opted to lead it into a nearby clearing instead, where she might have a chance of defending herself.

She made it two strides into the clearing when she was jerked back and thrown to the ground. The beast's great paw had come down on the hem of her cloak. It would have been comical if she wasn't a breath away from being torn apart. Clawing at the clasp at her throat, Nova managed to free herself. She tried in vain to crawl away from the creature, her fingers raking through the moss and mud.

It was no use.

The beast came down on her back with its massive front paws, its breath hot on the back of her neck. She heard the crunch of bone in her left shoulder, the sound chased by fiery pain as talon-like claws tore through her flesh as easily as the fabric of her shirt.

Hot blood rushed from the wound, soaking the tattered muslin, the sensation igniting a rabid desperation within her. The beast let up for an instant, and she twisted onto her back, facing the jaws snapping at her. Her left arm lay limp and useless at her side, but she lashed out violently with her right, her hand squeezed into a tight fist. The animal pulled back with a whine as she made solid contact with its snout. Suddenly, it dawned on her: Lycane, though monstrous, were flesh and blood.

Vulnerable.

All at once, she remembered the dagger sheathed in her boot. She yanked it out just as it settled on her again, its muscled foreleg pressing down on her injured shoulder.

Nova collapsed in on herself, swallowed whole by a memory conjured by the creature's crushing weight upon her. She struggled for air as a boy sat on her chest, his hands at her throat. Her forearms pinned beneath his shins, skin scraping against the rough dirt of the schoolyard. A group of children stood huddled around them, urging the boy on. Darkness seeped in from the edges of her vision, blocking out everything but the boy's crooked grin as he stared down at her.

Ripped back to the present moment, she cried out in pain, her high-pitched shriek sending the beast into a frenzy. She felt her energy ebbing away, like the tide receding from the shore. Gathering what little strength remained, Nova bucked and kicked until she had her legs between her and the lycane, the bottoms of her feet pressed flat against its chest and underbelly.

Gripping the dagger in her right hand, she held it over her chest with the blade pointed toward the starry sky. Her leg muscles quivered against the sheer weight of the creature, its gnashing jaws edging closer to her throat.

A roar spilled forth from somewhere deep within her.

Then, her legs gave out.

Nova's aim hadn't been perfect. Metal scraped against bone as the lycane crashed down upon her. The creature let out a sharp squeal, and she felt the rush of its blood on her chest. It twitched once and then was still. A rush of energy coursed through her despite the near exhaustion she'd felt only seconds before.

Pushing against its chest, she rolled the creature off her. Stunned, she rose up onto her knees, staring dreamily at the hilt of her dagger poking out from between the animal's ribs. She spied Callan at the edge of the clearing and reached out for him. Her vision narrowed down to a pinprick, and everything around her melted away as if the entire world had been snuffed out like a candle flame.

Callan was using the slain beast's coat to clean the blood from his blade when he heard Nova's scream. He sprinted in the direction of the sound, noting that it came opposite from where he'd left her. Within a minute, he arrived at a large clearing. Under the full moon's light, he saw Nova pinned to the ground by a second lycane. Fighting viciously, she braced her long legs, bent slightly at the knees, against the animal. Callan rushed to the clearing's edge, his sword raised. Then, Nova roared.

A battle cry. Wild and desperate.

Callan froze.

In the same instant, her legs fell, and the creature collapsed onto her, struggling briefly before going still.

A paralyzing fear seized him. He watched as Nova shoved the body of the lycane off her and it tumbled onto its back. Callan spied a dagger buried to the hilt in the creature's chest. Nova rose onto her knees, facing him, her shoulders hunched. She saw him. Reached out for him. Then fainted.

He closed the distance between them in a breath. She was unconscious, drenched in blood, and covered in mud. He knelt down beside her, making a hasty inspection of her injuries. There was a wound to her scalp. The hair on the right side of her head was sticky with blood, but head wounds often looked worse than they were. He turned her over gently to check her back and flinched at the deep gouges running down her shoulder blade, bone visible beneath the ruined muscle.

He needed to get her to Pyralis—fast. Callan cursed himself aloud for leaving her unprotected.

Lycane lived in groups but hunted alone. More might not be far off, especially once they scented the blood of two of their pack on the wind. Callan laid Nova flat on her back. With great effort, he freed the dagger from the beast's chest, securing it in his belt.

A mournful howl sounded in the forest, far too close for comfort. Callan whistled sharply, and Frost emerged, almost sheepishly, from the darkness between the trees. Growling a reprimand at his horse, he lifted Nova up, draping her over the animal's wide back and covering her with his cloak. Callan mounted hastily and gave a snap of the reins, sending Frost racing through the forest toward the Pyralis Estate.

Signaling to the sentries posted on the high stone wall, he passed through the tall wooden gates just as the sun crested the peaks of the mountains to the east. Dawn's first rays ignited the perpetually red and orange leaves of the surrounding trees, reaching out toward the horizon in every direction. Callan pressed Frost on at a gallop until they reached the small courtyard at the entrance to the residential wing reserved for the Noble family.

Dropping down from the horse, he shoved the reins into the grasp of a confused stable hand who met him at the foot of the steps. Hauling Nova down, he hoisted her over his shoulder, her head and arms dangling behind him, his forearm secured over the backs of her thighs. When he reached the entrance, he kicked open the massive wooden doors, bursting into the common area.

"Fawn!" His urgent shout reverberated off the lofted ceiling. "I could use your help down here!"

Six

It was not Fawn but Evander who first appeared, shirtless and bleary-eyed, on the landing at the top of the staircase. He leaned his elbows on the railing, squinting down at Callan.

"Cal, what in the name of the gods is going on?" he asked groggily, massaging his forehead with one hand.

Fawn jogged onto the landing seconds later and skidded to a halt beside her brother, tugging the sash of her robe tight around her waist. One glance at Callan and his strange cargo in the entryway and she was wide awake, skipping down the staircase two steps at a time.

"What's happened? Is that her?" she asked rapid-fire, darting behind him with the frenetic energy of a hummingbird and bending to get a better look at the female thrown over his shoulder like a shapely sack of potatoes.

"Yes, this is Nova. A lycane attacked her."

Evander, who had made his way to the foot of the staircase at a leisurely pace, circled them, inspecting. He was now fully awake but maintained his typical relaxed demeanor.

"There's hardly a drop of blood on you."

"She took down the beast herself," Callan said, twisting his neck to face him.

Evander's eyebrows lifted. "Impressive."

Fawn popped up beside Callan.

"How could you let this happen, Cal?" She pressed long, delicate fingers against her temples. "You only had one task."

"What do you want me to say? There were two beasts. I led one away not realizing another lurked nearby."

His patience was wearing thin. The two of them regularly made a habit of getting on his nerves.

"You were gone so long, I thought perhaps you'd decided to abandon your folk and live amongst the humans." Evander smirked.

"She's injured," Callan snapped. "Is there a bed available, or would you have me lay her out on the dining table?"

"Oh—of course—follow me!"

Fawn raced back up the stairs, her long auburn hair flying out like a cape behind her. Callan followed her into the hallway lined with chambers for the Noble family and their guests. Poking her head out of an open doorway halfway down the hall, Fawn waved him in wildly.

He laid Nova on the maroon velvet coverlet and adjusted her head so it rested atop a pillow, then sat on the edge of the bed beside her. In the bright candlelight, she looked far worse than he had originally assessed. Dried blood caked her hair and coated the right side of her face. Bits of moss and twigs clung to her thick braid. Nearly every bit of her was covered in blood, mud, or a mixture of the two. Gently, he lifted her right hand, laying rough fingertips against her wrist and finding a flutter of a heartbeat.

Fawn appeared beside him, balancing a basin of warm water in one arm and carrying a stack of cloth strips in the other. Evander flopped down into a brown leather armchair in the sitting area near the cold stone fireplace.

"Evander, make yourself useful," Fawn chided as she organized her supplies on the bedside table.

Evander waved a hand lazily toward the empty hearth. A blazing fire sprang to life, crackling and popping cheerily. Fawn leaned in close, inspecting Nova's head wound.

"I'm afraid that's the least of her worries," Callan said as he slowly rolled Nova onto her stomach, revealing the injury to her upper back.

Fawn gripped the thin fabric of Nova's shirt and tore it down the middle. Four deep, red slashes split the flesh of her pale back. And yet, it was clear the wounds had already begun to heal. The edges had puckered slightly, the tissue beginning to knit itself back together. Fae healed rapidly, but injuries such as hers typically required the aid of a healer. Evander pushed on the arms of the chair, briefly lifting himself up for a better look, and let out a slow whistle.

"That's it." Fawn clapped her hands loudly. "Show's over. I need to remove her clothing to clean her wounds, and I won't have you two standing around gawking."

Evander rose to leave at once, always eager to be reacquainted with his bed, but Callan remained frozen to the spot beside Nova. He wanted to be the one to clean the blood from her face. To be the one waiting when she woke. It was curious.

"Out, Cal." Fawn tugged on his arm, practically dragging him from the bedside and across the room, where she deposited him in the corridor. He turned, intending to ask her to send for him as soon as Nova woke, but she slammed the door in his face. Callan spun around to find Evander watching him.

"Did she take much convincing?"

"Actually, no. She was surprisingly receptive to the idea."

Evander's gaze appeared momentarily calculating. Callan's intuition flickered, but the flash of shrewdness vanished as quickly as it had appeared, replaced with Evander's usual mischievous glint.

"Get some rest, Cal—you look awful." Evander smirked and strolled down the hallway to his room.

Humming with agitation, Callan retired to the quiet of his own chamber. The fireplace was empty, but he didn't mind the chill. Hailing from the perpetual winter of Nivali, the crisp autumn air of his current residence was nothing compared to the frigid winds and swirling blizzards of his homeland.

He slipped his sword sheath over his head and laid it on the low table in his sitting area, disturbing a thin layer of dust coating the flat surface. The dagger he kept sheathed on his right thigh soon joined it. Callan examined the dagger Nova had used against the lycane, turning the weapon over in his hands. The blade was simple but well-made by human standards. He hadn't known she'd been carrying a weapon. She certainly was full of surprises. Clever, too. The echo of her battle cry rang out in his mind suddenly, the memory sending a chill through his entire body.

Sinking into a brown velvet armchair before the hearth, he fought the overwhelming urge to pace the perimeter of the room. An uneasy feeling coiled in the pit of his stomach as he dragged his hands over his face. Never before had he felt this way.

In the woods, the instinct to protect her had consumed him entirely, bringing her to safety his only concern. With Nova out of his sight, being cared for by someone else, he felt utterly useless and out of sorts.

Callan rose from his seat and crossed the room, throwing himself onto his bed, hoping for sleep. After two weeks of tracking Nova down in the Human Realm, coupled with the excitement of the past several hours, he should have been exhausted. Instead, he remained wide-eyed, restlessly tapping his thumbs on his chest as he watched the early-morning light creep across the ceiling. After an hour or so had passed, his stomach grumbled, and he resolved to get up and find some way—any way—to distract himself.

He rolled off the bed and entered the attached bathing chamber. Catching his reflection in the mirror, he noticed the shoulder of his gray tunic was stained with blood. A large rust-colored smudge marred his cheek as well. He yanked the tunic over his head, draping it on the edge of the tub. Having no patience to wait for the water to heat, he scooped a handful of icy water from the sink, splashing it on his face and running it through the length of his hair. His jaw was rough with a rasp of stubble, but, considering how jittery he was, he decided holding a blade to his throat was ill-advised.

He took a fresh tunic from the wardrobe, this one blue, and pulled it on before exiting his chamber, pausing in the hall just outside the door to fix the belt at his waist. He glanced down the hall toward the guest chamber where he'd left Nova. No sounds came from within.

The telltale clink of cutlery told him someone was helping themselves to breakfast in the common area on the lower level. He made his way down the wide-planked oak staircase. Evander sat alone at the long dining table crowded with platters of fresh bread and jam, boiled eggs, sausage, and fruit. Callan loaded up a plate and helped himself to a steaming mug of tea before taking a seat across from Evander.

Always dressing the part of a proper heir of Pyralis, Evander wore a finely tailored cream-colored tunic embroidered with gold thread, brown breeches, and shiny brown leather boots. His chestnut curls lay in a tousled mess atop his head, and his hazel eyes held their customary glint of mischief.

"Gods cousin, you still look a mess," Evander chided, rubbing a hand over his own clean-shaven jaw.

"I've slept in the dirt more than I've slept in a bed for a fortnight. What do you expect?" Callan speared a sausage and focused his attention on his meal.

"Quite the appetite this morning." Evander tossed a bit of bread into his mouth.

Callan rolled his eyes. "Any chance you wish to join me at the training field this morning?"

"Can't, I'm afraid. I'm overseeing preparations for Hayer. I promised Mother I'd see to it while she's away."

The Noble Lord and Lady of Pyralis were visiting allies in nearby Tundara but were expected to return for the harvest celebration in a few weeks' time.

"And an opportunity to shamelessly flirt with every eligible female at Court holds no sway over your decision at all, I'm sure."

Evander grinned and shrugged a shoulder.

"Cal," Fawn called out, leaning over the railing above. "She's all cleaned up."

Callan stood at once, practically knocking his chair to the floor.

"Get a hold of yourself," Evander said, shaking his head, but Callan was already halfway up the stairs.

Quietly, he entered Nova's chamber, pausing just inside the doorway. Fawn sat in the leather armchair near the fireplace.

"She's asleep." Fawn spoke without looking up from the thick book lying open in her lap. "She's a bit warm, but she'll live."

Callan crossed the room and sat on a wooden chair with an embroidered cushion at the bedside. Fawn had done well. There wasn't a trace of blood left on Nova. Her black hair was unbraided and lay in long waves on the pillow, framing her face. Her fair cheeks were flushed a pale shade of pink. Callan gathered frost in the palm of his hand and gently cupped the side of her face, flinching when she leaned into his touch and smiled in her sleep.

"She's certainly got Solar blood with how fast she's healing." Fawn appeared at his side, and he quickly drew his hand away from Nova's face. He stood, catching sight of Fawn's knowing look.

Callan cleared his throat. "She doesn't look like she's from Sonnend."

"Mother and Elena were friends when they were young. From what I heard, Elena was a gifted healer."

Fawn snaked her arm around his shoulders and guided him toward the door. He turned his head to glance back at Nova, still asleep in the bed.

"She needs rest, Cal. If you need me, I'll be in the library. For now, go swing your sword at something."

He felt an odd sensation, as if something was coaxing him back to the bedside. But Fawn was right. Experience had taught him the surest way to quiet his mind was to drown out his thoughts on the training field. So, he pulled the door closed and went to gather his blades.

SEVEN

Nova struggled to open her eyes. Through half-closed lids, a blurry canopy of golden leaves took shape above her. She tried to sit up, realizing with a start that she was unable to move. Dread covered her like a thick blanket, heavy and suffocating. Forcing her eyes open wider, she scanned her periphery, searching for the source of the unpleasant sensation.

She was in bed, her head propped up on a pillow. A quick glance to the left and right revealed wooden walls hung with ornate tapestries. Woven landscapes of orange-hued forests and innocently grazing deer. The lavish chamber was unfamiliar, but she saw nothing to explain the unease blooming within her chest. Her gaze traveled slowly to the foot of the bed. Wispy threads of black mist flicked over the footboard like snakes' tongues.

Nova opened her mouth to scream, but the sound caught in her throat. A flash of movement drew her attention beyond the edge of the bed to the far corner of the room. A swirling black mass loomed there, flickering in and out of focus. It had no defined shape and made no attempt to come closer, but Nova sensed the darkness was watching her.

All at once, she woke and regained the ability to move. She sat straight up in bed, chest heaving, skin prickling with sweat, fingers digging into the coverlet. She found herself sitting atop a wooden four-poster bed with thick velvet curtains tied at each corner with golden tassels. Leaves embroidered in gold thread fanned out across the canopy overhead. A low fire crackled pleasantly on the hearth of a gray stone fireplace. No menacing shadow figures to be found.

Fractured memories flashed in her mind. Her transformation. Falling from Frost and striking her head. The lycane. Her heartbeat quickened as she relived her struggle against the creature, recalling the sickening crunch of her bones under its forceful paws, its razor-sharp claws slicing through her flesh. It was as if all the air had been sucked out of the room, and, for a moment, she worried she might faint.

Sliding off the edge of the bed onto wobbly legs, she staggered to a gilded mirror hanging on the wall. Bracing her hips against the chest of drawers, she slipped the fabric of her silk nightdress off her left shoulder. In the reflection, four pearly lines, each one the width of her little finger, marred the otherwise immaculate plane of her back.

Scars.

Straightening to face the mirror, her hands flew to her scalp to check her other wound. She stilled as she registered the reflection staring back at her from within the mirror.

She almost didn't recognize herself. Her hair was full and lush, the darkest shade of black she'd ever seen. Her fair skin glowed faintly, and the tips of her ears tapered into delicate points. Her irises were light gray and ringed in silver, her gaze now infinitely more piercing than it had been before. Hands trembling, Nova gingerly traced the lines of her new face.

She spun at the turn of the doorknob behind her. A young Fae female stood in the doorway, palms held out in front of her. Slightly shorter than Nova and fair-skinned, her fiery auburn hair was half up and intricately braided, displaying her own pointed ears. A fine ankle-length dress, maroon velvet with sheer sleeves embellished with beaded leaves, hugged her slender frame.

Nova stared at the female without speaking, her breathing fast and shallow. Closing her eyes, she swallowed hard, willing her body into a disguise of composure.

"Callan," she demanded. "Where is he?"

"He's been to check on you several times, but I believe he's training at the moment. I'm Fawn," the female said, laying a hand on her chest and taking several slow steps forward. Her soft brown eyes were doe-like, large and expressive.

"H-how long have I been asleep? My wounds have healed." Nova assumed it must have been weeks, if not longer.

"It's been three days. It's quite remarkable, really." Fawn's voice swam with enthusiasm. "You're descended from Sonnend, the Solar Court, which is known for its healers. Though, I confess, I've never seen anyone heal as quickly as you have."

"Is this Sonnend?" Nova gestured vaguely to the room around her.

"No, darling. You're in Pyralis."

Fawn's kindness filled the chamber like a physical presence, practically palpable.

"When you're feeling up to it, I'd be happy to give you a geography lesson. And a history lesson. I'm sure you have many questions about the Fae Realm."

"Your offer is very kind."

"It's no bother. I've always been a bit of a know-it-all," Fawn said, approaching Nova with measured steps until she stood within arm's reach. "I'd love to learn about humans, if you'd be willing to teach me," she added, practically giddy.

"Yes, well, I suppose I was never truly human." Nova glanced quickly at the mirror and the unfamiliar face reflected there before turning back to Fawn. "But I could tell you about their customs and beliefs, if you'd like."

"It's lovely to finally meet you." Fawn placed a gentle hand on Nova's forearm, the touch warm and comforting. "You must be starving. Let's get you fed. Everything is better with a full stomach."

As if on cue, a maid entered the room, a tray of food balanced in her hands. She placed the tray on the edge of the bed and backed away with a quick curtsy. Fawn acknowledged the maid with a gracious nod before turning back and motioning for Nova to sit on the bed. Then she lowered herself onto the wooden chair at the bedside and smoothed her hands over her lap. Once settled, Fawn flicked her wrist, and the fire flared on the hearth, burning brighter as if she'd poured hog fat over the flames. Nova's eyes went wide at the casual display of magic.

But even the existence of magic couldn't distract her from the gnawing emptiness in her stomach. Nova turned her attention to the tray, piled high with roasted chicken, rosemary potatoes, braised carrots, and fresh bread. The aroma instantly set her mouth watering. She ate greedily, too overcome with hunger to concern herself with manners. She gulped down a mug of cold cider as Fawn sat quietly, biting her lip in what Nova assumed was an attempt not to laugh. When she was through, Nova dragged the back of her hand across her mouth, clearing her throat demurely.

"Better?" Fawn asked with a hint of a chuckle.

"Yes, much."

"Why don't you have a bath?" Fawn rose, leading the way into the attached bathing chamber. She filled the large copper soaking tub in the center of the wood-paneled room with steaming water. A pleasant, spicy scent filled the air.

Shrugging off her silk nightdress, Nova made a clumsy attempt to climb over the edge of the tub. She cursed under her breath, embarrassed by her coltish movements as she wobbled on foreign-feeling limbs. Fawn offered a hand, but Nova waved her off.

"I can manage," she said, trying to assure herself as much as Fawn.

After a moment of difficulty, Nova sank into the luxurious bath. Fawn excused herself, promising to return once Nova had finished.

Alone in the quiet of the bathing chamber, Nova slid down the tub until she was completely submerged, cocooned in the deliciously hot water. She opened her eyes and watched the small bubbles escaping from her nose dart to the surface. Squeezing her eyes shut, she held her breath until her lungs burned. The sensation was oddly comforting, the pain serving as proof she was alive. Bursting through the surface a moment later, she gulped down a deep, cleansing breath, smoothing her hands over the crown of her head and down her shoulders. Her fingertips grazed the raised lines of the fresh scars on her back—a permanent reminder of what she had survived.

Nova opened an amber bottle and poured sweet-smelling soap into her hands. As she scrubbed roughly at her scalp, she took stock of her current situation. While her physical transformation had been instantaneous when she crossed the Boundary, it would take time to acclimate to the ways of the Fae Realm. She needed to tread carefully as she learned as much as possible about the Fae folk and their customs. She questioned how much she could rely on the accuracy of her beloved faerie stories.

Nova dunked beneath the water and rinsed her hair clean. Rising out of the water, she grabbed a towel and tousled her hair before wrapping the downy fabric around her torso. She managed to step out of the tub on her own, a bit unsteady on her feet, but determined.

Three gowns lay draped over the edge of the bed when she returned to the chamber. After a quick inspection, Nova settled on the least extravagant option, a cinnamon-colored day dress with a fitted bodice and straps that fell off the shoulder. A gentle knock came on the door, and Fawn entered just as Nova finished fastening the row of tiny buttons on the front of the bodice.

"The color suits you," Fawn said, adjusting the drape of the straps. "I'll bring you to the seamstress for some gowns of your own. Until then, you may borrow anything of mine you like."

Nova accepted the offer with a nod; though she'd just met Fawn, she'd already gathered there was little sense in arguing with her plans. Nova tugged at the bodice, trying to shift it up higher over the swell of her breasts which fought against the confinement of the garment made for Fawn's willowy figure. In the Human Realm, Nova had preferred plain, modest dresses in a muted palette—an unsuccessful strategy she employed to blend into the background. In this gown, she felt like the focal point of the painting.

"I've never worn such a fine dress before," she said, squirming a bit more.

"You look lovely. Here, I'll fix your hair." Fawn guided her onto the cushioned stool and pinned her hair back with two golden combs shaped like leaves, displaying her new ears.

"I'm joining my brother and cousin for tea in the library if you feel up to leaving your room." Fawn looked down at her expectantly. Nova fiddled with the small buttons lining the front of her bodice.

"Of course." Nova stood, smoothing her hands over the fine fabric clinging to her hips. Fawn grinned as she took Nova by the hand and linked arms with her, leading her to the door.

The pleasant sound of male laughter drifted down the hall as they approached the library. Nova halted in the doorway, gawking at the floor-to-ceiling bookshelves lining the walls, each one stuffed practically to bursting with thick leather-bound volumes. Never in all her life had she seen so many. Her fingers tingled with the urge to gather a stack in her arms.

The high ceiling was ablaze, the entire expanse painted with a mural depicting Embra, the goddess of the hunt and harvest. Bright copper curls danced wildly around her face. Flames poured forth from her outstretched hands as she scorched a field of threshed wheat to enrich the soil for the next planting.

"Evander, this is Nova." Fawn stepped to the side, pulling her forward and presenting her to the room. "You've already met our cousin, Cal," she added, waving a hand in the air dismissively.

A male rose from a high-backed armchair, but Nova passed him over, her gaze immediately drawn to Callan's silhouette standing tall before a row of large windows. Bracers still on each wrist, he wore black breeches and a tunic of cobalt blue that pulled at the width of his broad shoulders. He turned to face her, and she joined him where he stood, bathed in the golden light of the late afternoon sun slanting through the glass. When they first met, she had thought his hair was black, but in the sunlight, she could see it was a deep brown, the color of freshly turned earth.

He brushed several strands of hair from his face and reached out his hand toward her, smiling warmly. A single dimple flashed on his left cheek. Nova took his hand, his fingers rough against the softness of her own. Her chest erupted with an intense flutter at the contact, like hundreds of papery butterfly wings beating.

While he was far more refined than the tracker who had appeared on her doorstep in Timberfell, he looked nowhere near as breathtaking as the regal Fae male he had revealed himself to be in the dim light of her kitchen. In the bright light of day, however, she could appreciate the finer details of his face. The flat brows and long, straight nose sitting over sensual lips. Those brown eyes flecked with gold, even more captivating than she remembered.

"It's nice to see you again, Callan," she said.

"Call him Cal, everyone does." Fawn tapped Nova's shoulder, gesturing to the sideboard set with tea service. The white porcelain teapot and dainty, flared cups were painted with a pattern of intricate gold leaves.

"I'm pleased to see you back on your feet," he said, his low voice like a caress as he made a slight bow. Callan released her hand, which hung in the air for a beat before she remembered to lower it.

Nova's eyes didn't leave Callan's until he shot a sideways glance at the other male, still standing in front of his seat. Shorter and leaner than Callan, the second male was finely dressed with fair skin. He had an impish look about him with hazel eyes and faint freckles dusting the bridge of his nose. One ear was pierced with a gold ring.

"I'm Evander." Taking hold of her hand, he brushed a soft kiss against her knuckles. "And you are positively delicious." Nova dipped in a quick curtsy and slowly drew her hand back.

Evander grinned wickedly and fell into his seat, leaning back and crossing one leg over the other.

"Ignore my brother, Nova," Fawn sighed with an exaggerated roll of her eyes, waving her over to take a seat. "Gods know, I usually do."

Fawn carefully poured a cup of herbal tea and delivered the saucer into Nova's hands. Nova watched the fragrant dried leaves swirl on the surface of the steaming water.

"So, Nova," Fawn began excitedly, raising her cup to her lips. "It seems we missed your birthday."

"Yes," Nova replied, taking a seat and stirring a spoonful of golden honey into her tea. "My twenty-fifth."

"I forgot entirely," Callan said, turning to her from where he still stood looking out the window. "Happy birthday, Nova."

"That's very kind of you," she said, before sipping from her cup. "In all the excitement, I had forgotten it myself."

She froze, realizing the three of them, who seemed to be roughly her age, were likely much, *much* older.

"Exactly how old are all of you—if you don't mind me asking?"

"I'm the youngest," Fawn said, her mouth full, gesturing toward the others with a half-eaten tea biscuit. "I'm only two hundred and fifty years old."

"I'm two hundred and seventy-five," Evander said. "That grandsire over there is three hundred." He pointed at Callan who closed his eyes and shook his head slightly, the corners of his mouth lifting into a ghost of a smile. Clearly, he was accustomed to Evander's teasing manner.

"I can't believe it." Evander's voice was suddenly close to her ear as he leaned in toward her, eyeing her with what seemed like amusement, as if she were a curiosity in a traveling carnival. "I've never met a human before. Or someone from the Human Realm, at any rate." He extended a finger and ran it lightly along her forearm.

"Oh, leave her alone, Evander." Fawn swatted her brother's hand away, and he sat back in his seat.

Thank the gods.

While Nova was newly arrived in Aemoria, she was fairly certain pulling away from Evander's touch would have been considered a slight in any realm.

"Are you feeling well?" Callan asked a moment later. Nova realized she must have been staring off at nothing in particular.

"Yes, I'm fine," she said, clearing her throat. "I didn't sleep well—nightmares."

"I'm not surprised considering all you've been through," Fawn said, patting the back of Nova's hand.

"It felt so real, I believed myself awake. But I couldn't move, and then, I saw a dark figure in the room, watching me." Nova shivered at the vivid memory.

She looked sideways at Callan, whose brows were drawn together.

"Cousin, tell me again about how you ushered Nova across the Boundary." Evander's tone was playful but noticeably sharp as he chimed in from where he lounged in his seat. "I especially love the part where you abandoned her to fend for herself against a bloodthirsty lycane mere moments after she took on her Fae form."

Nova's eyes flicked between the two males. Callan's expression was icy. A muscle in his cheek ticked as he clenched and unclenched his jaw.

"Actually, I would like to hear the story," she said, hoping to ease the sudden tension between the two males. She turned to face Callan. "From the time we crossed the Boundary, I have only flashes of memory."

Callan's cold gaze lingered on Evander for a beat. When he turned his attention to her, his expression thawed a degree, a faint warmth returning to his eyes.

"Perhaps another time, Nova. I must be going, if you'll excuse me." He stood at once, donning a thin smile, and made a quick bow before striding out of the library.

EIGHT

BRISK AIR WASHED OVER Callan as he burst out onto the high stone rampart surrounding the Pyralis Estate, the cold bracing him and tempering his anger marginally. Sentries stood posted at intervals along the wide walkway. All kept their distance, shrinking back and lowering their heads as he rushed past.

At last, he stopped inside an empty turret and rested his elbows on the half wall. Kicking the toe of his boot against the cold gray stone, he surveyed the sea of red, orange, and gold leaves of the surrounding forest.

It was a relief to escape the library. Confined in the space, he'd felt simultaneously energized and drained. Energized at seeing Nova safe and healed. Drained from keeping up the pretense that he wasn't keenly aware of her every movement.

Her soft bottom lip pressed against the rim of the porcelain teacup.

The way she self-consciously touched her ears three times.

The thrum of her pulse at her fair throat.

He'd forced himself to face the window to avoid openly staring. It felt as if he'd been enchanted.

What game was Evander playing? Callan was used to Evander's expert

54

needling and had often watched him wielding it as a weapon against romantic rivals. But he'd never before found himself on the receiving end of it. He flexed his jaw, thinking of how his cousin had behaved toward Nova. Testing the limits of how she would allow him to speak to her. Whether or not she would allow him to touch her.

She didn't pull away from his touch.

Callan fumed, his anger reigniting as he recalled Evander's mocking tone. He hadn't abandoned Nova. He'd defied every fiber of his intuition when he left her alone. He imagined pummeling Evander and sending him crying to his mother as he often had when they were younglings. The thought improved his mood considerably.

The sun had begun its slow descent toward the horizon. Callan scanned the shadows forming at the edge of the forest, the gathering darkness reminding him of Nova's midnight hair. He had no doubt she was descended from Sonnend. There was no other explanation for how rapidly her wounds had healed. But she bore no resemblance to the golden-haired Fae of the Solar Court he knew.

With her silvery eyes and fair skin, Nova looked quite the opposite, as if she were directly descended from Silvergard. But if that were the case, why had no one thought to tell him? Though he was not aware of any imminent conflicts, relations between the Lunar Court and the other territories had always been tenuous. Strained, at best. At present, they were practically nonexistent.

Callan groaned through his teeth. Why should he care where she came from? His assignment was simple: locate Nova Greenmore and return her safely to Pyralis. He'd done that. So why was he sulking in an empty turret, thinking about her hair and her eyes, and trying to invent any excuse to see her again?

He rubbed his forehead with both hands then dragged his fingers down his face, his head coming to rest wearily in his hands. It had been several days since he'd gotten any restful sleep. Longer if he counted his time on the road, bedding down behind hedgerows when there wasn't a room available at the inn of whatever hamlet he found himself in as night approached.

Callan resolved to take his evening meal in his chamber and turn in early for a full night's rest. Perhaps sleep and some distance from Nova was what he needed to get his head on straight. He planned to speak with Evander in the morning and knew it would be wise to be clearheaded if he hoped to get answers to any of his lingering questions. Although Fae couldn't lie outright, they were certainly capable of deception, and Evander could deceive with the best of them.

Rising at his usual time the following morning, Callan quickly dressed in a fresh tunic and breeches and pulled on the boots he'd buffed to a shine the night before. Surprisingly, Evander had already eaten and left for the Great Hall. It seemed he was truly honoring his mother's request to oversee preparations for the upcoming Hayer celebration in her absence. Normally, nothing short of an act of the gods would pull Evander from his bed before midday.

The long carpeted halls of the Estate were mostly empty, with the exception of servants going about their morning duties. Callan knocked on the massive wooden double doors leading to the Great Hall, and Evander's voice called out for him to enter. The large, open space was lit by the morning sun pouring in through the tall windows lining the far wall.

Evander sat on his father's gilded throne upon the dais before the wall of windows. He was alone except for a Fae commoner, a brewer by the looks of it. The male stood beside the throne, a tray with several glass steins containing a selection of amber ales balanced on his burly arm. The brewer cocked his horned head in Callan's direction as his footsteps approached the platform.

"Have you got a minute?" Callan asked his cousin, making a slight bow of greeting.

"For you? Of course." Evander waved the brewer away. "I'll send word of how many barrels we'll need."

Once they were alone, Evander rearranged himself, sitting up a bit straighter on his father's throne but casually resting an ankle on the knee of his opposite leg.

"What can I do for you?" He grinned broadly, clearly taking pleasure in playing the role of Noble Lord of the Autumn Court while his father was away.

"Just seeking a bit of clarity." Callan clasped his hands behind his back. Evander nodded, prompting him to continue. "Has it occurred to anyone that Nova might have ties to Silvergard?"

"Why the interest in her lineage?" Evander asked after a moment, avoiding the question by asking one of his own.

"I have no particular interest in her lineage. I'm simply wondering why, if she has Lunar blood, no one thought to share that information with me." Callan's tone was cordial, but a whisper of command churned just beneath the surface.

Evander pinned him with a stare, the corners of his grinning mouth beginning to slacken, his cunning eyes narrowing slightly.

Callan pressed on. "If there is a conflict brewing with Silvergard, and she is somehow involved, then the task I completed for Lady Estrid was much more dangerous than I was led to believe. For Nova and for me."

"You're both alive and well," Evander said. His tone was dismissive as he brushed his fingers over the top of his thigh. "In fact, the only harm that befell her resulted from your actions. Why the concern after the fact?" Evander asked, his head tilting to one side.

Callan crossed his arms over his chest, projecting an air of authority despite Evander's position above him on the raised platform.

"I won't play a part in any scheme that brings harm to her, Evander. And I won't stand idly by while she's used as a pawn in one, either." Callan wondered what had prompted his declaration. This line drawn in the sand.

"What sort of spell has she put you under?" Evander attempted levity, a smirk returning to his face, but his eyes remained calculating and trained on his cousin.

"There's no spell," Callan said, even as the memory of Nova's roar echoed so loudly in his mind, he could practically feel it reverberating in his bones. "It's a matter of honor," he added, hopeful his justification sounded as believable as he intended it to be.

Evander looked unconvinced.

"Don't be silly. Any fool could see you want her. She is a stunning creature, isn't she? Even now I can smell the faint reek of your desire. Tell me, Cal, what is she worth to you?" Evander perked up a bit, rubbing his thumb over the pads of his fingers, no doubt thinking he'd found his latest mark.

The conversation was going nowhere. Admitting Evander's suspicions were even remotely accurate could put both Callan and Nova in a vulnerable position. And Evander was the fool if he believed Callan would ever enter a bargain with him.

"Perhaps I'll wait and speak with Lady Estrid about this when she returns," Callan said, the casual mention of Evander's mother a thinly veiled threat to go over his head.

Evander shifted to sit taller on the throne, planting his booted feet flat on the wide oak planks of the dais, fingers grasping the golden arms of the throne. The threat clearly found its target.

"You would do well to remember, *cousin*, Lady Estrid is not your blood." Evander's voice was taut. All humor, genuine or feigned, had evaporated. His eyes glowed like live coals for an instant. "Although she may at times think of you in a motherly way, you are not her heir. You are a *blade*. Nothing more. A weapon she takes out when the need arises."

Callan's nostrils flared, but he managed to resist the impulse to climb on the platform and drag Evander from the throne. Evander's lips curled up on one side, pleased to see his words had struck a nerve.

"You fulfilled your duty bringing Nova across the Boundary into Aemoria," he said. "If she is truly nothing to you, as you suggest, then do try to remember your place here and stay out of my way. Unless, of course, you're ready to return to face your obligations in Nivali."

Callan stood frozen, inwardly raging at the fact that there was nothing he could do. And worse, that Evander knew it. He clenched his fists, ice biting at his palms and the tips of his fingers, a faint blue haze gathering at the edges of his vision.

"Breathe, Cal. I'd hate to see you lose that famous temper of yours." Evander chuckled and clapped his hands together once, the cunning in his eyes lifted for the moment. "Now then, I believe we have an understanding. If there's nothing else, I really am very busy."

Callan dipped his head in a hollow bow and turned away, storming out of the Great Hall without another word to his cousin. He charged all the way across the Estate to his chamber, a trail of fresh snow and jagged icicles forming along the fine carpets in his wake. The housekeeper would have his head if she happened upon the mess before the evidence of his anger had a chance to melt. Barging into his room, he slammed the door behind him with a blast of frigid air, driven by a harsh flick of his wrist.

Callan ran a hand roughly over his jaw, breathing deeply through his nose. It would be unwise to lose his temper. If he lost Lady Estrid's favor, he'd be forced to leave Pyralis. What use would he be to Nova then? He was taken aback by how much the thought pained him.

The exchange hadn't been a total waste. Evander was angry, and, though he said little, his emotion had revealed more than he likely intended. Callan was certain Evander had plans involving Nova somehow. Evander had never taken an interest in much beyond drinking ale, playing games with the courtiers, and pursuing females who were desired by others simply for sport. He'd never behaved in such a hostile way toward Callan before. It stood to reason that Nova's arrival was the catalyst.

Callan's eyes fell on a folded piece of parchment lying on the low table in the sitting area. He snatched it up. The seal of dark blue wax was stamped with crossed swords, the insignia of Nivali. Callan crumpled the letter in his fist and tossed it, unopened, onto the embers still glowing on the hearth. Flames licked at the edges of the dry paper before consuming it entirely. Callan slumped down in the armchair before the fireplace and massaged his forehead, uncertain whether he was angrier with Evander or himself.

Though he'd pushed himself to the brink of exhaustion on the training field earlier, sleep remained elusive. Callan lay on his back, staring at the ceiling as a brisk breeze blew in through the cracked window, ruffling his hair against his temple. A startled shout drew him from his bed and to the open pane. Sentries scrambled atop the stone rampart surrounding the Estate, gathering in a small cluster and peering into the darkness to the woods beyond. Like a gust of wind, Callan swept through his chamber, shoving his feet into his boots and taking his sword from its place on the mantel.

Minutes later, he had scaled the stairs to the top of the wall and approached the sentries from behind. They scattered to the left and right as he barged through their ranks to speak with the commander on duty. Callan had barely uttered a word when a hush fell over the group. He followed their collective gaze into the oppressive darkness beyond the reach of the flickering torchlight. It took a moment for him to spot them: a pair of lycane slinking along the edge of the forest. The creatures moved like water, their black coats barely distinguishable from the shadows around them. They kept to the tree line at first but eventually emerged, slowly creeping up the hill toward the Estate, muzzles low to the ground.

The sentries stood awestruck and unmoving, whispering to one another. An archer nocked an arrow, but Callan stayed his hand and hushed them all, curious to see what the beasts would do. The creatures reached the base of the wall a short distance away from where the group stood watch. Both appeared to sniff at the gray stone before rising up onto their hind legs and placing their forepaws on the wall.

"What the fuck are they doing?" a guard to Callan's left asked, his voice an agitated rasp.

"They can't scale the wall," a second said. No doubt intended as a confident statement of fact, the words came out as a fear-tinged plea for reassurance instead.

"Quiet—all of you," Callan ordered, his eyes never leaving the beasts. Their heavy paws dropped to the yellowed grass covering the hillside, and they turned, trotting back toward the forest.

Several soldiers released sighs of relief as the animals neared the tree line once again, but the relief was short-lived. Changing direction abruptly, the lycane charged full speed at the wall.

"What are they doing?" the commander asked in disbelief. Callan thought it was quite clear what the creatures were doing.

They're trying to breach the wall.

The monstrous beasts struck the wall in rapid succession, their broad sides colliding with the solid stone as forcefully as a pair of battering rams. Startled shouts rang out from the sentries, the sound quickly dissipating in the quiet night air. Two thuds followed as the lycane fell to the ground. Barely a breath later, they rose once again and readied for another running start.

"They can't get through," the commander shouted. "They'll never get past the shield."

Another faint reverberation rumbled beneath Callan's boots as the lycane crashed into the wall a second time, one yelping in pain.

"It makes no difference to them," Callan said absently, watching the beasts take position for a third strike.

The sentries shifted around him, uneasy. All their training and no one was prepared for this moment. Callan had never seen anything like it, either. After the third impact, one of the beasts remained on the ground, whimpering and unable to rise. Pity seized Callan's chest. The creatures were driven not by their own desires but by a power eclipsing even their instinct for survival. They would die in pursuit of their aim unless someone put them out of their misery first.

"Now," Callan said, signaling the archer whose hand he had stayed only moments before. "End its suffering."

The arrow sang as it sliced through the air, striking the wounded beast in the throat. The second lycane limped toward the trees, one of its forelegs clearly injured. Still, it readied for another assault.

"The other, as well," Callan ordered. The archer glanced at his commander, who nodded silently. A second arrow cut through the chill night, piercing the creature's eye.

Several minutes passed in silence with no movement from the trees. Callan sheathed his sword and took one of the torches, quickly descending the steps to the courtyard below. A handful of sentries followed close behind with blades at the ready.

After exiting the Estate through the wooden gates, Callan moved stealthily along the base of the exterior wall to the place where the two hulking beasts lay. Patches of blood marred their midnight coats, shining in the torchlight. The foreleg of one beast was obviously broken, bent at an unnatural angle. Callan held the torch close to the wall; a grisly painting of fresh blood and tufts of black fur splashed across the gray stone.

"Burn them and see that this mess is cleaned up." He jerked his chin at the soiled wall. "We don't want any of the residents to see this come morning."

Callan held the flame close to the remains, his brow furrowed and mind whirring. Four lycane sightings in as many days. The creatures were behaving abnormally: hunting in pairs, attempting to breach a fortified city guarded by both magic and solid stone. He couldn't help but wonder whether the strange occurrences were connected to the recent arrival of a certain raven-haired female in the Autumn Court.

NINE

Nova sailed along the carpeted hallway past countless candles mounted on gilded sconces. The flames flickered in her wake as she breezed past but never went out. Candles in the Autumn Court burned brightly until extinguished, the tapers never shrinking, the wicks never burning down. She'd learned a great many things over the previous seven days, sequestered in the library under Fawn's thorough instruction, intent on absorbing every detail she possibly could about Aemoria, its territories, the folk of each territory, and their abilities.

Nova had spent the previous day educating Fawn about the customs and beliefs of humans, as promised. Fawn was appalled to learn mortals no longer worshipped the ancient gods.

"What did you call them?" she had asked, shaking her head faintly as if she'd simply misheard.

"The Forgotten Gods," Nova repeated. "I read about them in an anthology of rare folklore my father once gave me. I'm afraid they've become as much a faerie tale as the Fae."

"Well, I suppose the Fae can't abandon the gods so easily when they are the very source of our magic." Fawn raised her hands toward the ceiling, gesturing to the mural of Embra overhead. The flames in the fireplace flared with her movement, and Nova marveled at her friend's power.

"Now then," Fawn said, returning to her lesson. "What are the two classes of Fae?"

"Noble and common."

"Can all Fae use magic?" Fawn tapped her chin with her forefinger.

"Common Fae can use magic on a small scale. The gentry of each territory can use magic to a greater degree, but the members of each territory's Noble bloodlines possess the most powerful abilities bestowed by their patron."

"Very good," Fawn had said, circling behind Nova's chair. "Name the patrons and abilities of each territory."

Nova began, ticking off each one on her fingers so as not to forget any.

"Aurore, the goddess of life and light, gifted Sonnend with healing and the ability to conjure sunlight. Nivali received snow and ice wielding from Brumal, the god of transformation."

"Keep going. You're doing well," Fawn had pressed.

Closing her eyes, Nova visualized the map of Aemoria she'd been studying in her room by candlelight long after her lessons ended each day.

"Elowen, the goddess of birth and growth, bestowed shapeshifting on the Fae of Maedwen. The Tundarans' ability to control water and conjure tempests comes from Brakos, the god of the sea and storms. Embra, the goddess of the hunt and harvest, granted fire wielding to Pyralis. And Orika, the goddess of change and influence, gifted Silvergard with the ability to read minds and influence thoughts and actions."

Fawn had applauded theatrically when Nova finished.

Distracted by her thoughts, Nova nearly collided with a servant carrying a tray of food as she rounded a corner, but she managed to sidestep at the last second. She shot the servant an apologetic look and continued on without stopping.

As for Raven's Isle, the isolated island territory off the northern coast of Silvergard? They hadn't discussed the Shadow Court yet.

Nova knew her mother came from Sonnend, the Solar Court, and she had asked about her when she first arrived. Fawn and Evander's mother, Lady Estrid, had known Elena when they were young. It was only Lady Estrid who could possibly provide information on her mother's current whereabouts, but she was away in the nearby territory of Tundara. And so, Nova sought distraction, immersing herself fully in her studies, and waited.

The chair behind Fawn's desk was empty when Nova reached the library. Instead, she found Callan seated in the armchair before the blazing hearth, a thick volume cradled in his large hands. He closed the book with a soft thud and stood when he saw her.

"Callan." He had caught her off guard. His name on her lips sounded like an accusation. Although she'd barely seen him since the day she first awoke in Pyralis, he'd been in her thoughts more than she cared to admit, even if only to herself.

"It's nice to see you again," she said, scraping together her composure. Could he sense the quickening of her pulse at the sight of him? "Sorry to interrupt. What genre?" she asked, gesturing to the book now cradled under his arm.

He held it out so she could read the title: *Compendium of the Beasts of Aemoria*.

His lips curled up ever so slightly at the corners. "Be honest. You were expecting a treatise on military strategy."

"Guilty," she said. The enticing scent of him, like fresh snow, found its way to her from across the room.

"I'm not much of a reader. In truth, I was hoping to find you," he said, his brows drawing together.

"Oh?" Her heart stuttered. "I've been practically living in here. Fawn usually hauls me in just after breakfast and doesn't release me until dinnertime."

But today Fawn hadn't sent for her. Nova had slept in until midmorning then spent several hours reading in bed. Finally, she decided to dress and seek out her friend in the library, assuming Fawn, too, must have gotten distracted.

"She can be a bit of a tyrant," Callan said conspiratorially.

"I'm a willing prisoner," she confessed. Despite Nova's customary resistance, the heiress of Pyralis had beaten past her defenses through sheer persistence and wedged herself into a budding friendship. Admittedly, Fawn had been a welcome comfort to her since her arrival in Aemoria.

"If you'd like to escape your cell for a bit, I could show you around the Estate." There was a brief flash of what looked like hesitation in his eyes, and she wondered whether he truly wished for her to accept his invitation.

"That sounds lovely." She was eager to see more of the sprawling, palatial estate she'd been calling home for more than a week.

"My pleasure." Callan set the book down and motioned for her to go ahead of him.

Before she knew it, nearly two hours had passed, and Nova found herself walking side by side with Callan through the Estate's courtyard, which featured several small ponds and fountains. An ancient white oak grew in the center, its bright orange leaves fluttering in the breeze like flickering flames. Nova imagined it would take at least three of her with arms outstretched to encircle its trunk.

She and Callan had passed the time, more or less, in companionable silence, which seemed to suit both of them fine. Several times when she'd risked a glance in his direction, she'd found his eyes already on her, flicking away immediately.

Vendors from the surrounding districts filled the courtyard, having come to trade with the common Fae who dwelt within the compound protected behind the high stone walls. Stalls crowded the open-air market, vendors selling everything from fabric and buttons to wine and ale. Nova closed her eyes, appreciating the pleasant hum of the crowd. It was deceptively similar to the bustling markets of downtown Timberfell, except for the variety of winged and horned residents and the wide selection of magical wares for sale. Nova browsed a tabletop laden with stones of various colors, the seller explaining the specific purpose of each: A shimmering gray stone for finding lost things. A polished amber stone for seeing loved ones over great distances.

She had only ventured out of the residential wing once since her arrival, when Fawn brought her to the seamstress to commission several gowns of her own. The sprightly female was a good deal shorter than Nova, with shining green eyes and a pair of incandescent, gossamer wings poking through the back of her own finely made dress.

She'd spent hours draping fabric samples over Nova's shoulders as she stood before a full-length mirror while Fawn shouted her approval or disapproval from a comfortable seat in the corner. In the end, Nova commissioned four gowns, simple by Fae standards but more extravagant than anything she'd ever worn in the Human Realm. Fawn insisted on ordering several silk shifts and stays for her. Nova discreetly requested the seamstress fashion a pair of simple black breeches and two loose-fitting shirts for her as well.

Just in case.

Nova wore one of her new gowns as she navigated the maze of vendor booths with Callan walking beside her. The floor-length silk dress was a deep purple and hugged her hips before flaring out slightly at the bottom. The boned bodice accentuated her waist and amplified her bust, and the sheer straps hung off her pale shoulders. A lightweight charcoal cloak shielded her from the crisp autumn chill in the air. She glanced sideways at Callan, who wore no cloak, seemingly unbothered by the falling temperature.

"You're not from Pyralis, are you?" she asked, gesturing to his clothing as she pulled her cloak tighter around her against the wind.

It wasn't merely his lack of outerwear that led her to believe he hailed from somewhere else. Callan's dress was practical—infinitely more utilitarian than the ruffled, beaded, and embroidered finery favored by the Pyralisins.

"No. Like you, I'm a guest here."

She began to climb a stone staircase leading to a covered parapet walk overlooking the courtyard on one side and the autumn forest on the other. Callan hesitated for a beat before following. When she reached the top of the wall, a sentry blocked her path, his palm held out in front of him.

"Only sentries are permitted access to the wall, miss." The male's gaze traveled above her head, and he shrank back, swallowed up in an instant by Callan's shadow as he rose up on the landing behind her.

"Apologies," the guard mumbled. "I didn't realize you were accompanying her." He dipped his head and backed away, allowing her to pass. Nova wondered, was the guard's deference to Callan born of respect or fear?

"But you're related to the Noble family?" she asked, continuing their conversation. Evander and Fawn called him cousin, but she didn't know if they were true blood relations or if it was simply a term of endearment. Her gaze danced over Callan's dark hair and rich brown skin. There was no family resemblance to speak of. She could certainly relate.

"The Noble Lady of Pyralis is a close family friend," he clarified.

The two of them stopped, and Nova stood facing the expanse of forest and the vast rocky mountain range beyond. Callan stood at her side with his body angled toward her. His eyes darted over the wall to the knoll covered in dry grass below before settling on her.

"Let me see." She took her time assessing him, raising one eyebrow and scanning him from the top of his head to the toes of his boots. Gods, she relished the opportunity to stare at him so openly. "No feathers or fur to suggest shapeshifting, so you aren't from Maedwen. You must be from Nivali."

"That's correct," he said. "I'm impressed."

"I've always taken my studies very seriously." A faint smile crept across Nova's face unbidden, and she turned her head away from him.

She stood silent, the feeling of Callan's eyes lingering on her like a soft caress.

"That's the first time I've seen you smile," he said. Though innocent, the observation stung her like a nettle. His voice was quiet, tone curious rather than judgmental. Still, her smile faded as quickly as it had appeared. Nova looked straight ahead over the treetops.

"I suppose there has been little for me to smile about," she said finally. Callan didn't speak but observed her intently.

"I was an outcast in the Human Realm. Folk found me odd and treated me horribly," she said matter-of-factly. "From the time I was a child, I promised myself I would never give anyone the satisfaction of seeing they'd hurt me. I became very skilled at hiding my emotions—both good and bad."

She glanced at him, her expression neutral. Silence hung in the brisk air between them.

Nova bit the inside of her cheek to prevent more words from spilling out. Why did it feel as though she could share her most closely guarded secrets with him, a stranger? It was reckless. And potentially dangerous. She suspected her ability to mask her emotions was as valuable a skill in the Fae Realm as it had been in the human one. Perhaps even more so.

"Well, it's lovely," he said after a moment. "Your smile. The world would be lucky to see more of it."

Nova looked to the east, feigning interest in the view of the distant gray mountains. In truth, she sought to hide the heat flushing her pale cheeks.

"So, the land of ice and snow," she said awkwardly.

"And steel," Callan added, shifting seamlessly with her change of subject. "The Winter Court is most renowned for two things: its forges that produce the finest blades, and its warriors who wield them." He reached down and proudly patted the dagger forever sheathed at his thigh.

"Why do you choose to remain in Pyralis?" She turned to face him directly again, more intrigued by him than any view, however breathtaking.

"Many years ago, I found myself conflicted. Feeling trapped. Not knowing what I wanted out of life. I traveled around the Realm for a time—adrift, you could say. When Lady Estrid invited me to the Autumn Court to train her elite guards, I fell into an uncomplicated life here, and I simply stayed."

The sideways glances from the sentries on the wall as they discreetly monitored Callan, their hands hovering a breath away from the hilts of their swords, suggested his existence was more complicated than he cared to admit.

"What was trapping you?" she asked, allowing her curiosity to get the better of her. At what point would she be prying?

"Expectations, I suppose." He shrugged, averting his eyes.

"I know what you mean." Nova nodded. "Females have little power in the Human Realm. I had an inheritance from my father that allowed me some freedom, but many are forced into unhappy unions simply for security."

"I can't say it's any different in Aemoria. Most matches are strategic alliances of sorts. Though the Noble Lady of Tundara rules over her territory alone."

"I read about her." Lady Samira had earned a reputation as a fierce warrior; a reputation Nova envied. Coveted. "My place in the world was so defined by my being female, I never even considered what I might do if I had a choice in the matter."

"And now?" Callan asked. "What would you like to do now that the choice is yours to make?"

Nova bit the inside of her cheek again.

"I want to learn to fight," she said with a resolute nod. "I've spent my life running and hiding from danger. I got lucky with the lycane—"

Callan laid his hand over hers where it rested atop the cold stone. A pleasant chill ran the length of her spine at his unexpected touch.

"It wasn't luck that saved you," he said. "I watched you defeat the lycane. You knew you were no match for its size and strength, so you got into position and you let it fall on your blade. Let its weight do the work for you. It was brave. And damn clever."

"You're very kind."

"I'm not saying it to be kind. I'm saying it because it's true. You're a fighter, Nova. You've earned your scars."

Nova stared at his fingers draped gently over her own. His touch was so warm against her skin she could scarcely believe he had the ability to conjure snow and ice in the palms of his hands. She blinked several times before drawing her hand away. Callan pulled his hand back as well, staring at it for a beat as if the limb had acted with a mind of its own.

"Look, I realized I brought you here without preparing you fully for what to expect. You're obviously a quick study, but I sought you out today to share some advice." He paused for a moment. "You should know that Fae can't lie directly. But they can deceive. There are many who would do so simply for amusement, or for their own gain. Promise me you'll be careful."

Nova searched his eyes, imagining what it would feel like to stroke the curve of his jaw. How the roughness of his stubble would feel against her fingertips.

Stop.

"Don't worry about me, Callan," she said dryly, turning her face away from him. "I can take care of myself."

She felt him bristle at the change in her demeanor. An awkward silence stretched between them.

"Why are there so many sentries?" she asked, changing the subject once again. "Expecting an attack?"

Callan rubbed his jaw, throwing a look at the guards stationed all along the crowded wall.

"They're guarding the Estate against lycane."

"Lycane?" A shudder rippled through Nova as she scanned the trees below. "Surely they can't get past the wall."

"Likely not. Lycane attacks are rare in Pyralis, though other territories haven't been so fortunate."

It was Callan's turn to fall silent.

"I nearly forgot. I have something for you," he said abruptly a moment later. Reaching behind his back, he removed something from his belt and held it out to her.

"My dagger!" she gasped, cradling it in her hands.

The blade had been sharpened and the hilt wrapped with a fresh strip of leather.

"I pulled it from the beast's chest. It would have been a shame to lose such a fine weapon."

Nova searched for adequate words but found none. If she remembered her faerie stories correctly, expressing gratitude was discouraged in the Fae Realm.

"It was my father's." It was all she could think to say.

Callan nodded and cleared his throat. They stood beside each other for another moment, neither one speaking.

"I can teach you," he said, breaking the silence once again. "To fight. With a dagger. A sword. Whatever you prefer."

"I'd like that." A thin smile played on her lips. He nodded, and they both looked out over the forest, the trees swaying in the chill wind as if dancing at their feet.

TEN

THE DINING ROOM WAS empty when they returned to the residential wing for the evening meal. A note from Fawn explained she had plans to dine with a friend, and Evander was occupied with matters to oversee at Court that would keep him past the dinner hour.

So, Nova and Callan dined together.

When Nova had eaten her fill and swallowed the last sip of her second glass of wine, Callan stood and offered to walk her to her chamber. Cheeks burning, she fought the peculiar urge to giggle as he accompanied her down the long corridor, his hands clasped behind his back.

"Finally," Nova sighed, leaning against her door. "Is it just me, or is this hallway entirely too long?"

She snorted involuntarily and clapped a hand over her mouth, swallowing the laugh threatening to spill from her lips.

Callan smiled faintly and shook his head.

"I think perhaps you are unaccustomed to drinking Fae wine," he said.

"Unaccustomed to drinking any wine—Fae or otherwise." Her third smile of the day spread across her lips, wider and more genuine than the previous two had been. What had gotten into her? Nova ceased smiling at once when she saw the intensity in Callan's eyes looking down at her. Taking a slow step closer so he stood within arm's reach, he raised his hands and held them with his palms toward her.

"May I?" he asked, voice low.

Nova responded with a jerky nod, unsure what Callan intended to do but certain she desperately wanted him to do it.

"Yes, of course," she murmured.

Reaching forward with both hands, Callan swept the loose waves of her hair behind her ears. Her breath hitched as his fingers brushed against the points. She hadn't realized they were so sensitive. Perhaps it was like being tickled, she thought, the sensation more intense when someone else was in control of the action. His crisp scent surrounded her, pulling her from her wine-induced musings.

Callan drew his hands back, and she stared in wide-eyed amazement as frost appeared, dusting his palms. Reaching out again, he cupped the sides of her face, gently stroking the apples of her cheeks with his thumbs. His frozen touch on her hot, flushed skin was jarring. Inhaling sharply, she looked down and away, interrupting the intimacy of the moment. Callan dropped his hands immediately and cleared his throat.

"Nova, I—good night, Nova." He turned, hastening down the hall toward his own chamber. Nova stared at the space between his shoulder blades, nodding, unable to force any words past her parted lips.

She slipped into her room and fell back against the sturdy oak door. Her heart pounded erratically, and she placed a hand on her chest, willing it to slow. Was the wine causing her body to betray her, to rebel against every defense she'd carefully crafted over the past twenty years?

Nova crossed to the dressing table, reaching awkwardly behind her back to undo the laces of her bodice. Shrugging out of her gown and leaving it lying on the floor, she loosened her stays and traded her undergarments for a white silk shift with straps of thin ribbon. The creamy fabric floated on a cushion of air atop her skin as she absentmindedly combed her hair, turned down the bedsheets, and blew out the candle on the nightstand.

She threw herself down on the bed, lying on her back in the dimly lit room. Moonlight streamed in through the open curtains. Tracing her fingertips over her cheekbones where Callan had touched her only moments before, she wondered if perhaps he was lying in his own bed thinking of her.

Nova's fingers slid lazily to her neck, drifting lower as if on their own. But she was no blushing maiden. The easy smile and near laughter she could blame on the wine. Not this. She knew her body. Knew what she desired. After a moment's hesitation, she decided to let herself have it. Nova lowered her hands to her chest, palms skimming over her breasts, full and tender. She squeezed them and shivered, her nipples hardening under the gliding fabric of her shift. Her eyes fell shut, and she imagined it was Callan's strong hands on her. She squeezed again, harder this time. Her breath came out in a soft gasp, a sensual thrill consuming her at the thought of his touch.

She continued her path, hands traveling lower along her abdomen, and she brought her knees up and apart, drawing the hem of her shift to her hips. Nova's desire urged her on as she slipped her hands between her legs, inhaling sharply as the soft pads of her fingers brushed against her clit. She began tracing slow circles around the sensitive spot.

In her mind, the specter of Callan's long body lay stretched out on the bed beside her, the solid weight of him pressed against her as he held her face in his hands, claiming her mouth with urgent, bruising kisses. Nova's pace quickened as she imagined his teeth nipping at her throat. His fingers finding a delicious rhythm between her thighs.

Her release took her by surprise, racing along her limbs with the wild force of a lightning strike. Nova cried out in the quiet of her chamber, turning her head to muffle the sound against her shoulder. Her chest rose and fell with rapid breaths as she looked around the darkened room, stunned by the intense pleasure brought on by a fantasy.

Which was all it would ever be.

All she could ever allow it to be.

Nova's eyelids fluttered. The air in her chamber was cold and still. She tried to rise up onto her elbows but realized with a jolt that, once again, she was unable to move. She stared at her right arm where it lay at her side and tried to lift it, but the stubborn limb remained frozen in place.

Terror laced the blood coursing through her veins, and her breath quickened, a growing panic clutching at her heart like a tightening fist. Frantically, she scanned the four corners of the room, searching for any sign of the darkness she was certain lurked nearby.

Nothing.

Nova raised her eyes to the canopy overhead.

Tendrils of black mist hung over the edge of the velvet canopy, swaying like the dangling branches of a willow. As if sensing her awareness of it, the dark fog crept closer, hugging the underside of the canopy as it spread out above her, inky black and limitless. A single coil extended from the mass hovering above her, reaching for her face. Nova panted with rapid, shallow breaths, powerless to turn away as it made contact with her forehead.

A surge of energy passed through her, sending her body into a painful spasm. At first, there was nothing but pitch blackness. Slowly, her vision cleared until she could see, though it remained hazy, as if peering through a veil.

Soaring under a bright moon, Nova circled above a fortress of shiny black obsidian. Hundreds of ravens swooped and dove amid the jagged spires crowning the structure, their croaking calls sharp and dissonant. The fortress sat at the edge of a rocky shore, backed by a forest of bare, sun-bleached trees, gnarled trunks rising out of the ground like great skeletal arms.

Nova's vision led her inside through an open window, and she floated along darkened hallways until she came to a Great Hall bathed in shadow. A throne of rough-hewn obsidian sat upon the dais.

Nova halted in the entryway, registering the silhouette of someone seated upon the throne, slumped to one side with an elbow resting on the wide arm. A lump formed in her throat as the figure sat up and leaned forward into a shaft of moonlight.

A flash of silver hair and piercing metallic eyes and the world collapsed into complete darkness once again.

"Nova! Nova, wake up!"

Someone shook her roughly and shouted her name. Nova woke to Callan seated on the edge of the bed beside her. His hair hung loose in front of his dark eyes, wide and flashing with concern. Nova bolted upright and wrapped her arms around his middle, laying her cheek flat against the thin fabric of his shirt. She pressed her fingertips into the firm muscles of his back, the solidness of his body against hers serving as proof she was awake. No longer in that desolate place where the air hung heavy with a sensation of pure dread.

Callan's arms hovered out at his sides for a breath before he wrapped them loosely around her shoulders. One hand stroked her hair while the other rested on her upper back, his fingertips grazing the pearly scars extending down from her left shoulder. They remained that way for several minutes, neither one breaking the silence.

"Another nightmare?" he asked once her heartbeat evened out, the breath from his whispered words tickling the shell of her ear.

Nova nodded, finally loosening her grip on him and pulling back to see his face.

"Did you see it? The darkness?"

Callan shook his head slowly.

"It felt so real." She brought her fingers to her brow. "The darkness—it touched me, and I was taken to another place. A dark citadel by the sea. There was someone there with me. It felt as if they could see me—actually see me." Nova shook her head, attempting to erase the memory of the silver eyes that seemed to see through to the very heart of her.

Callan's forehead creased briefly, the expression there and gone in an instant. A thin smile followed.

"It's all right. It's over now," he reassured her, laying his hand over hers. Nova glanced down. His shirt was untucked with the sleeves pushed up over his muscled forearms. Each wrist was marked with a thick ring of black ink.

"What are these?" she asked, running a finger lightly over one of the cuffs.

"I made a vow to Nivali long ago. To defend it with my life. These are a reminder of my vow." His voice was strained, and she wondered if the markings pained him. "You should rest," he murmured, guiding her down onto the pillow.

Nova's panic surged again. She couldn't bear the thought of him leaving. Of being alone in the dark.

"Will you stay with me?" The words fell from her lips before she could stop them. She winced at the neediness in her voice, grateful for the darkness that allowed her to hide her face from him.

"As you wish." Callan rose from the bed and made for the armchair in the sitting area.

"No, here," she said quietly. "Please?" There was that neediness again.

Callan paused briefly before turning back to face her. He lowered himself onto the bed beside her, stretching out on top of the covers and leaning back against the headboard. Nova rolled into him instinctively, her hand going to

80

the center of his chest. He was still at first but then wrapped an arm around her.

Nova lacked the energy to question the profound sense of calm that settled over her when Callan was nearby. As soon as she closed her eyes, she fell into a peaceful slumber.

ELEVEN

EARLY-MORNING LIGHT FILTERED THROUGH the windowpane, drawing Callan from his sleep. Confusion struck as he glanced around at the unfamiliar surroundings. He flinched at a quiet stirring beside him and found Nova nuzzling her cheek against the pillow, her face innocent and untroubled as she slept, her soft lips parted slightly. Callan rose from the bed as quickly as he could manage without waking her. He had intended to leave her chamber once she fell asleep, but he'd drifted off as well.

His thoughts returned to the night before.

After bidding Nova good night, he had first paced along the far wall of his chamber before forcing himself to sit beside the fire. He sank into the armchair and stared into the low, lapping flames. The sound Nova made when he touched her face in the hallway outside her room had bewitched him. He'd wanted to cover her mouth with his and drink in that gasp. To taste it on his tongue and swallow it down, keeping it for himself. He'd grown hard at the mere thought of it. It was unusual. True, he was no stranger to female company. But it had been many years since he'd lain with anyone, and he'd never desired anything beyond a single encounter.

Before long, his eyes had fallen shut, but not to sleep. Callan's hand drifted from the arm of the chair to the swell in his lap, growing evidence of his attraction to a female he barely knew. He imagined her in his chamber with him. Hair unbound and cheeks pink. Those long legs, her thighs, supple and strong, straddling his own. But most of all, he imagined that sweet, soft sound escaping from her mouth. He'd gripped himself through his breeches, hissing a breath between his teeth, desperate to relieve the pressure.

Nova's scream had ripped him from the fantasy, the sound slicing through him like an icy blade. The air in her chamber was thick with the scent of her terror when he threw open the door and raced to her side. Still, he hadn't expected her to wrap her arms around him, clinging to him as if his embrace was all that kept her from shattering into a thousand tiny pieces.

Gods help him, he enjoyed it.

Nova's breath had slowed as he stroked her hair, the scent of her fear gradually dissipating. It was then that he detected it: the scent of her desire. It was the same fragrance he already associated with her but highly concentrated, sweet and smoky, unique to her. It lingered in the corners of the room, faint but potent.

His chest had tightened with the foolish hope that he was the object of her desire. But he'd lived with Evander for decades. He'd seen time and again how females responded to his cousin's playful charm and ready smile. Surely, Nova had missed Evander at dinner and had been thinking of him as she lay in bed.

Callan left Nova sleeping and crept out of the room, returning to his own chamber. Raking a hand through his hair, he threw himself down on his bed, sprawling out on the cold, rumpled sheets.

What had come over him? While Evander's delivery had been harsh, Callan could admit his cousin was right. His responsibility for Nova ended once he delivered her to the Pyralis Estate. He had told himself he would stay away. He'd spent the past week intentionally keeping as far away from her as possible, a feat requiring no small measure of effort and restraint on his part.

Then he'd gone and *touched* her—several times in the span of a few hours. The slightest touch was all it took to set his heart racing, awakening something within him that had lain dormant for longer than he even remembered. Like a fool, he'd offered to train her, an activity that would bring them together as often as she wished it. Callan ran a hand over his jaw and chuckled humorlessly at his apparent newfound affinity for torture.

Nothing would ever come of it, he knew. But he couldn't deny that it felt right somehow. The two of them. Together.

Callan dragged himself from his bed and into the bathing chamber to make himself presentable before breakfast, welcoming the icy water as it rained down upon his heated body.

"And where have you been?" Evander asked when Callan entered the dining room a short time later, clapping him on the back as Callan took a seat at the table. It was as if their conversation the week prior had never happened. But Callan was too clever to believe his cousin had forgotten.

"Keeping busy on the training field, mostly."

"Training for anything in particular?" Evander arched an eyebrow.

"A true warrior ensures his blade is always sharp," Callan replied, a veiled taunt. Though Evander was a gifted bowman, he had come by the skill naturally and rarely bothered to train.

Evander held Callan's gaze for a beat; the jab had not gone unnoticed.

"Perhaps training is wise. There was an attack in Tundara. An entire patrol squad disappeared leaving no trace."

"How many taken?" Callan asked, his grip tightening around the end of his butter knife.

"Twenty or so. Lady Samira's elite guard followed the trail to the foot of the Gray Mountains, but the tracks ended there."

"Have you spoken with your parents?"

The Lord and Lady were guests in the Summer Court, which bordered Pyralis to the west.

"Yes. That's what kept me yesterday. Apologies I wasn't around to entertain you," Evander said, pouring himself a steaming cup of tea. "I'll have more time for diversions after the celebration."

"I managed to entertain myself, cousin. Nova allowed me to give her a tour of the Estate," Callan said, avoiding further conversation by making quick work of wolfing down all the food piled on his plate.

"How interesting. And where is our lovely guest this morning? Ah, there she is, looking good enough to eat. Is that a new dress, Nova?" Evander rose from his seat as Nova descended the staircase. "You look exquisite."

Evander intercepted her at the foot of the stairs and grasped her hand, once again pressing his lips to her knuckles. Callan drank in the stunning sight of Nova in a flowing gown of pale lilac. Her hair was gathered in a bun at the nape of her neck, a few strands hanging loose around her face.

"Charming as always, Evander," Nova said, her tone neutral as she removed her hand from his. "Fawn was kind enough to bring me to the seamstress."

She breezed past him and filled her plate with food, eventually settling into the empty chair next to Callan.

"Speaking of Fawn, has anyone seen my sister?" Evander asked, taking his seat again.

Fawn burst into the room just then, as if on cue.

"Good morning, everyone!" She flung herself down into the chair at the head of the table.

"How was your visit with . . ." Evander snapped his fingers in the air, a sausage speared on the tines of his fork.

"Josef."

"Yes, Josef."

"Quite enjoyable," Fawn huffed, her tone betraying her annoyance.

"Fawn has a suitor," Callan whispered to Nova.

"He still hasn't proposed," Fawn said, waving her hand in the air as she slumped further down in her seat.

"Perhaps he's waiting for the right moment," Evander suggested between bites of egg. "The upcoming celebration would be a grand event for announcing an engagement."

Fawn sat up at once, as if the thought had never occurred to her.

"Nova, you must come to the seamstress with me after breakfast. I suddenly feel as though I need an even fancier gown for Hayer," Fawn said excitedly, begging Nova with her big brown eyes.

"I can't," Nova said, her tone not quite apologetic. "I hoped to join Callan on the training field today."

"Why in the world would you do that?" Evander scoffed. "A dirt pit is hardly a suitable place for someone as lovely as you."

"I want to learn to fight," she said. "Callan offered to teach me, and I accepted." Callan's spine straightened as she turned to face him. "If you're free."

"Yes, of course," he said, hoping he didn't sound too eager.

"But what about my gown?" Fawn whined.

"Honestly, Fawn. You have much better taste than I do. I wouldn't even be any help," Nova said.

"Very well." Fawn rose from the table and climbed the stairs, pausing to call Nova a deserter before disappearing into the hallway above.

Nova passed beneath the archway leading to the training field, a wide expanse of dirt and yellowing grass rolled out under an open sky. She wore the black breeches and loose-fitting shirt she'd commissioned from the seamstress. The brown leather riding boots she wore the night she crossed the Boundary were free of mud, but three drops of blood marred the toe of the left one. Her dagger hung at her waist, held in place with a braided leather cord fashioned into a belt.

Nova threw her shoulders back, her thick braid swishing back and forth as she strode across the grass. She turned the corner around a wooden equipment rack but stopped short, shrinking behind it when she spied Callan already on the field.

He slashed and struck at an invisible opponent, his movements flowing as elegantly as a dancer's, contrasting sharply with the hard lines of his tall frame. His long, muscular torso was visible through his shirt, which stuck to the sweat gathering along his spine. Nova spied faint black lines beneath the thin fabric, evidence of more markings on his back. Her mind sprinted with imaginings of what they might be. Half up and gathered with a leather cord at the back of his head, some of his hair had come loose toward the front, the dark strands clinging to his forehead.

Callan was different on the training field. She had only seen him quiet and reserved, spine straight with hands clasped behind his back. She was uncertain what to make of this Callan—wild and unrestrained, grunting with the force of his strikes. Nova drew her bottom lip between her teeth and bit down, tracking his movements like a huntress concealed behind a blind. Disappointment washed over her when he completed the sequence and stood under the autumn sun, chest heaving as he swiped a shirtsleeve across his brow.

"What a fetching ensemble." Evander's teasing voice came from behind her, and she spun to face him. Though he'd changed from his fine clothing into more casual attire, he still wore his signature smirk. He carried a fine redwood bow in his hand and a quiver full of arrows at his back.

"It hardly seems practical to train in a gown and silk slippers," Nova replied, praying her cheeks didn't look half as flushed as they felt.

"Now *that* I'd like to see," Evander drawled, stepping in closer. "Honestly, why would you bother to train out here in the dirt when you've got me to protect you?"

He glanced away, spotting Callan on the field over her shoulder.

"Hello, cousin," he called out, waving Callan over. "What were you doing out there?"

"Nothing really," Callan answered, still a bit out of breath. "Just running through a strike sequence." He eyed Nova's training uniform and nodded approvingly.

Evander hooked a finger under Nova's chin, turning her face toward his. "Seek me out when you're ready to handle a superior weapon." His eyes went to Callan. "Any brute can swing a sword. It takes skill and precision to strike one's mark from a distance." With that, the heir of Pyralis sauntered past them toward the row of straw targets lining the far side of the field.

Nova bit the inside of her cheek and fiddled with the hilt of her dagger. "You're very skilled," she said, gesturing to Callan's sword.

His smile beamed, but he dipped his head toward the ground. "Would you like to hold it?"

He stretched out his arm, offering his weapon to her. Nova took it by the hilt; her arm dropped like a stone with the sheer weight of it. Hefting the sword up with both hands, she admired the craftsmanship and the shiny blade engraved with characters from an unfamiliar language.

"What does this writing say?" she asked.

"It's a charm of sorts. A Nivalian custom to ensure the blade always strikes its target."

"It's beautiful," she said, handing it back to him.

"It was my father's." His gold-flecked eyes found hers, and she instantly recognized the loss reflected in them.

Callan slid the sword carefully into its sheath and laid it on a wooden bench.

"So, what do you have planned for me?" she asked, aiming for a cheerful tone.

"I think it's best you start with your dagger and work your way up to a sword."

"Let's begin," Nova said. Callan turned to lead the way as Nova pulled the dagger from her belt. "*Shit.*"

The bite of the blade hurt less than her embarrassment at her clumsiness. Callan twisted to face her as she brought her forefinger to her mouth and drew the tip between her lips to stem the flow of blood. His eyes dimmed a shade darker for an instant, his jaw ticking once. The muscles in Nova's lower belly tensed at his reaction, but the sultry look in his eyes vanished, quickly replaced with concern, as he held out his hand to her. Begrudgingly, she allowed him to inspect her injury.

"It's nothing," she said, shrugging off the shiver rippling through her at his touch before pulling out of his grasp. "It will probably be healed in a few hours anyway."

Callan nodded and led her out onto the field.

TWELVE

TWO HOURS LATER, NOVA stood drenched with sweat, her arms unbearably heavy. Callan had kept her busy, first with learning different grips, then switching between grips, followed by practicing strikes on a sandbag strung up on a post at chest level. She'd nicked herself a couple times, but the shallow cuts on her knuckles would heal quickly.

Nova dropped onto the ground and leaned back on her hands, enjoying the cool breeze as it ruffled her damp shirt. Callan crouched beside her. Out the corner of her eye, she spied an iridescent glimmer flickering against the open sky over the field.

"What is that?" she asked, pointing to the phantom waves bobbing along the expanse of blue just as they disappeared from view.

"The shield," he replied matter-of-factly. Evidently reading the confusion written on her face, he shook his head. "Forgive me. I forgot you're newly arrived here. It's a guard of protective magic that defends the entire Estate from outside magic and attacks. Every Estate has one."

He tugged at a clump of yellowing grass, pulling the blades out at the root as he stared off into the sky, his dark brows drawn together.

"Where do they come from?"

"The rulers of each territory weave the shields around their Estates. The Noble bloodlines are powerful enough to cover large areas, though it requires considerable effort."

"How long have the Nobles been maintaining the shields?"

"Centuries."

"That's unbelievable," she said. "Why?"

"The Realm hasn't seen open war for more than a millennium. But the shields were raised as a defense against Omen of Raven's Isle. The Shadow-bringer."

"Omen of Raven's Isle?"

Callan lowered himself to sit on the ground beside her, leaning forward with his forearms resting on his bent knees.

"Do you enjoy faerie stories?" he asked. Nova nodded. "Then I'll tell you one, though I should warn you, this one is rather grim."

Callan shifted his gaze back to the cloudless sky.

"Omen was the middle son of Onyx of Silvergard, a Noble Lord known throughout the Realm for his cruelty. Omen was born with hair and eyes of silver. Those are rare features among the Fae of the Lunar Court, signifying great power. For this reason, folk said Onyx feared his son."

A chill crept like an icy fingertip along Nova's spine.

"He sent Omen away to Sonnend, where he served as an aide in the Court of Siris and Sienna. During his time there, it was rumored that Omen was taken with one of the courtiers and wished to wed. But his father soon announced the arranged union of the female and Omen's older brother, Sable, instead. On the day of the ceremony, Omen attempted to overthrow Silvergard in retaliation, murdering both his father and his older brother before vanishing.

"Not long after, a quake shook the ground of Silvergard. The northern peninsula of the territory broke away from the mainland, forming the island territory now known as Raven's Isle. For more than a century afterward, the other territories of Aemoria faced attacks by lycane and other dark creatures orchestrated by Omen. Sometimes entire villages would vanish, the residents disappearing without a trace."

"Why is he called the Shadowbringer?"

"Because his darkness consumes everything, leaving nothing but death and desolation in his wake."

Callan paused, seemingly lost in thought as he stared up at the shield, completely invisible for the moment.

"And so," he continued, "the Nobles concentrated their power, creating strongholds in the capital of each territory to protect as many citizens as possible behind the shields."

Callan tossed away the withered grass he'd been twisting in his hands. Nova swallowed hard, her throat suddenly bone-dry. She wanted to know more.

"The shields prevent anything dangerous from getting through, then?"

Callan shifted on the ground, squaring his shoulders as he glanced at the high stone walls surrounding the Estate. "In theory. Think of the shield as a bolt on a door. If someone with great power wished to get through, it wouldn't necessarily prevent them from slipping through the keyhole. I worry the Nobles have grown lax in their practices over the past several decades as Omen's attacks have dwindled."

Nova recalled the creeping black mist in her chamber and wondered whether she had only dreamt it, or if perhaps it had truly been in the room with her.

"How are you feeling?" Callan asked, startling Nova from her thoughts.

"Honestly?" She exhaled sharply. "Like a failure."

"You did well today. Don't be so hard on yourself." He nudged her with his elbow, and she bit back a smile.

A heavy sigh escaped her. "I'm just frustrated. Fawn refuses to help me develop my abilities. She says I need to learn about my magic before I can attempt wielding it. I should be able to harness the sun's light."

"And heal," he added.

"Do you know of anyone willing to maim themselves so I might practice?" she asked. "I confess, I sometimes find myself wanting to stab Evander."

Callan laughed, deep and loud, the sound ringing out across the field.

"Our abilities are second nature to us because we were born with them. We've had centuries of practice. Have some faith in yourself." He rose up beside her. "Here, let's give it a try now."

Callan extended a sturdy hand, and she accepted it, allowing him to pull her up from the ground. He stood at her back, placing his hands firmly on her shoulders.

"Close your eyes," he instructed.

Nova twisted her head to look back at him and rolled her eyes before she obliged.

"Now, breathe deeply and clear your mind."

Nova played along, filling her lungs completely before emptying them. She envisioned her thoughts being swept away, like dry leaves, with the rush of air.

Callan spoke from behind her, his voice low at her ear.

"Try calling the sun to mind—its light and warmth. Feel the sensation in your body."

A faint warmth came over her, though she suspected that had something to do with the closeness of their bodies. Chasing such thoughts from her mind, Nova allowed her consciousness to wander to her childhood days spent in the Wood, stretched out atop a bed of soft moss in patches of dappled sunlight. She imagined the summer sun sinking into her skin. Seeping into her bones. As she pictured it, she felt the unmistakable sensation of heat gathering in her chest and slowly spreading down her arms, as if the sun had emerged from behind thick clouds.

"You're glowing, Nova."

She lifted her hands before her face. A faint golden light flickered weakly in her palms. Eyes wide with surprise, she turned to Callan. The glow winked out in an instant, doused by her broken concentration.

"Gods be damned," she muttered, throwing her hands down at her sides. She thought she heard a laugh and shot a glance at Callan, arching an eyebrow at him. He managed to keep his grin from his face, but she could still see it shining in his eyes. She huffed in frustration, but her anger softened a bit.

An instant later, an icy breeze swirled around her, whipping at the damp linen of her shirt. Snowflakes drifted down lazily from the sky, and she tilted her head back to find a tiny snowstorm hovering just above her head. Fluffy flakes landed on her eyelashes and melted on her upturned cheeks. She spun to face Callan, who tipped his head in a bow.

"You may feel a bit unwell later. Tired," he cautioned. "Wielding magic takes from you; the more you use, the more it takes. With training, you'll be able to strengthen your abilities and learn to channel them, otherwise you risk draining yourself entirely."

"That sounds ominous."

Callan's expression turned serious. "It is. There's a reason Fawn insisted on training you. Without proper instruction, your magic could bleed you of every drop of your essence, leaving nothing but a husk behind."

Nova felt her face pale, if it was even possible. Perhaps it would be wise to stick to weapons training and leave the magic wielding to those with centuries of experience.

"We'd better make our way inside," Callan said as he gathered up his weapons. They walked back to the residential wing together, snowflakes from Callan's conjured flurry cascading down on them the entire way.

The sprawling halls of the Estate were silent as Nova padded along the plush runners leading to the library. The flame of her candle cast wobbly shadows on the walls.

Nearly a fortnight had passed since her arrival in Pyralis, and, in that time, she'd barely had a waking moment to herself. Though she was grateful for the constant company, which distracted her from her thoughts, she couldn't deny that part of her longed for solitude, the quiet nights she used to spend doing as she pleased.

Nova reached the library without encountering another soul. Twisting the smooth copper knob, she shouldered the heavy door, wincing as a creak cut through the quiet. She stood motionless for the span of a few quick breaths before slipping inside. Surely no one would object to her wandering the halls after dark, but her heart thudded away in her chest just the same.

A low fire crackled pleasantly in the fireplace; it was as if the room itself had been expecting her. Nova's thoughts turned briefly to Agnes. What had her friend made of the note she'd left behind? Had she believed the story about Nova visiting distant relations? What would Agnes think when she received no further communication from her? Never saw her again?

Nova sorted through the stacks of thick books piled on Fawn's desk, finally unearthing a text on Silvergard. Cradling the heavy volume under one arm, she settled into the armchair before the fire, hooking her legs over the side. The book was a relic. The cover of stretched black leather was cracked and weathered, its intricate silver foil accents flaking off. Flimsy pages threatened to tear between her fingertips as she carefully thumbed through them.

The first chapter contained general information about the Lunar Court. The Fae of Silvergard were nocturnal. The territory's primary export was something called moonstone. Interesting, to be sure, but not what she was searching for. She'd already learned that the nobility could read minds to varying degrees, with some members of the Noble bloodline capable of influencing the thoughts and actions of others.

The next several chapters detailed the Noble lineage of the territory going back nearly two thousand years. Nova flipped gingerly through the delicate pages, as fragile as moths' wings, until she found the section on Onyx of Silvergard. Famous for his cruelty, Onyx abused his ability to enter the minds of others in order to control any who would oppose him.

His mate, Luna, bore three sons: Sable, Omen, and Nox. Luna once petitioned the Aemorian Council to strip Onyx of his title and punish him for violence committed against his family and his subjects. The Council ultimately denied the petition, and Onyx continued his rule unfettered. Afterward, relations between the Lunar Court and the rest of Aemoria deteriorated until there was scarcely any interaction between them with the exception of trade.

The text told, more or less, the same tale of the formation of Raven's Isle as the one Callan had shared with her. She suspected so little was known about what truly happened when Omen assassinated his father and brother, that the accepted story was more legend than fact. The book provided no further information about the Shadowbringer.

Nova tilted her head back, staring at the fiery mural on the ceiling while she fiddled nervously with her mother's ring. Sitting up after a moment, she grumbled softly, disappointed her search hadn't yielded any useful informa- tion. Closing the book with a soft thud, she placed it on the desk where she'd found it and returned to her chamber, her mind weary.

THIRTEEN

FAWN BARGED THROUGH THE door like a battering ram on the morning of Hayer, humming gleefully as she tore open the heavy drapes.

"Good morning, sunbeam!" Fawn drummed her hands excitedly on the bed beside Nova, her voice an animated sing-song and entirely too loud for the hour. Nova threw an arm across her eyes to shield them against the bright light streaming through the window, announcing it was already midmorning.

"Did I miss breakfast?" she whimpered, her voice still hoarse with sleep.

A housemaid breezed through the doorway at that precise moment with a tray full of food, placing it on the foot of the bed.

"Clara, you are a gift from Embra herself!" Nova pushed herself up to sitting and dragged the tray across the coverlet toward her. The maid smiled and quickly left to see to her other duties, which Nova imagined must be numerous on such an important day as the harvest festival.

Fawn tempered her excitable energy a degree and plopped down with a bounce on the corner of the bed. Nova slathered a slice of warm bread with salted butter and sweet apricot jam. The butter had scarcely melted before she gobbled it up.

"I hope you're rested because I planned a day of indulgence for us to prepare for Hayer. Now, finish your meal. I'll be back to collect you in half an hour." Fawn stood and bent forward, curling her arms in a hug around Nova's neck before she left.

Nova pushed the tray away once she had finished, leaving only crumbs behind. She hauled herself out of bed, wincing as she raised her arms toward the ceiling in a deep stretch. She'd spent an hour training with Callan nearly every day for the past several weeks, and her muscles reminded her of her efforts.

She flexed her fingers, examining her knuckles. The cuts from her first day wielding a dagger had healed completely with no trace of any scars. Graduating to a wooden sword, she'd memorized the various positions for striking and blocking attacks, weaving the movements into a sequence she practiced for hours at a time until it started to become second nature to her. She had always approached her interests with an intense, unrelenting focus. Sword fighting, it seemed, was no exception. She was eager to get her hands on some real steel, but Callan insisted she wasn't ready yet. *A nick on the knuckle is one thing*, he'd cautioned, *but, healer or not, a severed limb is quite another.*

Nova plucked her maroon velvet robe from the foot of the bed and slipped it gingerly over her shoulders. By the time she finished cleaning her teeth and washing her face, Fawn appeared in the doorway, her auburn hair piled in a messy knot atop her head.

"Are you ready yet?" she asked, bouncing on the balls of her feet.

Nova tugged the sash of her robe snug around her waist and wrangled her own mess of hair into a twist at the nape of her neck.

"As ready as I'll ever be, I suppose," Nova said, following Fawn's excited steps out into the hallway.

The Estate hummed with an energy that matched Fawn's as they navigated the halls, preparations for Hayer fully underway. More staff than Nova had ever seen rushed around the residence. As they passed a row of tall windows, she peered out at the courtyard, bustling with activity. Vendors were making last-minute deliveries, unloading wooden casks of wine and ale from a horse-drawn wagon. Groundskeepers balanced on ladders hoisting banners of burnt sienna and gold, the colors of Pyralis, between the stone columns lining the Estate.

Nova followed her friend through a set of tall, carved wooden doors into a large bathing chamber. Fawn's day of indulgence consisted of soaking in tubs of steaming water infused with scented oils while gossiping about the gentry who would be in attendance. A massage followed, and, by the end, Nova's entire body felt supple and restored.

When they were through, Nova trailed dreamily behind Fawn on the way to her friend's sizable chamber. A platter of cheese, bread, and fruit awaited them, along with a bottle of wine, sweet and dark, tasting of blackberries. They lounged in the sitting area, chatting while their hair dried. Fawn giggled cheerfully, giddy from the wine and her excitement about the celebration.

"Tell me more about Josef," Nova prodded, taking a tiny sip from her glass.

"Well, he's from a respectable family, going back thousands of years. He's kind. Handsome." Fawn listed these qualities with little enthusiasm. "But most importantly, he's a poet." With that, the fire in her eyes flared.

"A poet?" Nova was surprised a member of the gentry would take an interest in the arts. In the Human Realm, creatives earned very little coin.

"Yes—a good one. He's been penning odes inspired by me for years now." Fawn threw her head back on the arm of the chaise in rapture. Nova smiled at her friend's playfulness. She wouldn't have thought Fawn was susceptible to grand romantic gestures.

"Enough about me," Fawn commanded, sitting up straight once more. "There will be many eligible males at the celebration tonight, Nova. You *must* dance with as many as you possibly can. Who knows, perhaps you'll meet your match tonight. Or at least a potential lover." She raised her eyebrows suggestively.

A vision of Callan the first time she'd seen him on the training field flashed in Nova's mind. Wielding his sword, he'd looked at once both undeniably lethal and painfully beautiful, his shirt clinging to the firm lines of his body.

Fawn gasped, and Nova flinched, momentarily afraid her friend had somehow read her thoughts. Fawn leaned in close, fiery waves falling loose around her face.

"You have had a lover before, yes?" she asked, her voice an exaggerated whisper.

Nova stared at her hands in her lap, scratching her thumbnail along the stem of her glass. "Only one," she admitted after a moment. Fawn bounced in her seat, nearly spilling her wine.

"Tell me everything," she demanded, smoothing her robe as if readying herself for the tale.

"I will, if you promise to slow down on the wine." Nova gently pried the crystal glass from Fawn's fingers and set it on the table between them.

"Of course! Whatever you want. Just don't leave out a single detail." She clapped her hands once, every bit an entitled heiress.

Nova shook her head, biting back a smile. "Very well. This was several years ago now, when I was about twenty years of age. His name was Tomas, and he'd come from another city to serve as an apprentice to the farrier in Timberfell, where I grew up. My father had several horses then, so Tomas and I spent many afternoons together in the stables behind my house."

Fawn listened intently with her fingers gripping the arm of the chaise.

"To me, he was magical." Nova's voice dipped lower, and she stared out the window as she continued. "I was charmed by his ability to coax the wildest horses into a calm stillness to carry out his work. The way he handled such powerful creatures as gently as if they were delicate sparrows."

Tears gathered at the corners of Nova's eyes as she recalled the young woman she'd been all those years ago. Incredibly lonely and desperate for connection.

Foolish.

"One afternoon, as we sat together, for once alone, he touched my cheek with that same tenderness."

Fawn was nodding, the movement almost imperceptible.

"The act itself was much less gentle." Nova flushed, embarrassed to be sharing such a private story. But perhaps, she thought, this was the kind of intimate talk shared between sisters. "You see, in the Human Realm, it's considered improper for unwed males and females to be alone together. We knew we didn't have the luxury of time, so it was a hurried affair with my skirts pulled up, pressed against a wall in the tack room."

Fawn's mouth fell open.

"The other times, in the hay loft above the stalls, were more leisurely, but we always kept our clothing on in case we were discovered."

A ghost of a smile crossed Nova's lips at the memory of the two inexperienced lovers. Of the girl who, when they'd lain together, felt a little less numb and alone. She omitted the end of the tale: how she had bared the wounded parts of herself to him. How he said he loved her and promised to take her away. How he abandoned her without a goodbye or a word of explanation when he found a position as a farrier in Faymere, leaving her alone once again.

"You'll no doubt find a male with more experience at the celebration tonight," Fawn cackled, wrenching Nova from her thoughts. She swiped away a tear with the back of her hand and snatched up the wine bottle, hiding it on the floor beside her seat.

Fortunately, two ladies' maids entered the chamber to help them dress, distracting Fawn from prying further. The one called Lilith, a wispy female with pearly, pale green skin, guided Nova to a cushioned stool before the gilded mirror above the dressing table. She combed Nova's hair, her long fingers quickly taming the tangled strands until they were smooth, then twisted it into a loose bun pinned at the nape of her neck. Using common magic, Lilith heated a metal rod, shaping several tendrils into loose curls to frame Nova's face.

Lovely by nature, Fae didn't require much in the way of decoration, in Nova's opinion, but Lilith insisted on lightly dusting her cheekbones and the bridge of her nose with a fine silver powder to accentuate the metallic ring within her eyes.

Nova gaped at her own reflection, turning her head from side to side to appreciate the maid's handiwork. "Lilith, it's perfect!"

"*Nearly* perfect." Fawn appeared in the mirror over Nova's shoulder, a wooden box in her hands.

"What's this?" Nova asked, running her fingertips over the intricate tree trunks and leaves carved into the lid.

"A gift, of course."

"Fawn, you shouldn't have."

"I wanted to. And I do what I want." She placed her hand on Nova's shoulder. "You cannot begin to imagine how dull it has been having only Evander and Cal to keep me company all these years. Having you here has been like having the younger sister I always dreamt of."

"I don't know what to say." Nova stood and wrapped one arm around Fawn's neck, cradling the box in the other.

"Open it," Fawn urged, pulling out of Nova's embrace and silently clapping her fingers together.

Nova lifted the lid to find a silver circlet adorned with luminous round stones the color of watery milk, and a pair of silver pendant earrings, each set with a single matching stone. Fawn took the box and laid it on the table, lifting the circlet and placing it on Nova's head. Lilith slipped the earrings onto Nova's ears, and Nova turned to the mirror again. Although she recognized the face staring back at her as her own, the regal female reflected in the glass was wholly unfamiliar.

A knock came at the door, and the sprightly seamstress who had made Nova's gowns entered, a garment bag draped over her arms. Fawn crossed the room and tugged at the lacing on the front of the bag.

"A final belated birthday gift." Fawn pulled the garment bag open, revealing an elegant dress made from a unique silver material.

"This is too much." Nova stood gawking at the brilliant gown. "Truly, Fawn. You're not allowed to get me anything for at least the next fifty years."

"Nonsense," Fawn shouted with a flourish of her hand as she removed the gown from the bag and held it against her body, twirling in Nova's direction.

A short time later, Nova viewed herself in the full-length mirror. The dress was exquisite, the metallic fabric glinting like armor in the candlelight. The neckline of the tightly fitted bodice dipped down to just above her navel, and the off-the-shoulder straps were each made up of several dainty silver chains. The fabric of the skirt hugged her body tightly through the hips but loosened at the bottom thanks to a slit reaching the middle of her left thigh. Lilith dusted the silver powder across Nova's shoulders and collarbones.

Fawn sidled up beside her wearing a brown velvet gown that matched her eyes. The long sleeves of sheer mesh fabric were dotted with gold beads, and the mesh dipped low, leaving the pale skin of Fawn's back exposed. A circlet of golden leaves rested atop her shiny auburn hair, a waterfall of loose curls cascading down her back.

"Shall we?" Fawn hooked her arm with Nova's and flashed a conspiratorial grin before leading her toward the night's festivities.

FOURTEEN

NOVA HAD NEVER SEEN the Great Hall before. The grand space boasted raw-wood beams spanning the high ceiling, gleaming oak floors, and a mezzanine above the main level. Across from the large double-door entryway was a dais, upon which sat two gilded thrones upholstered with plush velvet cushions. Two enormous fireplaces flanked the platform, one on each wall, both as tall as she was.

The room was dimly lit and teeming with noble Fae folk chatting idly. Only a dozen or so candles staggered along the walls were lit, and a low fire crackled in each fireplace. Fawn pulled Nova through the crowd by the hand, securing a spot at the foot of the platform as the court herald thumped his staff on the floor and announced the Noble Lord and Lady of Pyralis.

All at once, the twin fireplaces erupted with roaring fires, and hundreds of candles arranged on chandeliers ignited, bathing the Great Hall in bright, warm light. The crowd applauded the Noble Lord and Lady, who now stood before their thrones under the standard of the Autumn Court, a tree with flaming leaves embroidered in gold.

The copper-haired Noble Lord raised a hand to quiet the murmuring crowd. He wore a fine coat of chestnut-brown velvet secured with shiny gold buttons. Several of his fingers were adorned with gold rings.

"A hearty welcome and joyful Hayer to all!" the deep voice of the barrel-chested Lord boomed, carrying to the four corners of the room. He turned to the striking female standing beside him. "On behalf of myself and Lady Estrid, please eat, drink, and enjoy the fruits of the harvest."

The crowd cheered and readily dispersed, heading for the banquet tables situated along the perimeter of the hall and piled high with trays of roasted meats, one including an entire pig. There were roasted vegetables, cheeses, and fresh breads, as well as sweet and savory pies, tarts of every variety, baskets of fragrant apples, and large casks of wine and ale. Lively music burst forth from a band of stringed instruments, flutes, and drums set up in the far corner. Guests began to mill about, greeting one another with handshakes and warm embraces.

As soon as the first notes floated on the air, a group of males circled Fawn and Nova. Nova bowed politely as Fawn introduced her. However, her attention was divided between Fawn's introductions and the Noble Lady, who sat upon her throne. Lady Estrid smiled as she watched the Noble Lord speaking animatedly with a guest. There was little doubt as to where Evander's gregarious personality came from. The Noble Lady, on the other hand, appeared more reserved, though Nova wondered if that was truly the case, or if she was simply a keen observer like Fawn.

"What do you say, Nova?" Her name on the lips of an unfamiliar male drew her attention away from the dais.

"What?" she asked absently, blinking several times and realizing she'd lost track of the conversation entirely.

"I asked if you'd join me in a dance." The request came from a lanky, russet-haired male with twinkling green eyes who bowed before her, offering a hand with long, delicate fingers.

She was stalling, unsure how to politely decline his invitation, when he was suddenly shoved aside.

"Forget it, Hunter." Evander shouldered his way into the center of the circle. "The first dance is mine." He bowed and extended his own hand with a rakish smile.

Nova hesitated for an instant before accepting, wary of offending the heir of Pyralis. The others exchanged thin smiles and snickers, suggesting they were accustomed to Evander doing as he pleased. He took Nova to the far side of the hall, practically dragging her to where several other couples were already dancing.

The band picked out a jovial, fast-paced tune. Nova had had little experience with dancing during her life in the Human Realm, and she knew nothing of the style of dance in Pyralis. Fawn hadn't thought to cover that particular topic in her cultural lessons over the past several weeks. Nova glanced around at the other pairs occupying the dance floor, trying to get a sense of the movements. Evander pulled her tight against him, grasping one of her hands in his, his other hand holding her firmly in place at her lower back.

She leaned her shoulders away to put some distance between their faces.

"I don't know the steps," she protested through her teeth.

"Just let me lead you," he drawled as he began steering her around the floor in time to the beat.

Nova moved stiffly as Evander guided her through the dance, whirling around and around as the tempo quickened. It was as if she'd been swept up in a current that refused to release her. Her eyes darted between Evander's sly grin and the faces of the onlookers, bleeding into one another in a colorful blur as the pair spun faster and faster. When the song mercifully ended, she pushed against Evander's chest, dislodging herself from his hold. Out of breath, she muttered something about needing refreshment before rushing away.

Fists clenched discreetly at her sides, Nova scanned the sea of strangers, desperate for a familiar face. She spotted Fawn standing near one of the fireplaces, deep in conversation with a tall male with straw-colored hair, presumably the infamous poet, Josef. Nova raised her eyes to the mezzanine, searching the faces of the revelers in the gallery above. Relief flooded her chest when she found Callan in the far corner of the upper level, observing the celebration. He stood alone, the other guests seemingly keeping their distance.

His dress was uncharacteristically formal and finely tailored: a jacket of deep blue with silver buttons down the front and embroidered with silver thread, black breeches, and black leather boots buffed to a shine. He was clean-shaven. Several sections of hair were braided close to his head with silver beads woven into the strands. Nova was openly staring when his gaze wandered over to meet hers.

The Great Hall was already packed with folk standing shoulder to shoulder when Callan arrived. He ascended the stairs and pushed his way to a spot in the corner of the mezzanine to await the Noble Lord and Lady's arrival. He preferred to remain at the periphery at such celebrations. Though he'd resided in Pyralis for decades, he still felt like an outsider, especially when the gentry gathered under the banner of the flaming oak. He continued to dress in the blues and grays of Nivali, a place that both beckoned to him and no longer felt like home.

Callan had anticipated Rowan's parlor trick of igniting the fires and candles all at once. His uncle loved to make an entrance, even if it was the same entrance year after year. He found Nova the instant the candles flickered to life, as if she emitted a beacon that called out to him like a siren song. She was standing with Fawn before the dais, gray eyes wide and lips parted in surprise. His throat went dry at the sight of her in a brilliant silver dress that hugged every stunning curve of her body.

The eligible males of Pyralis began circling immediately. Eager to make her smile. Hungry to hold her close for the brief length of a dance. Why shouldn't one of them have the chance to make her happy? Nova deserved happiness. Someone kind who could give her stability. An uncomplicated life.

Callan wasn't surprised when Evander claimed the first dance of the evening. As much as his cousin infuriated him at times, Callan recognized the envy lurking behind his irritation. Evander behaved as he did because he'd never been touched by tragedy. Had never once had to contend with the cruelty of life. Callan could only dream of being so carefree.

He looked out over the crowd and caught the attention of Lady Estrid, who raised a glass to him from her seat on the platform. He bowed his head in response, a silent promise to speak with her before the night was through. When he scanned the dance floor moments later, he saw Evander had moved on to another partner but Nova had not.

He glanced over the sea of faces on the lower level until he found her once again. The raucous noise of the celebration fell away as soon as their eyes met. He tipped his head toward the nearby staircase and quickly descended to join her.

Nova was waiting for him when he reached the base of the stairs. From afar, she had been devastating. Up close, she was deadly. Callan strained with the effort of keeping his gaze on her face when it longed to travel down over the swell of her breasts to the spot at her midriff where her plunging neckline ended.

"I wondered where you were hiding," she said, standing practically toe to toe with him.

"I prefer to keep a low profile."

Nova tapped a finger against one of the silver buttons on his chest. "Yes, it certainly appears as though you're trying to blend in." A faint smile lifted the corners of her lovely mouth. "You look so different."

She ran her fingertips along her jawline absently, starting below her ear. He mirrored the gesture, stroking his own smooth chin and averting his eyes, suddenly self-conscious under her appraisal.

"I like it," she clarified.

She extended her hand in the space between them, and Callan thought she might touch him. But her arm dropped along with his foolish hope, and she laid her palm flat against her abdomen instead.

"Was that you I saw on the dance floor earlier?" he asked, knowing full well he could never confuse her with anyone else.

"Perhaps." She tilted her face up toward his, silvery eyes glinting under the light of hundreds of flickering flames. "Will you dance with me?"

"I'm afraid the sight of me dancing isn't a pleasant one."

"Allow me to be the judge of that." She smiled at him fully then, one eyebrow arched in challenge, and, gods above, he knew she could convince him to do anything she desired.

Before he could respond, he spied Lady Estrid approaching over Nova's shoulder.

"Callan, won't you introduce me to this jewel who has captured your attention?" Estrid stopped a short distance away as Nova turned to face her.

"Lady Estrid, may I present—"

"It's you," Estrid gasped, her face draining of color. She held her hand out, as if she meant to touch Nova, to confirm she was real. "I've been so eager to meet you, my dear."

"It's a pleasure, my Lady." Nova made a polite curtsy. Estrid regarded her silently for a moment, her eyes gone misty.

"Please, won't you come with me? I believe it's time we had a chat." The Lady forced a cheerful smile and a brief laugh, blinking away her tears as she took Nova's hand. "I'll have her back to you shortly, Callan."

"Yes, my Lady." He nodded, and Estrid guided Nova to the door leading to the antechamber where the Noble Lord and Lady had waited to be announced earlier. Estrid stopped short, throwing a look at him over her shoulder.

"I need to speak with you as well. Come find me in my study after breakfast tomorrow morning," she said, regarding him reproachfully.

Callan nodded once more, wondering what he was in trouble for this time.

FIFTEEN

THE NOBLE LADY CLOSED the door, reducing the celebration's cheerful roar to a dull drone. The quaint room was sparsely decorated with a small maroon sofa anchored on one wall and a low wooden table with a decanter and a set of crystal glasses against another. The wood paneling glowed in the light of several low-burning candles, creating a cozy atmosphere. Nova lowered herself onto the edge of a plush cushion and clasped her hands in her lap. She spun her mother's ring on her finger while Lady Estrid poured them each a glass of burgundy wine.

Estrid was lovely, short with soft, lush curves. Her auburn hair accentuated her creamy complexion, and her features, though striking, were severe. Her smile was friendly, however, partially offsetting the sharper lines of her face. The Noble Lady sat, angling her body toward Nova and handing her a glass before sipping from her own.

"I imagine you're eager to hear about your mother." Estrid rested her glass on her knee. Nova nodded and shifted in her seat, swallowing a mouthful of the sweet wine.

"Elena and I were about the same age. We saw each other every few years but mostly kept in touch through letters. She was always sweet tempered and kind. A gifted healer. I'm told you're also rather talented in that area."

"I'm learning, but I haven't had much success so far," Nova said before taking another sip of wine, forgetting to pace herself under the weight of her unease.

"You'll settle into your abilities in time, I'm sure." Estrid leaned back in her seat and crossed one leg over the other. "You remind me of her. Not your coloring, but something in the eyes." She studied Nova quietly for a moment before continuing.

"Because we didn't keep in touch regularly, many years passed before I realized her letters had stopped. I knew she didn't always see eye to eye with her parents, and I thought perhaps she'd run off and wed a commoner or someone who didn't meet their approval.

"By then, I had younglings and an entire territory to govern. We simply lost touch. One day, a letter arrived saying only that she'd made a bad match, and she was with child. That it wasn't safe for her in Aemoria, so she planned to travel to the Human Realm."

Estrid paused to drink from her cup, blissfully unaware of the significance of her words as each one sank like a stone in the pit of Nova's stomach.

Her mother was with child before she crossed the Boundary.

Nova's breath quickened. Anson Greenmore—the man she had cherished, cared for, and mourned—was not her father. She tipped her glass, swallowing the rest of her wine.

"I received another cryptic letter telling me her babe, a daughter, had been born. For your protection, she said, she planned to hide you amongst the humans until you came of age. She asked that I seek you out just before your twenty-fifth birthday, sharing only your family name of Greenmore and that you were living in a city along the border with Aemoria.

"I had no way of writing back, either to accept or decline her request, as she'd apparently gone into hiding. But I vowed to do what I could to honor

113

her wishes. I haven't heard a word from her since. I believe if Elena felt it was safe to return, she would. Clearly, she feels it's safest to remain hidden. As the twenty-fifth anniversary approached, I charged Callan with finding you and bringing you home."

Estrid laid her hand over Nova's and leaned in close.

"And I hope you will think of Pyralis as your home, my dear. Fawn speaks so highly of you. And I know you've caught Evander's eye, though he'd hate it if he knew I told you."

Nova's thoughts sloshed inside her mind like water in a bucket. A sudden, overwhelming urge to break out of the cramped warmth of the room took hold of her. She clumsily set her empty glass down on the table, righting it just before it tipped over.

"You are too kind, my Lady. Your family and your staff have been very generous." Nova stood slowly, her legs unsteady beneath her. "I hope one day I can repay your kindness. You've given me much to consider." Apparently catching her meaning, Estrid rose from the sofa as well.

"Of course, my dear. I suppose this could have waited until the morning, but I figured you'd already been waiting quite some time. Come, let us return to the celebration."

Estrid opened the door to the Great Hall. The dissonant sounds of the gathering crashed against Nova like a rogue wave, and she winced. Callan lingered close by, standing against the wall. His brow creased upon seeing her, and he hastened to her side.

"Now then," Lady Estrid said, making a sweeping gesture over the Great Hall with a graceful hand. "Fetch something to eat and enjoy yourselves. Celebrations like this are for the young." With that, the Lady returned to her place beside the Noble Lord, who sat on his throne watching the revelers as he drank from a stein of ale.

Nova clasped her hands into tight fists, the bite of her fingernails against her palms grounding her. Her eyes flitted around the room, landing briefly on the mass of couples twirling around the dance floor in time to thundering drums, then on a group of boisterous guests playing a game of cards along the far wall, their barking laughter cutting through the melody of the music.

"Do you mind if we leave? F-find somewhere a bit quieter?" she asked, turning to Callan.

"You read my mind." He leaned in close to her ear and murmured, "I can't stand these parties, either." He offered his arm, and she linked her elbow with his, appreciating the sturdiness of his body beside her.

Callan led her to one of the banquet tables and made a plate for each of them. Nova felt as though she was gliding along the floor as he guided her through the double doors to a quiet spot down the corridor where the sound of the celebration barely carried. Nova filled her chest with air, finally able to breathe fully again.

She and Callan sat side by side on the cushioned bench of a window seat overlooking the courtyard where the common Fae held their own celebration. An enormous bonfire burned brightly, sending countless glittering sparks into the night sky where they winked out into nothing. Nova had read that long ago, the celebratory bonfires of Hayer were used to make sacrificial offerings to Embra.

Callan set the plates on the cushion between them and handed her a roll. She took a bite and stared distractedly at the wall ahead of her as she chewed. Callan leaned back in his seat and tossed a grape into his mouth. His gaze wandered, but she felt it settling on her time and time again.

"I'm sorry," Nova said finally, plucking a wedge of hard cheese from her plate. "I've barely had a moment to myself since I arrived here."

"I can leave if you'd rather be alone." Callan made to stand and excuse himself, but she caught him around his wrist.

"No, I didn't mean . . ." She dropped her hand and motioned for him to stay. She bit the inside of her cheek.

"I've spent the better part of my life alone. I had my father and Agnes. And a steady stream of tutors once I was removed from school. But, for the most part, I've been on my own. And solitude suited me fine. I would read, wander the Wood, do whatever I wanted, really.

"Then I arrived here, and I seem to always be with someone. Someone with expectations. Fawn wants to quiz me or gossip. Evander's always trying to snare me in a witty back-and-forth. And they're both lovely—truly . . ." She trailed off, struggling to give voice to her feelings.

"I understand. Believe me, if there's anyone who knows how vexing my cousins can be, it's me." Callan shot her a smile.

"When I'm with you, I feel as though I can either tell you everything or say nothing at all. It's honestly an enormous comfort." She sighed, slumping against the wall beside her.

"This may come as a surprise," Callan said, lowering his voice and glancing down the hall in either direction. "But I've been described as the silent type on more than one occasion."

They fell into a comfortable silence then, both shifting on the bench to look down on the bonfire in the courtyard below and occasionally glancing at one another, as they ate. Nova knew it was silly to be melancholy on such a festive evening, but Lady Estrid's revelation weighed on her. She had so many questions, and it seemed no one had all the answers she sought.

"Something else troubles you," Callan said.

Nova shook her head, resigned. It seemed there was little sense in trying to hide anything from him.

"I grew up believing my mother had been taken from me. Stolen away. Whatever her reasons, it's painful knowing she chose to leave." She cast a glance in his direction. He regarded her intently, his expression unreadable. "I don't expect you to understand what it's like to have both parents choose to leave you—"

Callan held up a hand between them; his eyes squeezed shut for a heart-beat before he spoke, and his voice took on the same soothing lilt he had used to calm her the night they met.

"Your mother made a choice, it's true. But your father was well and truly taken from you."

With great difficulty, Nova managed to swallow. When she spoke, her voice was barely louder than a whisper, a rasp of raw emotion, like gravel raking over the back of her throat.

"My father—" She cleared her throat and tried once more, stumbling over the words she had never spoken aloud. "My father took his own life."

There had been no note. No explanation. No final goodbye or last words of affection. Only the cloying scent of poison lingering in the air and an emp-ty glass vial clasped in his cold, rigid fingers. A vial she had pried loose and discarded before the physician arrived and pronounced his death a natural one.

Callan said nothing. Nova turned away, hiding her face from him and hastily brushing away a single hot tear, the evidence of her shame. She had never blamed her father. Only herself. Her desire to escape her life had consumed her for many years. It had blinded her to the fact that he sought an escape of his own.

She felt Callan close beside her an instant before the familiar, crisp scent of him surrounded her. He held out his hand, and Nova glanced from his rough palm to his face. The hallway was empty apart from the two of them, the muted notes of a ballad meandering down the corridor.

"Dance with me." His voice was low and commanding.

"I'm a terrible dancer," she murmured. "You could find a much better partner back in the hall."

"Nova." He shook his head. "I'm choosing you."

Her breath caught, and her hand found his before she could overthink the decision. Callan pulled her close, their bodies not quite touching, separated by a breath of air between them. Nova longed to close the small distance, to press herself so tightly against him that discerning where she ended and he began would be an impossible task. She swallowed her longing, looking up to meet the gold-flecked gaze of the male so skilled at seeing past her mask.

Callan smiled, a dimple forming on his cheek, and began to lead her in slow circles around the fine runner lining the wide corridor. His hold on her was firm but gentle as the tempo gradually increased.

A tiny voice spoke in Nova's ear, whispering from a hidden place deep within her. It called her foolish and tried desperately to remind her she'd done this once before. To remind her how things had turned out the first time. Closing her eyes, she buried the voice for the moment. Her head fell back as Callan supported her in his arms, and for the brief length of a dance, she was happy.

SIXTEEN

CALLAN STOOD BEFORE NOVA'S chamber door, attempting to bid her good night. Their dance had been too short; his hands lingered on her when the song trailed off into muffled cheers and applause down the hall. Callan knew better. He knew what being so close to her would do to him, but his good sense did nothing to stop him. He knew the pain of losing a parent, hated that he couldn't take the pain away from her. But helping her forget for a moment or two? That was a service he could provide.

The silence hanging in the air between them began to feel heavy. Callan cleared his throat to speak, but a messenger owl sailed over their heads, dropping a letter to the floor between their feet. Nova's name was looped across the front in formal script. She snatched up the folded parchment, running her fingertips over the cream-colored paper.

"Secret admirer?" Callan asked as he watched her turn the letter over in her hands, noting the seal of pearly, white wax, stamped with a symbol of a six-pointed star. Nova slid a finger beneath the flap, breaking the seal. Callan averted his eyes as she silently read the message. When she finished, she gripped his arm, pulling him into her room and down onto a chaise beside her before pushing the parchment into his hands.

The writer, a Sister Iris from the Temple of Illora, claimed to have information about Nova's mother and invited her to visit in one week's time to speak in person. The letter itself would serve as an invitation, granting Nova access to the temple. Insisting on secrecy, the Sister requested that Nova tell no one.

"Where is the temple? Is it nearby? Surely, I have to go." The words tumbled from Nova's lips, falling on top of one another.

Callan was not so easily convinced. He turned the paper over and back and held it up to the light, bringing it closer to his face and squinting. The seal appeared legitimate. There was no evidence of a charm or enchantment concealed on the parchment, though any correspondence laced with dark magic wouldn't have been able to breach the Estate's shield.

"The Temple of Illora sits on an island off the western coast of Silvergard," he said, handing the letter back to her. She scanned the text again, as if it might somehow contain more information the second time.

Callan's mind whirred, assessing the situation for potential threats or trickery. He suspected Nova was connected to the Lunar Court. Perhaps the letter was part of a ploy to entice her across the border into Silvergard. Still, it was unlikely a sister from the temple would be involved in such a scheme. Though close to the Lunar Court, the temple housed an autonomous Sisterhood, not bound to the territory in any way.

"Please, take me, Callan." Nova's voice was an urgent plea, her slender fingers clutching his forearm.

Callan tensed at her words, desperate to hear her speak them again under entirely different circumstances. He wanted to agree immediately, but forced himself to consider for a moment longer before giving his answer. Leaving Pyralis to accompany her on the journey would undoubtedly complicate things for him, but he would never entrust her safety to anyone else.

"I will," he said finally. "I'll make the arrangements and bring you there myself."

"When will we leave? How long is the journey?"

"I promise to get you there in time for the meeting. It will be safer to travel to Nivali first, then sail up the coast to the Isle of Illora. But, before we go, I must speak with Lady Estrid."

Nova stood at once. "Should we return to the Great Hall to find her?"

"No, you should rest. It's better if I speak with her alone. The message said to tell no one of your plans, though Her Grace likely wouldn't approve of you traveling to Illora even if I could tell her."

"I'm fairly certain she wants me as a daughter-in-law," Nova said blandly.

"She said as much?" Jealousy flooded his chest, a prickly heat creeping up his neck.

"She told me I've caught Evander's eye. Not that he has been discreet." She shrugged as she crossed to the door, the gesture devoid of emotion. Callan rose from his seat and followed.

"Try and sleep." He stepped into the dimly lit hallway. "If I'm able to convince her of our plans, we'll leave at first light."

The festivities hadn't dampened in the time since Callan had left with Nova. If anything, the celebration had grown more untamed. A large group of guests had begun a drinking competition, and those occupying the dance floor no longer followed prescribed steps, opting instead to twirl and stomp wildly around the room.

Callan spotted Evander swaying on the dance floor, his body pressed against a chestnut-haired female. Her head was thrown back in a hearty laugh, and Evander's fingers grasped at her hips as they danced, their tempo much slower than the music. Callan clenched his jaw, grateful Nova was in her chamber, far from his cousin's greedy hands.

Estrid lounged on her throne, her full cheeks flushed from the wine she swirled in her nearly empty goblet. She stood and raised a hand when Callan approached the platform, beckoning for him to join her. He found an unoccupied stool and carried it onto the dais, placing it beside her throne and taking a seat. She flopped back down, chuckling to herself before tipping her head back and swallowing the dregs of her wine.

"And where have you been?" she asked, slurring her words ever so slightly.

"Around." Resting his elbows on his knees, he leaned toward her so she could hear him over the laughter and shouts filling the hall. "You know I prefer to avoid these affairs."

"Oh, Callan. Don't be so contrary," she tutted, waving a hand in the air between them as if his sobriety might be catching.

"Where's Uncle Rowan?" he asked, jerking his chin at the empty throne beside hers.

She pointed to the crowd gathered to watch the drinking competition. The bystanders parted, and he saw Lord Rowan was a top contender, downing an entire stein of ale in seconds and slamming it on the tabletop. Callan smirked as his uncle roared and embraced his subjects who cheered him on. Ale dripped from the ends of his ginger beard.

"You look so much like your father. Especially when you wear your hair like that," Estrid said, smiling faintly and running her fingers along one of his braids. Her smile faded seconds later, and she held a finger in the air, suddenly remembering she was cross with him.

"Thorn tells me you've been ignoring his letters," she scolded.

Callan shifted on the stool. He hadn't expected an opportunity to present itself so early in the conversation.

"I've been busy," he said, pitching his voice over the dull roar of the crowd. "But, speaking of Thorn, I've been thinking. Perhaps it's time I traveled to Nivali." Estrid pulled back and stared him down, eyes narrowed in vague suspicion.

"It's been some time since I last visited," he added.

"That's an understatement," Estrid scoffed. She tapped a fingernail on the rim of her empty glass, signaling to a nearby servant.

"At any rate, I'm resolved to make the journey." Callan paused for a moment while the servant filled her glass nearly to the rim. He continued once they were alone again. "I'd like to bring Nova with me."

Estrid sputtered, nearly choking on the sweet red wine. "Bring Nova? Why?"

"Fawn has been teaching her about the territories. I'd like to show her the Winter Court. Also, I've been training her in sword fighting, and where better to learn than in Nivali?" He kept his face blank as she considered him, her eyes squinted as if she knew he had omitted certain details.

"She's quite an intriguing female," Estrid said finally, looking out over the crowd and tapping her forefinger on the arm of her throne. "Very well. But I hope you'll speak with Thorn and seriously consider what he has to say. And I expect you to protect Nova as if she were one of my own. She and Evander would make a handsome pair. Don't you agree?"

Callan caught sight of Evander sipping ale with his friends, his scorching gaze following any female who happened past them.

"I'll leave the wisdom of matchmaking to you, my Lady." Callan stood and bowed before taking his leave to make arrangements and steel himself for the journey ahead.

SEVENTEEN

Crisp air greeted Nova as she stepped out into the stone courtyard. The bonfire from the night before had burned down to embers, but the stars still shone dimly against the purpling predawn sky. She wore a dark blue, fur-lined cloak, a sensible wool dress, and thick, thigh-high stockings under her brown leather riding boots, all pilfered from Fawn's armoire. She had hoped to bid her friend farewell in person but found Fawn's chamber empty and her bed still neatly made. Realizing Fawn must have been with Josef, Nova smirked and quickly penned a note, which she left on the desk.

Bending down, she adjusted the dagger sheathed within her boot, the crossguard digging into her ankle. Heavy footfalls descended the stone steps behind her, and then Callan was at her side. He whistled sharply, cutting through the stillness of the early-morning air. A moment later, Frost appeared, trotting through the stone archway, his mane and tail, as white as a snowsquall, bouncing behind him.

The horse came to a halt in front of them, and Callan stroked its graceful neck with one hand, murmuring softly as he took the reins in the other. Nova stepped forward and gently scratched behind the horse's ear. Callan tightened the straps of the saddle and hefted a brown leather saddlebag onto

Frost's broad back, securing it in place.

Dressed in his travel clothes, a heavy woolen cloak over a gray tunic and thick black breeches, Callan looked more like the rugged tracker she had first met in Timberfell, but his dark hair was still braided and woven with beads.

"I can't help but notice you've prepared only one horse for our journey," she said. "Again."

"You've never traveled by portal before," Callan explained, bending to hold the stirrup steady.

"Is that all?"

Callan lifted his brows. "Well, I thought it unwise to mention, but the last time you rode a horse, you were thrown."

He stared her down, the faintest hint of a grin tugging at the corners of his mouth.

"Yes, that would be unwise to mention," she huffed, hooking her booted foot into the stirrup and swinging her leg over. Shifting in the saddle, she adjusted her dress so it covered her legs as much as possible. Callan mounted behind her and took hold of the reins.

"You can have your pick of any horse in the stables when we arrive in Nivali," he murmured in her ear as he nudged Frost into a trot.

"I'll accept that as an apology," she said. The warm rush of his laugh brushed against her cheek, and Nova was thankful he sat at her back and couldn't see her blushing.

She tried to hide it, but the prospect of leaving the Estate's protective shield frightened her. Though the sun had fully risen roughly an hour after they'd passed through the Estate's massive wooden gates, Nova still flinched at the snap of twigs as they rode along the worn cart path beneath trees crowned with terracotta leaves. The only creatures she spied lurking in the forest were wood sprites flitting from limb to limb, no larger than hummingbirds, their gold-veined wings shimmering in the sunlight. Though the creatures had sharp teeth and could be vicious, swarming when provoked, they were mostly harmless, according to Fawn's lessons.

Callan tugged gently on the reins, steering the horse toward a row of apple trees lining the path. As they passed, he plucked a fragrant golden apple from a branch, buffing it on his cloak before handing it to her. Holding the ripe fruit in both hands, Nova brought it to her nose and inhaled deeply before sinking her teeth into it.

"Is it just my Fae senses, or does the food taste much better here?" she asked, mouth full of the sweet fruit.

"Legend says that long ago, when mortals could freely enter Aemoria, eating our food or drinking our wine enchanted them, making them vulnerable. It's one of the reasons the Boundary was created, barring humans from entering. But, to your point, I choked down enough mealy apples and stale bread while I searched for you below the Boundary to say this with a fair bit of certainty: The food here is much better."

A few moments later, Nova took a final bite of the apple and tossed the core into the brush. Movement caught her eye, and she tilted her head back to see a raven lazily circling high above them, a smudge of black against the expanse of clear blue sky. Callan nudged Frost into a canter when they reached a fork in the path, taking them deeper into the forest and only slowing to a walk once they were sheltered beneath a canopy of overhanging branches.

"Is something the matter?" Nova asked, twisting to look at him.

"A lone raven." He tipped his head toward the shadowy tunnel stretching through the trees behind them. "It's a bad omen."

Eyes wide, Nova twisted further to look over her shoulder, but nothing followed. There was no sound but birdsong and the rustle of leaves in the light breeze. The morning was comfortably warm. As they plodded along, crossing between cool shadows and patches of dappled sunlight, Nova leaned back, relaxing against Callan's chest.

"How much longer until we reach the portal?" she asked, absentmindedly combing her fingers through the snowy strands of Frost's mane.

"Not long now. See the crest up ahead?" He pointed at a gradual slope in the path before them. "The portal is in a clearing on the far side of that hill."

"How does it work, exactly?" The notion of traveling in minutes a distance that would have taken weeks in the Human Realm fascinated her.

"Portals sit on sites of ancient magic throughout the territories. Each portal is a gateway leading to a sacred site in another location. The one up ahead is connected to an ancient site in Nivali, not far from the capital."

When they reached the hill a short time later, Callan wrapped his left arm snug around her waist, clicking his tongue for the horse to pick up speed on the incline. When they descended the opposite side, he steered them to the right and off the packed-dirt path. Frost stepped nimbly over roots and overgrown brush. Callan loosened his grip on Nova, but his arm lingered, resting loosely around her middle.

At last, they crossed into a large circular clearing, the ground carpeted in spongy, green moss. At the center stood an ancient tree. Its knotted branches and thick roots reached out nearly to the edge of the circle. The wide trunk was split, as if it had once been struck by lightning, creating an opening large enough for them to pass through, even while seated atop the horse. The tree appeared hollow with a seemingly infinite blackness contained within it. As they approached, a glimmer ran across the opening, not unlike the ripple that had revealed the shield over the training field. The breeze stilled, and the forest birds went silent.

"Are you ready?" Callan asked.

The fine hairs on Nova's arms stood on end. "Y-yes," she answered, stifling a shudder triggered by her proximity to such concentrated magic.

Callan urged Frost on, and they entered the portal. The sensation reminded Nova of crossing the Boundary. All sound faded as if she'd been plunged underwater, and a great weight pressed in on her from every direction. The horse trudged forward slowly, as if fighting against the pull of a tide.

After what felt like only a matter of minutes, Frost carried them through a passageway and onto a snowy, windblown cliff overlooking a cove flanked by high bluffs. Nova twisted in the saddle. The portal entrance was a cave in the rock face, unremarkable except for the carved symbols around the opening. Nova recognized the characters as those she'd seen etched on Callan's blade. A weathered stone carving of Brumal, the god of transformation, stood to the right of the cave, arms held out with palms facing the overcast sky.

Moored in the harbor below, dozens of ships of varying sizes bobbed on the water. Large patches of ice, thick and opaque, dotted the cove. Set back from the sandy shoreline stood a great wooden structure, its peaked roof blanketed in pure white snow. A sprawling city of smaller wooden structures surrounded the main building with evergreen trees jutting up toward the sky like ships' masts between them. Dozens of tiny windows glowed with the flickering orange of firelight. Nova glanced up, realizing the sky was already growing dark.

"It's nearly nightfall," she said, pulling her hood over her head against a blast of icy wind. The soft fur lining tickled her chilled cheeks.

"Traveling by portal is much faster than traveling over land, but it still takes time." Callan's tone was serious, his expression somber, as he pulled up his own hood and opened his cloak, draping it over her shoulders. She leaned into him and pulled the material tight around them both, the combined heat of their bodies warming her immediately. "And days are much shorter in the Winter Court."

Frost snorted impatiently, pawing at the snow-covered rock. Callan made no move to start their journey down the mountainside.

Nova realized he was stalling.

"The wind's picking up," she said after a few moments. "Perhaps we should be going."

"Of course," Callan said. His voice had a faraway quality, as if her words had pulled him from a trance. With a nudge from Callan's boots to his ribs, Frost started off along the snowy decline toward the Estate.

The bite of the frigid wind against her face lessened once they made it down off the mountainside and were shielded by the dense evergreen forest. The air was thick with the sharp scent of pine and cedar as they traveled between the trees. Snow slid off the branches, landing with soft thuds on the forest floor, the freed limbs springing up and casting clouds of fine white powder into the air.

After a time, they came upon a fence with several collapsed sections. Callan pulled at the reins and stopped before a sagging wooden archway where a path led down a small hill to an abandoned village below. The thatched roofs of the buildings were caved in, the cracked panes of the windows dark. Callan shuddered.

"What happened here?" Nova murmured, a shudder running through her as well.

"You remember the tale I told you of the Shadowbringer?"

Nova nodded.

"This village was one of the first attacked during his campaign of bloodshed. Some of the residents were found dead, mauled by dark creatures. Most had simply vanished leaving no trace. The village stands as a monument to those who were lost."

Callan urged the horse on, understandably eager to put the ruined village behind his back.

"The attacks have lessened over the centuries. It had been many years since the last report, but a squadron of Tundaran soldiers disappeared just weeks ago under similar circumstances." He fell silent, and they rode on through the hushed quiet of the forest, even Frost's hoofbeats muted by the snow.

At last, the Nivali Estate came into view as they rounded a bend in the path. The grand three-story structure rose up before them built upon a raised platform. Several steps spanned the length of the building—each one a single plank hewn from an enormous tree—leading to a pair of towering doors. Dozens of chimneys speared the sky, plumes of gray smoke swirling out before dissipating in the frozen wind.

Callan brought Frost to a halt at the foot of the steps and dismounted, leading the horse to a post and looping the reins around it before offering a hand to help Nova down. He stared up at the entryway flanked by tall windows emitting a warm glow.

He was stalling again.

"How long has it been since you were last here?" Nova asked, hauling him from his thoughts once more. She accepted his hand and slid down smoothly from the saddle.

Callan shook his head. "You still think of time as humans do. It's different for the Fae." He clenched his jaw. "Let's say it has been far too long."

"How long?"

Callan blew out a breath.

"Two hundred years."

Before Nova could react, he started up the steps, one hand on the small of her back, guiding her beside him. When they reached the top, he lowered his hood and laid his palms flat on the doors but hesitated, turning his face to hers.

"There is something you should know before we enter."

His eyes found hers slowly, as if the weight of his emotion made it difficult to lift his gaze.

"I am the rightful Noble Lord of Nivali."

With that, he shoved his hands against the heavy doors and strode purposefully into the Great Hall beyond.

Eighteen

A HUSH FELL AS Callan entered, the gust of frigid wind snaking through the room in his wake nearly extinguishing the fire blazing in the center of the hall. Nova followed, halting inside the entryway and glancing timidly at the crowd gathered around tables laden with platters of roasted meat and fish, loaves of bread, and pitchers of ale.

The space boasted a high vaulted ceiling. Doors lined the gallery walks on the second and third levels, likely leading to private chambers. Some folk regarded Callan with distaste, crinkled noses and curled lips. Most wore looks of shock, particularly the male sitting upon a modest wooden throne on the low platform on the far side of the great room. As Nova watched Callan stride to the foot of the platform, two guards closed the doors with a bang, startling her.

"Callan?" Rising from his throne, the male moved to the platform's edge, looking down on Callan.

While he had the appearance of a young man, an air of wisdom clung to him, and Nova surmised he was considerably older than Callan. Dressed simply in black breeches, a loose cream-colored shirt, and a brown leather vest, he wore no ornamentation to indicate his status as being above his guests'. He descended the steps to stand at Callan's side.

"Uncle Thorn." Callan bowed his head.

The two males stood roughly the same height, but while Callan was solid muscle, his uncle had a leaner build. He had a full beard, and brown hair that fell to his chin, one side shaved close to his scalp. There was little resemblance between the two. Where Callan was clearly a trained warrior, his body a finely crafted weapon, his uncle had the look of a strategist. Nova suspected Thorn relied on a sharp intellect over brute strength.

"My last several letters to you have gone unanswered." Thorn addressed Callan, but pitched his voice so the gathered crowd could hear. "And, as welcome as it is, you sent no word to inform me of this . . . visit."

"There wasn't time. We've come urgently to take care of a personal matter concerning my companion." Callan motioned for Nova to join him.

She approached slowly, uneasy under the sea of eyes tracking her across the room, her footsteps echoing off the high ceiling. She reached Callan's side and lowered her hood. Startled gasps erupted from the crowd. Two guards posted at the base of the platform rushed forward, weapons drawn in a flash of steel caught in the firelight.

In a heartbeat, Callan pulled his own sword from the sheath at his back and swept Nova behind him, shielding her body with his own. The nearest guard halted just short of running onto Callan's blade.

"Anyone who even thinks of harming her will meet a swift death upon my sword. Without hesitation. Without mercy. Am I understood?" Callan's roar brought a dead silence to the crowded hall. None dared answer.

Callan's uncle raised his arm, signaling his guards to lower their weapons. The third and fourth fingers on his left hand were missing. The guards obeyed his command, shrinking back into position, wary eyes fixed on both Callan and Nova.

"Might we speak privately, Uncle?" Callan asked, his voice calm and even in spite of the blade still leveled before him. Thorn searched Callan's face for a beat before clapping his hands and glancing around at the onlookers.

"Clear the hall."

Abandoning full plates and half-empty cups, everyone rose from their seats, some climbing the stairs and others heading outdoors. Only when the room was empty did Callan return his sword to the sheath at his back. He turned to Nova, his dark eyes wide as he gripped her hand in his own. Under the circumstances, Nova welcomed the touch and clung to his hand with equal force.

"Won't you introduce me?" Thorn asked, his eyes narrowed on Nova.

Callan turned back to face his uncle. "Thorn, this is Nova. She's been a guest in Pyralis."

Thorn motioned to a male servant who stood like a statue close by, awaiting his Lord's instructions.

"Show *Miss Nova* to a guest chamber. Light the fire and prepare a tray with food and drink." He waved a dismissive hand in her direction, as if shooing away a fly buzzing in his ear.

"Nova remains with me," Callan said, his tone leaving no room for argument.

"Very well." Thorn addressed the servant again. "Prepare the fire. Bring food later."

The servant bowed before hurrying up the staircase and out of sight. Thorn sat on a stool beside the fire and motioned for them to do the same. Callan and Nova lowered themselves onto a long bench on the opposite side of the stone pit, flames dancing between them and Callan's uncle.

"Now then, what are you doing here, Callan?"

"I plan to accompany Nova on her journey north," Callan explained.

"To Silvergard?" Thorn's tone was wary as he studied her. "It's unwise to travel to the Lunar Court."

He held up an empty cup, which was promptly filled by a waiting servant holding a large pitcher. Thorn motioned toward them, and the servant filled cups for Nova and Callan as well. Nova sipped politely, realizing it wasn't ale but a sweet honeyed wine. In the bright light of the fire, she could better see Thorn's face, noting the faintest creases at his brow and the corners of his eyes—eyes pinning her with an appraising stare.

"How fortunate, then, that we're not traveling there." Callan swallowed a large gulp from his own cup.

"Ah." Thorn stared into his mug. "Then where *are* you going?"

"Nova has plans to visit the Temple of Illora. I offered to escort her by boat to avoid traveling through Lunar territory."

"So, this is only a temporary visit," Thorn said flatly. "I confess, when I saw you burst through those doors, I hoped you'd finally come to honor your responsibilities here."

Callan's jaw tensed, and Nova suddenly wished she had been whisked away to the guest chamber.

"I tire of this discussion," Callan said, words clipped. "It's the reason why I no longer even open your letters. I believe I've made my position clear."

"I understand your position," Thorn responded, voice raised. He paused to compose himself before continuing. "I mourn them too. So do your subjects. But you cannot continue to allow your grief to prevent you from fulfilling your obligations to Nivali. To your people."

"Everyone seems quite well under your rule." Callan gestured to the plentiful food and furs.

"I'm a regent. A good one, if I may say so, but I am not the rightful Noble Lord of Nivali. The folk do not forget this. It's you who has forgotten your oath."

Callan flexed his wrists as if the markings concealed beneath his bracers pained him.

"I have not forgotten!"

His shield slipped in his anger, and, for an instant, Nova once again beheld the raw power of Callan's true form. A bright light burst forth, like the blinding glare of sun on snow. Silver flecks glinted on his cheekbones, his dark hair blowing on an unseen breeze. Then his shield slammed back into place, the bright light vanishing as quickly as it had come. When he spoke again, his voice was a pained staccato.

"I cannot forget. I cannot move on. I cannot do what you ask of me." Callan hunched forward, as if weighed down by the burden of his uncle's expectations. Nova resisted the urge to reach out and touch him. The hall was silent save for the crackling of the fire as Thorn observed his nephew, his sharp mind clearly assessing the situation.

"You're weary from your travels," he said at last. "We'll speak again once you've rested."

Thorn clapped his large hands together, and a servant appeared, ready to see them to their quarters. Callan stormed off without another word to his uncle.

"Sleep well, Nova," Thorn said as she rose to leave. She made a quick curtsy before climbing the stairs to the upper level, keenly aware of Thorn's watchful eyes on her back.

Nova followed a trail of ice and snow to an ornately carved door at the far end of the hall. The door stood ajar, the knob encased in ice and the wooden surface coated in a thick layer of frost. She stepped into the room and closed the door behind her. Callan stood before the fireplace, an elbow resting on the mantelpiece beside his sword and dagger.

A large bed sat on a frame of carved wood, piled high with plump pillows, thick blankets, and plush furs. Two chairs and a small table sat tucked into the corner. Another doorway on the far side of the room presumably led to a bathing chamber. Tapestries of wintry scenes hung on the paneled walls:

snow-covered forests and green swirls dancing across midnight skies. An enormous white pelt covered the floor before the fire, with a small settee draped in woven blankets angled before the hearth.

Nova crossed the room, coming to stand beside Callan. Holding out her frozen hands, she flexed her reddened knuckles, joints sluggish from the cold. He kept his gaze trained on the fire. She undid the clasp of her cloak, draping it over one of the dining chairs. Tugging her dagger from her boot, she laid it atop the mantel beside Callan's blades.

"Well," she said. "That was quite a homecoming."

Callan huffed and continued staring into the flames. A moment later, he looked at her, his expression tight.

"I'm sorry." He shook his head, the action heavy with the same emotion she'd seen when he hesitated in front of the doors to the Great Hall. She now recognized it as shame. "I'm sorry you saw that."

"I'm not," she murmured, a thrill skipping down her spine at the memory of the beauty and power of Callan's true form. "Tell me what happened. What's kept you from your home for so long?"

Callan removed his own cloak and hung it on a hook beside the fireplace. He ran his hands roughly over his face as he sank onto the settee, slumping in the seat and focusing on the fire once again.

"When I was a youngling, all I wanted was to be like my father, the Noble Lord of Nivali," he began. "I trained eagerly, mastering combat with blades, growing stronger and more skilled with each passing year. But the older I got, the more I envied my father's emissaries who were permitted to leave the territory and visit new and interesting lands.

"I must have asked a hundred times to be granted leave to travel with his envoys, but he always refused, saying I was bound to the land and needed to stay close. To be ready for when my time came to rule. Like many young folk, I felt trapped and decided I knew what was best. And so, I set out on my own without my parents' approval, traveling across Aemoria. I wrote them regularly but never sent word before I'd moved on, so they couldn't track me.

"I was traveling in this way, cut off from the world, when Omen's attacks began. No one could reach me when my father and mother were killed defending the village we passed earlier. Their bodies were never found."

His voice had grown rough. Nova knelt on the floor, resting her shoulder against the empty cushion beside him. He avoided her eye as he continued.

"When I learned what had happened, I was mad with grief. At first, I refused to believe they were truly gone." He paused, shaking his head ruefully. "I didn't return for the rite to honor my parents, or the ceremony to formally name my uncle as regent. I spent decades seeking a chance at revenge, running from the truth. Running from myself. The longer I stayed away, the harder it became to return."

Callan stood abruptly, walking to the hearth and hiding his face from her.

"Even now, after all this time, I can't make myself do it." His voice broke. "I'm a coward."

Nova rose to stand directly behind him, laying a timid hand between his shoulders.

"That's not true," she said. "Grief is complicated. When my father died—" The memory of Anson's unblinking eyes stunned her for an instant. "I scarcely rose from my bed for nearly a year. I would have missed his rite if Agnes hadn't bathed and dressed me herself. If she hadn't propped me up on her arm and kept me standing as they lit the pyre."

Nova spoke as if soothing a frightened animal. The same way Callan had spoken to her the night he upended her entire existence and revealed her Fae heritage. Callan turned to her, eyes on the floor.

"You are no coward, Callan."

His gaze rose to meet hers, his dark eyes shining like river rocks, and Nova was certain no one had ever spoken those words to him before.

"Despite everything, you've kept your heart open. To Lady Estrid and Lord Rowan. Evander and Fawn. To me. You're so much braver than I am."

Nova's heart thundered in her chest at the closeness of their bodies. She took a shuddering breath and willed her hands to remain at her sides, but she found it was useless. Surrendering to the urge she'd felt countless times before, Nova raised her hand to his face, tracing the edge of his jaw to his chin. She felt his entire body tense under her fingertips. Causing such a response in him, a beautifully brutal warrior, made her feel incredibly powerful. Emboldened, she rose onto the balls of her feet and brushed a soft kiss against his lips. Pulling back, she held her breath, pulse racing, as she awaited his response.

Callan's chest rose and fell with several rapid breaths, his gaze fixed on her mouth. The next instant, he crashed against her like a wave, his mouth claiming hers. One arm circled around her, pulling her tight against his chest, his other hand cradling the back of her head. Nova returned his kiss, matching his frenzied pace. Though it had been years since she'd last been kissed, her lips quickly remembered how.

Gods above, it had never felt like this before.

Nova tangled her fingers in the soft strands of Callan's hair as she opened her mouth to him. He slowed, regaining some measure of control, and angled her head to deepen the kiss, his tongue caressing hers. The sensation sent a tremor of desire between her thighs, and she moaned against his mouth.

An abrupt knock sounded on the door, and a servant entered carrying a tray of food and a pitcher. Callan spun away as the male crossed the room and set the tray on the table. Clearing his throat, Callan snatched up his cloak and threw it around his shoulders before trailing the servant to the door.

"You should eat," he said, pausing in the open doorway, breath ragged. "I'll shield the door. Only I will be able to enter unless you invite someone in.

Don't wait for me. I'm sure you're tired." He managed a hollow smile before he left.

Nova stared at the door for several moments after Callan was gone, her body acutely aware of his absence. She brought her hand to her mouth, fingers lingering briefly on her swollen lips before she buried her face in her hands. Kissing him had been impulsive. Reckless. It violated a tenet she'd adopted years before, when her first lover abandoned her, leaving her heart battered and bleeding. A belief solidified by the sudden death of her father by his own hand.

Everyone—even those who claim to love you—will leave you.

No. The kiss was a mistake, one that could never be repeated.

Nova ate quickly and swallowed a cup of sweet wine before stripping down to her shift and stockings and crawling under the furs layered on top of the plush feather bed. As she lay there, listening to pops from the dry logs on the fire and waiting for sleep to come, she wondered where Callan had gone. She hoped he'd rejoined his uncle in the hall, or that he was sharing a drink with an old friend. But she knew him well enough to know he'd likely sought somewhere to be alone. Her heart ached for him, but she understood the impulse.

After all, she was no stranger to self-imposed isolation.

The wine had warmed Nova from within, and a loud rap on the door roused her from her sleep before she even realized she'd closed her eyes. Gray, early-morning light streamed in through the lightly frosted windowpane. The fire had died down to coals, and she shivered in the chill room as the blankets slipped down to her waist when she sat up. Callan wasn't there. The only evidence he'd returned at some point in the night was an indentation on the pelt before the fire.

"Come in," she called out, fairly certain an assassin wouldn't have knocked.

A female servant with a slight frame and dirty blond hair entered balancing a tray in her hands. She made a slight curtsy before making her way to the table in the corner.

"Would you mind putting it on the bed instead?" Nova stretched her arms lazily toward the ceiling as the servant set the platter at the edge of the mattress. Nova tried to smile in thanks, but the female wouldn't look at her.

"What's your name?" Nova asked.

Not answering, the servant crossed to the fireplace, hurriedly stirring the embers and adding fresh logs to coax the fire back to life. Her task complete, she took the tray from the night before and exited the room without ever looking Nova in the eyes. Nova tried to distract herself with the fresh oatcakes spread with golden honey and sticky berry jam, but the exchange unsettled her.

Once she had eaten her meal, she pulled on her woolen dress from the day before and gathered her hair into a loose braid. Draping her cloak around her shoulders, she left the room intent on visiting the stables. The Estate was still asleep with only household staff and a few early risers moving about the Great Hall. Nova bowed her head as she passed, but no one returned the gesture. Most looked away as they rushed past her.

Nova breathed a sigh of relief when she finally stepped out into the quiet solitude of the frozen morning. The sky was overcast, but the wind had died down since the night before. Fat snowflakes swirled around her, carried on a gentle breeze. She pulled her hood over her head and scanned the area to get her bearings. Trudging through the snow to the rear of the main building, she followed the winding lanes connecting the smaller outbuildings and homes of the common Fae until she arrived at the stables.

The familiar scent of hay comforted her as she strolled down the long row of stalls, each one housing a magnificent creature. Most were docile and friendly, reaching their velvety muzzles over the rails in search of scratches or a handful of feed. One reared back, snorting and pawing at the floor as Nova approached its stall. It was a mare, her shiny coat a deep charcoal, like a patch of cool shade.

Nova neared the gate, extending her hand as she murmured to the horse. The mare resisted at first, releasing an agitated whinny and stomping her hooves, but she moved closer to the railing after a few moments. Once the horse had calmed, Nova laid her hand flat on the side of the animal's neck. Slowly, the horse warmed to Nova, accepting pats along her graceful neck and scratches behind her ears.

"It seems you've made a friend." Callan's voice cut through the quiet, and Nova turned her head to find him standing in the archway. An intense flutter filled her chest at the sight of him, like the rapid beating of a hummingbird's wings.

"You did say I could choose any horse from the stables." She turned back to the mare and ran a hand along her smooth coat. "May I have her?"

"I'll have to ask Thorn," he replied, his voice close behind her. The crisp scent of him reached her, carried on the breeze. The horse snorted, drawing her head back behind the rail.

"Are you certain you want that one? She seems a bit . . . aloof."

"She's misunderstood," Nova tutted, holding out a handful of straw and laughing quietly to herself as the mare nibbled at it, lips tickling her palm. "She just needs a little patience and love."

"I'm sorry I left last night." Callan leaned against the rail, facing her. "I agreed to accompany you on this journey, and then I abandoned you in a strange place." He glanced around the barn, reluctant to meet her eye. "Returning to Nivali has unearthed feelings I thought I'd buried long ago, but it's no excuse."

"You don't owe me an explanation, Callan. Though your apology is appreciated."

"You shouldn't be wandering about without me." He shot an uneasy glance over his shoulder to the entrance.

Nova swallowed hard and cleared her throat, remembering how eager Thorn's guards had been to spill her blood before anyone had even learned her name. She tamped down her fear and took a step back to survey the mare, wild and beautiful and perfect.

"I think I'll call her Shade."

NINETEEN

CALLAN WOVE HIS WAY through the folk gathered in the hall, drinking and swapping stories as they awaited the evening meal. Nova had returned to their shared room to bathe after a day spent touring the Estate and the fishing village along the sandy shoreline. Callan had been away for so long, it felt as if he was seeing everything for the first time alongside her. He'd forgotten how the morning mist gathered around the tops of the rocky cliffs that guarded the inlet, the musical quality of the language spoken by the folk who fished the frigid waters and traded their catches on the docks each day.

Callan approached an area sectioned off with heavy woven curtains in the far corner of the hall. The guard posted at the entrance stared at him for a beat before bowing deferentially and granting him access to his uncle's private sitting area. Thorn lounged on a low sofa on one side. Pelts of varying shades and sizes lined the floor, and a low fire crackled in a brazier in the center.

"Callan, sit." Thorn straightened in his seat and motioned to the chair across from him. As Callan sat, he realized Thorn wasn't alone.

A slender female stood at the fringe of the firelight. A flowing robe of dark blue velvet accentuated her long flaxen hair, which hung loose down her back, silver beads and small white shells woven into several braided sections. The sharp, icy blue of her eyes and the evenly spaced diagonal lines below her ears identified her as one of the fisher folk whose gills allowed them to dive deep under water to fish with spears.

"Callan, meet Liv, a very important member of my Court."

Liv sauntered out from the edge of the shadows, stepping around the fire. Callan rose from his seat, and she dangled her hand before him as if she expected him to kiss it. He glanced down, and his intuition flared, cautioning him not to touch her. He bowed instead, and she dropped her hand to her side, an impish smile stretching across her full lips.

"Pleased to meet you, Your Grace," she said, her words carrying the accent of her people.

Callan only nodded, holding her icy gaze as he returned to his seat.

"Liv was just leaving." Thorn stood and guided her to the exit, placing a soft kiss on her lips before showing her out. "I'll join you later," he said, watching through the gap in the curtains as she slipped into the crowd and out of view.

"Is she your consort?" Callan asked once they were alone. His uncle returned to his spot on the sofa, lounging with one of his long legs stretched out across the cushions.

"Liv is my lover, yes," Thorn said. "And a gifted seer. Had you taken her hand, she might have glimpsed something of your future."

"Perhaps you should simply ask her what my future holds, since the subject interests you so greatly." Callan leaned back and stared down at the well-worn creases on his boots.

"It doesn't work like that, and you know it." Thorn sighed, rubbing a hand over the bristly hairs on the side of his scalp. "Perhaps you should get on with it and ask what you've come to ask."

"I need one of your boats and some of your sailors to work the oars."

Callan leaned forward, resting his elbows on his knees.

"For your friend's journey north," Thorn said, words sticky with skepticism.

"Yes. The journey should only take a few days if the weather is favorable."

Callan waited as Thorn dragged his hand down the length of his beard, twisting the ends between his thumb and forefinger.

"It's a dangerous journey to make." Thorn leaned forward, mirroring Callan's pose. "Tell me, why are you risking yourself to help her?"

"She is . . . important to me." Callan didn't fully understand his feelings for Nova, and he wasn't eager to discuss them with his uncle.

"If you want to bed her, there are far less perilous ways to get between her thighs." Thorn flashed his teeth in a lustful grin.

"That's not what this is about," Callan growled.

Thorn retracted his smile. "Of course not. But how much do you really know about her? She clearly has the look of a Silvergardian." Thorn flashed his teeth again, his lip curling disdainfully. He spat into the fire, eliciting a hiss from the coals. "You know more than most what those beasts in the North are capable of. Even now she could be poisoning your thoughts. Controlling you. Please tell me the notion has at least crossed your mind."

Callan gritted his teeth. He *had* been acting out of character since he'd met Nova. But his mind wasn't dulled. Quite the opposite. He felt awake for the first time in a long while.

"Her mother hails from Sonnend," Callan offered, hoping to ease some of Thorn's distaste. "I suppose it's possible her father had Lunar blood, but she has no connection to him."

"Blood is everything, Callan. Does it not spark your intuition that a female who looks as she does has entwined herself with the rightful Noble Lord of Nivali?"

"Nova knew nothing of my obligations until I told her on our arrival

146

here. She has no ulterior motives, I assure you."

"Forgive me. As the regent, I have a duty to my subjects to be suspicious." Thorn lifted his hands. His loose sleeves were rolled to the elbows, displaying the solid black cuffs inking both of his wrists.

"Will you loan me the boat or not?" Callan groaned, rising from his seat and looking down on his uncle. At this rate, he'd be better off renting a vessel from one of the fisher folk. Callan stood unflinching under his uncle's appraising stare.

"I'll loan you the boat since you seem so convinced." Thorn threw up his hands in a show of surrender. "But I have one condition."

"Which is?"

Thorn stood before him, placing a firm hand on his shoulder.

"When you return, you must remain in Nivali for one year. Get to know your subjects, Callan. Allow them to get to know you. It's what your parents always wanted. You've been away for far too long."

"If memory serves, you voted in favor of my proposal along with the rest of the Council."

"Because I thought it was what you needed at the time. I figured once you got it out of your system, you'd return home where you belong. Had I known you'd stay away this long, I never would have agreed." He regarded Callan expectantly, for once abandoning his posturing. "Please, Callan."

Callan stared into the fire, considering his uncle's proposal for a moment before countering.

"Six months if you'll part with the charcoal mare in the stables. Nova has taken a liking to her."

"We have a bargain." Thorn grinned, gripping Callan's hand firmly.

An icy sensation slithered along the markings on his wrists, magic binding him to the terms of the agreement.

His uncle clapped him roughly on the back. "Join the feast

tonight—both of you—as my guests."

"Of course, my Lord." Callan bowed and took his leave, winding his way through the smoky hall and back to Nova.

Nova's travel dress needed washing. Bits of straw and sand clung to the sodden hem after her day spent grooming Shade in the stables and wandering along the shore. She wrinkled her nose and tossed the garment into the corner before rummaging through Callan's saddlebag for a fresh gown. A member of the household staff had drawn her a steaming bath as soon as she'd returned from touring the village. The scenery was breathtaking, but nearly every resident she encountered throughout the day shied away from her. Their obvious unease stirred up a familiar anxiety in the pit of her stomach, like a layer of silt disturbed at the bottom of a pond.

Finally finding her olive day dress, she shook out the wrinkles as much as she could. It wasn't the most practical gown for the weather, but it would have to do. Nova tightened the laces of her stays before gathering the skirt and stepping into the dress, easing the straps up over her shoulders. The doorknob twisted behind her, and Callan entered, averting his eyes when he realized she was dressing.

"Apologies—I'll wait outside."

"No." She held up a hand to stall him. "I could use your help." She turned her back to him, her stays peeking out from between the row of tiny buttons waiting to be done up along her spine.

Callan closed the door before coming up behind her. Nova held her breath, listening to the soft thud of his boots on the fur carpet as he approached. He made quick work of fastening the delicate buttons, with a tenderness out of character for a trained warrior.

Her breath caught at the brush of his knuckles against her skin. She wondered if the touch had been intentional. Callan lifted her hair over her shoulder, smoothing the strands down her upper back. Neither had spoken of their kiss during the many hours they'd spent together earlier. But an attraction that had perhaps always passed unseen between them now felt awake and alive, a forceful pull drawing them close to one another repeatedly throughout the day.

"Nova?" His voice was hushed.

"Yes?" She turned to him, steeling herself for him to broach the subject.

"I . . . made the arrangements with my uncle." Callan retreated. The change was almost imperceptible, but Nova felt as if a curtain had been drawn between them. "He's agreed to lend us a boat and a crew of sailors."

"That's wonderful news," she said, at once relieved and disappointed. She looped the silver earrings Fawn had gifted her through her ears and slid her mother's ring back onto her finger.

"You're welcome to have Shade, as well. And all for the price of six months of my life."

"What do you mean?"

"I agreed to remain in Nivali for six months after we return." He shrugged. "Perhaps it's time."

"Your uncle must be pleased."

"He's invited us to join the feast tonight as his guests. If you'd like, of course."

"How kind of him." Nova's voice lacked the enthusiasm she'd hoped to muster. She worried the ring around her finger, a nervous habit she'd developed since arriving in Aemoria.

"I can have our meal brought up if you'd rather not go," he offered.

"I don't wish to cause anyone discomfort." She attempted a casual laugh, but it came out a bit choked. "Most folk I saw around the Estate today would barely glance in my direction, let alone speak to me." Her eyes found his, trying to read his reaction there.

Callan's brow furrowed, and he shook his head, the muscle in his jaw ticking.

"Nivali shares a border with Silvergard. Even before the reign of Onyx and Omen's attacks around the Realm, there had already been mistrust between the territories for thousands of years. Onyx's youngest son sits on the Lunar Throne today. I'm sorry, Nova—their suspicion is based purely on your appearance."

Nova gathered her hair and busied herself with weaving the damp strands into a braid. What a fool she'd been to believe she'd finally found acceptance. What did it say about her that even in a world teeming with magic and mythical creatures, she was still wrong somehow? Still didn't belong? Callan's gaze lingered on her. Nova bit the inside of her cheek, willing her face into a neutral expression.

"Nova." His tone was apologetic. She couldn't bear the thought of him pitying her.

"Don't trouble yourself, Callan. Gods know it isn't the first time I've been judged for my looks." She secured the end of her plait with a black leather cord and smoothed her hands over the front of her gown. "Let's join the feast. I'm starving."

Nova knew her performance hadn't fooled him. Knew he could see right through her carefully crafted exterior. But he said nothing and simply offered his arm.

The air in the hall was tinged gray with smoke from the fire. A cheerful buzz of laughter and conversation filled the space. Upon the dais sat a long table with several chairs arranged behind it, the surface covered with platters of steaming food and large pitchers.

Thorn presided over the feast wearing a formal blue jacket embroidered with silver thread, though the buttons remained unfastened, revealing a loose-fitting shirt underneath and a patch of dark chest hair peeking out at the collar. A striking blond sat on his left, dressed in a robe of luxurious blue velvet cinched at the waist. The two reclined lazily in their seats, their faces close together. The female whispered in Thorn's ear. Callan tilted his head close to Nova's as they descended the stairs.

"The female beside my uncle is his consort, Liv. She's one of the fisher folk." Liv's piercing blue gaze fell upon them as they reached the bottom of the staircase. "Thorn says she's a seer."

The notion intrigued Nova, but she kept her expression blank as they approached the base of the platform. Thorn rose from his seat and held his arms wide in welcome. He clapped his hands loudly, immediately drawing the attention of the feasting crowd, whose voices died down in anticipation of their lord's address. Thorn raised his cup in the air.

"I welcome my nephew, Callan, and his companion, Nova, as my guests this evening. A toast to our honored guests."

The room filled with a mix of genuine and half-hearted cheers as those gathered hoisted their own cups high. Callan bent forward at the waist, holding his fist over his heart. Nova followed his lead and curtsied, bowing her head respectfully. Thorn motioned for them to join his table, and the room was, once again, filled with laughter and animated chatter. Callan pulled Nova's chair out for her before taking the seat beside his uncle, leaving the chair on her other side empty.

Nova was ravenous, and Callan wasted no time filling a plate with roasted pheasant and root vegetables, which he placed before her. Nova listened absently as Thorn regaled some of his guests with a tale of a perilous sea voyage, made many years before, when his ship was nearly capsized by a run-in with a sea serpent. Scanning the crowd in between bites of food and sips of wine, Nova observed several folk watching her with uneasy sideways glances.

For all the gods' love, smile, she chided herself.

She lifted the corners of her mouth, baring her teeth in an expression she hoped was pleasant. Eventually, she was forced to look down at her lap to rest her cheeks, which had begun to ache with the effort of appearing likable. Nova's head snapped up as Thorn's consort, Liv, slipped into the empty chair beside her. She was a stunning beauty. Her skin was a pearlescent white, and sections of her long blond hair were woven into intricate braids.

Liv held her cup loosely in her long fingers, tilting it toward Nova.

"A toast to the outcasts," she murmured, a conspiratorial smile gracing her lovely face.

Nova lifted her own cup, hesitating for an instant before tapping it lightly against Liv's. They both drank.

"Half the folk in this room don't believe I deserve to be here," Liv said, jerking her delicate chin at the crowd. "I'd wager many more are questioning what you're doing here." Her accent gave her voice a musical quality.

If anyone else had spoken to her as Liv had, Nova might have taken offense, but it was clear Liv considered them equals.

"I suppose it must be odd to see someone who looks as I do dining in this hall. At the Noble Lord's table, no less." Nova shrugged one shoulder, setting her cup down and nudging her food around her plate with her fork.

"Those who fear you will one day celebrate you."

Nova looked up, barely able to keep the surprise from her face.

"It doesn't take a seer to recognize that there is something remarkable about you," Liv said.

"I'm no one special."

"You have many questions about the past. Those I cannot answer." Liv tilted her head to one side, her brows pinched as if in thought. "But, if you'd like, I can try to spy something of your future." Liv laid a hand palm up in her own lap beneath the table.

Nova wavered for a breath. She glanced at Callan on her right, engrossed in his uncle's tall tale. The other folk gathered in the hall were occupied with their own conversations. Turning back to Liv, Nova took her hand.

Liv's eyes fell shut as her fingers closed around Nova's, then snapped open again an instant later. Her icy blue irises were clouded over with a milky sheen, gleaming like luminous pearls. Her voice was low and monotonous when she spoke. Nova leaned in close to hear her over the noise of the crowd.

"You are born of sun, moon, and shadow. Wherever your path leads, death will follow. Do not despair, for you are the light that casts out the darkness."

Liv blinked slowly, her eyes returning to their normal color. She released Nova's hand and straightened in her seat with a casual sigh.

"It appears my cup is empty," Liv said, picking up her mug. She stood from her chair, bending down beside Nova and speaking low in her ear. "Stay close to Callan. The thread of your life is woven together with his."

Liv breezed across the platform, returning to her seat beside Thorn on the other end of the table and leaving Nova stunned. Thorn's epic tale concluded to a chorus of cheers from his captivated audience. Callan turned to her, smiling wide enough to show off the dimple in his left cheek. Nova swallowed past the lump in her throat and forced a smile of her own, tight-lipped and hollow.

The rest of the evening passed in a blur, the noisy gathering muted around her as Liv's words echoed in her mind, part riddle and part warning. Fear twisted in the pit of her stomach as she envisioned the specter of death stalking her like a shadow. But an inconvenient anticipation took root within her, a faint warmth spreading from her chest and out along her limbs, at the confirmation that she and Callan were connected. Nova studied him from under her lashes. He appeared happier and more at ease than she'd ever seen

153

him, as though he was exactly where he belonged.

She was staring unblinking into the dancing flames of the fire some time later, her empty cup cradled near her chin, when Callan laid a hand on her shoulder. The sounds of the feast suddenly returned to full volume around her, and she blinked several times.

"Are you well?" he asked, his brow creased.

"Yes, of course," she assured him. "A bit tired."

"I'll bring you upstairs," he said, offering her his hand. They bid his uncle good night before leaving. The cheerful voices of those who continued drinking in the hall faded to a low hum as they neared their chamber.

Callan closed and shielded the door, sealing them away from the rest of the world. Gathering several blankets from the arm of the sofa, he crouched and arranged them into a makeshift bed on the pelt before the hearth.

"It'll be a few days yet before we're able to set sail for Illora." He smoothed his hands over the blankets and moved to the sofa where he tugged off his boots. "I thought we might spend some time training before we leave."

"I'd like that," Nova said distractedly, removing one of the plush pillows from the bed and tossing it at him.

He caught the pillow against his chest and set it aside before slipping the bracers off his forearms. "I saw you met Liv. What did you speak about?"

Her heart stuttered. "I allowed her to tell my future."

Callan was silent for a beat. "And?"

Nova bit her lip. "She told me death will follow me wherever I go, but those who fear me will one day celebrate me."

Nova remained silent, bracing for Callan's reaction. She chanced a brief look in his direction. He said nothing, his expression unreadable.

"I know," she said, forcing a dry laugh. "It's ridiculous." She gripped the layers of blankets and tugged, roughly turning down the bed.

"I didn't say that," Callan protested, his voice quiet.

Nova pinched the bridge of her nose, hot tears stinging at the corners of her eyes. "I wouldn't fault you for thinking it."

"Nova—"

"Don't, Callan." She couldn't bear the tenderness in his voice as he spoke her name. She turned to him, her face a mask of cold indifference. "I'm not a child. I know there's nothing remarkable about me. Liv was simply having a bit of fun at my expense."

"Nova, look at me." He was beside her then, his fingers loosely circling her wrist. She wrenched her hand away from his touch.

"Forgive me." He stepped away from her, clasping his hands behind his back. "I thought . . . last night—"

"Last night was a mistake," she said, lacing her words with as much ice as she could summon. "It never should have happened."

"I see." Callan's face fell, and she was taken aback by the depth of pain conveyed in such a simple look. Her rejection had cut him deeper than any blade ever could.

Callan didn't try to speak, his jaw tight and face drawn. Nova spun, forcing herself to turn away from the hurt shining in his eyes. She rushed into the bathing chamber and closed the door against the overpowering attraction intent on drawing her to him no matter how fiercely she fought against it. When she came out a short time later, Callan had blown out the candles. He lay on the floor with his broad back to her, silhouetted against the glow of the fire.

Nova crept into bed quietly and buried her face in the soft down of the pillow. Only then did she allow her tears to fall, silent and hidden, the evidence of them quickly vanishing into the pillowcase. She desperately needed Liv's premonition to be false. Her words had confirmed what Nova already felt. Already feared. There was *something* between her and Callan. She'd already allowed herself to grow too close to him. Too fond of him.

Nova had known love before. Knew what it was to accept someone into your heart, into your body. She also knew the bitter taste and hollow ache of heartbreak; it was a pain she feared she wouldn't survive a second time.

She peeked over the covers to where Callan lay motionless. Her awareness of his anguish twisted like a knife in her chest. But she knew it was nothing compared to the suffering she would endure if she allowed herself to love him. If she gave herself to him entirely and he left her.

As everyone else had.

A full minute passed before Callan realized he was staring at the door through which Nova had disappeared. His fists hung clenched at his sides, palms dusted with a biting frost, the blue haze swirling in his field of vision. He crossed to the fireplace, standing in the spot where he and Nova had kissed the night before. No, it was more than a kiss. It had awakened something in him, something buried deep and long forgotten. He'd felt more alive in that fleeting moment with her wrapped in his arms than he had for centuries.

She'd returned his kiss with a passion that seemed to burn as intensely as the one blazing within him. Or had he imagined that? If they hadn't been interrupted . . . Well, they had been interrupted. It was no use speculating. But now, the connection he'd felt earlier in the day, passing like an invisible thread between them, seemed to have been severed. Something had changed, but what?

Liv.

There must have been more to her premonition.

He approached the bathing chamber door, intending to knock, but stopped short, his hand hovering in midair. Nova had kissed him after he told her the story of how he'd lost his parents. Callan winced. She hadn't kissed him out of passion at all.

It was pity.

A prickly heat crept up his neck, and he blinked against an unwelcome sting at the corners of his eyes. How could he have been so foolish? She'd felt sorry for him, and he'd taken advantage. He'd been out of control since the night he met her. Confronting Evander, unleashing his magic, returning to Nivali on a whim after two hundred years. And that godsdamned kiss.

Callan spun away from the door, sending a brisk gust of wind racing through the room, extinguishing all the candles. He lay down on his blankets before the hearth, staring into the flickering flames. He heard Nova slipping into bed a short time later but made no attempt to speak to her. He closed his eyes tightly and realized his anger had already dissipated, leaving only hollow regret in its place.

TWENTY

CALLAN WAS ALREADY GONE when Nova woke, his blades missing from their spot on the mantel. She pressed the heels of her hands against her red-rimmed eyes, wishing the events of the previous night had been nothing more than another bad dream. After splashing several handfuls of cold water on her face and cleaning her teeth, she dressed quickly in breeches and a shirt, then threw her cloak around her shoulders.

The morning was brisk but bright as she exited the Great Hall, tilting her face up toward the sun and savoring the warmth of it upon her skin. She hastily covered the short distance to the training field, which Callan had shown her the day before. The clash of steel grew louder as she approached the covered area enclosed by a wooden post and rail fence.

In the center of a ring of packed earth, Callan sparred against a male with tightly braided black hair and dark brown skin who stood at least a head taller than him. Both appeared to be fighting with their full capability, neither one holding back for the other's sake.

Nova studied Callan as he deftly swung his blade and blocked his opponent's forceful strikes, his hair clinging to beads of perspiration on his temples. The larger male lashed out over and over again, pushing Callan backward toward the fence. With his back nearly pressed against the wooden rails, Callan dropped into a crouch and ducked under the horizontal arc of the blade. Callan swept his foot behind his opponent's ankles, sending him tumbling to the ground, then sprang to his feet, holding the tip of his blade against the male's throat.

The male lay like a fallen tree, panting heavily for a moment before a rumble of laughter rolled forth from his broad chest. Callan grinned and sheathed his blade, extending a hand to help his sparring partner to his feet. They embraced, clapping each other roughly on the back. Wiping sweat from his brow with the sleeve of his shirt, Callan turned to Nova, as if he'd sensed her watching, and meandered over to where she stood.

"Good morning, Nova." His tone was more formal than usual. Distant. "Are you ready to begin?"

"After that display, I'm a bit intimidated." She nodded at the massive warrior, as solid as a brick wall, running through a sequence of strike positions in the center of the training area, his movements less elegant than Callan's, but no less brutal.

"That's Arik. We trained together when we were young." He gestured to a nearby break in the fence. "Shall we get started?"

Nova entered the training area and removed her cloak, draping it over the railing. The icy wind ruffled the light fabric of her shirt, tucked securely into her breeches. Her dagger, sheathed within her boot, hugged the inside of her left ankle.

"I have gifts," Callan said, motioning for her to follow.

He kept his distance, remaining just out of arm's reach at all times. He led her to a wooden bench at the edge of the field and picked up a small black leather sheath on a strap.

"For your dagger." He knelt before her and cinched the band around her thigh, careful not to touch her any more than was necessary to accomplish the task.

Nova stared down at him as he did so, her fingers itching to tunnel into the strands of his rich, brown hair. But she resisted. He skillfully drew the short blade from her boot and slid it into its new home. Another sheath of black leather lay on the bench, affixed to a belt. From it, Callan drew an exquisite sword and held it out to her, the blade lying flat on his outstretched fingers.

"I had this made for you," he said, eyes fixed on the weapon.

Nova took it by the hilt. It was a smaller version of the sword he carried, shorter and lighter. The hilt was wrapped with brown leather, the same writing, a charm for accuracy, etched along the blade.

Nova's lips parted, but words escaped her. When had he commissioned the sword, and how much did a blade of such fine quality cost? She cleared her throat, blinking away tears.

At last, she spoke. "It's beautiful, Callan. Truly."

He nodded, a thin smile crossing his lips. Reaching around her waist, he fastened the belt with the sheath at her left hip. She carefully slid the blade inside and briefly rested her chilled fingers on the back of his warm hand in a silent apology. His posture relaxed a degree.

The following days were consumed with training. Callan began with the bare basics of unsheathing her sword and lifting it out in front of her. Though her blade was much lighter than his, it was heavier than the wooden sword she had been using in Pyralis, and her untrained muscles struggled to draw it and hold it extended.

She spent hours practicing swiftly getting onto her feet from the ground. Callan insisted getting pinned during a fight, whether with swords or fists, must be avoided at all costs. He taught her several maneuvers for escaping an opponent's grasp, starting with attacks from the rear. Coming up from behind, he would wrap his arms tightly around her, trapping her arms at her sides. He instructed her to throw her head back into her opponent's nose, or to drive her heel into the kneecap.

Each time his arms encircled her, Nova was overcome with the desire to lean her head back and melt into him. To allow herself to be engulfed by the crisp scent of him, like freshly fallen snow. Fortunately for her, Callan held on for only as long as was necessary to practice each maneuver and then, mercifully, released her before she could do anything she would regret.

The days melded in a blur of training, eating, and collapsing into bed fully dressed, too exhausted to dream. She was so absorbed in her study of swordplay that she nearly forgot the purpose of her trip to Nivali all together until she stood beside one of Thorn's sturdy wooden boats lashed to the dock.

Narrow at the bow and stern, the boat had a wide belly in the middle. A single mast extended from the center of the vessel, a dark blue sail tightly rolled midway up the thick pole. Seats lined the perimeter of the hull beside openings for oars to pass through. Callan was busy loading provisions onto the ship, securing them in an enclosed cabin at the rear, and speaking with some of his uncle's sailors who would accompany them on the journey.

Nova gazed across the water to the mouth of the inlet where the sea opened up, blue and vast under a clear sky dotted with wispy clouds. The wind fluttered the hem of her cloak, and Liv's premonition echoed in her mind.

Wherever your path leads, death will follow.

Nova shivered, gritting her teeth and pulling her cloak tight around her shoulders. She ran a hand over the hidden pocket she'd sewn into the lining, confirming the letter from Sister Iris remained safely concealed within. She wore her training clothes for the journey, her dagger and sword fastened at her thigh and waist. A gown had seemed impractical for a sea voyage, but she wore her silver earrings and her mother's ring, items too precious to leave behind. Callan appeared at her side, and she felt the insistent pull stretching between them despite all her efforts to dismiss it.

"We're ready to leave." A mix of males and females boarded the ship, including Arik from the sparring match a few days earlier. "We should arrive at the temple tomorrow morning if the weather holds."

Heavy footsteps fell upon the wooden planks behind them. Nova turned to see Thorn and Liv, who had come to bid them farewell.

"It's a fine day for a sea voyage," Thorn said blandly, looking down his nose at Nova. Clearly, she'd failed to endear herself to the Noble Lord during her short stay in his Court. He turned to Callan, gripping his shoulder.

Liv approached, her blond hair and red robe billowing in the breeze.

"Remember my words, Nova. There is something truly remarkable about you."

Nova bowed her head briefly and boarded the vessel, making her way to a wooden bench at the stern.

Callan dropped onto the deck shortly after and freed the lines. Several hands on the dock shoved the boat forward over the water's choppy surface as Callan took his place at the base of the mast. A moment later, he shouted a command, and the sailors slid the oars through the hull, rowing in time with one another and propelling the ship across the cove.

Nova glanced back at the shore once they reached the open sea, the fishing village reduced to a speck on the horizon. The sailors pulled the oars inside, and Arik helped Callan raise the sail. The dark blue fabric unfurled and caught the wind, carrying them farther out to sea.

Callan joined her at the stern to monitor the tiller and keep the ship on course. With the wind blowing from directly behind them, the raised stern buffered them from the breeze. He motioned for her to slide down the bench toward him. When she was close, he positioned her so she sat with her back to him, gathered her hair in his hands, and braided it, securing the end with a leather cord.

"You'll be glad your hair is tied back if the wind picks up," he said.

"Where did you learn to braid?" she asked, twirling the end of her hair around her index finger.

"We're taught as younglings. Warriors often braid their hair before battle or for special ceremonies," he explained, readjusting his cloak. "Who did you think braided my hair for Hayer?"

Nova shrugged, and he smiled, turning his attention to the horizon.

The daylight hours passed uneventfully with clear skies and favorable winds. The sailors busied themselves with card games and twirling daggers. Everyone shared a meal of bread, smoked meat, and ale as the sun began to sink toward the horizon.

Nova leaned over the side of the ship, staring into the choppy water gone murky in the growing dusk. She dangled her arm overboard, the cold spray of saltwater misting her sleeve as she tried to dip her fingers into the sea.

An unfamiliar voice, deep and rich, came from behind her. "Careful you don't fall in."

She turned her head to find Arik, the solid height of him towering over her like a marble statue.

"Our legends tell of Laika, a great sea beast that roams the ocean. She shipwrecks those who fail to make an offering in exchange for safe passage." Nova had never heard the legend. She gathered he was teasing, trying to frighten her.

"What sort of offering?" she asked, rising to stand beside him. She craned her neck to meet his dark eyes.

Arik shrugged. "A blood sacrifice. A goat, perhaps." He grinned at her, his teeth standing out against his dark skin in the fading light. "But some gold or jewels might do the trick."

Nova brought her hands to her face, running her fingers over the earrings from Fawn. They were silver, but the pale stones were lovely and seemed to glow faintly. She removed them with some hesitation and held her hand over the side of the boat, closing her eyes.

"Laika, please accept this offering in exchange for our safe journey," she murmured solemnly. She tipped her cupped palm, and the earrings dropped with a plunk, sinking into the seemingly endless depths below. Arik nodded in approval.

Callan's voice carried on the wind, drawing Nova's attention. He stood at the bow with one of the sailors, gesturing at the sky and the empty horizon sprawled out before them. She noted that several of the crew appeared to be keeping a watchful eye on him. It suddenly occurred to her that perhaps she should have been keeping a wary eye on the crew.

"Do they not trust him?"

Arik followed her gaze, then leaned forward, resting his elbows on the rail.

"Many who don't know him, fear him," he said, voice quiet.

A laugh nearly passed her lips, but his expression had grown serious.

"Why should anyone fear Callan?" she asked, leaning forward and extending her hand toward the water once again.

Arik shot a quick glance to where Callan stood, still occupied.

"Has he told you of his parents' deaths?" he asked, his voice barely audible over the sound of the vessel cutting through the waves.

Nova nodded. Arik tapped his thumbs together a few times before continuing.

"When Omen of Raven's Isle murdered his own father and brother, he became a threat to the authority of the Aemorian Council."

"The Council of the leaders from each Court?"

Arik nodded. "But Omen wasn't alone in defying them. Separatist groups had operated in secret for centuries. For them, Omen's act in defiance of Aemorian law was a catalyst to band together, conspiring to overthrow the Council in favor of each Court's right to govern itself, free from oversight. The Council was desperate to find the leaders of the movement and bring them to justice.

"Tensions between Silvergard and Nivali had been high for generations. After his parents were killed in an attack orchestrated by Omen, Callan wasn't himself. Wasn't thinking clearly. He appeared before the Council less than a year after his parents died and convinced them to task *him* with tracking down the separatists. The Council agreed unanimously.

"I told him it was unwise. I'd never seen someone so utterly empty yet so full of rage. I offered to go with him, so I could keep an eye on him. Eventually, we located our first target, Ithan Greylock, a separatist leader from Maedwen. He was hiding out with a group of eight high-ranking members in an abandoned temple in the Wylds.

"The Council granted us authority to bring the targets in alive or dead, with a preference for the former, so they could answer for their treason. When Callan tried to detain him, Greylock provoked him. Spewed vile things about Callan's parents. Praised Omen for his courage to act. When Greylock drew his sword, Callan's rage boiled over. It consumed him."

Arik fell silent, pursing his lips.

"He killed Greylock. Killed them all." He exhaled sharply. "And when he was through, I didn't see my friend behind his eyes. It was as if he wasn't there. Didn't realize what he'd done."

Nova imagined the scene Arik described: a slaughter with Callan, dazed and blood spattered, at the center of it. The bite of her fingernails against her palms brought her back to herself. She splayed her fingers wide and rested her hands on the wood rail. Perhaps she ought to fear him as others did, but she didn't. Her heart ached for him. For the son who felt he had failed his parents. For the young male desperate to absolve himself of his shame.

"Did it ever happen again?"

"No," Arik said firmly. "We tracked fugitives for the Council for decades afterward, and he always maintained control. That's not to say he never took another life, mind you. There's plenty of blood on Callan's hands. But he never lost himself again. Callan was haunted by what he'd done. The Council spread the tale throughout the Realm, thinking it would serve as a deterrent. They called him Aemoria's Blade. Unfortunately, the name, and the reputation, stuck."

Nova studied Callan in the fading daylight. His spine as straight as the ship's mast. The tension between his broad shoulders strung as taut as a mooring line. She wondered if it tired him, keeping his shield in place and maintaining constant control. Perhaps he'd grown so used to hiding his true self that he barely noticed. But she had peeked behind the shield. A shiver bloomed at the base of her spine at the thought of Callan unrestrained.

As if sensing her gaze, Callan glanced in her direction and returned to the stern. A crewmember had climbed up and sat perched on the peaked bow. The rest of the crew had laid themselves out on the deck for rest. Arik nodded a silent goodbye and returned to his position by the mast. Nova joined Callan on the bench. Shifting in his seat, he removed something from the pouch at his hip: a smooth, cloudy stone the size of a robin's egg that emitted a pale light.

"It's a moonstone. They glow brightest at night," he explained, placing the stone in her palm. "They're native to Silvergard. The Lunar Court exports them as light sources."

Entranced, Nova passed it between her hands several times before returning it to him, realizing the earrings she had sacrificed to Laika must have been moonstones as well. She slumped down on the bench, leaning back against the side of the ship and tilting her head to stare at the seemingly endless expanse of dark sky sprinkled with gleaming stars overhead. One star shone with a light that put all others to shame.

"What star is that?" she asked, pointing.

"*That* is Illora."

"As in the Temple of Illora?"

He nodded. "Do you know the legend?"

Nova shook her head.

"Illora was a day goddess. Her sister Aurore, the goddess of the sun, always shone brighter than she did. Illora envied how her sister's light nurtured the first beings of the world, providing them with warmth and strengthening their crops. She wished to be of use to the vulnerable creatures, but she was always invisible next to her sister.

"At night, the beings were swallowed by darkness. They had Orika, of course, whose moon shone brightly when it was full. But the moon was inconstant, at times dimmed or not visible at all. So, Illora renounced her position as a day goddess and gave up her proximity to her sister to become a permanent fixture in the night sky.

"She winked out into nothing, vanishing for a full day before finally reappearing once the sky grew dark to become a light in the darkness for the beings of the world. In fact, she's the patron goddess of sailors, who rely on her for navigation. Tomorrow you'll be standing in the temple dedicated to her."

A shiver ran through her as he finished the tale, and she pulled her knees to her chest, wrapping her cloak around her legs. Callan fell silent, lost in thought as he, too, stared up at the sky, his dark brows drawn together.

"What troubles you?" she asked.

"When I look up at the stars—" He shook his head as if he thought himself foolish. "They remind me of the night I met you. After we crossed the Boundary."

Nova shifted on the hard bench.

"Of how I failed you. How you nearly died because I left you alone."

"It wasn't your fault," she murmured, looking at him from under her lashes.

He shook his head again, the corners of his mouth drooping into a frown before he turned away from her. Nova hugged her knees tighter against her chest, afraid she would reach out and touch him if she didn't.

Turning her eyes skyward, she stared at Illora, glinting against the black canvas of the sky, until her eyelids grew heavy and drifted shut, the motion of the boat on the waves lulling her to sleep.

TWENTY-ONE

NOVA STIRRED AT THE shrill call of gulls overhead. She straightened in her seat, glancing around the deck and blinking the lingering fog of sleep from her eyes. The sea breeze ruffled her hair, brisk and refreshing but noticeably warmer than when they set sail from Nivali.

A strong wind blew at their backs, propelling the boat toward an island just coming into view. The crew was already awake and enjoying a breakfast of cold oatcakes. Callan and Arik stood at the bow, taking turns peering through a spyglass at the island emerging on the horizon. Off the starboard side, Nova could barely make out the dark, jagged line of a rocky coast in the distance.

Silvergard.

Her chest swirled with equal parts intrigue and unease as they sailed close to the infamous Lunar Court. Callan approached, holding out some oatcakes and a flask of water, which she gladly accepted.

"Did you sleep well?" he asked.

"Surprisingly well," she replied through a mouthful of food. She took a gulp of water and swallowed it down. "Thankfully the sea agrees with me."

"We should reach the temple in another hour or so." He pointed toward the island, which had grown slightly since she'd last looked.

"Is it dangerous to sail this close to the coast?" She tipped her head toward Silvergard, barely visible to the east.

"We won't draw their attention. Even if we did, we're traveling outside their borders."

Nova took a final sip of water and handed the flask back to Callan. He took up position at the foot of the mast while she set to work making herself presentable, rebraiding her hair and smoothing out the fabric of her rumpled clothes. Lowering herself onto the bench, she pulled the piece of parchment from the concealed pocket inside her cloak and read the message before stashing it away again. A nervous energy coursed through her, her body refusing to sit still as she watched the Isle of Illora slowly come into view.

Up close, the island was massive. Carved out of a stark white rock formation jutting up from the sea, the temple consisted of a large central structure, round with a domed roof, flanked by two smaller structures of the same design. High walls around the perimeter connected the three domed buildings. Tall, arched windows dotted the exterior walls. The only entrance was an enormous gate at the end of a long jetty, made from the same white rock as the temple, shaped over time by the sea.

When they were a short distance out, the crew lowered the sail and rowed the rest of the way, pulling up skillfully alongside the dock and tying off the lines to secure the ship. Callan climbed off the boat first and extended a steady hand to help Nova disembark.

She turned to the temple and observed a male walking along the dock toward them. Roughly her height, he was slim but muscular and dressed in a spotless white tunic, breeches, and boots. His platinum-blond hair was cut close to his scalp and contrasted with the deep brown of his skin. He greeted them with a slight bow, his hazel eyes warm and welcoming.

"Greetings. My name is Daví," he said. "Only Sisters and invited guests may enter the temple."

Nova reached into the folds of her cloak and produced the letter requesting her presence.

"My name is Nova. I've been invited by Sister Iris." Daví smiled as he scanned the message.

"Very well." He handed the letter back, his eyes lingering on her blades. "Weapons are forbidden inside the temple walls." His gaze shifted to Callan, who stood protectively at her back. "As are males, I'm afraid."

Nova unfastened her belt and laid her sword across Callan's ready hands before pulling her dagger from its sheath and passing it to him as well.

"Don't leave without me," she whispered before turning back to Daví, who motioned for her to follow.

The walk to the entrance took several minutes. While the structure had seemed enormous from the dock, it positively loomed over her as they neared the gate.

"If males are not permitted inside, where do you live?" she asked.

"There's a modest barracks carved into the rock where I reside along with several other Brothers. We belong to a sect whose members dedicate their lives to serving and protecting the Sisters of this temple."

"That's very . . . noble of you . . ." Her voice trailed off as she gaped at the vertical wall of white rock before her. Daví halted at the foot of a set of stone steps leading up to the gate.

"In my mind, there is no cause more noble than defending those who cannot defend themselves." He bowed and motioned for her to enter.

As soon as she set foot on the first step, the ground trembled beneath her, and the stone gate slowly swung open, leaving just enough space for her to enter before rumbling back to life and sealing her inside. Shortly after, a petite female arrived to greet her, dressed head to toe in white. Her high-necked robe had long belled sleeves and was cinched at the waist with a braided silver cord. Her light brown hair was pulled back from her face in a tight braid.

"Welcome, Nova. I'm Sister Iris." She bowed her head and laid a hand over her heart. "Please come with me."

Sister Iris turned and led Nova across a vast courtyard toward the largest domed structure. The ground underfoot was the same white rock. Potted trees and plants filled the courtyard, and awnings provided cover from the sun. White-robed figures roamed about the grounds, some tending to the greenery, others reading.

"Who are the Sisters of the temple?" Nova asked as they passed a group kneeling in a bed of soil and tending the brightly colored flowers.

"Most have troubled pasts and seek sanctuary within these walls. We overcome our own struggles by dedicating our lives to a common purpose."

"Common purpose?"

"Serving as a light for those in darkness."

Nova followed Sister Iris in silence, past a large pool of pristine water with a magnificent fountain and through a high stone archway into what Nova gathered was the main temple.

The structure was open all the way to a curved ceiling so high above that Nova had to tip her head all the way back to see the constellations painted across it, mirroring the night sky. The air was thick with the murmured prayers of the Sisters gathered to pay homage to the goddess Illora. The rap of Nova's boots echoed loudly off the stone walls as Sister Iris approached the base of an oversized statue of the goddess carved from the gleaming stone. Illora's flowing hair and robes floated out around her, her kind face lowered, smiling lovingly at those who worshipped at her feet.

Sister Iris approached one of the figures kneeling before the statue, tapping her lightly on the shoulder and whispering in her ear. The female rose and turned to face Nova.

Nova's heart stopped for an instant before stuttering back to life.

She knew the face staring back at her as well as she knew her own. The face she had seen on canvas, nearly every day of her life, was now cast before her in flesh and bone. The face of her mother, Elena.

TWENTY-TWO

Nova's chest tightened. "I-I don't believe it," she stammered.

Elena's chin trembled. She reached a hand out toward her daughter, who pulled back at first. "Nova, you came," she said, taking a tentative step closer.

Elena looked exactly as she had in the painting. The gold flecks in her green eyes matched the tone of her skin. When she reached out a second time, Nova remained motionless, allowing her mother to run a hand over her hair and down to her cheek. Nova blinked several times, completely numb. Elena drew Nova to her, stroking her hair as Nova stared wide-eyed over her mother's shoulder. After a moment, Elena pulled back, holding her daughter at arm's length.

"Come," she said, glancing around the crowded temple. "Let us find somewhere to speak in private."

She led Nova outside to an isolated stone bench at the edge of the fountain. Several minutes passed in near silence, no sound but the the fountain's spray falling onto the surface of the shimmering water. Nova studied Elena's profile from the corner of her eye. How strange to be sitting with her mother, who barely looked older than she did. There was an aura of wisdom about her, but otherwise, Elena could easily have passed for her sister.

Finally, her mother spoke. "I'm certain you have many questions—"

"How?" Nova demanded. The initial shock of seeing her mother had withered, and anger rose within her to claim the space it left behind. "Why? Why did you leave me?"

"My heart broke when I left you. You must believe that." Elena slid closer to her on the bench.

"And what of my father's heart? Do you think he felt nothing when you died? When you *left*? It changed him. I was all he had." Nova thought of Anson's kind smile. "Did you even love him?"

Elena stared down at the refracted sunlight, darting like bolts of lightning across the bottom of the pool.

"I cared for him. Deeply. Anson was kind to me. Before I met him, I had known only cruelty for a very long time."

"Cruelty?" Nova barely contained her scoff. "I was a *monster* in the Human Realm. Ridiculed. Beaten. Alone."

Anger surged in her chest at the memory of the frightened, lonely girl she had once been. Nova clenched her jaw and turned her face away from her mother.

Elena laid a hand on Nova's shoulder. "You must believe me, my darling. Leaving you was the only way I could protect you."

"Protect me from what?" Nova shrugged out from under her mother's touch. "Your selfishness?"

"From your father," Elena said, her voice dropping lower. "From Omen."

Nova's breath caught as if all the air had been siphoned from her chest. She tried to stand, but her legs refused to cooperate, and she dropped back onto the hard surface of the bench. Elena grasped her shoulders to steady her.

"I don't understand," Nova said, brows pinched. "Omen of Raven's

Isle? He is my true father?"

"He wasn't always as he is now," Elena said, as if it might quell the fear gathering like storm clouds in Nova's chest. "He was once caring and idealistic, but deeply angry. His entire life, he'd been tormented by his father and older brother. I'm sure you've heard stories of Onyx."

Nova nodded vaguely, recalling the night she'd crept to the library in Pyralis and learned of Silvergard's dark history.

"Omen's father despised him—feared him. He knew Omen's abilities would one day eclipse his own. So, he sent him away to Sonnend to serve as an emissary. That's where we met. We were young. We fell in love. We wanted to be wed, but our parents needed to arrange the union.

"Omen begged for his father's blessing, but Onyx refused. Shortly after, my parents told me I had been promised to Omen's older brother instead. There was nothing I could do. I was duty bound to marry Sable. Omen was blind with rage. He vowed to kill Onyx and Sable himself. He frightened me.

"I heard nothing from him until the day of the ceremony, when he appeared in the temple out of nowhere and slaughtered his father and brother before my eyes. He came for me, and I cowered before him. When I looked up, he was shattered. Utterly devastated. As if my rejection had broken him. He stumbled back into the shadows and vanished."

Nova finally looked at her mother. Elena's eyes were clamped shut, bronzed cheeks wet with tears. For a brief moment, a spark of shame flickered in her chest at making her mother relive the terrible memory. But she had waited long enough for the truth, so she urged Elena on.

"If what you say is true, then how did I come to be?"

"The quake that created Raven's Isle happened the same day. In the weeks that followed, attacks occurred throughout the Realm, including one in Nivali that claimed the lives of the Noble Lord and Lady. I felt responsible. I offered myself to Omen, begged him to stop the bloodshed."

Elena crumpled in on herself, her shoulders shaking with the intensity of her sobs. Nova flinched when her mother straightened suddenly, wiping her eyes roughly on her sleeve and swallowing the rest of her tears.

"I thought I could save him, but he was no longer the Omen I once loved. He was violent and controlling. Full of rage. I endured five years with him. A prisoner locked away in a dark tower of his black fortress.

"We coupled to seal the union, and he made such demands of me a handful of times over the years. He said he would never father an heir and vowed to kill the child if he did. I never allowed myself to believe it would come to pass. But, one day, I knew. Deep in my bones. I could feel you, shining like the faintest ray of sunlight breaking through dark clouds."

Nova sprang to her feet, striding to the pool's edge and peering into the water. Her mind raced, trying to make sense of the new information, her mother's voice fading in and out in the background.

"... left me alone, and I managed to escape... he killed my parents ... fled to the Human Realm..."

Elena appeared beside her and took Nova's hands, her grip bordering on painful. Their eyes locked, and Nova found she could not pry herself away. How many nights had she studied her mother's portrait trying to identify the look in her eyes? She'd always thought Elena was hiding something, but nothing could have prepared her for the extent of her mother's secrets.

"The glamour convinced Anson and the community that I'd died in childbirth. But I hoped you and I could be reunited one day."

"How is this possible?" Nova asked, recalling the story of how the Shadow Court was formed. "The quake that created Raven's Isle happened centuries ago."

"Time is different in the Human Realm. While only twenty-five years passed for you there, nearly two hundred years passed here."

Callan had said time was different for the Fae; she'd thought it was a figure of speech. Nova's legs threatened to buckle, and Elena held her firmly by her upper arms. Certain her mind could not endure another revelation, Nova wrenched herself out of her mother's grasp and staggered away. Her grip on reality was tenuous as it was, like grasping at smoke. Elena reached out and caught Nova's wrist, her fingernails piercing Nova's skin. Her mother's words rushed past her lips, as if she knew she'd pushed Nova to the brink.

"He started killing again as soon as I left. As long as he lives, I can never leave this place. Powerful magic protects Illora's temple. He'll never find me here. Please, *stay*. If he discovers you in Aemoria, discovers who you are, I won't be able to protect you. I can't even protect myself."

Nova's gaze narrowed on the open sky above the courtyard. There was no shield around the temple, but she could feel it—a faint vibration emanating from deep within the solid rock beneath her feet. Visions flashed in Nova's mind. Fragmented images. Callan's dark eyes and the curve of his smile. Fawn peering at her over the top of a book. Even Evander and his smug grin.

"No," Nova murmured, shaking her head. "*No*," she repeated, more forcefully. "I'm through running. I'm through hiding. I have people who care about me now."

Sorrow flooded Elena's features, her gaze falling under the weight of it. She nodded solemnly, loosening her grip on Nova's arm.

"I wish I could convince you." She clung to Nova's hand weakly, rubbing her thumb over the smooth white stone of the ring that had once been hers. "Wear this ring always, my darling. It's my last gift to you."

Elena squeezed once, then let go, her hand dropping to her side with a sense of finality.

Sister Iris approached and stood behind Nova. Her time with her mother had reached its end. The Sister motioned for her to follow, and Nova turned to leave.

"Goodbye, Nova. My sweet child," Elena called out weakly. Nova glanced back over her shoulder.

"Goodbye," she murmured.

She forced herself to turn her back on her mother, wondering if it was the first and last time she would ever see her.

Nova barely registered the walk from the temple building to the front gates. Sisters breezed by in a blur of white like doves in her periphery. Sister Iris spoke as she guided her toward the entrance, but Nova didn't register her words.

She managed to reach the bottom of the wide stone steps before she collapsed, landing on her hands and knees. Her breath came fast and shallow. She didn't know whether to sob, scream, or laugh like a madwoman. Lifting her head, she saw Callan standing at the end of the dock, his stature dwarfed by the distance.

Nova rose to her feet and started toward him. Relief washed over her at the sight of him there waiting, but countless emotions churned within her chest. Disbelief, frustration, sorrow, and anger all battled to be given a voice. Her first instinct was to bury each and every one. To slip on a mask of indifference and pretend she was unaffected. But she knew she couldn't manage it.

Not this time.

Callan jogged halfway down the dock to meet her, his smile morphing into a look of concern as she drew closer. A scowl pulled hard at the corners of her mouth, but she was powerless to erase it. Nova strode past him without a glance, and he turned on his heel, following close behind.

"Nova? What's wrong?"

She spun around, and he stopped short.

"What's wrong?" she snapped. "I just met my mother."

"What?" Callan shook his head.

"My mother, Callan. The one who abandoned me. Who lied to my father—no—he wasn't my father." She was rambling, words spilling out in a confusing mess.

"Slow down. What is going on?" Callan spoke softly, his hands held out with palms facing her, as if to remind her he wasn't a threat.

"Did you know?" she demanded coldly.

"Know what?" His hands hovered above her shoulders, but he didn't touch her.

"About my father?"

"I see that you're angry, and I want to help, but I don't know what's going on."

Nova shoved against his chest, forcing some distance between them. If she couldn't hide her emotions, she'd cling to her godsdamned rage. She refused to let anyone see her pain.

"Of course I'm angry!" She struck his chest again with all her strength. His body barely registered the assault. "Everything I've ever known has been a lie."

Nova's restraint crumbled, her anger giving way as she collapsed to her knees a second time. Her breath was too fast. Too shallow. She couldn't get enough air. A rush of tears flowed from her like a burst dam. Tears caused by more than the shock of seeing her mother alive, or the revelation about her true father.

Tears she never shed during the torment she endured as a child.

Tears she silenced when her first love cast her aside.

Tears she bit back when she lost the only father she'd ever known. The only person who had ever truly loved her.

Tears she swallowed when she left the Human Realm and the life she'd created for herself, however lonely it had been.

Callan knelt before her, gathering her in his strong embrace. He anchored her and kept her from blowing away like a scrap of parchment on the cool breeze swirling around them. Stroking her hair, he held her close, his low voice a soothing rumble in her ear pressed against his chest.

"I'm here. I'm here. I've got you."

Nova clung to him until her tears ran dry and she sagged in his arms, utterly drained.

TWENTY-THREE

PANIC SEIZED CALLAN FOR the span of a single beat of his heart when Nova went slack against him. With the next beat, his mind cleared and he took action, lifting her into his arms and racing back to the ship. The crew looked on, baffled, as he boarded the vessel cradling a motionless Nova. He called for someone to open the hatch at the stern and carried her inside the small cabin, laying her down on a lumpy straw cot made up with woven blankets.

"Food and water—now," he ordered. The sailor rushed out, returning soon after with a hunk of bread, some smoked meat, and a flask of water.

Callan crouched beside the mattress and patted Nova gently on the cheek, repeating her name. He poured a trickle of water into the corner of her mouth before emptying some into his hand and dabbing it over her face and neck. Nova stirred and rose onto her elbows, blinking rapidly as she looked around the cramped cabin.

"Are you all right?" He cradled her chin in his hands and ducked his head to meet her gaze. After a few seconds, her eyes focused on him, and she nodded slowly.

"Thank the gods." He dismissed the sailor, who then left them alone.

Callan held the bread out to her, and she ate it quickly before moving on to the slab of dried meat. Washing it all down with several gulps of water, she sighed when she was through, then threw herself down onto the mattress and flung an arm across her eyes.

"I'm such a fool," she muttered.

"You're not a fool."

"You really didn't know?" She lifted her head, her face open and innocent. "About my father?"

"I know nothing of your father. Apart from my suspicion that he's a Silvergardian."

"So, you suspected he wasn't human?"

"Not at first," he said. "But once I saw your Fae form, it was difficult to deny."

"Well, your instincts were correct. My father was from Silvergard." Her eyes flitted around the tight quarters, avoiding his. "My mother told me that my true father is Omen of Raven's Isle." Nova winced, turning her face to the wall.

Callan's spine went rigid. Although he'd considered Nova might have ties to the Lunar Court, which could make her a target, he never imagined she was the daughter of the Shadowbringer. In the wrong hands, this knowledge could mean her death.

Callan jumped to his feet and burst through the small hatch onto the deck. Several crew members snapped their heads in his direction at the sudden noise. He rushed to untie the lines securing the ship to the dock.

"Arik, give me a hand." He waved his friend over, and they worked together to shove off.

"We must return to Nivali immediately," he said. Arik nodded and took his place at the base of the mast.

"Oars!" Arik bellowed his command, and the sailors dipped their wooden paddles into the sea, quickly turning the vessel around. Callan stood beside Arik as the boat cleared the dock, and the two of them raised the sail, adjusting the angle on the mast to account for a strong wind pushing in from the west.

"I need to see to Nova. I'll be back on deck as soon as I'm able," Callan said.

"This wind is going to push us closer to shore. Storm's coming out of the west." Arik jerked his chin toward the thick gray clouds gathering off the starboard side.

"Perhaps we can skirt the storm if we cut in closer to the coast. Not too close, though," Callan warned. "The last thing I need is Silvergard breathing down our necks." Arik accepted his orders with a fist over his heart, and Callan slipped back through the hatch.

Nova sat hunched forward, her face buried in her hands. She lifted her head when he entered, steel eyes red-rimmed and puffy, pale cheeks damp with fresh tears. She ran her sleeve over her face and coughed once, clearing her throat.

"I'm so sorry, Callan. My father is the reason your parents are gone." She looked down at her hands. "You must hate me."

Callan sat on the cot beside her.

"Look at me."

Slowly, she lifted her face to his.

"Nothing in this world could ever give me cause to hate you," he murmured. "But I am worried for you."

He brushed a thumb over her cheek, and she leaned into his touch.

"How is this possible?" he asked.

Nova dabbed at her eyes with the cuff of her shirt and recounted her mother's story, shooting glances at him from the corner of her eye.

"I can't believe this secret remained hidden for so long," he said, mind whirring. "You must never share this information with anyone else. Omen is every bit as dangerous as your mother said he is. If the truth got out, your life could be at risk."

"I never want anyone to know about this." She shook her head rapidly, twisting her hands together in her lap. "I can't bear the thought of anyone believing I'm a monster."

"You're no monster." He wrapped an arm around her shoulder, drawing her close.

"But what if I am?" she whispered, as if she feared speaking the words aloud. "My mother said he wasn't always as he is now. What if something happens, and I . . . change?"

"You are *nothing* like your father," Callan insisted, hopeful his certainty would be enough to put her at ease. Convince her that he could never fear her. He cursed Omen and his vile shadow that seemed to fall on those Callan cared for most. First his parents, and now Nova.

She tilted her face up at him, wide eyes searching his.

Gods, he wanted to kiss her.

"You should rest," he said, releasing her.

Nova obeyed, laying her head down on the cot and closing her eyes. Not long after, her breathing slowed to a measured rhythm, and Callan knew she was asleep. He reached out and gently tucked a lock of hair behind her ear.

Callan sat beside her for a long time, watching her forehead crease and relax in her sleep as he considered all she'd shared with him. For a moment, he wondered if this was what Evander had been so secretive about, but he quickly dismissed the idea. The simplest answer was the most likely: Evander desired Nova and saw Callan's obvious attachment to her as an inconvenient obstacle. The ship took a sudden hard turn, nearly sending him tumbling off the edge of the cot. Nova remained asleep. Callan barged through the hatch and onto the deck.

They'd managed to avoid the storm. The swirling mass of dark gray clouds lay to the south. But the rockbound coast of Silvergard loomed little more than a stone's throw away.

"We tried to avoid it," Arik said, defeated. "The storm moved too fast, and we got caught up."

Callan twisted his neck, following Arik's stare off the stern to the swift Silvergardian ship slicing through the water and gaining on them. It was more than double the size of his own vessel and with twice the speed. Callan growled, glancing around at the open water surrounding them. Outrunning the ship would be impossible. Grabbing the spyglass, he peered through the viewfinder at the approaching vessel. The tiered deck of the sleek, double-masted ship boasted at least thirty armed Silvergardian soldiers posted along the rails, many whose bows were already nocked with arrows.

Callan shouted a curse that was quickly carried away on the wind. He lowered the spyglass and gritted his teeth, unable to do anything but wait for the enemy ship to complete its approach.

Nova lay flat on her back on a bed of soft green moss. Strips of clear blue sky peeked through the canopy overhead. She stretched, gazing contentedly at the crowns of the trees, marveling at how they swayed in the breeze but never seemed to touch. Rays of dappled sunlight fell across her face, and her eyes drifted shut as the chirping of the birds began to lull her to sleep.

All at once, the birdsong ceased, and Nova's eyes shot open. A churning, dark mist rippled over the roots and rocks, tendrils reaching out like long, slender fingers as it approached her.

Dread settled over her like a shroud as the darkness reached the toes of her boots. She willed herself to stand—to run—but she remained rooted to the forest floor. The mist crawled along her body, swallowing her up, an icy sensation creeping along her skin as if she were sinking bit by bit into a frigid pond. Her breathing grew frantic as the mist drifted to her chin and over her mouth. It was going to suffocate her. Before it could steal her breath, the ground crumbled away beneath her, and Nova plunged into darkness.

A series of jarring thuds ripped Nova from her fitful sleep. A moment passed before she realized someone was pounding on the hatch. She stood unsteadily, crouching to avoid striking her head on the low plank ceiling. Forcing the hatch open, she stepped out onto the deck, blinking rapidly as her eyes adjusted to the sunlight.

As her vision cleared, she saw Callan with the curved blade of a stranger's dagger held against his throat. The entire Nivalian crew stood restrained by armed guards. The strangers wore black leather uniforms and silver metal breastplates embossed with the symbol of a crescent moon hooked around a six-pointed star. Black powder darkened their foreheads and the skin around their eyes.

An impressive ship bobbed directly beside theirs, the railing considerably higher than the vessel on which she stood and lined with nearly two dozen additional soldiers. Some had arrows trained on her and her companions, the arrow heads carved from luminous white stone. Others held swords, the steel blades slightly curved. Nova glanced at her own sword still in its sheath on the nearby bench but thought better of it. She was no warrior, and the strangers had every advantage.

The guards parted, and a male emerged from the center of the line, pinning Nova with a hard stare. He was tall and muscular, clad in the same uniform and breastplate as the others, with his sword sheathed at his hip. He was pale with jet-black hair cropped close to his scalp on the sides, wavy locks sweeping over the top. An unsettling glint shone in his eyes, the fair skin around them smudged with what looked like soot. He smirked at her, his lip curling back to reveal slightly elongated canines.

"Welcome to Silvergard." He held his arms out wide at his sides. "It looks as though you ran into some bad weather, Miss . . ."

"My name is Nova," she said, her voice mercifully flat as she willed her face into her practiced mask of detachment. "And you are?"

"Commander Lucan," he said with a grin, flashing those teeth again. "Head of the Noble Lord's private guard."

"Perhaps your guards could lower their weapons, Commander. As you can see, I am at a disadvantage." She held up her hands and gestured to her general lack of weapons.

He seemed to consider her request, an intense, faraway expression clouding his eyes for a moment, before signaling to his guards on the Silvergardian vessel. All sheathed their blades and lowered their bows on his command, but the Nivalian sailors remained held at knifepoint. The commander widened his stance and clasped his gloved hands together in front of him.

"The Noble Lord of Silvergard seeks an audience with you."

"What could he possibly want with me?"

"He's heard of you. He'd like to meet you. He asks you to join him at his Estate for a time. As his guest."

"If this is truly an invitation, I'm afraid I must decline," she said.

Callan shifted on his feet, and his captor tugged his head back by his hair, pressing the blade closer to his throat. A thin line of crimson bloomed against the warm brown skin just below the curve of his jaw.

"It's a polite request." The commander's smirk faded a bit. "One I strongly suggest you accept."

"Nova, don't." Callan's voice was at once desperate and commanding. The Silvergardian archers raised their bows once again, training their weapons on him.

Nova moved swiftly, placing her body between Callan and more than a dozen taut bowstrings. She held her palms up to the commander, indicating her submission, then shot a glance at Callan over her shoulder, silently pleading with him to keep still.

Be quiet.

Callan's brows drew together, his eyes widening.

"And how long would I remain a guest of the Noble Lord?" she asked, turning back to the commander and mustering as much indifference as possible under the circumstances.

"Until the next new moon."

Roughly one month.

Nova thought quickly, devising a bargain she hoped would see everyone out of the godsforsaken situation safely.

"I will accompany you if you agree to allow my companions to return to Nivali immediately, and you personally guarantee no harm of any kind will come to them at the hands of any citizen of Silvergard." She held her breath.

"I don't think you're in a position to be making bargains. From where I'm standing, I've got the upper hand," Lucan said, cocking his head to the side.

"Then I appeal to your honor, Commander."

His eyes flashed for an instant before his sly grin returned.

"I should warn you, I'm more animal than man. You may be disappointed to find my honor somewhat lacking." He paused for a beat before giving a resolute nod. "Very well. I agree to your terms." Nova released a slow breath as Lucan relayed his orders to the guards.

"This crew is under my protection. No harm is to come to them." He turned back to her and made a mocking bow. "But you, Miss Nova, you're coming with me."

The guards released the crew at once. Callan's captor shoved him roughly, and he fell onto his knees on the deck. Nova rushed forward and knelt before him, reaching instinctively for the superficial wound on his throat.

Callan laid his hand on top of hers, their faces hovering close together.

"Don't do this," he whispered.

"I have to. It's the only way to keep you all safe. You need to go—now." Her words rushed past her lips just ahead of the panic creeping up her throat. The longer they lingered, the more she worried the commander might change his mind. "I'll contact you as soon as I can."

Callan's dark eyes stormed, but he released her hand, his chin dropping to his chest. Fearing she might never see him again, Nova took his face in her hands and rested her forehead against his. She longed to kiss him, to feel his mouth against hers once more, but she denied the impulse.

I will return to you, she thought. A vow she couldn't bring herself to utter aloud.

Nova dragged herself away from him, defying the undeniable pull connecting them. Callan's eyes shimmered, his chest rising and falling rapidly, his brow furrowed as he watched her leave. One of the soldiers gripped Nova's arm, ushering her to the railing where a second soldier pulled her up onto the deck of the Silvergardian vessel.

She couldn't bring herself to look back at Callan as tears welled in her eyes. She hoped she would live to keep her promise.

TWENTY-FOUR

CALLAN'S FURY SIMMERED FOR the entire journey back to Nivali. Leaving Nova in danger, *again*, pained him like a blade twisting in his side. He would have chosen death happily if it meant shielding her from harm. It took every bit of will he possessed to keep himself from ordering the crew to turn the small vessel around. All that stopped him was the grim understanding that his motley band of sailors, none of them warriors besides Arik, wouldn't stand a chance. So, he manned the tiller and kept the boat on course, his anger sitting like a crushing weight on his chest all the while.

Thorn was waiting at the base of the steps leading to the Great Hall after the ship docked. Callan stormed past his uncle and several curious onlookers, heading directly to his chamber, where he locked himself away for the remainder of the night. He was still in bed when Arik knocked the following morning.

"Are you through sulking?" Arik asked.

Callan exhaled slowly, the tension in his shoulders as unyielding as it had been when he watched Nova being taken from him. He couldn't shake his suspicion. His fear. He flung his legs over the side of the bed and stood, snatching up a clean pair of breeches and tugging them on.

"Where do you think you're going?" Arik asked as Callan searched for a fresh shirt. Callan ignored his friend, continuing to dress. In his haste, he nearly toppled over tugging on one of his boots, and Arik steadied him by the arm. Callan wrenched out of his friend's grip.

"What in Brumal's name do you think you're doing, you fool?" Arik barked. Callan returned to where his other boot sat, the worn leather folded over and drooping dejectedly. He threw himself onto the settee and kicked the boot away.

"Nova is in danger," he snapped, glaring at Arik, who now stood between him and the chamber door, stance wide and thick arms folded across his chest.

"You don't know that," Arik said, with entirely too much confidence for Callan's liking.

"You trust those soldiers who stole her away?" Callan rubbed a hand roughly over his face.

"If their aim was to harm her, why allow any of us to live? The commander kept his word. They could have devised a way to be rid of us as soon as she was out of sight."

Callan groaned. He didn't remember Arik being the sensible one when they were younger. In fact, it was usually the other way around with Callan keeping Arik out of mischief and ridiculous scrapes. Under other circumstances, he might have applauded his friend for his levelheadedness, but in the moment, Callan wanted to act, however reckless and ill-advised his actions might be.

Callan pinched the bridge of his nose, his thoughts turning to his last moments with Nova. The feeling of her forehead pressed against his.

It felt like a goodbye.

But then, he could have sworn he heard her voice inside his mind, distorted and faraway, promising to return to him. Had he imagined it? When she'd pulled herself away from him, it was as if she'd taken a piece of him with her. He felt the absence of it, a gaping hole in his chest. Callan rubbed a hand over his heart, but it did nothing to ease the ache. Arik spoke again, pulling him from his thoughts.

"You're staying put, Callan. There's no way your uncle is going to send armed soldiers to storm the Silvergard Estate to rescue her. And you can't go alone. Even if you could, there's no evidence she's in any danger. I'm sure she'll write."

Callan sighed gruffly.

"Your uncle is asking for you. He hasn't had a chance to gloat yet."

Callan narrowed his eyes on his old friend. "I could get past you in a heartbeat," he said, smiling despite the vague twinge of unease still gnawing at his gut.

Arik's laugh filled the room. "You could try." He uncrossed his arms and left Callan alone.

Callan shook his head. Best to face his uncle's reprimand before attempting to ease his frayed nerves on the training field. Opening the wardrobe, he ran his fingers over the silk and velvet of Nova's gowns before selecting a gray tunic for himself. Once he finished dressing, he exited the chamber.

When he entered the Great Hall, Callan spotted Thorn seated on his throne. He was engaged in a game of strategy with one of his courtiers, the two taking turns moving small carved figures around the wooden board. His uncle's face held a poorly concealed look of boredom, and he perked up immediately upon spying Callan at the base of the stairs. Thorn dismissed his opponent, waving his nephew over to take a seat on the stool beside him. Small groups of courtiers lounged about the great room, talking quietly among themselves. Thorn grasped Callan firmly by the shoulder as he sat.

"I'm pleased to see you," his uncle said with a genuine smile. "After hearing what happened, I'm surprised you returned at all."

"We owe our lives to Nova." Callan left it at that, not eager to revisit the unpleasant memory.

"Indeed." Thorn swigged from a mug of something and wiped at his mouth with the back of his hand.

"The soldiers drew upon us, but to be fair, we were trespassing in their territory," Callan said, eyeing a nearby tray of fresh bread and sliced cheese. He had missed breakfast. "They were surprisingly forgiving."

"Well, it would have been unwise to kill a Noble of Nivali."

"I don't believe they knew who I was. They came for Nova."

"Curious." Thorn twirled the end of his beard between his thumb and forefinger.

"Not so curious." Callan snatched up a thick slice of bread and tore off a large bite. "As you suspected, she discovered her father had Lunar blood."

He would never share the truth of Nova's paternity, but it was no use denying what was obvious to anyone who possessed a functioning pair of eyes. Callan thought of Nova's raven hair, infinitely dark against her milky-white skin, and the delicate pink of her flushed cheeks. He found himself wondering if other parts of her blushed a similar shade.

Thorn was silent for a time, turning one of the carved game pieces in his fingers as Callan ate. Finally, he placed the piece down on the board, gesturing for Callan to join the game. Callan surveyed the board for a moment before moving one of his own tokens.

Thorn prodded absentmindedly at his teeth with his tongue as he pondered his next move. Callan eyed his uncle with mild skepticism. He'd been expecting something akin to the wrath of the gods, but Thorn hadn't so much as raised his voice. It was entirely out of character.

"I recall you said she is . . . how did you phrase it? *Important* to you?" He nudged a token across the board with his index finger.

"She still is," Callan said, not looking up.

Even more so, he thought.

Sliding a token to an occupied space, he flicked one of his uncle's pieces off the board.

"It occurs to me, quite spontaneously, of course, that a union between the two of you could be mutually beneficial for Nivali and Silvergard." Thorn tapped a finger on the edge of the table, glancing sideways at Callan.

Callan scoffed. "A week past, you would have seen her slaughtered in the middle of this very hall. Now you wish for me to wed her?"

"I'm simply suggesting she could be useful, Callan." Thorn nudged a token into place and leaned back in his seat, drinking deeply from his mug.

"Nova is not a tool, and I will never seek to manipulate her." Callan toppled Thorn's final token with his own, ending the game. "If anything becomes of us, it will be because Nova desires it, not because I orchestrated it."

Would she ever desire it? While Callan had come to believe something existed between them, she'd certainly given him cause to think he might be mistaken.

Callan stood and stepped down from the platform. He made a low bow before striding through the doors and out into the morning air, thick with heavy flakes, beyond. Rounding the corner, he leaned his forearms on the railing of the covered veranda that wrapped around the building. The frigid wind whipped around him, tugging at his clothes, but he found comfort in the stinging bite.

A sea of small wooden cabins stretched out before him, from the Estate to the docks, countless windows shuttered against the cold. Gray smoke rose from chimneys, commingling against the overcast sky. Callan stared at the distant, snowcapped Nephari Mountains to the north. A wall of solid rock separating Nivali from Silvergard.

Separating him from Nova.

TWENTY-FIVE

THE NIVALIAN VESSEL QUICKLY disappeared from sight as the Silvergardian ship sailed swiftly up the coast, eventually mooring in a rocky inlet alongside several other ships. A small band of guards disembarked with Nova and the commander, taking a skiff to shore. The group hiked to a copse of bare trees at the summit of a rocky incline where several horses had been left tied to the gnarled limbs. Commander Lucan led Nova to a stunning gray horse with a silvery mane and gestured for her to mount. She stared at him blankly.

"It's a long walk to the Estate," he said, annoyance flashing in his amber eyes.

"You're too kind, Commander."

Once she had mounted, the commander swung himself up behind her. He covered his nose and mouth with a black kerchief, then gave the animal a nudge under the ribs, urging it into a gallop.

The horses carried them away from the cool mist of the desolate, craggy coast. Farther inland, the air turned warm and dry, and the landscape morphed into dunes of gritty, charcoal-colored sand dotted with patches of hardy desert bushes and more of the same twisted, fruitless trees. The pounding of the horses' hooves kicked up a cloud of fine dust, and Nova quickly understood why all the riders wore face coverings like the commander's, their foreheads and the area around their eyes appearing smudged with soot.

An imposing structure carved into the side of a mountain loomed in the distance. The sun glinted off the enormous panes of glass covering the front of it. A high wall of black stone rose up before them, a fortification stretching along the horizon in both directions. The pack of riders halted briefly, and the horses pranced impatiently as a metal portcullis lifted, granting them access to the capital.

A city of dark stone structures sprawled out around the base of the Estate, dwarfed by its size. The empty shop-lined streets were eerily quiet. Nova spotted a market, an apothecary, and even what appeared to be a confectionary as they thundered past. Somehow, she hadn't expected to find such mundane establishments within the Realm's most notorious territory.

As they rode past residences and businesses, Nova spied a raven soaring on the wind high above them. Recalling what Callan had said about the significance of a single raven, she sincerely hoped it was only a silly superstition. Callan had also said the reigning Noble Lord of Silvergard was Omen's younger brother. Her uncle. She knew nothing of his temperament, but if his father and brothers were any indication, she certainly had reason to be fearful.

Nova shook off her apprehension and reached back into her memory to her evening in the Pyralis library and the thick book with its brittle pages, trying to recall anything useful. Silvergardians were nocturnal. The sun's position overhead told her it was late afternoon.

"You're up early." Her shout was loud enough for the commander to hear over the wind and the rhythmic beating of the horses' hooves.

"Our scouts spotted your vessel as soon as it crossed into our territory. They alerted me to your presence." His mouth was close to her ear, his voice calm and even. "The rest of Silvergard will rise with the moon."

They rode on, and, before long, the Estate stood menacingly before her, all straight lines and sharp edges. The commander dismounted and tugged her down by the waistband behind him. The others turned over their steeds to several stable hands waiting at the base of the wide stone steps leading to an enormous black metal door. Nova craned her neck to the sharp spires crowning the Estate, stabbing at the sky. She saw no glimmer of magic overhead.

"There's no shield."

"We have no need for one," the commander answered. "In two hundred years, Raven's Isle has never attacked Silvergard." He waved impatiently for her to ascend the steps.

Nova moved slowly, stalling the inevitable. The commander grabbed her arm above the elbow and climbed the stairs, dragging her along. The heavy metal door swung open with a groan that rattled her teeth, and the commander guided her into the great room within. The floors and walls of the massive space were carved from the black rock of the mountain, smoothed and polished to a shine. The floor-to-ceiling windows lining the front wall looked out over the surrounding city and the shifting black sand beyond.

The space was sparsely decorated with small area rugs anchoring black, low-backed sofas and armchairs. Along the far side sat a dining table crafted from a slab of petrified wood large enough to seat forty. A chandelier of round moonstones hung suspended in midair over the tabletop. And in the back corner, a twining staircase led to several levels above, drawing Nova's eyes to a ceiling made entirely of glass.

A life-size statue of Orika stood atop a platform in the center of the room sculpted from a block of gleaming moonstone. The staff in her hand was carved to depict the lunar phases. The goddess and the folk of Silvergard alike revered the moon, which represented both change and influence—on the ebb and flow of the tides and the cycles of fertility.

Nova only realized she'd halted her steps when the commander whistled sharply and pulled her along to the staircase. As they climbed to the upper level, Nova wondered where he could be taking her. Certainly prisoners would be kept in cells on a lower level, perhaps underground.

They reached the second floor and turned down a high-ceilinged hallway, their footsteps echoing loudly as they walked. Moonstone globes hung at intervals along the shiny stone walls. The commander stopped before a tall black lacquered door and released her arm to hold it open for her.

Nova poked her head into the room before taking a few cautious steps inside, surprised to see not a cell, but a beautifully appointed chamber. A large bed made up with black satin sheets sat atop a platform anchored against the wall to her right. Sheer black curtains hung from the ceiling, encircling the bed. There was a blackwood wardrobe with a matching vanity and writing desk. A sliding glass door on the far wall led to a small terrace. The door stood slightly ajar, and a warm breeze blew through the room, fluttering the curtains.

"The bathing chamber is through there," Commander Lucan said coolly, indicating an arched doorway to his left. "I'll send someone up to help you bathe and dress."

Nova said nothing, and he turned for the door.

"You're expected to join the Noble Lord for breakfast," he called over his shoulder before pulling the door closed with a resounding click.

Alone at last, Nova's mask slipped, and she staggered to the stool at the nearby vanity. Shielding her face with sweaty palms, she breathed heavily, in and out, through the cracks between her trembling fingers. Her thoughts swarmed. Could she trust the commander to keep his word? Would Callan arrive in Nivali safely? Would she ever leave Silvergard? Allowing herself only a brief release of emotion, Nova swallowed several deep, gulping breaths and swiped her sleeve across her eyes and cheeks.

A knock sounded on the door a few minutes later, and Nova sprang to her feet. Her hand flew to her thigh, reaching for a blade that wasn't there. A sprightly female entered, so pale Nova could see her veins, faint purple branches under nearly translucent skin. She paused in the entryway, her papery, white wings fluttering like those of a moth, her irises so dark they looked like the glassy eyes of a bird. The female scanned Nova from head to toe, taking in her windswept hair and the fine black powder coating every bit of her exposed skin.

"Don't you look dreadful," she said, immediately clapping a hand over her mouth. "Pardon me, miss. I'm Isla. Your lady's maid. Though, truthfully, I'm just a kitchen maid as there's no Noble Lady at the Estate. I'm afraid you're stuck with me."

Nova's fear ebbed a degree, and she nearly smiled in spite of herself at the maid's honesty.

Isla motioned toward the bathing chamber with an apologetic smile and tucked a lock of pale gray hair behind her ear. While Nova undressed, Isla filled the oval black stone tub with steaming water and added oil infused with jasmine and primrose. Nova lowered herself into the hot water, dunking her head beneath the surface. When she came up for air, Isla was ready with a soapy cloth and silently set to work washing Nova's hair and gently scrubbing the remnants of sand from her skin.

Back in the main chamber, Isla slipped a black satin robe over Nova's shoulders and tamed her hair, styling it with delicate silver combs shaped like crescent moons. The wardrobe held a number of fine gowns, as well as breeches and shirts, though the garments appeared to be designed specifically for females, rather than simply mimicking the styles typically worn by males.

"Would you prefer a gown or breeches?" Isla asked, her hand hovering before the rack. Nova imagined a gown would be proper for her introduction to the Noble Lord.

"A gown, I think."

Isla nodded and chose one, draping it over her forearm.

The dress featured a black leather bodice with silver stitching and a multilayered skirt of sheer black fabric. Thankfully, the skirt's many layers ensured it was not entirely see-through. Finally, Isla helped her into a pair of black silk slippers.

"His Grace should be ready to see you now." She looked Nova up and down and nodded in approval. "Much better. Follow me, miss."

Once in the corridor, Isla took to her wings, fluttering several strides ahead of Nova. Rather than descending the stairs to Great Hall, as Nova had expected, Isla led her to the wing on the opposite side of the Estate. The maid ushered her into a private chamber, past a large bed and stately furniture, and out onto a wide terrace overlooking the seashore in the distance.

The sky had darkened, and several moonstone orbs lit the space with pale light. At the center of the terrace sat a black metal table with a glass top set with tiered platters of fruit, boiled eggs, and fresh sliced bread with butter and jam. Nova's stomach growled at the sight. Two males sat at the table, but only one rose on Nova's entrance. She'd already had the displeasure of meeting the one who remained seated: Commander Lucan. Nova looked past him, focusing her attention on the other male.

Nox. Her uncle. The Noble Lord of Silvergard.

He was nothing like what she'd expected.

Straight white hair fell past his shoulders, and the genuine smile on his wide mouth warmed his charcoal eyes. He wore a loose shirt and black leather breeches on his tall frame. Studs of glowing moonstone and several silver rings pierced his ears.

"Nova," he said, extending a hand to her. "Welcome." His voice was a soothing baritone.

Nova crossed the terrace and stood beside the table, taking his offered hand.

"Your Grace." She bowed her head. He squeezed her fingers gently and motioned for her to take the seat beside him.

"Please, call me Nox," he said as he settled back into his chair. The commander slouched in his seat, ignoring her. To her surprise, Nox swatted him lightly on the shoulder.

"Say hello to our guest, Lucan."

The commander straightened and forced a thin smile. "Welcome, Nova." He resumed his slouching immediately afterward.

Nova thought she caught Nox roll his eyes. "You must be hungry. Please, eat," he said. "Lucan tells me you had quite the journey."

Nova glanced at the terrace doors, realizing Isla had silently taken her leave. She was on her own. Lowering herself into her seat, she quickly scanned Nox's breakfast of melon, eggs, and tea. She helped herself to servings of the same foods, assuming those items would be safe to eat.

"Yes, your guards boarded us and took me hostage," she said calmly as she leaned forward, reaching across the table for the silver teapot. Lucan tensed, his eyes lingering briefly on the scars running down her shoulder blade and disappearing beneath her bodice.

"You should see the wolf that did it," she said.

Lucan glanced warily at Nox, who chuckled quietly before sipping his tea.

"How did you know I was on the vessel? Your commander came prepared with an invitation for me to remain here as your guest." Nova poured herself a cup of steaming tea and took a sip. Strong and bracing. *Thank the gods.* Her day should have been ending, while Nox's day was just beginning.

"Lucan showed me," he replied.

"Showed you?"

"I'm sure you've heard whispers of the abilities I possess. Abilities I don't often use. But when Lucan saw you on the ship, he allowed me to see you through his eyes."

Nova casually sipped her tea, marveling at what it must be like to possess such power.

"Believe it or not, word travels fast in Aemoria," Nox continued, observing her closely. "The sudden arrival of a mysterious, raven-haired female with pale skin and silver eyes in the Autumn Court set tongues wagging. Word of you first made it to me after you attended the Hayer celebration dressed like Orika herself." He set his drink down on the table before him. "You certainly glow just like a moonstone."

"I can see how my arrival may have caused a stir, given my appearance and the reputation of your Court." She bit into a juicy slice of fresh melon.

"Surely you mean *our* Court," Nox said, a faint smile tugging at the corners of his mouth. Nova kept her face neutral, politely chewing her food.

"I suspected you were descended from Silvergard when I heard the description of you. But I knew you were my niece, last of the Elsever bloodline and heir to the Lunar Throne, the instant Lucan showed me your face."

Nova swallowed dryly, then tried and failed to clear her throat.

So, Nova Greenmore was Nova Elsever all along.

"I've only just learned the identity of my father."

"What was your plan for coming to Silvergard?" Lucan interjected, amber eyes narrowed on her.

"Coming to Silvergard was never part of my plan," she said icily. "I sought to return to Nivali before we inadvertently sailed too close to shore."

Lucan nodded mockingly, as if to say it was a likely story.

"Speaking of which, what has happened to my companion? To his crew? I trust you were true to your word." Nova struggled to keep the tremble from her voice.

"Oh, yes. Your *mate*." Lucan's lip curled up in a sneer.

"Enough," Nox ordered, his tone calm but authoritative. The commander's unfriendly demeanor shifted, and he looked at her, his expression almost apologetic.

"He's alive. On his way back to Nivali." He glanced at Nox, seemingly seeking approval.

Relief crashed against her, and Nova dipped her head, hiding the raw emotion on her face.

"Leave us, Lucan." A gentle order, but an order nonetheless. "I'll join you shortly," Nox added, a bit softer. Lucan nodded and rose from his seat, slinking across the terrace and back inside.

"Your commander is an ass. I hope you don't mind me saying so."

Nox chuckled softly. "Lucan is many things. He comes from an ancient race of walking wolves." He paused, presumably to gauge her reaction.

As usual, she showed none.

"And you're right, he can be an ass."

Nova didn't respond and instead sipped her tea. She felt Nox's gaze lingering on her as she ate in silence for several minutes.

"You're a lot like him, you know. Intelligent. Stoic."

Nova scoffed. "Are you talking about Lucan?"

"No. My brother," Nox said. "Omen."

"My father is a monster."

Nox nodded slowly. "You may be right. But experience has taught me monsters are often made, not born."

Nova twisted the gauzy fabric of her skirts in her lap.

"You must be tired," Nox said finally, rising from his seat. "Why don't you return to your chamber to rest. I'd like it if you would join me again later so I might show you around the Estate."

"As you command," she said, standing to leave.

"You are not a prisoner here, Nova. Please don't feel obligated to do anything you don't wish to do."

"May I have some parchment and ink? I'd like to send word to Nivali."

"The desk in your room should be stocked with whatever you need. I hope to see you later."

Nova nodded and left the Noble Lord of Silvergard to his breakfast.

Lucan stood at attention in the hallway when he saw Nova exit, stepping to the side and allowing her room to pass.

"Commander," she said, pausing in front of him. "I've been training in sword fighting, and I'd hate to stall while I'm a guest here. Can you spare anyone to instruct me during my stay?"

"Call me Lucan," he said, apparently growing resigned to her presence. "And I'll train you myself. We can begin tomorrow."

"I look forward to it." She turned and started down the hall in the direction of her own chamber. When she glanced back, Nox had joined Lucan in the hall, the two of them speaking quietly with their heads bowed close together.

TWENTY-SIX

THE MOONSTONE LAMPS SHONE brightly when she returned to her room. Nova wished she knew how to shield the door as Callan had in Nivali. A warm breeze blew in from the terrace doors, swirling the sheer curtains surrounding the bed. Nova searched the drawers of the writing desk and quickly inked a message to Callan, reassuring him that she was safe. That her uncle was not what she expected and she truly seemed to be a guest, not a prisoner. Rolling the parchment, she tied it securely with a length of silver twine.

A gentle wind ruffled her hair and her skirts as she walked to the edge of the terrace. A piercing screech split the night air, and a large mottled owl landed on the railing beside her, its talons gripping the polished stone. Yellow eyes glinted in the moonlight as she secured the letter to one of its scaly legs. Nova stood back as the creature spread its great wings, launched off the railing, and soared gracefully into the sky.

Leaning her elbows on the rail, she followed the bird with her eyes until it faded from view on its way south. In daylight, the landscape had been barren and lifeless. In darkness, Nova found it mysterious and hauntingly beautiful, the coarse, black sand dotted with deposits of moonstone, glowing like ethereal jewels under the light of the moon. Exhaustion drew her back into her chamber, where she stretched out on top of the sheets. Sleep overtook her before long, her mind so weary she didn't even dream.

A firm knock on the chamber woke her many hours later. Sliding off the edge of the tall bed, Nova rubbed her eyes groggily and opened the door. Nox stood alone on the other side, a smirk spreading across his face when he saw her, eyes rising to the air just above her head. Nova clapped her hands on top of her wayward hair, combing the strands flat.

"I can return later if you'd like some time to freshen up," he offered as she toed on the shoes she'd kicked off inside the doorway earlier.

"No, I'm ready now." She smoothed the front of her gown and stepped out into the hallway, pulling the door closed behind her.

Nox held a hand out to his side, directing her toward the sounds of music and muffled laughter. She paused at the railing overlooking the Great Hall. Courtiers crowded the area below, some lounging on the furniture, some feasting at the enormous table laid with platters of food, others dancing to a melody emanating from a string quartet stationed on a low platform in the corner. Nox's guests certainly seemed to be enjoying themselves.

Her uncle led the way down the staircase to the main level, where they meandered through the gathered crowd. Nox smiled and chatted with his subjects as they went, but he made no introductions.

At the rear of the great room, Nox held open a tall door, and Nova crossed the threshold into an impressive library. The high glass ceiling created a frame for the moon as it crawled across the sky. Shelves crammed with books reached all the way from the polished floor to the edge of the starlit canopy above. Rolling ladders sat at intervals, granting access to the highest stacks.

A large black sofa sat on the far side of the room, anchored by a plush white rug. A fireplace framed by onyx tiles served as a focal point, a low fire crackling on the hearth and a portrait hanging above the mantel. Nova crossed the open space to stand before it, tipping her head back to view the realistic detail of the oil painting. In the center sat a brawny male with a head full of inky-black curls and dark, fathomless eyes.

"It's a family portrait," Nox said, joining her. "In the middle is my father, Onyx. That's me and my mother, Luna, on his right."

Nox looked to be about fourteen in the painting, his white hair cut short and his ears unpierced.

"And to his left, my older brothers, Sable and Omen."

Sable took after his father, with the same hair and eyes, though his build was leaner. Nova lingered on the image of her own father. Her skin prickled. Though younger, the silver-haired male with metallic eyes in the painting was, without question, the same male who had appeared in her dream shortly after she arrived in Aemoria.

There was no denying she was his daughter. She recognized the arched eyebrows, prominent cheekbones, and angular chin. All were features she saw reflected in the mirror every day. But how was it possible she'd dreamt of her father before she knew he existed? And what else, if anything, had she inherited from him? Nova inhaled sharply and tore her gaze away from the portrait.

"Come, have a seat." Nox placed a hand on her shoulder and guided her to the sofa.

She sat, folding her hands in her lap. Nox paused before a glass cart and filled two glasses with red wine from a crystal decanter. Handing one to her, he sat, angling his body toward her. Nova peered into the glass and tried to discreetly sniff the contents while she waited for her uncle to take the first sip.

"I can't kill you, Nova." Nox chuckled and sipped from his glass.

"How comforting."

"I should say, I would never kill you. But, in any event, it's not possible for Fae to kill members of their own bloodline. It would threaten the preservation of the nobility if we could pick each other off at will."

"But then how . . ." She glanced at the painting and lifted her glass to her lips, drinking deeply.

"How was Omen able to murder our father and brother?" Nox's tone was jarringly nonchalant, and Nova sputtered, nearly choking on her wine. Her uncle regarded her with an amused expression as she composed herself, wiping a trickle of wine from her chin with the back of her hand. He took another sip, savoring the liquid in his mouth for a few seconds before swallowing.

"I don't know exactly. All I know is on the day Sable was to be wed, Omen appeared in the temple wielding a black sword. Before my father could speak a word, Omen ran the blade through his heart. Then, Omen turned on Sable and beheaded him where he stood on the altar.

"He tried to take Elena, but she refused him. She was terrified—we all were. Omen backed away into the shadows and simply disappeared. One instant he was there, and the next, he was gone."

"How terrible."

"Yes, well." Nox sighed deeply before throwing back the rest of his wine. He refilled his glass and relaxed into his seat once again, propping one elbow on the back of the sofa and resting his head on his hand.

"My father was a terrible father. A terrible ruler. I think he felt most powerful when inspiring fear in others. He was cruel to us all, but he seemed to delight in harming Omen most. As the years went on, my father and Sable became a team of sorts, working together to torment him."

"Why did your father despise him?" Nova asked, shifting to curl her legs on the cushion beside her.

"Our bloodline carries different abilities and levels of ability. My father was unmatched when it came to mind control, but he was unable to read minds. I can read minds remarkably well, but I've never been particularly skilled at controlling them. Omen excelled at both. My father resented him. Feared him, really. Most feared Omen. They found his appearance unsettling."

"I was raised in the Human Realm, concealed with a glamour. But the humans weren't fooled. They could sense something unnatural about me," Nova said, the words coaxed from her by both the wine and Nox's candor. "They taunted me. Beat me. Even once threw stones at me. All because of how I looked."

"And yet, here you sit. A strong, capable female, despite how you were treated."

"I don't know why I'm sharing this with you." She shook her head, setting her glass down on the low table in front of them. "It's not something I like to think of, much less discuss."

"I didn't always speak so openly about my past, either. I preferred to keep it buried. But over time, I discovered my anger had begun to fester inside me. I realized it would likely consume me entirely if I didn't find a way to stop it. Then, I met someone I trusted enough to share even the darkest parts of myself."

Nova studied the painting again, her eyes roaming over the shadows and highlights skillfully formed by the artist's brush, bringing vibrant life to the composition.

"Why display this portrait when it's a reminder of so much pain? Why not commission a new one?"

Nox considered for a moment. "It's important to me to remember my past. It keeps me focused on the future I want, for myself and for my Court." Nox leaned toward her. "I know we've just met, but I'm hopeful you'll come to see that I am not my father. That Silvergard is so much more than it once was. I'm aware of our reputation throughout the Realm. What is whispered about me.

"This perception keeps my people isolated. Isolation is what allowed my father's cruelty to go unchecked. Unpunished. You've already made connections in Pyralis and Nivali. I had hoped you might use those connections to improve relations between Silvergard and the other territories. Whatever you may have thought of me or my Court before you arrived here, you are the rightful heir to the throne of Silvergard."

Nova's spine straightened.

"I hadn't even considered the prospect," she insisted. "I wouldn't know the first thing about being a ruler."

"And I would never force you to take on such a responsibility. But perhaps you'd be willing to serve as an emissary between Silvergard and the other territories?"

Nova pressed her eyes shut and pinched the bridge of her nose, the weight of her exhaustion settling over her all at once.

"I'm asking a great deal, I know," Nox said apologetically. "We can discuss it another time."

"Yes, I think that would be best. Good night, Nox."

The fire crackled faintly as she padded across the thick rug. Nox called her name just as she took hold of the carved stone doorknob. She looked back over her shoulder at her uncle.

"I'm very glad you're here," he said quietly.

She dipped her head in a bow of acknowledgment before making her way toward the privacy of her chamber and the alluring promise of sleep.

A handful of minutes later, she was slipping out of her dress, which she left in a puddle on the floor, and into a black satin nightgown that trailed behind her as she crawled onto the bed. The moonstone lamps began to dim with the coming dawn. Nova's eyes burned with fatigue as she curled up on her side, quickly falling into what she hoped would finally be a deep and restful sleep.

Nova glided down a long hallway lined on both sides with tall windows. She knew she was dreaming. Moonlight streamed in through the windowpanes on either side of her as a warm breeze billowed the sheer black curtains.

A heavy door swung open before her, revealing a throne room beyond. A full moon shone brightly through the glass ceiling overhead, bathing the room in its silvery light. A throne of carved moonstone sat on a raised platform at the far end of the room, glowing faintly.

A voice spoke her name, the sound a vaguely distorted murmur seeming to rush at her from all directions at once. Nox appeared at her side clad in a black robe. His hair was tied back, charcoal eyes solemn.

"I wish to show you something." His voice sounded slow and muffled, as if it came from far away. Nox extended his hand. Nova hesitated for an instant, staring at the feathered lines creasing his palm, before laying her own hand in his. His slender fingers closed around hers, and a flash of white filled her vision as a shock ripped through her body.

Nova blinked against the blinding light as the pain evaporated. Her vision cleared, and she found the once-empty throne room full of folk standing shoulder to shoulder. Her vantage point was lower than normal, as though seeing through the eyes of a child. The crowd stood gathered around the dais, where her grandfather Onyx sat elevated above them all, the great throne dwarfed by his large frame. A silver crown set with luminous stones lay atop his inky-black curls. His wide mouth curled in a hateful sneer.

An earsplitting scream cut through the murmur of the crowd, and Nova's chest seized. Stifled gasps erupted as the crowd fanned out to the edges of the room, leaving an open space just before the dais. A male lay on the stone floor, crying out in pain and thrashing about, his limbs contorted grotesquely as if he were being speared with hot iron.

Onyx's voice boomed. "Those who refuse to kneel before me will writhe at my feet instead." A rumble of vile laughter flowed from his broad chest, mixing with the tortured cries of the male and echoing throughout the throne room.

The blinding light flashed a second time, and the folk who had crowded the throne room only an instant before were gone. A female knelt weeping at Onyx's feet. Nova recognized her from the portrait in the library; it was her grandmother, Luna. Onyx struck her cheek with the back of his hand, and she fell to the floor. A young Omen ran to her and crouched by her side, his silver hair glinting under the light of the moon. Omen stood and turned from his mother's crumpled form to face his father, his hands balled in defiant fists at his sides, chest heaving. Onyx towered over him.

A moment later, Omen began to twitch. He staggered toward a black stone column at the edge of the dais, his movements jerky, like a marionette manipulated by an invisible puppeteer.

Omen halted before the pillar and slowly raised his hands, arms trembling as if struggling against the movement. Suddenly, his fist shot out in front of him, connecting solidly with the stone. His other hand followed close behind. Omen roared through clenched teeth as his fists increased their pace, forcefully striking the column over, and over, and over again.

The thud of the strikes grew wet as Omen's knuckles split and bled before the sickening crunch of shattered bone rang out in the air. Only then did Omen stop, slumping to his knees. Onyx prowled up behind him, chuckling to himself and nudging his son forward with the toe of his boot. Omen fell to his side on the floor, rolling onto his back and cradling his mangled hands against his chest. A wave of nausea washed over Nova, and her vision faded to black.

She bolted upright in bed, the bitter tang of bile clinging to the back of her throat. Her hands flew to her chest, where her heart thundered like the wings of a great bird.

It was only a dream.

She slid out of bed and stumbled into the bathing chamber. Running the tap, she splashed a handful of icy water over her face, rubbing the bracing liquid over the back of her neck. She rested her elbows on the cool stone counter, letting her head roll forward and breathing deeply for several minutes, willing her pulse to slow.

After a time, she returned to bed, crawling under the smooth sheets and drawing them up to her chin despite the warmth in the room. Sunlight streamed in through the terrace doors. Nova focused her attention on the long gossamer curtains dancing in the breeze, the rhythmic motion eventually lulling her back to sleep.

TWENTY-SEVEN

NOVA AWOKE AT DUSK to the steady rustle of beating wings. A messenger owl swooped in from the terrace clasping a folded piece of parchment in its talons. The bird deposited the letter on the bedsheets beside her and flew back through the gap in the doors. She snatched up the paper, sealed with dark blue wax stamped with an insignia of crossed swords, and tore through the seal, nearly rending the parchment in her eagerness.

Nova released a sigh of relief. Callan was alive and well.

> *I owe my life to you, Nova. I'm relieved to hear you're being treated well, but I worry. How much longer is your stay? I'll come and steal you away myself if you ask it.*

Not for the first time, Nova imagined Callan hefting her over his shoulder. The needling anxiety in the pit of her stomach, which she'd been doing her best to ignore, eased a bit. She feared the unpleasant sensation wouldn't fade completely until they were reunited.

Flinging herself off the bed, she rushed into the bathing chamber, needing to physically distance herself from Callan's words and the feelings they stirred within her. She tidied herself at the sink, first cleaning her teeth, then dousing her hair with rose water and wrangling it into a braid.

Rifling through the wardrobe, she settled on a pair of fitted black breeches and a leather bodice cinched over a loose linen blouse. She tugged on a pair of boots, then ventured into the corridor, where she wandered for a bit before getting herself hopelessly lost. Fortunately, she was able to flag down a passing servant who told her she could find Nox in his private garden and kindly offered to escort her there, chatting amiably at her the entire way.

Nox's back was to her when she passed through the wrought-metal gate into the open-air garden. Similar to the Temple of Illora, the area was crowded with potted trees, shrubs, and flowers in ornate arrangements. With the exception of a few acacias and juniper bushes, Nova assumed most of the garden's greenery was likely imported.

Her uncle stood pruning the limbs of an impressive magnolia tree. From what she'd seen of Silvergard, very little sprouted from the dry terrain, but this tree was firmly rooted in the coarse black sand. Delicate white moths fluttered around the white and pale pink petals, attracted by the fragrance. Nova crossed the garden to stand beside Nox, quietly watching as he snipped off any wilted blooms. After a few moments, he finished his task and set the shears down on a table.

As Nox turned to face her, Nova took in his platinum hair gathered at the back and his black satin robe. She took a step back, stung by a barb of recognition.

"I saw you," she murmured, recalling her dream. A shudder ran through her at the memory of Omen's ruined hands.

"Yes," he said, eyes downcast. "I influenced your dream. It's not something I do often or that I take lightly, I assure you. I know it was an invasion, but it was the only way to make you see—"

"Through your eyes," Nova finished, the pieces falling into place. "You showed me your memories." She'd thought the visions were from the perspective of a child.

"It's one thing to hear stories of my father's cruelty. It's quite another to witness it firsthand." He met her gaze, guilt written across his face.

"It was horrific," she said, aware the word was wholly inadequate to describe the sickening visions he'd shown her. The residual terror of seeing a child powerless to stop the abuse rushed through her.

Nox nodded in silent agreement. "I promise you, Nova: I will never enter your mind without your consent again." He laid his hand on her shoulder, squeezing gently.

Nova bit the inside of her cheek. "I think I'd like to get to know your, I mean, *our* people while I'm here."

"You would?" He grinned. "That's wonderful. I'll arrange a welcome dinner for you."

The heavy gate groaned behind them, and she turned to see Lucan, who'd halted in the entryway, one boot hovering mid-step.

"Lucan," Nova said flatly. "It's you."

"It's me." He made a mocking bow of his head. "Sorry to intrude."

"There's no intrusion," Nox said, smiling faintly.

"I thought Nova might want to see the training yard. I'm headed there now for drills."

Lucan was dressed in light armor of black leather, his curved sword sheathed at his hip.

"Excellent," Nova said.

Traces of nervous energy still rattled like loose coins in the pit of her stomach, and physical exertion sounded like the perfect distraction.

"Very well. We can fetch some food and eat on the way."

"You read my mind."

Lucan scoffed and turned to lead her out of the garden.

"Play nicely, you two," Nox called after them as they left.

A handful of minutes later, Nova and Lucan walked side by side, each gnawing on a roll stuffed with thick slabs of ham and slices of cheese. Both were silent except for Lucan, who occasionally identified points of interest through mouthfuls of food.

"Those are the stables. Obviously. The barracks. And here we have the training yard."

Nova surveyed the sandy field enclosed by a tall metal fence. A force of roughly fifty guards stood in formation, running through a defensive sequence in unison.

"This is Nox's personal guard," Lucan said, throwing his shoulders back and puffing out his chest. "We have squadrons running patrols all around the territory. Most of our forces live in districts outside the Estate. They report for training several times per year, and we can raise them at any time if necessary."

Lucan led her through the gate to an area along the side of the field with equipment laid out on racks and tables. He sorted through a stack of chest and shoulder armor, selecting the smallest one he could find and tossing it to her.

"That should be a good fit for a lady," he said as he sauntered over to a cabinet and yanked the doors open. Nova slipped the chest plate over her head and fastened the straps along her ribs. It was a bit loose around the waist and not designed to accommodate breasts, but it would serve its purpose.

"Are there female soldiers?" she asked, tugging at the stiff leather material.

"Of course there are. But most have their armor specially made to accommodate their *unique qualities*." He shrugged and removed something from the cabinet.

"I believe these belong to you." He held her dagger and the sword from Callan.

Snatching the weapons from his outstretched hands, she unsheathed her sword at once, checking the blade for damage.

"I took them from the Nivalian vessel. Both are passable weapons," he conceded, though admitting it was clearly a challenge for him. "Do they have sentimental value?"

"The dagger belonged—" Nova caught herself before she referred to Anson Greenmore as her father. "To the man who raised me. The sword was a gift. Forged by the legendary smiths of Nivali," she added proudly.

Lucan held his hands up, palms facing her.

"Too bad they're known for their steel and not their ships. Otherwise, you might have outrun us," he quipped, cracking a smug grin.

Nova stared at him, stone-faced, until he cleared his throat and moved on.

"If you insist on using those blades, then I have something else for you." He produced a small sheath and pulled out a dagger of Silvergardian steel, the blade slightly curved like a crescent moon. Nova ran her thumb over the pommel, inlaid with a small, round moonstone, as smooth and shiny as a marble.

"It's beautiful," she said, raising a wary eyebrow at him. Lucan waved a hand in the air as if sensing her gratitude and deeming it unnecessary.

"I'm only hoping to prove a point that Silvergardian blades are far superior. Now, follow me to the sparring ring. No need to have an audience before you're any good."

When they entered the training room, Lucan instructed her to show him what she'd learned so far. He observed her silently from the edge of the ring, scrutinizing her every move as she performed the various sequences and maneuvers Callan had taught her with a wooden sword.

The moon ambled lazily across the dark sky. Before she knew it, hours had passed, and the drills concluded. Nova stood watching Nox's guard, a mix of males and females as Lucan had said, as they filed off the field toward their other duties.

"So, does agreeing to train me mean you like me?" She panted, beads of sweat gathering along her hairline and rolling down her forehead, stinging her eyes.

Lucan smirked and threw himself down on a dusty incline at the edge of the field.

"It means I've decided to tolerate you. You're important to Nox. Nox is important to me. So, I'll tolerate you."

"But you don't trust me."

"I told you already: I'm more animal than man. My primary concerns are food, fucking, and defending my territory." He held up a finger for each item as he listed them off.

"In that order?"

Lucan continued, ignoring her. "I'll protect Nox until my dying breath. Given your family's legacy, you can hardly blame me for not welcoming you with open arms."

He brought out a flask and took several gulps before tossing it in her direction and wiping his mouth with the back of a gloved hand. Nova caught the flask against her chest and lowered herself to the ground beside him.

"I don't blame you." She tilted her head back and drank greedily, the cool water easing her parched throat. A twinge of pain brought her fingers to her mouth, gently prodding at the split in her bottom lip. She'd caught Lucan's elbow while sparring.

"Sorry about that," he said, though his grin suggested he wasn't particularly sorry.

Nova pressed her fingertips against her lip and closed her eyes. Recalling Callan's instructions, she emptied her mind and visualized the injured flesh knitting itself back together. Warmth bloomed in the tips of her fingers and passed to her lip. When she drew her hand away a moment later, the wound was gone. She turned to Lucan, allowing herself a cocky raise of her eyebrow as she showed off her handiwork.

"How did you manage that?" he asked.

"Solar blood."

Lucan clicked his tongue. "I suppose that explains how you walked away from a fight with a wolf."

"A lycane, actually."

Lucan's brows shot up. He puffed out his cheeks and let out a slow whistle.

"But you're right," she said. "I nearly died. And I hope to never face one again."

Lucan nodded, his expression almost sincere. "For your sake, I hope you never do either." The sly glint returned to his eyes. "Because after what I saw today, we've got a lot of work to do."

"Gods above," Nova groaned. "You truly are an ass."

TWENTY-EIGHT

DUSK WAS BEGINNING TO purple the sky when she woke. Nova quickly slipped into the breeches, shirt, and leather armor of her training uniform, securing her weapons in place. Lucan met her at the foot of the staircase holding an enormous savory hand pie for each of them, which they wolfed down as they headed for the sparring ring.

Just over a week had passed since her arrival in Silvergard, and Nova had already settled into a comfortable rhythm in the Lunar Court. For the first seven days of training, she faced off against Lucan, both of them wielding wooden swords as he taught her how to strike and block against an opponent in the style of a Silvergardian soldier. The Nivalian style Callan practiced was rooted in brutal offensive techniques and maneuvers, leveraging one's size and strength against an opponent. The Silvergardian method incorporated evasive maneuvers, using speed and agility to best one's opponent. Not being exceptionally large herself, Nova found she preferred the Silvergardian style.

Lucan never took it easy on her. In fact, she got the distinct impression that her trainer derived a sizable measure of joy every time she tumbled face-first onto the smooth stone floor of the sparring ring. Still, there was no denying her skills had already improved significantly under his instruction.

Following their most recent session, he'd lost his patience and accused her of holding back.

Nova stood at the edge of the sparring ring, resting her hand lightly on the hilt of her sword. She would finally be training with a real blade, but Lucan wasn't foolish enough to offer himself up as her first victim. She watched through narrowed eyes as he dragged a training dummy into the center of the ring. The figure was slightly taller than she was, stuffed with straw, and clothed in the traditional dress of Nivali. How Lucan had come by the garments, Nova didn't wish to know.

"Friend of yours?" she asked, attempting to douse her irritation with sarcasm as Lucan steadied the mannequin on its round base.

He stood back with a hand on his hip, admiring his handiwork, and shook his head.

"Nah, he looks more like your type to me." Lucan playfully flicked the insignia of crossed swords embroidered in silver thread on the chest of the faded, blue jacket.

Nova gritted her teeth.

"What?" Lucan clapped the mannequin on the back, a cloud of dust exploding into the air. "Isn't he the spitting image of your wintry warrior?"

"His name is Callan."

"Whatever." Lucan snapped his fingers. "Tear him apart."

Nova didn't move, her breath quickening as she stared Lucan down.

"I want to see what you've got, Elsever." His patience was wearing thin, but Nova remained motionless.

Lucan drew his sword, the metal singing as he pulled it from its sheath. "I wonder what you'd do if it really was Callan." He raised his blade to the dummy's neck. Drawing her own sword, Nova took two quick steps toward Lucan. He leapt back as she brought her weapon down, slicing through the air and slashing the mannequin's blue jacket cleanly down the front.

Lucan sputtered as a laugh burst from his pursed lips, and Nova turned her blade on him, pressing the tip against his leather chest plate, just below his breastbone.

"Whoa, whoa, whoa!" Lucan held his hands out in front of him, his laughter drying up in an instant.

"What's wrong, Commander? Afraid to feel the kiss of Nivalian steel?" Nova asked, tight-lipped. "Remove the jacket." Her instruction was calmly delivered through clenched teeth.

Lucan sidestepped her blade, reaching behind the mannequin and cautiously peeling the slashed coat from its shoulders. Nova lowered her weapon.

"It was a joke, Nova. A bit of fun." He tossed the garment off to the edge of the ring. "Though it's nice to finally see a little spark from you. Perhaps we'll make a killer out of you yet."

Nova spun and took a few steps away from him. She rolled her shoulders and shook out her sword arm, attempting to banish the anger that had her gripping the hilt so tightly her knuckles had gone white.

"Don't do that," Lucan instructed, motioning for her to come back. "Whatever you're feeling, use it."

Nova took his advice and used her anger for the next hour, slashing and stabbing at the training dummy until its thick burlap skin hung in ribbons and the polished stone floor was littered with straw clippings. When she was through, she walked the perimeter of the ring, chest heaving and bits of golden straw swirling in her wake. Slowly, she backed against the wall and lowered herself to the floor, struggling to regulate her breathing. She laid her sword on the floor beside her, aware of Lucan tracking her movements from his position across the ring with narrowed amber eyes.

"I'm s-sorry." Nova gasped for air, hating herself for the whine of weakness in her voice

Lucan shoved off the pillar he'd been leaning against and joined her, his back sliding down the wall until he sat beside her.

"Sorry for what? Getting pissed off?" He shrugged, tilting his head back against the smooth stone behind him and looking up at the ceiling. "Look, when I was young, I had to hide certain parts of myself. Gods, it pissed me off. I lashed out constantly, picked fights, aching for a bit of physical pain to distract me from what I was feeling."

Nova's breathing slowed a bit, intrigued by this chink in the commander's armor.

"When I met Nox ..." A faint smile. There and gone, quicker than a blink. He shook his head and continued. "When I first joined his guard, I was still simmering away. This rage I kept trying to put a lid on was always there, threatening to boil over. Rather than letting it get the better of me, I poured it into my training. Anger can be useful. But you've got to channel it. Otherwise, it's just chaos. Do you see what I'm saying?"

A slight nod. Her breathing was returning to normal.

"Your anger, your fear, your pain—you can let it fuel you." Lucan spoke softly, brows low as he nodded, staring into the empty air in front of him. "But you can't let it burn you up."

Nova flexed her fingers and ran her damp palms over her face before smoothing down the riotous flyaway hairs that had escaped from her braid. Lucan nudged her shoulder with his own.

"Seems my plan to bore you with my sob story worked." He clapped once and hefted himself up, standing over her and extending a hand. "Let's go, kid. I think you've done enough damage for today."

Nova took hold of his hand and pulled herself up beside him.

"Don't call me kid, grandsire." She slipped her sword back into its sheath.

"Try and have some measure of respect for your elders," Lucan chided as he playfully shoved her toward the door.

Nova skipped breakfast, opting to ease her nerves by sinking into a hot bath instead. Once clean and relatively calm, she dressed for the day in a sleek black gown with black leather straps crisscrossing her back and wrapping around her ribs.

A message from Callan had arrived while she bathed. It was brief. He was making an effort to fulfill his bargain with his uncle by getting to know his people. Thorn had roped him into attending an upcoming Assembly, a special gathering for the citizens of Nivali to make appeals for aid or seek the Noble Lord's wisdom in settling disputes over land and fishing rights. And, as Callan put it, *for Thorn to address many other* incredibly important *matters that require the input of a Noble Lord.* Nova smiled to herself as she imagined Callan speaking the words with his customary seriousness. She shook her head and laid his letter atop a stack of several others beside her bed. Nox would be expecting her to join him in the library.

Nova and her uncle spent several hours together most days, often sitting in companionable silence in the grand library while she read and he drew in a sketchbook. Occasionally they would socialize with members of the Court, many of whom were patrons of the arts, either creating works themselves or supporting others in their artistic pursuits.

The Estate itself was like a museum. Abstract paintings and realistic landscapes hung on nearly every wall, the pieces beautifully lit by moonstone orbs. Ornate sculptures carved from onyx or moonstone dotted the halls and chambers.

As Nova learned, it hadn't always been so. Nox broke with thousands of years of tradition over a century earlier, slashing spending on Silvergard's armed forces and investing in the arts and education for all. He'd worked with district leaders to end mandatory conscription for males across the territory, though one or two districts still upheld such laws. Nox had told her of his efforts to persuade the remaining holdouts to abolish the practice as well.

Nova pushed open the door to the library but found it empty. She slumped down on the sofa next to Nox's sketchbook lying open on the cushion next to her. She flipped idly through the pages, admiring the detailed sketches of flowers and plants, delicate, lifelike images captured in lines of smudged charcoal. She closed the book and ran her fingertips over the stretched fabric of the cover. A shared love of plants had initially sparked their friendship, though Nova's interest was in medicinal applications while her uncle's was purely aesthetic.

Nova tossed the sketchbook onto the table with a thud and glanced up at the portrait hanging above the fireplace. The image of her father never failed to unnerve her, his piercing eyes often seeming to stalk her as she moved about the room. The sound of muffled voices carried through the cracked door of Nox's study. Nova rose to her feet, forcing herself to turn her back on the painting and rush toward the study. In her haste to escape Omen's eerie gaze, she burst through the door without knocking, skidding to a halt just inside.

Nox sat behind his desk, knees spread wide with Lucan stood between them. Lucan leaned over her uncle, his hands braced firmly on the carved wooden arms of the chair. She might have found the position threatening if not for Lucan's sly smile and Nox's slender fingers gripping Lucan's forearms, his face tilted expectantly toward the commander's.

Lucan stepped back at once, his hands going to his sides as he stood at attention. Nox shifted in his seat and stumbled his way through a greeting. Nova had never seen her uncle flustered before.

"I . . . I'm sorry I missed breakfast," she said.

"I wondered when you'd turn up." Nox motioned for her to take a seat.

A faint flush seared his pale cheeks, and Nova wondered how often her own complexion betrayed her thoughts despite her best efforts to hide them.

"How was training?" Nox asked breezily.

"Fine." She flopped down onto one of the twin leather wingbacks sitting opposite the desk, shooting a sideways glance at Lucan.

"Come now, Nova. Don't be so modest," Lucan teased, sinking into the seat beside hers. "You would have been so proud, my Lord. She nearly gutted me." Lucan grinned, showing off his pearly white fangs.

Nox arched an eyebrow. "I can't imagine why."

Lucan set to work cleaning his fingernails with his dagger, and Nova breathed a silent sigh of relief that he'd omitted the part about her outburst.

A knock sounded at the door with a servant announcing a visitor. "General Idrian has arrived, my Lord."

"A bit earlier than expected," Nox sighed, pushing his chair back and walking around to the front of his desk. "Please show him in."

Lucan rose from his seat as the general entered. Nova remained seated but twisted in her chair, her eyes landing first on a pair of black leather boots, hitting just below the knee and buffed to a shine. Her gaze traveled upward over finely tailored black breeches and a meticulously pressed tunic to match, before finally settling on the general's face.

His black hair was cut close on the sides but kept longer and combed back at the crown. A thin streak of silver mixed with the strands above his left eye. Full brows crowned his slate-gray eyes, and his mouth formed a serious line above a deep cleft in his chin.

"My Lord," the general said, bowing low while his spine remained as straight as an arrow.

"General Idrian. Welcome back to the Silvergard Estate. It's been many years, hasn't it?"

"Indeed, it has."

Nox leaned casually against his desk while the general maintained a soldier's posture.

"You remember Commander Lucan, the head of my guard?"

"Yes, of course." Idrian nodded politely in Lucan's direction before taking notice of Nova, peeking out like a child from behind the wing of the chair.

"Allow me to introduce Nova." Nox held out his hand, and she took it, rising to stand beside him. "Nova is a relative visiting the capital after many years spent abroad."

Nova didn't flinch at her uncle's practiced evasion to explain her presence at the Estate. He was always very careful to avoid revealing the truth of her paternity to anyone. She smiled faintly, more than happy to play along. She'd never had a knack for lying, even in the Human Realm, but she'd certainly been learning the fine art of dancing around the truth since arriving in Silvergard.

"Pleased to meet you," she said, making a quick curtsy.

"Likewise," Idrian replied, bowing his head briefly.

"I'm afraid I won't be able to meet until tomorrow, General." Nox held his hands out at his sides apologetically. "But please, make yourself at home while you're here. I've had my staff prepare a chamber for you."

"You are very generous, my Lord. But I've come with twenty of my best soldiers, and I would prefer to bunk with them in the barracks."

"As you wish," Nox replied.

With a final low bow, Idrian turned to take his leave but halted in the entryway. He made an abrupt about-face, locking eyes with Nova. She shrank back slightly at the sudden movement and the intensity of his stare.

"You've been living abroad?" he asked.

"That's right." She pressed her shoulders back and lifted her chin, praying to the gods he wouldn't prod for details about her supposed travels.

His eyes narrowed on her. "How fortunate that you've returned home," he said after a beat.

"Indeed," she replied, the word *home* conjuring images of Agnes and her cozy, firelit den in Timberfell for an instant.

"I hope our paths will cross again during my time here," Idrian added. A ghost of a smile passed fleetingly over his austere features.

Nova blinked at the unexpected expression.

Perhaps there is more to the general than meets the eye.

TWENTY-NINE

THE FEUD WAS OVER livestock. Or was it property lines? Callan couldn't recall and, honestly, didn't care either way. His agreement with Thorn obligated him to attend Assembly held in the Great Hall. But while Callan's attendance was required, his participation—gods be praised—was not. Each appeal bled into the next, continuing on with mind-numbing monotony, until he found himself weighing whether dozing off for a bit was worth the reprimand he'd surely receive from his uncle. He decided it probably was not.

Thorn dispensed his latest wisdom, and the griping landowners parted ways, disappearing into the crowd. It was standing room only in the hall. Callan squinted, then opened his eyes wide, rubbing a hand over his face to keep himself awake.

The herald announced the next complainant, and the crowd parted, allowing a disheveled male with long, stringy hair and wrinkled clothing to approach the platform where Callan sat on a simple chair set back from his uncle's throne. The visitor's bloodshot eyes suggested it had been some nights since he'd last slept. Intrigued for the first time in the hours since the meeting began, Callan shifted in his seat as his uncle acknowledged the male and asked his reason for coming before the throne.

"I am Anders, my Lord. I've come from the ice fields of the Whitepeak District."

Callan knew the place. Roughly two days' ride from the capital.

"Three days past, my village was attacked."

"Attacked?" Thorn asked.

"Yes," Anders said. "By a pack of yaesira."

Murmurs and whispers rose from those standing closest to the dais, a wave of disbelief rippling out to the four corners of the room. The predatory cats were massive and covered with thick, armorlike scales in place of fur. Native to Silvergard, it was almost unheard of to encounter yaesira in Nivali; the creatures rarely strayed from their established hunting grounds north of the Nephari Mountains.

"How can you be certain?" Thorn raised his voice and held up an authoritative hand to silence the crowd.

"I observed the tracks myself, and some of the townsfolk managed to kill one of the beasts. Its body lies there still." Anders turned to address the gentry gathered in the hall. "The yaesira slaughtered at least three, but the rest of the townsfolk are missing. No bodies. No footprints in the snow."

"This is the Shadowbringer's doing!" The shout came from a stocky, blond male with a long braided beard. Callan didn't recognize him. "He controls the wicked beasts and sends them to do his bidding."

"The Realm hasn't seen an attack by Raven's Isle in decades. Why would the Shadowbringer suddenly strike again?" a female warrior questioned, her muscled arms crossed over a chest plate of thick brown leather.

"I'm sure there's a reasonable explanation. There's no sense in spreading needless panic," Thorn reassured the crowd. "Perhaps the creatures simply tracked a herd of elk down through one of the passes. Gods only know what the conditions are like beyond the northern border."

Callan rose from his seat and approached the front of the platform.

"If I may speak, my Lord," he began, bowing his head to his uncle. Thorn waved a hand, granting him permission to continue. "A similar attack was carried out in Tundara only a few weeks ago—"

"That proves it!" the blond male interrupted, instigating the folk around him until everyone was shouting and swearing angry oaths.

"Enough!" Callan yelled, his command instantly bringing silence over the room. Realizing he had overstepped, he glanced at his uncle. Thorn's mouth hung open for an instant before he collected himself.

"Karlsen, I'll have you removed from the hall if you can't respect the rules of Assembly." His authority re-established, Thorn nodded at Callan to continue.

"The attacks in Tundara and Whitepeak may be unrelated. Or they may be related but have nothing to do with Raven's Isle. And, yes, there is a possibility both attacks were carried out by the Shadowbringer."

Callan turned to his uncle.

"My Lord, I ask to travel north to Whitepeak to investigate the circumstances of the attack and determine whether or not Nivali is at risk."

"You." Thorn pointed at Anders. "How did you survive to bring this news before Assembly?"

"I was out with a hunting party when the creatures attacked. The others in my group stayed behind in Whitepeak, guarding the bodies in the hopes that someone would be sent."

"Very well." Thorn turned to address Callan. "Accompany him north to the ice fields and return with your findings."

Thorn clapped his hands, and a servant stepped forward.

"See that this man is fed and given a bed."

The servant led Anders away, and Thorn dismissed the crowd.

Callan turned to leave and make preparations for the journey, but his uncle caught him around the wrist.

"Keep your wits about you, Callan. These are strange times, indeed."

Less than an hour's ride remained before Callan and his guide would arrive at the ice fields of Whitepeak. Mercifully, the clear weather had held since they departed the Estate, though the gusting winds blew bitterly cold. Callan had cobbled together a few hours of sleep the night before, stretched out on the hard ground beneath an awning of ancient spruce, his cloak pulled tight around him.

Few words had passed between them on the journey. Callan wasn't particularly talkative under normal circumstances. His nagging unease about the scene awaiting him had him clenching his jaw too tightly to engage in idle chat. Anders didn't seem to take offense, giving Callan the wide berth to which he'd grown accustomed. He sensed the apprehension emanating from the hunter, who rode a short distance behind him, his watchful gaze fixed on Callan's back. On the weapon sheathed there.

The path cutting through the snowy wood widened, and Anders picked up speed, bringing his horse to ride alongside Callan.

"I know who you are," he said, the slight tremor in his voice proof it had taken him nearly two days to gather the courage to speak.

"Do you?"

"You're Callan Nyhauslen. Aemoria's Blade." The hunter's voice held a hint of childlike wonder.

Inwardly, Callan recoiled at the name forced upon him, a name he had never once claimed. The Council hadn't spared even a fleeting thought for the part of him that'd been lost in the Wylds all those years ago. The Council only cared about maintaining its image of authority and control throughout the Realm. He had no choice but to bear the title, even if it cut him like the flick of a knife each time he heard it uttered.

"I go by Callan," he said, voice low and words clipped, refusing to look at the awestruck male keeping pace beside him.

The gods heeded Callan's prayer for silence, and Anders went quiet again. They rode on for a time, the trill of the birds making the journey almost pleasant.

"Is that it? The blade that slayed Ithan Greylock?"

For an instant, Callan was back in the abandoned temple in Maedwen, kneeling in a pool of blood on the cold stone floor. Hands shaking and stained red as he struggled to focus on the tall columns of speckled granite swirling around him. On the face of his friend Arik, dark eyes flashing with concern, as he came to kneel before Callan.

"Yes," Callan snarled, returning to the present moment and snapping his head toward the hunter. "And it always thirsts for fresh blood."

Anders fell back once again, his chestnut mare following a short distance behind Frost. Callan exhaled sharply through his nose, his breath a cloud of steam rising in the frigid air. He preferred to think of his sword as the one that had once belonged to his father. A reminder of the male Callan had been before fate intervened, leaving him forever changed. When Nova had admired the blade on the training field in Pyralis, simply appreciating it for what it was with no knowledge of its history, he'd hoped she viewed him the same way. Exactly as he was. Unmarred by the many mistakes of his past.

Frost trotted through the tree line, and a vast expanse of ice, thick and tinged with blue, spread out before them. On the opposite side of the field, Callan spied wooden structures. Anders pulled ahead, leading the way across the frozen ground.

They reached the village a short time later, and a corpse greeted them as they passed through the high wooden gates. The female's eyes were cloudy, staring at the sky, her mouth open in a silent scream. A pool of frozen blood surrounded her, still bright red nearly a week after her death, stemming from a savage wound to her throat. Callan trembled with a shudder that had nothing to do with the icy wind racing across the flats surrounding the village.

He slid down from the saddle, his boots landing with a crunch on the packed snow covering the roadway. A male and a female emerged from a trading post: the rest of Anders's hunting party. They greeted the hunter with silent nods and made no attempt to speak to Callan as he crouched beside the body.

The female's skin was tinged blue, like the ice. She'd been mauled by a beast of considerable size. Callan raised the apron tied at her waist, draping the bloodstained fabric over her face. Before he could stand, something caught his eye—a streak of black against the pool of garish crimson. He pinched the object between his gloved thumb and forefinger, holding it before his face. The wind ruffled the black barbs of a raven's feather.

"Where is the creature?" he asked, rising to his feet and securing the feather in the leather pouch hanging at his hip.

The female hunter gestured with a jerk of her chin, turning to lead Callan farther into the settlement. The wind swept along the ice fields, producing a faint, high-pitched whistle, an eerie sound without the bustle of a village to mask it. His guides turned onto a narrow alleyway between the trading post and tavern. Two more bodies lay on the ground with injuries similar to the first. A short distance away, nearly stretching from one side of the alleyway to the other, lay the yaesira.

Callan approached cautiously despite knowing full well the creature was dead. A large ice hook protruded from the side of its neck. The beast was huge, not so different from the snow cats of Nivali. But instead of a coat of soft white fur, the yaesira had thick scales, black and shiny.

Callan returned to the bodies, both males, one older, the other little more than a youngling. The older one lay curled around the younger, shielding him with his body. Bile rose in Callan's throat as he confronted the horror laid out before him, the village so similar to the one where his parents met their ends. His head swam with the acrid, coppery tang of blood in the air. Callan swallowed hard, his mouth twisting into a grimace.

"We need to burn them," he said, clenching his fists at his sides.

"We'll gather the firewood." Anders and his companions hurried out of the alley, leaving Callan alone to see to the dead.

He found several bolts of finely woven fabric inside the trading post. After gathering the bodies in the village square, Callan set to work carefully wrapping each one in a shroud of deep indigo.

Twilight painted the sky purple by the time the others had finished constructing the pyre. Together, they laid the bodies on top. Callan touched a torch to the dry wood, flames fully engulfing the bodies within seconds. He took several steps back, the scorching heat singeing his cheeks as he watched the thick smoke billowing into the sky, bearing the souls of the dead to the After Realm.

There had been nothing to burn after his parents' deaths. Even if there had been, he had lacked the courage to return home. Perhaps if there had been a pyre for them, if he'd seen the smoke carrying them away, he would have been able to accept that they were truly gone. The intervening centuries had done little to ease his doubt. Callan whispered a prayer for his parents and the souls of the villagers to the darkening sky.

Anders and the others felled an elk on the hunting trip that had spared them from the attack. They all took refuge within the tavern for the night, the female called Bronna roasting cuts of meat over an open fire. Callan ate out of necessity but struggled to get the food down past the taste of ash and iron clinging to the back of his throat.

He was certain the attack was Omen's doing. The similarities were glaring, and there was the raven's feather. As he chewed on a hunk of meat, he puzzled over why the Shadowbringer had suddenly resumed his aggression against the Realm after lying dormant for so many years. It was uncommon for yaesira to leave their territory in the North, just as it was uncommon for lycane to hunt in pairs. Perhaps Nova was the catalyst for Omen's reawakening. Had Omen sent the beast that nearly took Nova's life only minutes after she crossed into Aemoria? Callan's brows pinched together. He was thankful he was the only one, apart from her own mother, of course, who knew the truth about Nova's paternity.

Callan shoved his plate of half-eaten venison across the tabletop stained with rings from countless overflowing mugs of ale, then stretched himself out on the floor at the edge of the fire's light, tucking his hands behind his head. He watched the flicker of the fire as it danced across the ceiling, listening to the hushed voices of the hunters whispering tales of Aemoria's Blade.

THIRTY

NOVA BURST INTO THE library fresh off a training session with Lucan, an excitable energy crackling just below the surface of her skin. She'd gotten him on his back, the tip of her blade pressed against the hollow at the base of his throat. She paused for an instant as a celebratory smirk tugged at the corners of her mouth. Lucan struck her sword with his own, sending it flying from her hand and skittering across the polished floor.

"Where's your killer instinct, Nova?" He rose to his feet as he scolded her. "You *cannot hesitate* when the opportunity presents itself. If you do, even for a heartbeat, your opponent will take advantage."

Nova knew there was a kernel of pride buried somewhere underneath his criticism. She was eager to tell Nox all about it, but, once again, she found the library empty. The door to her uncle's study was closed, and she didn't find him there when she knocked and eased the door open a crack to peek inside.

Nova spun on her heel, the fabric of her gown swishing across the floor as she entered a shadowy aisle between the towering stacks. Immediately comforted by the calming presence of thousands of books, Nova ambled along, running a finger over the creased leather spines. Pausing in front of the familiar section of botany and herbology, she rested her hands on her hips and scanned the titles. Only a few remained that she hadn't yet devoured.

Perhaps, she thought, it was time for something new.

A soft thud sounded in the still air, coming from somewhere behind her. Nova twirled and ducked slightly, peeking into the next aisle through a narrow gap above the row of stacked tomes.

"Hello?"

Her voice startled her, the sound jarring in the quiet. She'd overheard Lucan and Nox discussing rumors of spies and whispered threats against the Lunar Throne a few days past. As far as the commander was concerned, the rumors were just that and nothing more. Still, Lucan had increased the number of guards posted throughout the Estate, their presence simultaneously reassuring and unnerving.

A moment passed with no other noise. Nova chided herself and blew out a sharp breath, turning her attention back to her search and striding farther into the stacks. She was absentmindedly perusing the faded section labels when a thin shaft of faint light near the floor of the darkened aisle caught her attention.

On closer inspection, she found the light came from a crack along the base of the wall. Nova ran her hands over the smooth surface; it was solid. Laying her palms flat, she gave a gentle push, letting out a gasp of delighted surprise when a panel popped open to reveal a hidden room beyond.

Nova poked her head through the opening, noting a single central aisle with several smaller aisles branching off of it. She took a small book from a nearby shelf and used it as a makeshift doorstop. Throwing a quick look over her shoulder, she entered the dimly lit space.

The low ceiling was stone, not glass like the rest of the library. The air was cold, and the only light came from dust-covered orbs of moonstone mounted on the end of each row. The farther she went, the older the books became, a

241

thick film clinging to the cracked leather covers and delicate cobwebs strung up in every corner. Some shelves held dozens and dozens of scrolls of aging parchment, piled haphazardly on top of one another.

Nova chose one scroll at random, unfurling the crinkling paper and holding it out in front of her. Faded lines crisscrossed the surface, but she immediately recognized the map of Aemoria. Each territory's boundaries were slightly different than a present-day map would show. Raven's Isle was noticeably absent, which meant the map had to be more than two hundred years old, at least.

An unfamiliar landmass north of Silvergard caught her eye. She brought the map close to her face, squinting to decipher the text. While time was responsible for dulling the majority of the ink on the map, the writing on the landform appeared to have been intentionally rubbed out.

"C-y-r . . . ?" She couldn't make out the rest.

A rustle startled her, and she dropped the map on the floor. Kneeling, she hastily rolled up the scroll and tossed it back onto the pile. She wondered if there were bats in Silvergard, and, if so, whether some of the creatures might be roosting in the dark, forgotten section of the library.

"Is someone there?" She laid a hand over the swift thump of her sprinting heart.

The unmistakable sound of boots scraping against polished stone sent her rushing deeper into the stacks. She risked a look over her shoulder when she reached the end of the aisle, slowing to round the corner. Nova cried out as she collided with a solid mass, and something took hold of her arms.

Drawing back, she recognized General Idrian at once. She hadn't seen him again in the week since his arrival. Eyes wide and nostrils flared, his face was a mask of alarm she was certain matched her own. His gaze flicked down to where he clutched at her bare skin just below the capped sleeves of her gown. He dropped his hands to his sides, the ghost of his warm touch vanishing within seconds in the cool air.

"Apologies," he said, glancing down at his boots. "I only meant to keep you from falling."

"It's nothing," she said. "I'm sure there's no permanent damage."

She stepped back and placed a hand just below her collarbone, willing her breathing to slow. The action had the unintended effect of drawing the general's attention to her heaving chest.

"I thought I was trapped in here with a horde of bats," she said, dropping her hand as a nervous giggle bubbled up from inside her. Her laugh trailed off, the sound dampening as it reached the stone ceiling.

General Idrian didn't laugh.

"And I thought I heard a little mouse scurrying around between the stacks."

A mischievous smile crept across his face, which Nova had to admit was rather handsome. He was clean-shaven with a proud, if slightly blunted, chin. His full brows gave him a youthful appearance.

"What are you doing here, General?" She shifted from one foot to the other, unnerved by his quiet observation of her, as if he were assessing her. Trying to see through her somehow.

"Call me Idrian," he said after a moment, his voice low. "And, to answer your question, I was simply searching for some records."

His eyes flicked to a nearby alcove where a hefty book lay open atop a lectern. Nova breezed past him, the bare skin of her arm brushing against the metal studs dotting the sleeve of his black leather tunic.

"Did you find what you were looking for?" she asked, dipping her head to read the small script looping across the book's frail pages. It appeared to be a record of Noble lineage. A ledger detailing the branches of an ancient family tree.

"As a matter of fact, I did." Idrian came up close behind her and shut the book with a resounding thud, sending dust motes swirling into the air and dancing in the light of the moonstone.

"We shouldn't be here," he murmured, his mouth hovering close to her ear. "This is where they hide the records documenting Silvergard's dark history. An archive of conquest and bloodshed."

Nova shivered at his breath on her cheek and pulled away. His playful expression disarmed her, and she flashed a thin smile, pushing aside the flicker of unease sparking in the pit of her stomach.

"Is war your preferred subject? A bit predictable, don't you think?" she asked, clicking her tongue. The corners of her mouth went slack when she saw the intensity with which he regarded her.

"It's an occupational interest. But, I'm an avid reader with varied tastes. What were you looking for?" he asked, eyeing her.

"Actually, nothing. I found myself here by accident. Though I am on the hunt for something new."

"Perhaps I can make some recommendations." He motioned toward the exit at the far end of the central aisle.

Nova walked ahead of him, the sound of their footsteps overlapping as they approached the hidden door. Idrian caught her elbow before they reached it, and Nova inhaled sharply.

The general's mannerisms reminded her of Callan's, his straight spine and his habit of clasping his hands behind his back. But while being close to Callan immediately put her at ease, with Idrian it was wholly different. Being close to him felt like standing near the edge of a cliff—thrilling but dangerous.

"I meant it when I said we shouldn't be in here, Mouse. The Noble Lord might overlook your transgression. You're family after all. I'm afraid he might not be so forgiving toward me."

Nova bristled slightly at his mention of her relation to Nox. Had he been looking for evidence of her in the ancestry records?

"Nova?" Her name on his lips pulled her from her thoughts.

"Your secret is safe with me, General," she whispered.

"I told you to call me Idrian."

"Of course . . . Idrian."

Nova pushed the false wall open silently, looking both ways before stepping out into the main library. The general exited after her, sealing off the secret wing with a quiet snick behind them.

THIRTY-ONE

NOVA GROANED THROUGH HER teeth, clutching her abdomen and wishing, for the briefest of moments, that she were dead. It was only a matter of time before it arrived: her first cycle since taking on her Fae form. Nova had always found her courses unpleasant, but this was godsdamned excruciating.

Her lady's maid entered her chamber to find her rolling around on top of her bedsheets, trying to find a comfortable position.

"You really ought to be dressed by now," Isla tsked as she fluttered about the room, tidying up the clothing scattered on the floor and hanging from every knob. "Commander Lucan will be cross if you're late."

"Please inform the commander that I'm ill and I don't wish to be disturbed," Nova said, sighing as she finally found a mildly contorted pose that relieved her discomfort for the moment. "Could you bring me something sweet from the kitchens?" she whimpered.

Isla leaned down and ran a hand across Nova's forehead, brushing several wayward strands from her eyes.

"I'll see what I can manage," she said before flitting out into the corridor.

Another spasm rippled through Nova's lower abdomen, and she folded in on herself. Grabbing one of her pillows, she clamped it between her thighs and curled into a ball in the center of the bed. The pressure of the bedding between her legs felt surprisingly pleasant, briefly distracting her from the pain.

Nova stilled at the sudden overwhelming feeling of arousal mingling with the throbbing ache inside of her. Sliding her hands over her breasts, she squeezed gently through the thin satin of her nightdress. They felt full and tender, but it was a delicious sort of pain that had her biting her bottom lip. Nova threw her legs over the side of the bed and headed for the bathing chamber, stripping down and leaving the garment in a pile on the floor as she went.

The steaming water cradled her, and she released a contented moan as she lowered herself into the tub. An old letter from Callan sat on the small side table beside an empty teacup. She unfolded the paper along the well-worn creases and read his message for what was likely the twentieth time, absentmindedly tracing the lines of his script with her fingertips.

It had been nearly two weeks since he'd last written her. The sting of rejection took her by surprise. *Perhaps out of sight* is *out of mind*, she thought. The tone of his messages was always casual, but she knew he remained suspicious of her uncle's intentions, offering several times to come steal her away. She always wrote back, her replies matching his tone. Still, she sensed the pull stretching between them, drawing her thoughts back to him again and again, despite time and distance.

Nova set the letter back on the table and sank lower until the water lapped at the hollow below her bottom lip. She raked her fingers along the surface of the water, miniature whirlpools swirling in their wake. She thought of Callan's hands, strong enough to wield a longsword but gentle enough to braid her hair.

Her eyes drifted shut, and she imagined it was Callan's hands sinking beneath the water, massaging her breasts and gently rolling her nipples between his fingers. She sighed, envisioning those same nimble fingers moving lower, brushing against her inner thighs and stroking her clit before sliding inside her, again and again, until her entire body shuddered with pleasure.

Nova teetered on the edge of a Realm-shattering release when a series of knocks sounded on her chamber door, wrenching her from the fantasy.

Her vision flooded red, and she rose out of the water, yanking on her black silk robe without bothering to towel off first.

"Godsdamn it, Lucan," she growled, storming to her chamber door. "I said to leave me—" Ripping the door wide open, she found not Lucan but Idrian standing on the other side. "Alone," she finished, blowing a loose strand of hair out of her eyes and refusing to look as mortified as she felt.

A half smile curled on Idrian's lips as he glanced down at her robe. The fabric was damp in spots and clung to the curves of her body. Nova ducked behind the door and cleared her throat.

"I heard you weren't feeling well," he said.

Isla was nothing if not a gossip. That and Idrian had already charmed his way into the good graces of every member of the household staff in his short time at the Estate. They were all too happy to grant whatever request he made of them, her lady's maid included.

"I come bearing gifts." Idrian held out his hands, a book in one and a small paper box in the other. Nova took both items, looking up at him with a vaguely skeptical expression.

What is he after?

"Something to read, and something to eat," he explained as she lifted the lid of the box, revealing a handful of dark chocolates nestled inside. "There's a shop in the city known throughout the territory for making the most decadent little treats."

Nova inhaled deeply, the aroma of sugar wafting out of the decorative box.

"How unexpected," she said, maintaining a neutral expression.

"I do enjoy defying expectations," he replied, his voice low as he stared at her intently.

Idrian cast a quick glance down the hallway before stepping in closer and leaning his shoulder against the doorframe.

"Is there any other way I may be of service to you today, Nova?" His eyes dimmed a shade darker, his words laced with hidden meaning. The open, youthful expression he normally wore morphed into a heavy-lidded stare. It felt like a challenge.

There was that feeling again. Like she was standing too close to the edge. Nova gripped the doorknob with her free hand.

"No," she said finally, her tone friendly but firm. "I believe I've benefitted from your kindness enough for one day."

"Very well." Idrian's gaze brightened, and he shoved off the doorframe. "I've accepted an invitation from Lord Nox to dine with you all. I hope you'll be feeling better by the dinner hour."

"We shall see. I should rest."

"Of course." He took a step back and bowed formally before taking his leave.

Nova shoved the door closed with her hip, balancing the book and the chocolates in her arms, and went to the bed. Easing down onto her stomach, she opened the small box and brought one of the treats to her lips. The chocolate was delicious, dark and slightly bitter as it melted on her tongue; it was precisely what she craved.

She rolled onto her back, flipping through the pages of Idrian's book. A small square of black parchment fluttered out and landed on her chest. A note was written in silver ink, the lettering boxy and masculine.

Will they, or won't they?

Nova opened the book to the title page and read through the first several chapters, chuckling out loud from time to time in the quiet of her room. The decorated general had brought her a romance novel. She shook her head, entirely unsure what to make of him.

Defying expectations, indeed.

The Great Hall thrummed with lively conversation, occasional peals of laughter ringing out above the hum. Nova swirled deep red wine around the globe of her crystal glass. She sat flanked by Nox, seated at the head of the table on her right, and Lucan, lounging in his chair on her left.

She tilted her head back, drinking in the view of the moon visible through the glass ceiling. A waxing crescent hung against the dark sky, casting minimal light, but the ornate moonstone chandelier brightened the space. The terms of Nova's bargain stipulated that she remain in the Lunar Court until the next new moon. With the end drawing near, she wasn't certain she wanted to leave.

The grand table was packed to capacity with members of Nox's Court. Many were painters and sculptors, though there were a few musicians and composers peppered in. Every one of them had welcomed her with open arms—no trace of fear in their eyes when they looked at her. For the first time in her life, Nova felt as though she belonged. As if she was precisely where she was meant to be.

Discreetly, she observed Idrian at the far end of the table seated on the opposite side. His gaze locked on hers, and Nova wondered whether he had been watching her, too. He ran his fingertips along the stem of his glass before lifting it to his lips and taking a sip, his eyes not leaving hers. Nova flashed a thin smile and looked away, shifting in her seat.

"What's wrong with you?" Lucan asked, tearing into a crusty roll with his sharp teeth.

"Nothing. I'm fine," she said, waving him off. "I sometimes find it difficult to sit through these five-course meals."

"Maybe you wouldn't be so restless if you'd made it to training earlier."

"As I already told you, Commander, I was dealing with female troubles—"

"Spare me the details, please." Lucan tossed his half-eaten roll onto his plate.

Nova chuckled to herself. It was endlessly satisfying to get under Lucan's skin; he preferred to be the one ruffling feathers.

The delicate tinkling of a knife against stemware drew everyone's attention to the far end of the table where Idrian stood, wineglass in hand.

"I'm a soldier and not accustomed to making flowery speeches," he began, glancing around at the other guests. "But I hope you'll all indulge me, as I'd like to make a toast to our Noble Lord."

All eyes flicked briefly to Nox, a casual but commanding presence.

"Silvergard is no longer what it once was," Idrian continued. Many of the guests lowered their heads, no doubt recalling the dark times they had lived through. "Change happens slowly, but the Lunar Court has turned a page over the past century. So, let us raise our glasses to Lord Nox—the one responsible for changing . . . everything."

Cheers and applause burst forth from Nox's guests, and Idrian lifted his glass. Nox tipped his head and drank from his own cup, but his charcoal eyes narrowed slightly, his gaze lingering on Idrian. Nova imagined her uncle respected the general but would never entirely trust him. While both males were idealists, they had vastly different worldviews.

Lucan snorted beside her, the sound mercifully muffled by the trailing applause.

"Have some manners," she hissed, nudging his knee with her own.

"Oh, please," he muttered, twisting his torso to face her, his back to the general. "Surely you can see what a flatterer he is. He's here to ask Nox for coin for his troops. He'd say anything to get what he wants."

"Don't be so cynical."

"It's my job to be cynical," he said, turning back to monitor Idrian, who had returned to his seat. "It's how I've managed to keep Nox safe all these years."

Nova rolled her eyes and leaned back in her seat, bringing her glass to her lips again. She watched Idrian closely as he chatted with the guests seated around him, a charming smile stretched above his proud chin. Perhaps she'd missed it thanks to Lucan's antics, but she couldn't recall if she'd seen the general drink to his own toast.

THIRTY-TWO

THE AIR WAS HEAVY, thick with steam and the scent of jasmine. Callan slowly waved a hand in front of his face, scattering the mist that hung in the air and clouded his vision. Parting like curtains drawn open before him, the haze faded, revealing Nova reclined in a soaking tub carved from polished black stone.

Her head rested on the lip of the tub, her long raven waves cascading over the edge like a shadowy waterfall. Callan took a step toward her, silencing the voice in his head accusing him of trespassing. His eyes drifted down, lingering on the soft swell of her breasts barely peeking out above the glossy surface of the water. A breathy moan passed her lips, almost too quiet for him to hear. He shot a glance at her face. Eyes closed. Dark lashes fanned out over cheeks flushed pink.

This wasn't right. He should leave. Callan turned to go when she spoke, murmuring his name. His name. His body responded immediately. Long strides quickly closing the distance between them. His knees hitting the floor of gleaming black stone. Eyes still closed, Nova tilted her face toward him. A lazy smile stretched across her lips. He reached out and slowly traced a finger over her forehead, tucking a stray lock of hair behind her ear.

Acting without thought, Callan dipped his head and pressed a kiss to the apple of her cheek. Her skin was hot under his lips. Nova moaned, a soft command escaping into the humid air: "Kiss me, Callan."

He stared at her mouth for a beat, then did exactly as he was told, lowering his head again. When their mouths joined and he felt the light brush of her tongue against his bottom lip, it was impossible to judge what was harder: the beating of his heart, or his cock straining against the fabric of his breeches. Nova gently lifted his hand from where it gripped the edge of the tub and laid it on her breast. She squeezed her hand over his, encouraging him to feel her.

Callan pulled back to drink in his view of her, the peaks of her nipples breaking through the surface of the water. He kneaded her breast, his eyes wandering to the shadowy depths concealing the rest of her body from view. As if reading his thoughts, Nova took his hand again and guided it beneath the water, along the softness of her stomach, and brought it to rest against her inner thigh.

Callan held his breath, his arm submerged past his elbow, hot water drenching his sleeve and lapping at his skin. He kept his gaze trained on her lovely face as he touched her, slick and inviting under his fingertips. Her mouth fell open and she moaned softly, eyebrows pinching together as he stroked her. Callan swallowed hard, his throat suddenly gone dry. Nova languidly lifted her foot out of the water, bracing it on the edge of the tub and opening herself to him.

Callan's breath was ragged as he slowly eased his middle and ring fingers inside her. Nova gasped, lifting her hips and clamping her hand down over his, sending him deeper.

Callan awoke with a low groan caught in his throat. He was in his bed. Alone. The echo of Nova's moans sounded in his mind. He rose onto his elbows and peered out the window at the midnight sky scattered with shimmering stars. With an agitated growl, he threw himself down onto the damp pillow.

He ran his palm over his cock, hard and aching with want for her. Taking himself in his hand, he closed his eyes, stroking himself roughly as he imagined what the water had hidden from view. The sweet, yielding heat between Nova's thighs. It wasn't long before he found a frustrated release, sweat clinging to his brow as he chased the memory of the female who seemed to have enchanted him.

The next day, Callan wandered along the winding laneways that meandered around the Estate. Two weeks had passed since he returned from the ice fields, but his uneasiness hadn't diminished. A persistent sense of dread remained tucked away inside his rib cage. Despite his insistence that the Shadowbringer was responsible for the attack in Whitepeak, his uncle refused to act. In fact, Thorn seemed preoccupied with trivial matters, constantly pestering Callan about the damn bargain he'd made.

The folk of the Winter Court seemed to be warming to him. They bowed their heads as they walked past him, fists laid over their hearts. Callan smiled but always averted his eyes, certain they'd see him for what he truly was. A fraud.

Eventually, his aimless walking led him to the docks, with the fish vendors counting coins and stacking their wooden crates. Did Thorn truly wish for him to take his rightful place on the throne? Callan didn't know the first thing about being a ruler. He'd left Nivali long before his parents could start preparing him for leadership. He could wield a sword and not much else. The Council had reduced him to a weapon long ago. He was beginning to fear they may have been right.

Leaning against a wooden post, Callan stared out over the water. He felt untethered, a ship without a mooring. He wished someone could simply tell him what to do. An icy wind rolled in off the sea as a vessel pulled up alongside the dock, the captain calling out to one of the vendors in the lyrical language of the fisher folk. Callan stood at attention. Perhaps there was someone who could tell him where his path would lead.

Though Liv was his uncle's consort and resided with him in the Estate, Callan learned she kept a small cottage of her own at the edge of the woods. A female exited as he arrived, pushing past him, her eyes wet with tears. He considered turning back. Did he truly wish to know his future? Nova had seemed deeply troubled by what Liv shared with her.

Gathering his resolve, Callan knocked on the doorframe and stepped over the threshold. The space was cramped but cozy, a hearty fire blazing on the hearth. A daybed took up one side of the room. A workspace with a loom and hundreds of spools of colorful thread occupied the other. Liv sat at the loom, weaving a thin thread of midnight blue through the taut vertical strings, then brushing the thread upward with a wooden comb.

"Hello, Your Grace," she said without looking up. "Please, sit." She gestured to a wooden stool opposite her and set aside her weaving. Leaning back and resting an elbow on the low worktop, she eyed him for a moment.

"What brings you to my cottage?" she asked, though Callan suspected she already knew the answer.

"I hoped you could . . . assist me," he said, pausing when a knowing smile flashed on her lips. His intuition flickered; he was never quite certain whether he should trust her.

"And what assistance could I offer a Noble of Nivali?"

Callan rubbed a hand over the stubble at his chin. "I wish to know my future." He wanted to snatch the words from the air and swallow them back down as soon as he'd uttered them.

"Ah," she breathed, sitting up straight in her seat. "And if I were to share your future with you, what would you give me in return?"

Callan furrowed his brow. Did his uncle compensate Liv for her premonitions? Had Nova?

"I have nothing to give." He meant it. He'd lost track of how long had he'd been drifting through life, relying on the generosity of those around him.

"Not now, perhaps. But you might have something I want one day," Liv drawled. "Promise me a favor, and I'll give you your future."

"A favor?"

"Yes. A simple favor. To be granted at the time of my choosing."

She folded her hands in her lap and stared at him through the tense threads strung on the loom. Callan suspected she knew he would agree to her bargain, just as she had known it was he who darkened her doorway moments before. He didn't like her terms. It was precisely the kind of trap he had once warned Nova about. But he hadn't felt this adrift since his parents' passing. He was desperate for something—anything—to hold on to.

"Very well," he agreed. "I will grant you one favor."

The corners of her mouth lifted in a coy smile. "Hold out your hand, Your Grace."

Callan reached around the loom, his palm up toward the ceiling. Liv placed something in his hand: a smooth blue stone.

"You will return this stone to me on the day I invoke my favor."

Callan nodded once, his expression turning grave under the meager weight of the thing. He dropped it into the pouch at his hip. Liv extended her hand again, inviting him to take it. Recklessly, Callan reached out, laying his hand in hers before he could think better of it. She gripped him with a strength he didn't realize she possessed, her fingernails biting into his flesh. He shot a glance at her face and saw her eyes had gone milky white. Her voice was a low drone like a swarm of bees.

"Your path is obscured by shadow. The way forward is for you, and you alone, to choose. You may one day sit upon a throne, but never one of snow and ice."

Liv released him from her grasp, and he flexed his fingers against the lingering pain, the marks of her nails etched like half-moons on his skin. Her eyes cleared, pale blue once more, and she returned to her weaving without another word.

Callan rose from his seat and strode out into the cold, rubbing his hand and wondering whether the information she had shared was worth the price he would one day pay.

THIRTY-THREE

ONLY TWO DAYS REMAINED until Nova's bargain would expire. Nox flagged her down in the hallway as she rushed to meet Lucan for training. She barely stopped when she reached him, turning in his direction and continuing to jog backward as he spoke.

"I have something special planned for today. Isla will help you dress after training." He sent her on her way with a wave of his hand. "Try not to take any hits to the face," he called out a second later.

Nova grinned like a fool, recalling the elbow to the mouth that had left her with a split lip after her first day in the sparring ring. It felt like ages had passed since then.

As she reached the base of the stairs, Lucan tossed her an apple, his raised eyebrow a reminder that he didn't appreciate being kept waiting. Without a word, he turned and marched toward the front door, and Nova rushed to keep pace with his determined stride.

Having reached the end of her training session unscathed, Nova headed back to her room several hours later, finding Isla already waiting inside.

"Gods, you look awful. This will never do," Isla tutted, shoving her into the bathing chamber.

Nova glanced at her reflection in the mirror. Large sections of her hair had come loose from her braid and lay plastered with sweat to the sides of her face. Wispier strands flared out around her crown in a dark halo.

Once Nova had been scrubbed to Isla's satisfaction, the lady's maid dried her hair and gathered it into a sleek twist with several long tendrils. A circlet of fine silver set with a single teardrop moonstone was laid on Nova's head, the stone dangling in the center of her forehead. Isla reached into the armoire and brought out a new gown of fine silk, the color a deep oxblood. Nova stepped into the sleek skirt before slipping her arms into the dress.

The sleeveless gown had a high neck and a keyhole cutout extending from the hollow at the base of her throat to midway down her abdomen. The fabric clung to her chest and hips before belling out around her legs and trailing in a short train behind her. Black silk slippers and twin silver cuffs, one for each wrist, completed the ensemble. Nova rubbed her thumb over the smooth white stone of her mother's ring. It had become a talisman of sorts, easing her anxiety whenever it flared.

Satisfied with her handiwork, Isla nodded and headed for the door, taking to her wings and beckoning Nova to follow. Floating along a short distance ahead, Isla led Nova to the main level, stopping at the rear of the Great Hall in front of a door which Nova had never passed through. Inside a small antechamber, she found Nox waiting for her on a low sofa. He sprang to his feet as she entered, taking her hands in his.

"You look stunning." He beamed as he held her at arm's length.

"It's not me," she said, awkward under his focused attention. "It's the dress."

"I'm certain, in your case, the opposite is true."

He dropped one of her hands but held fast to the other, leading her toward a second door. Through it, they entered a long corridor lined on both sides with floor-to-ceiling glass. A warm breeze blew in through the open windows and set the long gossamer curtains dancing as Nova and her uncle passed. Suddenly Nova froze, tugging on Nox's hand as a swell of recognition crashed against her: This was the hallway he had shown her in a dream. A prickly sensation crept along the length of her spine.

Nova shuddered.

Nox turned to face her. She stared past him at the large double doors looming at the far end of the hall. He spoke her name softly and bent his head to meet her eyes, which flicked from him to the doors and back again.

"I know this place," she murmured.

"Yes," he said, placing his hands firmly on her upper arms. "On the other side of those doors is the throne room."

Nova nodded, her breath quickening as she recalled Nox's memories made real by the visceral sensations of terror and nausea she'd felt in her dream.

"All is well, Nova," he assured her. "You're safe with me."

Nox held his hand out to her, palm up. An invitation. She held her breath for an instant before she accepted.

The great doors swung open before them, and a shiver ran through her as she laid eyes on the ornate moonstone throne, glowing where it sat upon the dais. After a time, she vaguely registered that Nox was speaking to her. With great effort, she ripped her gaze away from the throne.

An easel and a worktable sat at the foot of the platform, the surface of the table crowded with charcoal sticks, brushes, small trowels, and paint pots of various colors.

"You inspired me with something you said your first night here," Nox explained. "I'd like to paint a portrait of you."

"Of *me*?" she scoffed.

"Yes. A portrait of you," he repeated, ascending the steps of the platform. "You are part of the Noble Family of Silvergard, and, as such, you deserve a place of honor, proudly displayed within the Estate."

He stopped before the throne and motioned for her to join him.

"Besides, when you leave me and return to the ice and snow of Nivali, I'll need something to remember you by."

Nova dipped her head as a smile bloomed on her face, a smile that faded as she beheld the throne before her, even larger and more imposing up close. Nox urged her to take a seat. Her lips parted wordlessly as an image of her grandfather seated on the same throne flashed in her mind, a vicious sneer splitting his stony jaw.

"This throne is your birthright," Nox said, watching her expectantly. "Just take a seat."

Nova took a reluctant step forward before turning and cautiously lowering herself into the seat. All the air flew from her chest, and a forceful rush of energy coursed through her body. Nova laughed nervously, half surprised she hadn't been struck down by a bolt of lightning.

"Excellent," Nox said, clapping his hands together once as he descended the steps and took his place behind the easel.

He proceeded to direct Nova as to how she should sit and the precise placement of her hands. Once she was properly posed, he set to work sketching on the canvas with a bit of charcoal. Sitting for a portrait was tedious and lasted several hours, though her muscles, fatigued from her increasingly intense training, were grateful to be resting. Nox distracted her as best he could while he worked, sharing harmless gossip about happenings around the Court.

"Perhaps you could relax a bit," he suggested at one point. "You're looking a bit stiff."

Dipping her chin, Nova realized she was gripping the arms of the throne, and her shoulders had crept up toward her ears. She rolled her neck and splayed her fingers wide before laying her hands back down upon the carved stone.

Just then, a servant entered the throne room, delivering a letter into Nox's hands. He turned it over once and stood, climbing the steps of the platform to pass the letter to her. Immediately recognizing the insignia stamped in blue wax, Nova broke the seal and unfolded the parchment, smiling faintly as she read Callan's latest message.

As you and your uncle have had ample time to get acquainted, please come back to Nivali and rescue me from mine. I don't know how many more games of strategy I can endure.

Her fingers grazed her chin, and her smile blossomed even wider on her face.

"Just like that," Nox said suddenly, drawing her attention. "Don't move a muscle."

Nova was silent, keeping as still as possible while her uncle's skilled hands flitted around the canvas.

After a few minutes had passed, she spoke. "Nox," she began, anxiously tapping her ring against the arm of the throne. "May I ask you something?"

"Anything," he replied distractedly, sweeping his paintbrush across the canvas like a conductor leading an orchestra. He bit his bottom lip as he worked. A smudge of ruby-red paint marred the fair skin of his cheek.

"How long have you known Lucan?" In the time she'd been in Silvergard, Nova had gathered that the connection between her uncle and his commander extended well beyond friendship.

"A hundred years or so, I suppose," he said, glancing at her with a curious look.

"And how long have you been together?"

His hand halted. A look of apprehension flashed on his sharp features for an instant before he shook it off and let out a breathy laugh. His brush started moving again.

"A hundred years or so."

"Is it meant to be a secret between the two of you? There are plenty of folk who enjoy others of the same gender at Court."

Nox dropped his paintbrush into one of the little pots littering the tabletop and folded his hands in his lap.

"I suppose it's a bit of an open secret," he said. "My staff knows. The members of the Lunar Council know." He paused, first tilting his head back to view the night sky through the glass ceiling, then dropping his gaze to the throne on which Nova sat.

"It's a tricky thing when so much in this world is wrapped up in blood," he sighed. "To outsiders, my being with Lucan could signify weakness. The end of the Elsever bloodline. Some might seek to usurp me. The Elsevers weren't always the keepers of the Lunar Throne; our ancestors took it by force to become Orika's favored bloodline. I've made too much progress for me to allow Silvergard to fall into the hands of another. The safety and prosperity of my people is worth the price of my secret."

"Did you always know?" Nova asked timidly. "That it was love, I mean."

One side of Nox's mouth curled into a smile and he chuckled. "At first, it was pure attraction. This undeniable pull. Like a riptide. Like I couldn't have stayed away from him even it meant I'd drown. As time went by, I realized it was much more. I could tell him anything. He stood beside me. Backed me fully in everything I did and encouraged me to strive for more. Never in my life had I experienced such unwavering support. In the beginning, that felt more terrifying than the prospect of drowning." He paused. "Why do you ask?"

Nova stared at the letter resting in her lap, tears pricking at the corners of her eyes at the thought of how she'd treated Callan. How she'd pushed him away. She'd been treading water. Fighting against the pull of the same relentless tide her uncle described. Her heart and mind were weary with the struggle. She longed to let go, to allow herself to be swept away by her feelings for Callan. But she didn't know how to surrender when there was a chance she could sink beneath the surface forever.

Nox's brows fell, his lips forming a thin, sympathetic smile as he leaned forward around the easel.

"You deserve love, Nova." His voice was kind but firm, as if issuing the formal decree of a Noble Lord. "If it has found you, let it in."

The doors to the throne room swung open, the sudden sound startling them both. Nova's head snapped to the entryway to find Idrian striding purposefully into the room. The general froze when he caught sight of her. His eyes went wide for an instant, but Nova couldn't read his expression. He could have been enchanted or horrified.

"My Lord," Idrian said, gathering himself and bowing his head to Nox. "I've come to inform you that I plan to depart for Stargrave tomorrow. You have been most generous these past weeks."

"Safe travels, General. I've found our conversations to be very enlightening. I'm hopeful we can continue a positive relationship going forward."

Idrian brought his feet together and made a formal bow. Once he rose, he nodded briefly in Nova's direction, then turned on his heel and exited through the double doors without a backward glance.

Nova was unsettled by Idrian's reaction to her seated on the throne. Had the sight finally brought her resemblance to her father into focus? Had he pieced together the truth about her connection to Nox? To Silvergard?

Seemingly unbothered by the interaction, Nox caught her attention and beckoned for her to join him. She stood slowly, muscles tight after sitting in one position for so long. She nearly gasped when she reached the easel and beheld Nox's creation.

Nova had never seen a likeness of herself before. Her uncle was an incredibly talented artist. Though unfinished, the portrait was remarkably lifelike and rich in detail, from the matte black of her hair to the ring of silver around her steel-gray irises. What struck her most, however, was the expression on her face. Nox had captured a genuine smile on her full lips, the warmth of it reaching all the way to her eyes.

"Is that truly what I look like?" she murmured, unnerved by the smile so unlike the stony mask she'd gone to such great pains to perfect over the years.

"Yes, my dear niece," Nox replied. "You have a lovely smile, and I think we both know what coaxed it from you."

Nova curled her fingers tightly around the parchment she still held in her hand. Her mind flickered to Callan and the evening they stood perched atop the stone wall surrounding the Pyralis Estate. To what he'd said about her smile as his tiger's-eye gaze lingered on her.

It's lovely. The world would be lucky to see more of it.

THIRTY-FOUR

NOVA WOKE TO THE taste of leather and the stifling sensation of something being pressed over her mouth. She cried out, but the sound was smothered by a gloved hand clamping down even harder against her lips. She clawed at the attached wrist, fingernails scraping against the soft material. Her breath came rapidly through her nose as her eyes adjusted in the darkened room, lit only by a sliver of daylight creeping in through a gap in the curtains.

After a few seconds, Idrian's face came into focus, hovering above hers. Nova widened her eyes at him. His expression was grave, his mouth a grim line and his brows knitted together.

"I'm going to remove my hand, but you must be quiet," he said, his voice a rough whisper.

Slowly, he lifted his hand from her mouth, and Nova bolted upright, swiping the back of her wrist over her lips.

"Idrian, what are you doing here?" she hissed.

"Quiet." He shot a glance over his shoulder at her chamber door. His hand hung in the air as if he meant to cover her mouth again, and Nova leaned away out of his reach. "Spies from Raven's Isle have infiltrated the Estate. Come with me—now. You are in grave danger."

"Nox." Her stomach turned, immediately fearing the worst. "Where is Nox?"

"Commander Lucan is with him. The Noble Lord is not my concern. My only concern is getting you out of the Estate without being spotted."

"Where will we go?" She rubbed a hand across her forehead, her thoughts still foggy with the cobwebs of sleep. How long had it been since she'd retired to her chamber?

"I know of a secure location. No one will find you there. Come, we'll join up with some of my soldiers on the way." He stood beside the bed, his hand resting on the hilt of his sword. His eyes flicked back and forth between the chamber door and the terrace. "Get up."

Nova obeyed, scooting along the satin sheets and sliding her legs over the side of the mattress. Her sleep-addled mind struggled to process all he'd said as she crossed to the armoire. He grabbed her arm and tugged her back.

"There's no time to dress," he cautioned, his tone growing impatient. "Here." He snatched her black woolen cloak off its hook and tossed it at her. "Put this on and follow me."

Nova threw the cloak over her shoulders, fastening the clasp with trembling hands and slipped her feet into a pair of flats she'd carelessly discarded beside the bed.

Idrian gripped her painfully around the wrist as he dragged her across the room. Nova nearly asked him to loosen his hold on her, but she bit her tongue. He was clearly distracted.

As quietly as possible, Idrian eased the door open enough to peek his head out, surveying the hallway for a breath. The Estate was silent. Not necessarily surprising, Nova thought. Everyone was likely asleep. Even so, there were usually at least a few servants awake and walking the halls at all hours, weren't there?

Idrian opened the door further, allowing them to pass through into the corridor. Instead of heading left toward the main staircase, he turned right, rushing toward a dead end. They moved soundlessly, apart from the soft rustling of Nova's nightdress dragging on the floor.

"You're going the wrong way," she whispered in protest. Wrenching her hand from his grasp, Nova spun in the opposite direction and headed for the stairs. A cry rang out in the Great Hall below, the sound quickly followed by the scrape of a blade being drawn. Nova halted immediately and listened as ragged, wet gasps trailed off into silence. Idrian grabbed her by the wrist and pulled her down the hall. Nova followed without question, hastening her steps to keep pace with his long, determined strides.

When they reached the far wall, Idrian laid his free hand on the smooth stone and pressed. A section of the wall gave way like the one in the library, revealing a hidden doorway in the black rock. Idrian stood aside and shoved Nova into the gaping mouth of the secret passageway. Following immediately behind her, he pulled the stone slab closed with a click, the sound echoing in a blackness that swallowed her whole.

Wherever she was, it was chilly and smelled of damp. A trickle of water dripped rhythmically in the distance. Nova heard the faint clinking of metal behind her, and suddenly she could see, though not very well. Idrian took hold of her wrist again, and she twisted to face him. A silver medallion inlaid with a moonstone hung on a long chain around his neck. The cloudy stone was engraved with the crescent and star insignia of Silvergard. It barely gave off any light as it was still daytime.

Idrian pushed past her, and Nova turned back to find herself perched at the top of a steep staircase and caged in by a low ceiling. The stone steps disappeared into the darkness looming at the edge of the moonstone's pale light, only a few strides ahead of them. She took a deep breath of stale air and followed Idrian, as if she had a choice in the matter.

They descended the staircase for what seemed like an eternity. The train of Nova's nightgown gathered all manner of dirt and grime as it mopped each step behind her, erasing her footprints as she went. Moisture seeped through the soles of her silk slippers. Her toes began to go numb. It was clear they were the first souls to pass through the tunnel in ages. Nova wanted desperately to prod Idrian for information, but she continued to bite her tongue, afraid to speak in the oppressive silence.

Finally, they reached the bottom, and Idrian hurried her along the narrow passage. The glow of his moonstone bounced off the walls as they ran. Nova lost her balance once and fell to the ground. Idrian barely paused long enough to haul her back up onto her feet, then kept going.

He stopped short suddenly several minutes later, and she nearly collided with his broad back. They'd hit another dead end. As he had before, Idrian pressed his hand against the wall of stone, and a hidden doorway opened. Daylight drenched Nova, temporarily blinding her as she burst out into the fresh air.

When her vision cleared, Nova threw a glance over her shoulder, craning her neck to take in the massive black mountain rising behind her, the jagged peak silhouetted against the gray blanket of the overcast sky. The passageway had led them through the heart of the very mountain into which the Silvergard Estate was carved.

"Where are we going?" Nova asked, a bit less afraid of the sound of her own voice.

"A horse is waiting for us up ahead," Idrian said, looking back at her with a stern nod.

Within minutes, they arrived at a copse of leafless trees. Slipping between the bone-white trunks, they walked until they spotted a gray stallion tethered to a low branch. Idrian finally released Nova and rushed to the horse, swiftly untying the reins. Nova cradled her tender wrist against her chest, brushing her fingers over the reddened skin where a bruise would likely form.

Idrian turned to face her, scanning the forest around them and urging her to mount. Something caused her to hesitate. A flicker of apprehension in the pit of her stomach. She looked back in the direction they'd traveled, nervously spinning her mother's ring on her finger. Nova sensed Idrian's presence beside her an instant before his gloved hand clamped down firmly on her shoulder. He gripped her chin with his other hand, forcing her to look at him.

"Nova, I know you're frightened and confused, but I need you to trust me. Get on the horse." His words had a sharp edge to them. He smiled weakly and released her chin, his hand dropping to his side.

Nova swallowed hard, forcing down the lump in her throat, and gathered the filthy fabric of her nightgown. She hoisted herself into the saddle. He mounted behind her and kicked the horse in the ribs, sending the animal racing between the trunks of the skeletal trees.

Nova stared back over her shoulder as they rode north, the distance between her and the Silvergard Estate growing with each passing minute. After a time, her eyelids grew heavy and fell shut despite her better judgment, the rhythmic pounding of the horse's hooves lulling her to sleep.

The horse slowed suddenly, the abrupt change in pace waking Nova some hours later. She couldn't determine the exact time of day through the thick cloud cover, but she estimated dusk was only a few hours away. She tried to sit up higher in the saddle, but Idrian's arm lay coiled tightly around her ribs.

He released his hold on her, taking the reins in both hands to meet a rocky incline a short distance ahead. The horse picked its way carefully up the steep slope toward a ruined structure at the summit. Idrian dismounted when they reached the cover of the partially collapsed walls of ashen stone. He grabbed Nova around the waist and pulled her down from the saddle, setting her on the ground in front of him. The warmth of his rapid breaths puffed against her forehead.

Nova backed away and turned in a slow circle, surveying her surroundings. The Estate was no longer visible in the distance. She silently scolded herself for falling asleep. It was impossible to gauge how far they'd traveled or if they'd changed direction. An unfamiliar mountain rose out of the horizon to the north. She couldn't see what lay beyond from where she stood.

"This is where we agreed to meet," Idrian said distractedly, coming to stand beside her. He raked a hand through his hair as he scanned the barren landscape stretching out around them in every direction. "Something is wrong. They should have been waiting for us."

Nova bit the inside of her cheek, suddenly feeling exposed and vulnerable under the wide, gray sky, clad in nothing but a thin nightdress. A chill wind blew through the ruins, and her skin prickled, sending a shiver darting along her limbs. Idrian slung an arm around her shoulders, guiding her to an intact corner sheltered from the wind.

"Rest now," he told her.

Nova sank onto the damp ground, gathering her cloak around her bent knees as she huddled against the remnants of cold stone. Pulling her hood over her head, she studied Idrian as he paced back and forth, wearing a groove in the sand. Her stomach cramped with hunger, but they'd brought nothing to eat. Her eyelids grew heavy, and, before long, her body defied her by drifting off to sleep once again.

A drizzling rain fell, the cool drops moistening Nova's cheeks and waking her from a dreamless sleep. The sky had gone dark. The moon was new, the stars obscured by thick clouds. Idrian sat on the ground nearby, leaning against a crumbling stone column. He appeared to be resting, but Nova sensed he was fully alert, sharp eyes scanning the perimeter, keen ears listening for any indication of an approach.

The faint sound of tumbling rocks startled them both. Nova swallowed a gasp, and Idrian sprang to his feet, hunching low as he silently drew his sword from its sheath. He took several measured steps in the direction of the noise, turning his head to Nova, a finger pressed firmly against his lips. Nova nodded wordlessly as he disappeared from view.

Minutes ticked by slowly with no further noise and no sign of Idrian. The rain came down heavier, fat drops gathering into rivulets that rushed down her hood and onto the shoulders of her cloak. Nova thought of her blades, laid out on the vanity in her chamber—gods only knew how far away and utterly useless to her. She flexed her fingers, sluggish and slightly numb, before clenching her hands into fists.

My only weapons, she thought wearily and cursed under her breath.

A male voice rose above the pattering of the rain. A grunt of pain. She was on her feet in an instant, crouching low to the ground. Her heart thumped wildly, an untamed bird flinging itself repeatedly against the cage of her ribs.

Nova willed herself forward across the sodden ground toward the source of the noise. She peered over the collapsed wall on the eastern edge of the hill. Without the light of the moon, the world was blanketed in darkness. Nova's breath halted as she stared silently into the night.

A sudden flash of pale light.

Idrian's medallion.

By the glow of the moonstone, Nova spotted him halfway down the incline, sprawled on his back in the sand, scrambling for his sword. Two figures emerged, their cloaks peeling away from the surrounding darkness as they loomed over him. One kicked the sword out of his reach and yanked Idrian up by the neck of his armored vest. Steel glinted as the other produced a dagger from the folds of his cloak.

A gasp escaped from her lips before she could stop it. She clapped a useless hand over her mouth as the hooded figures turned their heads in her direction as one. She didn't think they could see her, but her blood iced over just the same. The figure with the dagger hauled Idrian onto his knees, tugging his head back by his hair and pressing the blade against his throat.

The second figure began an unhurried climb up the hill toward Nova's hiding place. She remained rooted to the spot. Idrian struggled against his captor and shouted into the darkness, a single word cutting through the thrum of the blood rushing in her ears.

"Run!"

Nova shot to her feet and stumbled backward, immediately bumping against something solid. A pair of sinewy arms wrapped around her middle, pinning her arms to her sides. Her mind flashed to her early training sessions with Callan, and she threw her head back instinctively. A sickening crunch was chased by a pained cry. She'd broken her assailant's nose.

The arms around her loosened but held fast despite her violent thrashing. She struggled to get free, growling through clenched teeth like an animal caught in a snare. The night was so dark and her voice so loud that a second figure appeared directly in front of her before she even realized someone else was there. She saw the fist wrapped around the hilt of a dagger as it sailed through the air before striking her in the temple.

Then she saw nothing.

THIRTY-FIVE

CALLAN BOLTED UPRIGHT, FURS sliding down his bare chest and gathering around his hips. Confused, he scanned the four corners of the room. The fire still blazed on the hearth, the flames casting a wobbly orange glow on the walls and ceiling. No more than an hour or two had passed since he'd gone to bed. He was alone. But the voice that had roused him from his sleep echoed in his mind. He'd heard it as clearly as if there had been someone in the room with him.

Nova is in danger. Come to Silvergard at once.

He threw back the covers and dressed quickly, pulling on thick black breeches and a dark blue tunic before stepping into his boots. He slipped a breastplate of thick brown leather over his head, tugging it down so the pauldrons lay flush against his shoulders, and secured matching bracers at each wrist. All the while, he willed his heartbeat to remain steady.

Pulling each of his blades from their sheaths, he squinted, checking them for readiness. As usual, both were lethally sharp. With his dagger strapped to his thigh, Callan finally threw a heavy cloak of midnight blue around his shoulders and strode out onto the gallery, carrying his sheathed sword in his hand.

Dozens of folk remained gathered in the hall, drinking. Upon the dais sat Thorn, contentedly observing the revelry and, judging by the lopsided grin on his face, already deep in his cups. Callan shoved his way through the crowd to the foot of the platform, drawing his uncle's attention.

"Where are you headed dressed for battle?" Thorn asked, speech slurred.

"Silvergard." Callan said, his tone inviting no argument. "I do not seek your permission. I merely wished to inform you of my departure."

Thorn's merry smile melted into a scowl. "What foolishness is this? For how long?"

"I can't say. Nova needs me."

"Running, running, running," Thorn mumbled, lazily tilting his head back. "Always running away."

Callan tensed at his uncle's words but said nothing.

"When will you stop, Callan?" He shook his head, the drink preventing him from masking his disappointment.

"I'm not running away. I have no choice," Callan said, his voice a low growl. He glanced from side to side to see whether anyone was watching their exchange. "Nova is in danger."

Leaning forward, Thorn stared down at his nephew, his brow creased in thought.

"Are you bonded to her?" Thorn's forehead relaxed a degree as if he'd finally uncovered the solution to a vexing riddle. "I see no other reason why you so readily risk yourself for her time and time again."

Callan opened his mouth to respond, but nothing came out.

He had never known a bonded pair. While common Fae honored the bond, an all-consuming pull toward another, nobles favored strategic alliances, ensuring the preservation of ancient bloodlines. His own parents' union had been an arranged one. One where love and devotion bloomed after they were joined and not before.

The noise in the hall faded to a low hum. Callan stood frozen, unable to hear anything above the insistent, rapid beating of his own heart. Was this what it felt like to be bonded to someone? Wanting to protect them and desiring their safety and happiness regardless of the cost?

Finally, he found words to answer his uncle. "She means more to me than my own life."

Thorn rolled his eyes but nodded once.

"Let us hope you return to Nivali in one piece," he said. "Don't think I've forgotten about the five months left on our bargain."

The magic binding Callan to the agreement slithered along the markings on his wrists. He nodded silently in farewell and strode through the hall, past the drunken onlookers and out into the frigid night.

The mouth of the tunnel lay gaping before him, unused for centuries and all but forgotten. Nearly hidden by a patch of overgrown evergreen bushes and partially blocked by the trunks of several fallen trees, it was indistinguishable from the dozens of caves dotting the landscape roughly an hour's ride north of the Nivali Estate. As Callan sat and stared, gently stroking the side of Frost's neck, a faint glimmer of magic rippled across the opening. Frost snorted nervously, and Callan murmured a few words to calm the beast. Clicking his tongue against the roof of his mouth, he urged his horse forward and into the portal connecting Nivali and Silvergard.

He emerged in a clearing mere minutes later, surrounded by leafless trees, their gnarled trunks the washed-out color of driftwood. The guiding star, Illora, shone bright overhead. Callan followed it north to the capital, pushing Frost at a gallop the entire journey, lasting several hours. The guards on the city wall granted him entry without delay, as if he'd been expected. When

Callan finally came to a halt in the black stone courtyard in front of the Silvergard Estate, his horse was nearly spent, white froth gathering at the corners of the animal's mouth. Fortunately, they hadn't encountered any dark beasts along the way. Frost would have been too drained to outrun a lycane or yaesira.

Callan slid down from the saddle and handed his mount off to a waiting stable hand, impatient strides carrying him toward the entrance. He'd reached the base of the massive stone steps when a figure emerged from the shadows, quickly descending to meet him. The starlight illuminated a face Callan recognized from the day Nova was taken from him. It belonged to the Commander of the Guard.

"Am I glad to see y—"

Callan's fist shot out without warning, hammering the commander solidly in the jaw. The male's torso twisted with the impact, but he remained on his feet. Two guards rushed down from the top of the steps, but the commander waved them off, swiping his hand across his mouth and turning back to Callan. Callan shook his own hand against the stab of pain radiating up his forearm. If he hadn't been wearing gloves, he might have split his knuckles on the male's sharp canine.

"Suppose I should have expected that," the commander said, amber eyes glinting, his bloody lip curled in a faint smile. He extended a hand. "Gods know I deserved it. I'm Lucan. Come with me. We don't have much time."

Callan followed Lucan inside the imposing structure and through the Great Hall, its high ceiling made entirely of glass. Callan fought the urge to gawk at the countless orbs of moonstone fixed to the walls and hanging from enormous chandeliers suspended above the large open area. He fixed his attention on the commander's back, but took note of the flurry of guards posted around the edge of the room in his periphery.

Lucan led him through a grand library to a door tucked in the back corner. A comfortable study lay beyond it. Callan stood at attention just inside the room as Lucan closed the door. Sitting behind a wide desk was the Noble Lord of Silvergard, severe in appearance with alabaster skin and sharp features. His dark eyes widened as he registered the commander's blood-stained teeth. Lucan said nothing but shook his head dismissively, dabbing at his mouth with his sleeve.

The Noble Lord grinned.

"Apologies for the intrusion." He tapped a long finger against his temple. "I had no other way to reach you as quickly, and time is already against us."

Callan recognized the warm, low voice as the one that had pulled him from a dead sleep.

The commander fell into a leather armchair opposite the desk.

"I appreciate you summoning me, my Lord," Callan bowed his head.

"Please, call me Nox." He motioned for Callan to take a seat.

Though he felt too anxious to sit and had spent the past several hours riding hard in a saddle, Callan obliged, not wanting to offend Nova's uncle. He perched on the edge of the cushion, his elbows resting on his knees as he leaned toward Nox.

"I'd like to see Nova," Callan said, getting straight to the point.

"She's not here," Lucan replied, and Callan bristled with worry. "She was taken while everyone slept. We didn't realize she was gone until she missed training earlier. I went to her chamber and found it empty."

"Who has taken her?" Callan asked, barely leashing his anger and willing himself to remain calm. Though he was a skilled tracker, he'd need to set his emotions aside if he hoped to find her.

"We believe she was taken by General Idrian of the Stargrave District, a decorated and well-respected soldier," Nox explained. "He stayed as a guest here for the past several weeks, but informed me he planned to depart for Stargrave today."

"There's no shield around the Estate. How do you protect your folk?" Callan asked, thankful his tone came out only mildly critical.

"We've never had a need for one," Lucan said defensively. "In any case, Idrian accomplished his aim without the use of magic. He carried out his plan with good old-fashioned deception and brute strength."

Nox picked up the story. "As I said, General Idrian arrived several weeks ago, accompanied by roughly twenty soldiers. They remained in the barracks alongside the members of my guard. We now believe they were learning their routines, taking note of the changing of the guard, identifying gaps in our practices."

Lucan shifted in his seat. Callan imagined it must be distressing for the commander to hear, knowing faults in his procedures had contributed to Nova's abduction. *Good.* Callan hoped it pained the bastard.

"Idrian seemed to take a liking to Nova," Nox continued. "More than once, I found him loitering around the library, waiting for her. She mentioned he'd been sharing books with her. I believe he did so to earn her trust."

"If you can read minds as folk say, how did you fail to uncover the general's plans?" Callan's voice rose, something primal crackling within him at the thought of another male pursuing Nova.

Nox's face fell. Callan realized he'd given voice to a question the Noble Lord had likely asked himself a thousand times in the hours since discovering Nova was missing.

"As you may have gathered from my apology, my ability to enter the minds of others is one I choose not to use unless absolutely necessary." Nox pressed his lips together. "I consider it an invasion. I allow myself to go so far as a cursory glance to get a general sense of someone."

Callan wondered if Nox's speech was an explanation for him or a reaffirmation of his beliefs for Nox himself. Perhaps a bit of both, he decided.

"For instance," Nox continued, "I feel the rage and fear warring within you at this very moment. However, there are those who are difficult to read. Idrian is one such individual. As is my niece."

Callan nodded. He supposed it was honorable of Nox to respect the privacy of others, though his decency provided little comfort with Nova missing and no indication of where or for what purpose she'd been taken.

"Though it was Idrian who took Nova," Nox said, "I believe my brother may have had a hand in the plot."

Callan followed the two males to Nova's chamber where the scent of her fear still lingered. He clenched his fists at his sides when the acrid tang of it found its way to him. The room was in order—by Nova's standards. Discarded clothing hung over the back of a chair and on the knobs of the armoire. Beside the bed, a precarious tower of books created a makeshift table where a cup of forgotten tea sat next to a stack of his letters.

No signs of a struggle. Nothing to suggest she'd been taken by force.

Callan scanned the chamber, lingering first on her hairbrush lying next to her blades on the vanity, then the bed where she'd been sleeping all the weeks they'd been apart. He ran a hand along the sheets discreetly, the intoxicating scent of her wafting up to meet him.

"No blood," he said gruffly, shaking his head. "He didn't harm her."

"Thank the gods," Lucan said. "Eight of my guards were slaughtered at their posts along with three servants who happened to be walking the halls."

"She may have gone willingly," Nox added. "I believe she considered him a friend."

A stab of pity pierced Callan's chest. Nova didn't have many friends. He gritted his teeth. If the general had betrayed her trust, a gift Nova rarely gave to anyone, it was grounds enough for Callan to punish him. Very slowly.

Pushing past Nox and Lucan, he exited the chamber, following Nova's scent to the wall at the end of the corridor. He looked left and right before turning to the others, arms held out at his sides, his posture demanding an explanation.

Nox approached and pressed his hand against the polished stone. A concealed door appeared, leading to a hidden passage. Callan poked his head through the doorway, sniffing at the air within. The scent of Nova's fear, more potent in the enclosed space, combined with the stale smell of ancient stone, undisturbed for gods knew how long. Lucan held out a moonstone, round and flat, hanging from a silver chain affixed to his pocket.

The stone's light illuminated a landing and the first several steps of a staircase leading deep underground. Callan observed boot prints in the thick dust on the landing. The layer of dust on the few visible steps, however, was disturbed, as if someone had swept the surface.

"Where does it lead?" Callan asked pointedly, his eyes pinned on Nox.

"The passageway is a relic, an emergency egress from a time when the Estates of every territory were regularly under siege. No one has used this passage for centuries. No one in my guard even knows it exists. But Omen knew. When we were young, he would open the door and dare me to go inside. Pretend to push me in, try to frighten me." His brow creased with the memory.

"Idrian has always been ambitious," Lucan said, taking over for his Lord. "Chasing fame and desperate for recognition. Maybe Omen enticed him into abducting Nova in exchange for ruling all of Silvergard."

"What would your brother want with Nova?" Callan asked, certain the Shadowbringer couldn't simply be interested in a reunion with his long-lost daughter.

"I can't say, but I don't expect his intentions are good." Nox took a deep breath and blew it out. "We can't spare any soldiers, not with the potential for a full-scale attack on the capital looming. I would go myself if it weren't for the imminent threat to the throne. I know how important Nova is to both of you. There's no one I trust more to find my niece and bring her home safely. But the two of you must leave at once. Idrian and his soldiers already have the advantage of a sizable head start."

"Where does the passage lead?" Callan asked again, his jaw set in determination.

THIRTY-SIX

THE TUNNEL CUT THROUGH the mountain itself. Callan and Lucan needed their horses for the journey, so they took the long way around. Roughly an hour passed with them guiding their steeds over the rocky terrain, galloping when they could, before they reached the point where the passageway terminated at the base on the far side of the mountain. Both males dismounted and crouched close to the ground, surveying the scuffs and footprints in the dense black sand.

"She was still going willingly at this point," Lucan noted, pointing to the sweeping marks made by the train of her nightgown. "He hadn't thrown her over his shoulder yet."

Callan tensed at the image. "What did Nox mean?" he asked abruptly. "When he said Nova is important to you?"

Lucan's face contorted for an instant, as if he'd never heard a more ridiculous question, then understanding washed over his features.

"It's not what you think." He chuckled but choked on the sound and cleared his throat instead. Callan was far from laughing. Lucan paused thoughtfully before continuing.

"Nova reminds me of myself. She's lonely. Angry. She wants to connect, but she's afraid to trust. I can tell she's been hurt. I want to see her overcome that. To rise above it and learn how to live with it. That's all." He held his palms out in front of him.

Callan nodded. Nova had shared some of the painful details of her past. The desperate urge to shield her and take away her pain consumed him, transforming into a physical ache in his chest. He rubbed a fist uselessly over his armor directly above his heart.

Lucan rose to his feet and pointed at a spot far off in the distance.

"They went north," he said, heading for his gray stallion. "I'd recognize the reek of her anywhere."

Lucan stopped short before he reached his horse, glancing over his shoulder at Callan.

"Sorry," Lucan added, a bit sheepishly. "I'm sure you like it."

Callan couldn't help the brief smile that flitted across his face as he mounted up next to the odd commander, the two of them taking off, chasing Nova's trail.

Several grueling hours passed as they rode on through rainstorms rolling across the barren landscape. At last, they reached the base of a small hill with a ruined temple at the summit. Callan dropped down from the saddle, allowing Frost to wander, and started up the hill directly in front of them. Lucan circled around the base to inspect the far side. The plentiful tracks preserved on the wet ground told Callan a strange story under the light of the moonstone Lucan had given him.

Roughly halfway up the incline, Callan discovered signs of a struggle. A sizable body, likely that of male, had lain on the ground, his large boots carving grooves into the damp sand as he fought for purchase. He'd been overtaken by at least two males, based on the size and number of the boot prints.

Callan continued up the slope, following a single set of tracks to the top. No statues or markings indicated which deity the temple honored. The most likely patron was the moon goddess Orika, but the structure was ruined. A crumbling stone archway still stood, inlaid with a large, round obsidian, the glassy surface cracked like a shattered black mirror. How could a temple be left to fall into such disrepair? Callan stepped carefully over a collapsed rock wall and crouched on the opposite side. Leaning in close to the wet gray stone, he immediately detected the faint scent of Nova's fear. Impressions from her hands and knees were clearly visible on the ground.

He rose to his full height, noting the indentations likely made by her heels as she was dragged backward. A single pale pink slipper lay abandoned in the center of the ruins, the toe stained with several drops of blood. Callan squatted and picked up the shoe, cradling it gingerly in one hand. Lucan entered the ruins from the northern side and stood over him, not speaking.

"It's not much," Callan murmured, holding up the slipper, the blood standing out starkly against pink silk. "But it's hers."

Callan swallowed the bitter taste of his dread, burying it so he could focus on finding her.

"It's not enough for a serious injury," Lucan reassured him. "A broken nose. Maybe a split lip. It'll be healed by this time tomorrow."

Callan appreciated his hopeful tone and made a low grunt of agreement, discreetly scrubbing his sleeve over his eyes to wipe away the tears that had gathered in his eyelashes.

"Did you find anything?" He lifted his head in the direction from which Lucan had come.

"A group was gathered there on horseback. Four mounts. Only hoof and boot prints. No bare feet. Someone must have carried her."

Callan stood and ran a hand roughly over his face, scratching at the stubble on his jaw.

"Someone—a male—was attacked by two others halfway down the hill. General Idrian, I assume. A third must have approached from behind, taking Nova by surprise," Callan said, thinking out loud. "It doesn't make sense. If Idrian planned the abduction, who attacked him, and why?"

"You're right. It doesn't make sense," Lucan agreed, shaking his head slowly, amber eyes fixed on Nova's bloodstained slipper.

"Which way did the horses go?" Callan walked to a collapsed section of wall facing north, surveying the circle of hoofprints below.

"North. If I had to guess, I'd say they're taking her to Schadwen Mountain." He pointed at the jagged black peak rising out of the horizon. "The Gloaming Sea sits on the other side. There's a cave system beneath the mountain. A good spot for anyone looking to hide out for a bit of rest before heading on to their final destination, wherever it may be."

"It'll be dawn before long." Callan shot a brief look at the sky. "I've never staged an ambush in broad daylight before."

"You're in Lunar territory," Lucan reminded him with a half-hearted smile. "They'll be bedding down at dawn. Besides, it'll be dark in the caves no matter the hour."

Callan nodded in silent agreement. He followed Lucan down the hill to where their horses drank from a splintered bucket beside a crumbling well. Callan hoisted himself into the saddle on Frost's broad back, looking east where the sun would soon be rising. *Everyone has to rest eventually*, he told himself. Catching Nova's abductors while they slept in a few hours would be their best opportunity to strike. He only hoped they weren't too late.

THIRTY-SEVEN

NOVA'S HEAD THROBBED IN time with her heartbeat. She reached her hand to her right temple, the source of the pain, but discovered she was shackled at the wrists. Her eyelids fluttered weakly before opening fully.

The ground beneath her was hard and damp, the ceiling above, rough-hewn stone. Forcing several deep breaths through her nose, she rose slowly, pausing when her blood surged in her veins, briefly worsening the pressure in her skull. She sat in a small cavern lit by a single torch fixed to the wall beside an opening that led out into darkness. Another torch burned further down at the bend in a narrow tunnel. A simple wooden stool sat against the far wall beside the entryway. There was no door, though one was hardly necessary with her chained up.

Bending her arms, Nova examined her wrists. Only then did she register the searing pain there, the sensation previously eclipsed by the ache in her head. The skin beneath the shackles was raw and blistered. Iron cuffs, she gathered.

Once, when she was a child, she'd grabbed the handle of an iron skillet sitting on the worktop in the kitchen. Her palm and fingers had been badly burned. Agnes scolded her as she loosely wrapped a bandage around the scalded skin, warning Nova not to touch a pan straight out of the fire. But Nova had read countless faerie stories that told of the Fae's vulnerability to the dense metal. She'd kept her distance entirely afterward.

A drop of liquid landed on her forearm, and she twisted her neck to inspect the ceiling. After a moment, she realized it was blood. *Her* blood. She pressed her fingertips to her temple, crimson coating them when she pulled her hand away. The iron was suppressing her ability to heal.

Nova lifted her hands once again, but they halted in midair before she could raise her arms above her head. The cuffs were fixed to the stone floor with a length of chain secured by a thick pin hammered deep into the solid rock. She shifted her position so she rested on her knees. Clasping her hands together, she wrenched her arms upward several times. It was no use. Her head swam with the effort, and she collapsed onto her back on the uneven floor.

Dragging deep breaths in through her nose, she battled the waves of nausea crashing down upon her, one after another. As black dots began to dance at the edges of her vision, she thought suddenly of Idrian. The terrified look on his face, illuminated in the ghostly glow of the moonstone, as he shouted for her to run. She rolled onto her side and pushed herself up into a sitting position.

What had happened to him? Was he being held in another cell?

She rose up onto her knees again, the soiled train of her nightdress tangling around her ankles. Gripping a section of the gown near the hem where the thread had already started to come loose, she tugged hard, rending the seam and removing the excess fabric.

Nova groaned as she pulled against her restraints again, the iron rings cutting into tender skin. She fell onto her backside with a grunt. Holding her hands aloft, she kept the chain taut and kicked at it over and over. The pin didn't budge, and the chain held fast. Nova threw herself down flat and

289

roared through clenched teeth, the sound bouncing off the walls of the small cavern.

Her chest heaved as the steady thud of boots sounded in the dark passageway outside her cell, growing louder as they neared. Nova sat upright and scrambled back as far as her restraints would allow. She hadn't seen the faces of her captors, but she vividly recalled the pain they'd inflicted.

Finally, the footsteps drew close enough for her to hear the scrape of sand under leather soles. A tall cloaked figure stepped through the darkened entryway and into the flickering torchlight. The hood was pulled low, the face hidden. The visitor's movements were unhurried, almost casual, as they dragged the stool away from the wall and took a seat.

Nova reached deep within herself and slipped on her practiced mask of detachment, disguising the fear threatening to consume her entirely if she'd only let it. She held her breath as the figure lowered the hood, revealing a crown of black hair. A single streak of silver ran like a bolt of lightning through the inky strands.

Nova pressed her lips together.

Idrian. Her *friend*.

Nothing about his appearance had changed, but his manner was wholly different. The slate-gray eyes, once so open and seemingly sincere, sat narrowed and calculating beneath his full brows. His lips curled up on one side in a cruel sneer.

"Don't look at me like that, Mouse," he mocked, clicking his tongue at her. "I told you I enjoy defying expectations."

"I trusted you."

"Yes, and it was quite foolish of you, wasn't it? Though I can't say I expected much from a vapid female who spends her time lounging about in fancy gowns and reading all day." His nose crinkled, as if he found her very existence repulsive.

"You deceitful prick," Nova spat. "Your toast to Nox—it was all lies." Tears stung her eyes at his betrayal. At her stupidity for trusting him even as her body repeatedly tried to warn her something wasn't right.

"You've got quite a mouth on you. And I never lied to anyone." He lifted his chin proudly. "Silvergard *is* no longer what it once was. It was once a force to be reckoned with, a formidable power feared throughout the Realm. Now, thanks to that feckless uncle of yours, this once-mighty territory is a joke."

Nova flinched at the word *uncle*.

"That's right," Idrian said, chuckling low in his throat. "I knew Omen's heir had arrived at the Estate. Though, even if I hadn't, one look at you would have given it away. The two of you thought you were so clever, skirting the truth. But you're the spitting image of your father."

Nova didn't respond right away. She bit the inside of her cheek to keep from losing the sliver of composure to which she desperately clung.

"Why the charade? Why pretend to rescue me when all along you were abducting me?"

"Honestly, it was such fun deceiving you. Seeing how far I could go. Wondering if you'd ever catch on. Certainly, I'm biased, but I'd say my performance was damn near perfect. Who knows, I might have made a good actor if I believed any of Nox's 'art over conquest, creation over destruction' horseshit."

Idrian dragged a hand through his hair, preening like a cat taming its fur. Nova's resolve flared. She'd be damned if she let this arrogant ass see the fear and dread crackling just below the surface of her skin.

"What's your plan, then?" she asked dryly, her mask righted after her brief slip. "Am I to remain chained to the floor until I rot? Surely you have something more grandiose planned for me."

"I do," he said, leaning forward with his elbows resting on his knees.

"You're my key to the throne."

When Nova showed no reaction, Idrian leaned back against the rock wall, stretching his legs out in front of him and crossing his boots at the ankles. She swallowed a groan, realizing he was readying himself for a speech.

"I grew up poor in Stargrave," he began, his face tilted toward the low ceiling. "My father was a low-level soldier and a piss-poor one at that. He wasted what little wages he earned on drink and female company, never aspiring to be anything more than he was. He disgusted me. We had little food in those days, but my mother fed me a steady diet of stories about the once-noble blood flowing through my veins—a noble bloodline overthrown by your ancestors nearly two thousand years ago."

She supposed that explained his interest in the ancestry records stored in the hidden wing of the library.

"As I grew older, I vowed I would be nothing like my father. I would aspire to greatness, to be worthy of the throne stolen from me long before I was born. Everything I have, I've earned through struggle. My rank. My reputation. You can't imagine what a slap in the face it was to see the future of Silvergard laid at Nox's feet, only for him to piss on it."

Idrian leaned forward again. Nova nearly flinched at the abruptness of the movement.

"Your uncle is a spoiled, fucking brat," he spat, jabbing a finger at her. "He's not worthy to sit upon the Lunar Throne. And neither are you. When I saw you upon the dais, it took every shred of my self-control not to end your life that very moment."

He paused briefly to compose himself, wiping a drop of spit from his chin with the back of his hand.

"But I made a bargain, and I must honor the terms of the agreement. I've always dreamt of taking back what is rightfully mine. But, for reasons that are lost on me, Nox is beloved by the folk of Silvergard. I never could have amassed the support I needed to carry out my plans. That is, until your father presented me with an offer that was simply too good to pass up. A simple exchange, really: your life for the backing I need to retake the territory."

Her mother's voice rang out in her head.

If he discovers you in Aemoria, discovers who you are, I won't be able to protect you.

"What does my father want with me?" Nova asked, barely able to keep her voice from trembling.

"Nothing," Idrian said matter-of-factly. "Make no mistake, your father wishes you dead. And while he may not be able to dispatch you with his own hand, he certainly means to watch."

A sinewy soldier with close-cropped white hair entered the room, passing a rolled bit of parchment into Idrian's hand.

"From one of his birds," the soldier muttered, shooting a hateful glance in her direction. His nose was swollen and slightly crooked, the bridge flecked with remnants of dried blood. Fresh bruises purpled the pale skin around his eyes. Nova realized she was responsible for the injury. She held his rage-filled stare for a moment before dropping her eyes, taking note of the ring of keys dangling from his belt.

Nova recoiled as Idrian jumped up from his seat, unleashing a vicious snarl. He kicked the stool, launching it across the cell where it crashed against the far wall.

"The bastard is either too weak or too paranoid to leave his Estate. He won't be meeting us here as planned," he informed his lackey, crumpling the message and casting it aside.

Idrian spun to face Nova. Inky strands of black hair hung loose over his forehead, his gray eyes gleaming like white-hot coals. Lowering his lids for an instant, he calmly ran both hands through his hair, taming it once more. When he looked at her again, it was as if his outburst had never happened.

Nova found his ability to shift so rapidly from seething rage to eerie stillness deeply unsettling.

"I suggest you get some rest, Nova Elsever. We depart for Raven's Isle at dusk."

Idrian left, disappearing into the dimly lit tunnel. The light-haired soldier glared at her for a moment before he followed the general. Nova waited for the echo of their footsteps to fade. Finally, she released the breath she'd been holding; hot tears followed close behind.

She threw herself down flat on her back, striking the stone floor with her shackled hands. How could she have been so stupid? Nox, Lucan, Isla, all the folk of the Lunar Court—her Court—were in grave danger, all thanks to her foolishness.

She pressed her palms against her eyes and saw Callan's face in the sea of glittering blackness, her shoulders shaking with silent sobs. She cursed herself for all the times she'd pushed him away and denied their connection. The times she'd allowed him to believe he was unworthy when, in truth, it was she who felt undeserving. Her regret sat like a stone on her chest, making it difficult to catch her breath.

Had she lived long enough to join her life with another's—and she now wished desperately to have had the chance—she could think of no one more perfectly suited for her than Callan Nyhauslen. She'd been handed a death sentence and would never be able to tell him how she truly felt. To tell him what his kindness had meant to her. That she was falling in love with him.

Nova rolled onto her side on the chill, damp ground. She fought to hold back her tears, and an uncomfortable heaviness grew within her chest until she could have sworn she felt her rib cage crack. Tears spilled forth then, soaking her cheeks as she wept for the life she'd wasted and all that would never be. She wept until her tears ran dry, then smeared the tracks staining her cheeks with grimy fingers. Unmoving, she lay there in the silence. As seconds dragged into minutes, minutes into hours, a hollow sensation spread slowly from the center of her chest, creeping along her spine and down her limbs, until she could feel nothing. Until she was nothing. Dreamily, she wondered whether the numbness stemmed from the iron or her despair.

Nova curled her knees to her chest, eyelids growing heavy as she watched the dancing flame of the torchlight. As exhaustion and the effects of the iron overtook her, she imagined she felt the warmth of a body nestled against her back. The comforting weight of an arm wrapped around her waist. It was only a hallucination, she knew, but she could have sworn she heard Callan's voice, murmuring softly in her ear.

THIRTY-EIGHT

THE HORSES WERE EXHAUSTED by the time Callan and Lucan reached the rocky outcrop, not far from the base of Schadwen Mountain. It was shortly after sunrise when they tethered the animals to the branches of a twisted acacia, hidden from view. Quickly scaling the formation of black bedrock, Callan lay flat on his stomach atop the slanted summit, pulling a spyglass from the folds of his cloak. Lucan joined him a moment later, crouching beside him as Callan scanned the base of the mountain for a point of entry.

"There," he said, passing the spyglass to Lucan and pointing. The cave entrance was nearly hidden by several desert trees springing out of the sandy ground in front of it. Lucan nodded and glanced up at the brightening sky overhead, handing the spyglass back to him.

"I say we give them another hour to settle in for a rest, then we make our way inside."

"You said the general traveled with twenty soldiers?" Callan's mind whirred, making mental calculations, formulating a plan of attack.

"Yes. I imagine he'll have two or three guards wherever he's bedded down. Several more posted near Nova. The remaining soldiers will be divided, with some sleeping and the rest on watch."

"We're going in blind. Don't know the layout. It'll have to be a stealth attack. We kill anyone we encounter as quickly and quietly as possible. I'd like our odds much better if we're not fighting all twenty at once, especially in such close quarters."

"Agreed," Lucan said, seeming slightly surprised. "Since you've taken care of logistics, I suppose I'll find some water for the horses."

As the commander descended, boots scraping rough stone, Callan narrowed his eyes on the cave entrance. He could almost hear Nova's essence calling to him like a beacon from the darkness within.

An hour later, the males hiked to a spot a good deal west of the cave, planning to make a covert approach along the foot of the mountain. Once they rescued Nova, they'd make a run for the horses hidden behind the outcrop.

The skinny acacias marking the cave entrance came into view, and Callan sank down into a low crouch, signaling for Lucan to do the same. He watched the entrance for several minutes, not observing any movement. He rose to walking height but remained hunched forward as they crept into position near the mouth of the cave.

Callan picked up a stone and lobbed it a short distance up the rock face. It rolled down, bringing a few smaller rocks tumbling with it. A single soldier poked his head out in response, craning his neck to investigate the source of the noise. Not seeing anything of concern, the guard disappeared back through the darkened entryway.

"I'll take out the first guard when we enter," Callan whispered. "You watch my back—there's likely at least one more just inside." Callan pulled his dagger from the sheath at his thigh, his leather glove groaning faintly as he tightened his grip around the hilt.

Lucan produced his own dagger, the curved blade glinting in the sunlight. "If our plan falls apart, I'll shift. It won't be stealth, but I'll clear a path straight to her."

Callan nodded once. A moment later, he entered the cave, surprising the soldier leaning against the wall. Before the male could draw his sword, Callan pulled him to his chest and ran the blade of his dagger across his throat, killing him instantly. Farther down the tunnel, a second guard emerged from the shadows, his weapon in hand, but Lucan was ready, overpowering him and slitting his throat efficiently. They left the bodies where they fell and crept farther into the darkness.

A small chamber off the main tunnel contained two soldiers sleeping on the ground, both easily dispatched without a struggle. Callan and Lucan exited the chamber, each hugging the wall as they proceeded along the stone corridor, following Nova's scent deeper into the caves.

They had just crossed into a ring of orange light cast by a single torch mounted on the wall when a guard emerged from a narrow opening in the rock, his head lowered as he fiddled with the laces of his breeches. The male was out of reach when he looked up, spotting the intruders. Callan sent forth a burst of frigid wind, hurling the soldier against the wall, but his warning shout was already reverberating off the damp stone.

Callan rushed forward, drawing his sword from the sheath at his back as he quickly closed the distance between them, and separated the soldier's head from his body with a single brutal blow. But the damage had already been done. Echoes of faraway shouts rang out, overlapping with the sound of running footsteps.

Callan sheathed his dagger and shot a glance at Lucan. The commander flashed his teeth in a smirk and shrugged casually, as if to say, *Oh well*, before throwing his arms out wide at his sides.

In the blink of an eye and a cascade of crunching bones and rippling muscles, Lucan's form shifted to that of a walking wolf, covered from head to toe in thick black fur. He looked much the same as a lycane but with longer limbs and a greater range of motion, which allowed him to walk on his hind legs and lash out freely with his front claws.

Lucan unleashed a deafening howl that vibrated Callan's rib cage, the haunting sound instantly raising the tiny hairs on Callan's arms and the back of his neck. Three guards skidded to a halt at the edge of the torchlight, staring wide-eyed at Callan and the beast before drawing their own weapons. One lunged at Lucan, the other two preferring to take their chances on Callan.

Callan lifted his sword arm and sent forth an icy blast from his other hand, throwing one of his opponents against the wall. The second guard continued to rush him, and they crossed blades in a crash of steel. Callan spun quickly, coming to rest behind the guard and running him through the back with the point of his sword. He pulled his blade free and switched his grip, thrusting his weapon behind him and plunging his blade through the chest of the second guard, who had managed to get back on his feet.

Callan scanned the tunnel ahead, only vaguely aware of the third guard's screams quieting on the heels of a sickening squelch as Lucan tore out his throat. Callan locked eyes with the creature and jerked his head to the left. The two of them took off running into the darkness, headed for the next ring of light.

A moment later, two more guards appeared, blocking their path. Lucan leapt on one, tackling him to the ground. The guard cried out as Lucan's claws slashed him across the throat. The second guard froze. Callan seized the opportunity and lunged at him, coming down with his blade from above. The Silvergardian soldier had the sense to raise his own weapon and block Callan's attack. Lucan charged up from behind, clawing at the back of the soldier's legs. He collapsed, and Callan brought his blade down forcefully, piercing him through the heart.

A faint roar rang out in the darkness. The familiar sound frightened

Callan more than Lucan's howl had.

Nova.

Callan pressed his boot against the dead guard's shoulder and yanked his blade free. He took off sprinting in the direction of Nova's voice, jaw clenched, blood laced with pure ire coursing like glacial water in his veins. Around a bend in the tunnel, a figure emerged from the shadows ahead of him. Callan swung his sword, splitting the soldier's throat open without stopping. He barely registered Lucan overtaking him as they careened toward a dimly lit cavern at the end of the passageway.

Thirty-Nine

Gasping for breath, Nova woke from a nightmare, her skin slick with a cold sweat. In her dream, the lycane hovered over her, its great paws crushing her chest. Stealing her breath. In an instant, the creature transformed into her father, his metallic eyes flashing wildly and strands of his long silver hair brushing against her cheeks as he strangled her with his bare hands.

Only a dream, she assured herself, swallowing hard and sitting upright on the ground. Her stomach twisted with a painful hunger. The torch in her cell was dying, and shadows gathered at the edges of the room.

An ominous howl echoed in the distance, and her head snapped to the entryway. A shiver rippled across her skin as she recalled the searing pain of the lycane's claws against her flesh. If one attacked her now, she simply wouldn't survive. She was an easy target. Chained to the floor. Without weapons. The iron impeding her ability to heal. Nova crawled as far back into the shadows as her restraints would allow, crouching low and staring into the void, bracing herself for whatever monster was coming for her.

To her surprise, it was not a creature but an ordinary male that rushed into her cell. As he stepped into the faint light, she heard the clink of metal and recognized the battered face of Idrian's second-in-command.

She was in serious trouble.

"There you are," he sneered as his eyes settled on her hiding in the darkness along the cell's back wall.

"The whole plan's gone to shit," he said, panting slightly as if he'd been running. He took several more steps until he loomed over her. "Came to collect what I'm owed while I'm still alive to claim it."

He moved swiftly, grabbing her by the hair and hauling her away from the wall. She tried to strike him, but the chain halted her hands.

The guard laughed, lifting his foot and forcing her onto her back with his boot. He lowered himself to the ground, roughly wedging his hips between her thighs. One forearm pressed against her chest, holding her down, while his free hand fumbled with his breeches. Nova heard the key ring knocking repeatedly against the floor as she struggled beneath him.

"Don't worry," he rasped, his breath coming out in short puffs against her cheek as she turned her face away from his. "It'll all be over soon."

He cursed under his breath, rolling his body off of hers a bit to grapple with his laces. Seizing the opportunity, Nova slammed the iron cuffs into his nose. Hot blood spurted onto her chest as he cried out, bringing both hands to his face and releasing his hold on her.

Nova squirmed out from under him and scrambled to her knees, quickly looping the chain around his neck once and pulling it taut. The guard sputtered and choked, clawing at the chain cutting off his breath and blistering the skin at his throat. Nova shoved a knee between his shoulder blades and settled her weight on top of him, roaring as she fought her exhaustion and the pain of the iron cutting into her already-scalded wrists.

Less than a minute later, her attacker ceased struggling. Nova slumped forward, her vision blurring. She heard the faint tinkling of metal and realized her hands were trembling. Her vision went in and out of focus as she stared at the body beneath her, her heartbeat pounding in her ears.

Someone entered the cell, and Nova twisted to face whoever else had come for her. In the light of the dimming torch stood the terrifying form of a wolf-like beast on its hind legs. The creature dropped to all fours and approached her. As it neared, Nova lowered herself to the ground, using the guard's body as a shield. A paralyzing fear ran through her for a breath before she saw the creature's amber eyes.

"Lucan?" Her voice was an exhausted whimper. The animal dipped its head low in a submissive pose and came to her side. Nova didn't know whether to laugh or cry, so she did both as she gently petted the bristly black fur on his snout.

Nova flinched as another figure flew into the cell, skidding to a halt just inside the entryway.

This time she could only cry as Callan fell to his knees before her, wrapping his arms around her shoulders and pulling her tight against his chest.

"Are you all right?" He tilted her face up toward his, quickly scanning her for injuries and hissing through his teeth at the wound on her head.

"I'm alive." They both let out a choked laugh.

The clink of metal reminded her she was restrained, the iron chain still looped around the neck of the guard who lay dead on the ground between them.

"The keys. On his belt," she said.

Callan set to work releasing her from her shackles, his gloves protecting him from the iron's ill effects. The second key he tried turned in the lock, and the cuffs fell away, landing on the guard's back with a soft thud.

Callan cradled her wrists in his hands, and she winced at the lingering burning sensation.

"Did he hurt you?"

Nova shook her head weakly. "I broke his nose yesterday. I managed to rearrange it again just now before he could get what he came for." She forced a frail smile.

Callan's nostrils flared, and he pulled her to him again, pressing a firm kiss to the top of her head as she sagged against his chest. Lucan emitted a low yowl beside them, and Callan pulled away.

"We have to get out of here. Can you walk?"

"I think so." He helped her to her feet, and she kicked off her remaining slipper. "The iron—I wasn't able to heal."

"The effects will fade. I won't let anything happen to you," he assured her. "Take this."

Callan pressed his dagger into her palm, and she closed her fingers tightly around the hilt, relishing the feeling of a blade in her hand.

Lucan stood at the cell's opening, sniffing at the darkness beyond. Nova and Callan joined him. Idrian barked orders in the distance, his voice an unhinged roar rumbling through the tunnels. The clamor of rushing footsteps was nearing with every passing second.

Lucan lunged forward into the darkened passage, leading the way to the exit with Callan and Nova close behind. Nova registered several dead bodies, slashed or torn open, as they sped through the winding corridor of stone.

They could see daylight brightening the opening a short distance ahead when they were set upon by guards, three of them pouring out of an adjoining tunnel from the right. One swung his sword horizontally at Nova, but she ducked beneath the blade, crouched behind him, and thrust the dagger up and under his ribs through a crease in his armor. She twisted the blade as she pulled it free.

The guard fell to the ground, and she looked up to see Callan fighting against a second soldier who had him pinned close to the wall, their blades crossed. Callan kicked his opponent's kneecap, sending him stumbling backward.

"Run, Nova!" Callan bellowed. "Get out of here!"

She got to her feet and sprinted for the light. Lucan's deep, guttural growl and the wet, choking gasps of his victim mixed with the clash of steel and a pained cry from Callan, echoing in the tunnel behind her.

Nova's chest was ready to burst by the time she emerged into the sunlight. Collapsing onto the ground, she twisted to face the cave, sweat dripping down her forehead and into her eyes as she willed Lucan and Callan to come into view. Perhaps it was another hallucination, but, for an instant, she thought she glimpsed a raven, wings spread wide and stark black against the bright sky, before it disappeared behind the mountain's peak.

An agonizing minute passed before Lucan appeared, the sun glinting off the midnight strands of his coat, his muzzle and the fur at his throat shimmering with fresh blood. Callan stumbled out soon after, falling to his knees. He buried the tip of his sword in the ground and turned to the cave with his arms outstretched. Flowing forth from his hands, a thick wall of ice began to form, covering the mouth of the cave entirely and sealing Idrian and what little remained of his forces inside.

When he was done, Callan fell forward, bracing himself on the ground, and Nova crawled to his side. A faint blue glow faded from his eyes, leaving them dark brown once again. Tiny red droplets freckled his skin, a constellation in blood spattered across his face. Starting at his shoulders, she ran her hands over his body. He caught her wrists gently just as she reached his ribs.

"I'm fine," he said, still breathing heavily through his nose.

Lucan appeared beside them, leading a large gray stallion by the bridle. He'd returned to his Fae form, his chin and neck still wet and stained crimson. Nova glanced down at her chest, covered with blood from the guard's broken nose.

"We make quite a crew," she chuckled weakly, lightheaded with the imminent threat to her life having been thwarted for the time being.

"We need to leave," Callan said. "That's a wall of solid ice, but it won't hold forever."

"I found their horses tethered in a grove to the east and freed all except this one." Lucan grinned, patting the animal on the side of the neck. "Nipped at their ankles a bit, too, to get them good and scared. It'll be a while before they're able track them all down."

"Good thinking." Callan rose to his feet, grunting with the effort. He pulled his sword from the ground and sheathed it. Nova handed him his dagger, which he slipped back onto his thigh. He held out his hand and helped her up.

"We left our horses there." He pointed to a large rock rising out of the ground in the distance. "How are you feeling?"

Nova briefly touched her temple and examined her wrists and forearms, taking stock of her injuries. Her mind already felt clearer in the short time since the iron cuffs had been removed.

"Well enough to get there," she said.

Callan gave a close-lipped smile, the rest of his features drawn tight.

"You two take the horse," Lucan said, handing the reins over to Callan. "I'll run alongside."

Callan agreed with a nod and proceeded to help Nova mount. He struggled to get himself onto the horse, exhaling sharply once he settled into the saddle behind her.

"How are *you* feeling?"

"It's been a long couple of days, and that ice took a lot out of me," he said with a dry laugh. "Let's get you home."

The word conjured an image of the Silvergard Estate in her weary mind. Nova closed her eyes and breathed a sigh of relief. The strange horse whinnied nervously as Lucan sprinted past, a blur of black in the sunlight. Callan nudged the stallion in the ribs, and the animal took off at a gallop.

They reached the rocky outcrop a short time later, circling behind to where their horses waited, somewhat rested. Lucan shifted in the blink of an eye, leaving Nova momentarily stunned, and untethered the animals. The stolen mount carrying Nova and Callan slowed to a halt. Behind her, she felt Callan slump to the side. She grabbed uselessly at his cloak as he fell from the horse, landing in a heap on the ground beneath her.

In an instant, she slid down from the saddle and crouched on her knees beside him, shaking him by his shoulders and shouting his name. Callan's eyelids fluttered. His skin was ashen, lips dry and tinged with blue. Nova threw open his cloak and frantically ran her hands over his chest and arms.

"Lucan, help me get this damn thing off him," she ordered, pulling at the thick leather armor hugging Callan's solid torso.

They worked together to remove Callan's chest plate, revealing his blood-soaked tunic. One of the soldiers must have thrust a sword underneath his armor. Nova shoved the darkened fabric aside, finding a deep wound on his right side. Blood flowed from it like a spring, pooling in the sand beneath his body.

Too much blood. Too much blood.

Nova's teeth chattered, as much from the wind fluttering her flimsy nightgown as the dread taking root in the pit of her stomach, tendrils of it climbing like ivy into her throat.

"We need to get him back to the Estate," Lucan said soberly, eyes wide. Nova had never been more desperate for Lucan to make one of his jests. The grave expression on his face chilled her to the bone.

"He can't ride like this," she said, voice trembling. "He won't make it."

Steadying herself with a deep breath, she leaned down to further assess Callan's wound. It was the width of a few fingers, entering through his abdomen right above his hipbone and exiting his back just below his rib cage. Gods only knew what the blade had struck internally.

Instinctively, Nova placed her quivering hands on either side of the wound and pressed down with every shred of strength remaining within her. Callan's body jerked beneath her.

"What do you think you're doing?" Lucan demanded.

"Healing him."

"No. You're not. You're too weak. We'll throw him over the horse, and Nox's healer can tend him." He tried to pull her from Callan's side, but she shoved him away.

Laying her hands on Callan's wounds a second time, Nova closed her eyes and visualized his flesh knitting back together, stemming the rush of blood. Soon, a warm sensation bloomed in her chest and snaked down her arms to her palms, where the heat intensified. Nova grew dizzy, as though she might faint. She breathed deeply through her nose and shook her head against the alluring pull of oblivion.

Her body temperature continued to rise. In her mind's eye, she saw herself drifting closer and closer to an endless black pool. An all-consuming darkness. It was surprisingly warm and comforting when she began to sink below the surface. Nothing like the dreadful, biting cold she felt when the black mist had swallowed her bit by bit in her dream.

Nova, stop.

Lucan's voice floated around her, faraway and fading in and out. She blew all the air from her chest as the enveloping darkness reached the hollow beneath her bottom lip.

I said, stop!

The next instant, something hooked under her arms and hauled her back forcefully. The scorching heat on the surface of her skin dissipated, and she drew a ragged, painful breath, as if breathing for the very first time. Nova thrashed wildly, blinking as her vision returned. She found herself on top of Lucan, who lay on the ground, arms wrapped tightly around her waist.

"Let me go!" She tore free from his hold, throwing herself down beside

Callan. She scrambled onto her knees, wobbling with the effort, and shoved the hem of his tunic up to his chest.

The flow of blood had stopped.

The straight edges of the wound were red and raw but slightly puckered, the tissue beginning to reach toward itself like a plant reaches toward the sun. Callan groaned, and she gripped the fabric of his tunic, resting her forehead against his and letting out a shuddering breath. He wasn't fully healed, but she had kept him alive. He curled his fingers around her forearm and squeezed weakly.

"You saved my life," he whispered. The bluish tinge still clung to his lips.

"I suppose you owe me a debt."

Nova cupped Callan's face, her hands sticky with his blood, and pressed her mouth softly against his.

"Hate to interrupt," Lucan said bitterly, rising onto his feet. "But we need to get going."

Nova pulled her lips from Callan's and glanced around, dazed, having forgotten for a moment that anything existed outside the two of them. She stood and, with Lucan's help, hoisted Callan onto Frost's back. Nova settled into the saddle behind him. She took the reins in one hand and wrapped her other arm tightly around his waist, determined never to let go. He was weak, but she'd make sure he stayed astride.

"What were you thinking?" Lucan scolded, bringing his horse alongside Frost.

"I wasn't thinking. I had to save him."

"You had next to nothing to give, Nova. You're fucking lucky I was here. You could have drained yourself. You . . ." Teeth bared in a silent snarl, he looked over his shoulder at the hulking black mountain behind them. "Let's get moving. Try to stay on the horse."

Lucan took off galloping south, and Nova followed close behind, the three of them racing back to the Silvergard Estate without pausing for rest.

FORTY

THE JOURNEY BACK TO the capital passed in a hazy blur punctuated by the sensation of his insides being ripped apart. Though the pain tearing at Callan's side was excruciating, it paled in comparison to the uncertainty and fear he had felt not knowing if Nova was alive. He would have died happily, knowing he'd brought her to safety.

Now that he lay convalescing in a comfortable bed within the Silvergard Estate, Callan was very glad he wasn't dead.

Nova's uncle kept the territory's best healer in residence—a short, wizened female with black curls streaked with white and fingers like gnarled tree roots. The crone, called Eir, finished what Nova had started, cleaning Callan's wound and encouraging the edges to join and scar over. After only a few hours of uninterrupted sleep, he felt much improved, but Eir ordered him to remain in bed and rest for several days more.

Not likely, he thought.

If the general and what remained of his guard were still hiding out near Schadwen Mountain, Callan intended to return and finish what *he'd* started. To punish them all for what they'd done. He needed only to consult with Lucan to devise a plan. They couldn't allow Idrian to escape, free to plan another attempt on Nova's life. Another plot to seize the Lunar Throne.

Callan heaved his legs over the side of the bed, wincing at the twinge of pain in his side. He raised his right arm above his head and looked down, running his fingers along the fresh scar. The healer had washed him with a cloth and a basin of warm water, but he was eager to soak his sore muscles in the bath. Callan limped carefully into the adjoining bathing chamber.

As soon as he entered the room, he was struck with an uncanny sense that he had been there before. He filled the black stone soaking tub with hot water and lowered himself beneath the surface. His sizable frame sent water sloshing over the edge to pool on the polished stone floor, his kneecaps peeking out from underneath the water.

Draping his arms over the sides of the tub, he tipped his head back and closed his eyes. Despite all that had happened in such a short period of time, the one thing his mind kept returning to again and again was that kiss, soft but crackling with intensity. Had Nova simply gotten carried away in the moment, overcome with relief at saving him? Gods, he hoped not. He hoped she was ready to acknowledge the thread stretching between them. Even if she wasn't, Callan knew he would wait as long as it took. For the rest of his days if it came to it.

A short time later, he sat on the edge of the bed drying his hair with a soft towel, clad only in a fresh pair of breeches. A quiet knock came at the chamber door an instant before it opened. Callan expected to see the healer coming to check on him, but he found Nova standing in his room instead.

Nova *needed* to see him.

More than she'd ever needed anything in her life.

As soon as they had arrived back at the Estate, Callan had been carried off to be treated by an expert healer. Twice Nova attempted to visit his chamber, but the stern female shooed her away.

Callan's brush with death, and her own, for that matter, had solidified something within her: a depth of feeling she hadn't known was possible. One impossible to deny.

She *desperately* needed to see him.

And so, Nova waited patiently in her own room for the healer to leave Callan's, noting Eir's distinctive footsteps as they slowly shuffled past her door. After forcing herself to wait several more minutes, she slipped out into the corridor and rushed down the hall to Callan's chamber, her robe and unbound hair trailing behind her.

Nova knocked softly and eased the door open to find Callan sitting on the edge of the bed, shirtless and running a towel over his damp hair. His head snapped up at the sound of the latch, and he stood immediately when he saw her, wincing slightly, his hand going reflexively to his side. Relief flooded his features, and his eyes fell shut. Nova's heart swelled almost painfully in her chest at the sight of him.

Alive.

Callan's long strides erased the distance between them, but he stopped just in front of her.

"You're alive." Her voice wavered as she met the heat radiating off his body, her eyes dancing over his bare chest and shoulders. Brown skin marked here and there with the faint scars of long-healed wounds.

"I feared I would never see you again," he murmured. "That I wouldn't get the chance to apologize."

"What for?"

"For kissing you. In Nivali. It was wrong of me—"

"Callan." She took hold of his hands. "I kissed you first."

"I know. It was kind of you to offer me comfort, but I took it too far. The next day, you were angry with me. I apologize."

"I wasn't angry with you. I was . . ." Nova inhaled a steadying breath. "Afraid."

"Afraid of what?"

"The night we argued . . ." She paused, distracted by both the memory of the first kiss they'd shared and Callan's full lips hovering so close hers. "Liv told me we are connected. You and I. That the threads of our lives are woven together."

"And this frightened you?" His forehead creased as a faint smile crept across his face.

"It did. It *does*. Though I've tried to drown it out, I feel you . . . calling to me somehow. When my mind races and my emotions threaten to consume me, your words and your touch soothe me. Gods, how I crave your touch." Her breath ran out, and she inhaled shakily. "And yes, that frightened me because I knew someday, I would lose you. As I've lost everyone else."

Nova attempted to swallow, her throat suddenly as dry as the midnight dunes surrounding the Estate. Her skin was hot, blood racing in her veins. She was both terrified he might not feel as strongly for her and exhilarated at the thought that he might.

"After all that's happened, I realized nothing could be more frightening than losing you without getting the chance to love you first. And I do, Callan." She tilted her face up to his, focusing on his mouth, too nervous to meet his eyes. "I love you."

Callan laid his hand on her neck, brushing his thumb over her pulse, thrumming beneath the sensitive skin of her throat.

"Nova," he murmured, a wide smile spreading across his lips and revealing the dimple on his cheek. "I've been drawn to you since the very first night I met you. I should have known it was love I felt the moment Thorn's guards raised their blades, because I knew then that I would do anything, give anything, even my own life, for you."

He bent his head and kissed her then, softly at first, her lips melting into his as she lifted her hands to his broad shoulders. Tilting her head back, she eagerly opened her mouth to him, deepening the kiss. The velvety swipe of his tongue against hers sent a rush of desire between her thighs. The kiss grew possessive. Urgent. His tongue questing farther into her mouth, as desperate to be inside her as she was to have him there. Breaking the kiss, Callan slid his hands to her chest. He traced his fingertips lightly over the smooth fabric of her robe, which hung open, revealing a strip of pale skin between her breasts.

Nova ran her hands from his shoulders to his biceps, muscles rigid beneath her fingers. She looked up into his face. His jaw was clenched, his brow creased. She could see he was holding himself back, restraining his desire until he was certain she wanted them to come together as much as he did.

"You never have to hide from me. You never have to hold back," she murmured. "Put your hands on me, Callan."

Every muscle in her own body tensed with the anticipation of finally getting what she had been denying herself for months. She wore nothing under her robe; she had wanted this to happen.

Callan eagerly obliged her, sliding his fingers beneath the robe and pushing the fabric aside. A low groan escaped his lips at the sight of her breasts, and he immediately took them in his hands.

"Gods, you're beautiful," he said, his voice a reverent whisper.

Pressing his forehead against hers, he kneaded her breasts, pinching her pale pink nipples between his fingers. Nova moaned softly at his rough hands on her skin, a sensation she'd imagined countless times before. Her fingertips found the firm cord of muscle running from his neck to his shoulder, her fingernails digging in, earning a sultry smile from him. She let her head fall back as he lavished her throat and chest with soft kisses and warm swipes of his tongue.

Callan glided his hands down her back, cupping her ass and lifting her into his arms. She wrapped her legs around his waist, relishing the feeling of his firm chest against the smooth softness of her own. Carrying her to the bed, he laid her on top of the bedsheets then leaned over her, untying the sash at her waist. He took his time laying the robe open around her as if he were unwrapping a gift.

Callan knelt between her legs, sitting back on his heels. His eyes were shadowed through half-mast lids as they traveled along the curves of her naked body. One hand went to his lap, gripping the obvious swell barely contained behind his breeches. Nova shuddered. She had bared her heart to him, and now she lay before him, her body completely bare as well.

Callan smiled faintly, though the intensity of his gaze never wavered. He dropped his hands, curling his fingers around her ankles. "I've imagined you in my bed so often, Nova. Now that I have you here, I can't decide. Should I take my time exploring every exquisite bit of you with my tongue?" His eyes fell, lingering on her cunt, already wet with her desire. He swallowed, his throat bobbing, before he pulled his gaze away to meet hers again, his voice rough when he continued. "Or should I bury myself inside you, which we both know is where I belong?"

Nova was kindling ignited by flame. She sat up, reaching for his waist-band. Callan caught her hands and guided her back down onto the bed, clicking his tongue at her.

His tongue.

Nova's brows pinched as her breath quickened. How was it possible his tongue already had her on the edge when he'd used it for nothing but words?

A soft whimper escaped her. "Please, Callan."

"No need to rush," he crooned, releasing her wrists and lowering himself to kneel at the foot of the bed.

His sturdy hands ran up the length of her soft thighs, taking hold of her hips and pulling her toward him until her ass was flush with the edge of the mattress. The satin sheets bunched up beneath the small of her back. Nova rose on her elbows, their eyes meeting across the pale canvas of her body.

His eyes remained locked on hers as he cradled her foot in his hand. He placed a soft kiss on the arch before nipping at the sensitive skin. Nova inhaled sharply, her head falling back as a bolt of pleasure raced up the length of her leg to her cunt. Her entire body trembled beneath Callan's lips as he kissed and nipped a painfully slow path from her foot to her ankle, along her calf, and up to her knee. As his mouth roamed higher, she clutched at the sheets at her sides, the anticipation of what awaited her nearly tearing her apart.

"The scent of you," he murmured, his lips ghosting along her inner thigh. "It's been driving me mad since the night we met."

Gods, he was going to kill her. Nova was certain this teasing approach of his would be the end of her. The growing ache inside her was nearly unbearable.

"I've pictured this moment so many times. I wonder if you taste as sweet as I've imagined."

Callan slid his arms under her hips, crossing his forearms over her lower abdomen and pinning her in place. He dipped his head, kissing her clit as eagerly as he'd kissed her mouth minutes before. Nova moaned, collapsing back onto the bed as Callan feasted greedily between her legs. He groaned as he savored her, his tongue alternating between long, slow licks and gentle tugs on the sensitive spot.

Propping herself up on one elbow, Nova wound her fingers into his dark hair, still damp from his bath. She rocked her hips, panting as Callan drew out her pleasure, brilliant stars dancing at the edges of her vision as she watched him. He followed her lead and increased his pace, removing one arm from beneath her hip and easing a finger inside her. Nova cried out and pressed herself against his mouth. His responding growl vibrated against her cunt. He added a second finger, plunging in and drawing out. Laying his other hand on her lower abdomen, he pressed down firmly. Fingers curling, he rubbed against a needy spot deep inside her while his tongue danced over her swollen clit.

She wanted to keep her eyes on him, to watch what he was doing to her, but they clamped shut as each exhale that passed her lips carried a wild moan. Nova's body tensed as her climax built low in her belly, winding tighter and tighter until it snapped. She came apart on his tongue with his name on her lips. Callan trailed his fingers lightly over her stomach, gliding his tongue between her legs until the tiny shudders of her release ceased.

Nova eyed Callan hungrily as he stood, loosening his laces and shoving his breeches to the floor. He rose to his full height, revealing his impressive cock, hard and ready for her, angled up toward his muscular stomach. A giddy rush sent her head swimming, knowing she had that effect on him. That his desire for her was that strong.

Though she'd lain with another before, Nova had never seen a male fully undressed. Her gaze roamed over his body. His broad shoulders and firm chest. His solid abdomen and the trail of dark curls leading down to his perfect cock. For a moment, she was stunned by the beauty and power of his form. Her eyes dropped, catching briefly on the image of a dagger inked in black on his right thigh. Callan leaned forward, bracing his arms on the mattress, and Nova snapped to attention, scooting backward as he prowled along the bed toward her. He brought his fingers to his lips and drew them into his mouth, savoring her taste before lowering himself over her.

"You're even sweeter than I imagined." He kissed her deeply, his tongue stroking hers, and she tasted herself on him.

Callan knelt between her parted legs again, sitting back on his heels and firmly gripping the base of his cock with one hand. Slowly, he pumped the hard length of it while she watched. She bit her lip, aching with the need to be filled by him. Lowering himself over her again, he caged her in with a muscled arm braced on either side of her head. He pressed his face into her neck, breathing deeply as he placed a kiss over the thundering pulse at her throat. His cock brushed against her clit, and she swallowed a moan. Callan pulled back, flecks of gold shining in his dark eyes.

"Do you want me, Nova?" Though his voice was rough, commanding, the vulnerability in his question was a naked thing. She nodded jerkily, her mouth gone dry.

"Tell me," he urged. "I need to hear you say you want me."

"I want you. Only you. Please, Callan." Her voice was little more than a whimper. A plea for him to end her suffering.

Callan groaned, hooking one of her legs over his hip. He entered her then, but not all at once. He drew himself out and eased in again, a bit deeper the second time. Nova wanted all of him. The way he was giving himself to her by degrees was akin to torture.

A growl passed her lips, a frustrated sound she'd never heard herself make before. Callan entered her fully then in one powerful thrust. He stayed motionless for an instant, and she thought she might come apart again simply from the intimacy of it all, how perfectly their bodies fit together.

"Fucking perfect," he whispered, as if he'd read her mind.

Resting his forehead against hers, he began to move inside her, slow and measured. When she gasped, Callan captured her mouth with his own, cutting off the sound with a swipe of his tongue.

"Gods, I'm selfish." His dry laugh danced across her lips. "I want every sweet sound you make for myself."

"They're yours."

Her words seemed to ignite something primal within him, and he began to move with abandon. Nova crossed her ankles behind his hips, pulling him into her and meeting every thrust.

"You're so beautiful." His voice was an awe-filled rasp. "I've dreamt of taking you like this. Dreamt of your pretty cunt . . ." His words trailed off into a moan trapped low in his throat. The sounds of his pleasure inflamed her.

The exquisite feeling of him so deep inside her sent Nova plummeting over the edge, and she cried out his name, her body tightening around his cock. Callan thrusted once more, burying himself within her and finding his release with a moan that rumbled against her chest.

As they lay there, bodies still joined, Nova sifted dreamily through all the moments she had spent with him since the rainy night he appeared on her doorstep. Moments when he'd supported her, standing beside her though she'd grown accustomed to standing alone. Moments he'd made her feel safe and accepted in a world that told her she didn't belong.

Their time together had been like the slow turning of a key, each moment shared allowing another tumbler to fall into place. Now, the lock had been opened. Her heart exposed. She knew it belonged entirely to him.

FORTY-ONE

TIME CEASED TO HAVE meaning.

Callan didn't know how long he'd been lying beside Nova on the bed; it could have been seconds, or perhaps hours. He slid off the mattress and entered the bathing chamber. Returning with a soft, wet cloth, he knelt before her again. Gently parting her knees, he ran the warm towel over her upper thighs and between her legs. She moaned appreciatively, smiling with her eyes closed. The sight of her open to him sparked his arousal, and he fought the urge to pull her close. To have her again that very moment. Releasing a slow breath, he brought her knees back together.

"Lay with me." Nova tugged on his forearm and pulled him down onto the soft sheets beside her.

Callan rolled onto his back and tucked one hand behind his head, resting the other on his chest. Perhaps he'd died on that soldier's blade, and this was his eternal paradise in the After Realm. He ran his fingers over the newly formed scar tissue on his side before tracing them along the soft arc of Nova's hip.

He grinned.

No. He wasn't dead.

Nova turned onto her side to face him, propping herself up on one arm. She touched the solid black marking on his wrist, then moved lower, her delicate fingers dancing along his right hip to the dagger inked on his thigh. His muscles tightened in response.

"Show me the one on your back," she ordered playfully.

Callan grunted as he pushed himself up into a sitting position, resting his forearms on his bent knees. Nova shifted to kneel behind him, examining the ornate design of a sword running diagonally from his right shoulder along the length of his back, the point ending at his left hip, just above the curve of his ass.

"It's beautiful," she said softly, tracing the black lines. "Are these markings part of your vow to Nivali?"

"The sword and dagger ensure I'll always have my weapons, even in death." He turned his face toward her. "A charming custom."

She wrapped her arms around his neck, as if needing confirmation that he was not a figment of her imagination, but warm and alive. He closed his eyes, appreciating the softness of her breasts and stomach pressed firmly against his back. He loved that she was soft in all the places he was hard. His cock stirred at the thought.

"The warriors of Nivali certainly take combat seriously." Nova nuzzled against his neck, just below his ear, and breathed deeply. "You always smell so delicious, like the air before a snowfall."

"I love the scent of you, too," he said, shifting onto his hands and knees and crawling toward her, guiding her down onto her back. Lowering himself onto her once again, he rested his hips between her warm thighs. Starting at her shoulder, he planted a trail of slow kisses along her collarbone and up the side of her neck, nipping lightly at her throat. "It led me right to you."

"And what do I smell like?" Nova asked as he peppered kisses along her jaw, making his way toward the waiting softness of her lips.

"Sweet, like vanilla, mixed with something darker. Something smoky. It's intoxicating."

She smiled before their lips met in a kiss, tongues exploring one another curiously. Callan broke away, rolling onto his side and drawing her to him, so their bodies lay nested with his chest at her back. Her body had changed somewhat since they'd been separated, the muscles of her arms and back firmer and more defined.

"What are you thinking about?" she asked.

"Just admiring your figure." He pulled her tight against him.

"I've been training for four hours a day with Lucan." She stretched out her arm and twisted it, inspecting the toned muscles of her forearm and bicep.

"He's quite a character," Callan said. "We became friends of sorts while we tracked you."

"Did he tell you he thought I was an assassin at first? Once our training began, I think he quickly realized how wrong he'd been." Nova chuckled, and Callan laughed along with her.

"The look on his face the first time I landed a solid punch to his jaw . . ." She broke into a fit of laughter. "The shock. And . . . outrage."

She squeezed her eyes shut, struggling to catch her breath. Callan himself didn't dare breathe, afraid to break whatever spell had her showing emotion so freely. He'd never seen her so expressive, apart from the anger and sorrow she'd unleashed outside the Temple of Illora. Callan watched her quietly, smiling to himself and wondering what he could possibly have done to deserve her. Nova regained her composure after a moment.

"When I bested him with a sword for the first time, he was proud." She swiped at a tear with the back of her hand. "He'd never say it, of course. But I knew."

Callan's chest swelled with gratitude for the odd commander who'd taken Nova under his wing and become a friend to her. He traced Nova's markings—the pearly scars stretching from the top of her left shoulder down to the middle of her back. The markings of a warrior.

"These remind me of the moment I first felt connected to you," he murmured. Nova perked up, turning her head so her ear lay close to his mouth. "I found you in the clearing beneath the lycane, and I started toward you. But you cried out, and the sound froze me in place. You were so powerful, so beautiful, in that moment. I can't explain what happened to me. It was as if I'd been trapped beneath a sheet of ice. In that instant, you shattered the ice, and I began to breathe again." He placed a light kiss over her scars and watched her skin prickle in response.

He brushed his lips against the back of her neck. "Thorn asked if I'm bonded to you."

She shifted on the bed, twisting to face him.

"What does it mean to be bonded?" she asked, one eyebrow raised.

Callan took a lock of her hair between his thumb and forefinger.

"It's like being two parts of one whole. Fated to find each other, and destined to be together."

"What, like a soulmate?"

"Is that what they call it in the Human Realm?"

"If you are bonded to me, does that mean you have no choice but to be with me?"

"Of course I have a choice. As do you." He tucked her hair neatly behind her ear. "Common Fae still honor the bond, but for nobles, bonding has been out of fashion for thousands of years. But I believe my heart and my body will always call out to you. Will always be connected to you. And I will choose you every day for the rest of my life. I can't imagine denying what I feel for you. I don't believe such a thing would even be possible."

A smile bloomed on her face, and he reached over, brushing away a tear as it slid down her cheek.

"I choose you, too," she whispered. "I was a fool to deny this. To deny us."

"The gods have never favored me, Nova, but if they've decided to make you mine, I'll travel the Realm and make an offering to each one," he said, stroking her bottom lip with his thumb.

Nova kissed him softly, then pushed him down onto his back and straddled his thighs. His cock rested a breath away from her core. Callan shot a glance at the sacred space between her legs, pink and wet, nestled below a patch of soft black curls. His cock stirred, instantly hardening against her inner thigh. He growled low in his throat and reached out to grasp her hips, but she swatted his hands away, a playful smile tugging at the corners of her mouth.

"You took your time with me, my love," she teased. "You can hardly deny me a chance to return the favor."

She dragged her hands down his chest at a leisurely pace, alternating between the soft pads of her fingers and the scratch of her nails. Callan's back arched when, finally, her fingers curled around the base of his cock. Moving her hand up and down, she pumped him slowly with a firm grip as she had watched him do before. Her mouth hung open slightly as she kept her eyes trained on him, intently observing his every reaction to her touch, as if pleasing him was a skill she intended to master.

When she brushed her thumb over the glistening tip, he bucked his hips beneath her, inhaling sharply through his teeth. He spoke her name aloud, his voice choked and pleading. Nova shushed him before leaning forward and kissing him deeply.

Repositioning herself over him, she rocked her hips so his cock slid against the waiting warmth between her legs. She teased him mercilessly, pulling away each time he tried to enter her. Taking his hands in hers, she kissed and nipped at the tips of his fingers before placing them on her breasts. She threw her head back as he massaged them, moaning softly before her gaze connected with his once again.

"I've touched myself with you in my thoughts, guiding my hands, but nothing compares to this."

Callan gritted his teeth at her admission, resisting the urge to roll her over and pin her beneath him. To claim her as his own. She hovered over him for an instant. Just when he thought he couldn't withstand another second of being so close to her but not inside her, she lowered herself onto him, taking him fully.

Nova let out a soft gasp, and her eyes fell shut as she began riding him in earnest. Her hands covered his on her chest, cupping and kneading her breasts along with him. Callan couldn't tear his gaze away as she rose and fell above him, taking his cock deep into her warm cunt. He was so godsdamn close to her. As close as two bodies could be. And still he craved more. In truth, he knew very little about her; he hungered to know everything.

Nova's movements intensified, and she moaned softly as a pale glow shone beneath the surface of her milky skin. Callan's own climax built as he watched her in complete awe, afraid to blink. Nova cried out as she took him fully a final time and ground against him. The sound, a wild whimper, ignited something primal in Callan. He grasped her hips then, thrusting but finding he was as deep as he could go, and spilled himself inside her.

A moment later, Nova stretched out beside him on the bed, her head resting on his shoulder and an arm thrown over his chest. The room was silent except for their labored breaths. As Callan lay there with the length of her body pressed against his, he prayed to the gods—the same ones who had taken nearly everything from him—that he wouldn't wake and find it had all been a wonderful dream.

FORTY-TWO

BY THE SECOND DAY following their return from the northern shore, there was little more than a slight twinge in Callan's side when he moved. Other than an itchy sensation around the newly formed scar, he felt more or less normal. Eir, the healer, had practically chased Nova from his room when she discovered them in bed together, limbs tangled. She'd dealt Callan a severe tongue-lashing for ignoring her strict orders to rest.

It was worth it.

After breakfast, Callan found himself in the Noble Lord's study again, the intimate space crowded with Nox seated behind his desk and Nova and Lucan occupying the twin leather armchairs across from him. Callan tucked himself away across the room, leaning an elbow on the mantel and wondering why every room seemed to be outfitted with a fireplace despite Silvergard's mild climate.

Nova had allowed her uncle to peer into her mind to hear for himself every word General Idrian had spoken to her. Callan was glad he would never hear the general's words firsthand. The flames of his anger had been sufficiently fanned by the brief synopsis Nova had shared with him. The general was a coward, eager to sacrifice Nova's life to fulfill his own selfish desires.

"Our scouts have returned," Lucan reported. "Idrian remains near Schadwen Mountain. A small number of reinforcements have arrived there. The troops have set up an encampment beside the Gloaming Sea."

"How many reinforcements?" Callan asked, looking up from the needless fire.

"Roughly fifty additional soldiers," Lucan answered, twisting in his chair to face him.

"More will follow," Nova said. "My father may only want me, but Idrian wants all of Silvergard. If he succeeds in taking the throne, he won't stop at our borders. Nivali and Sonnend will be next."

"I believe we're all in agreement: There is no scenario in which Idrian can be left unchecked," Nox said, steepling his fingers before his face, eyes narrowed as he stared off into the middle distance. "As I see it, we have no choice but to head to the Gloaming Sea and put down this rebellion."

"I saw many more soldiers posted around the Estate today." Callan leaned his back against the wall, crossing his arms over his chest. "How many have arrived to protect the capital?"

Lucan launched into a further report. "Two hundred troops arrived yesterday from the Shadowcrest District. We've placed them throughout the Estate and the surrounding city. Patrols are riding out in shifts to monitor the coast to the west and the dunes to the north, east, and south."

"More are coming," Nox added. "Unfortunately, with such a credible threat against the throne, it will be at least a week before we can afford to spare any forces to travel north."

"We don't have a week," Nova insisted. "Idrian knows he's lost the element of surprise. He knows his only option is to amass whatever forces he can cobble together and strike as soon as possible. Before we're able to form a strong defense or launch an attack of our own."

The room fell silent for a moment, the three males nodding in agreement with Nova's assessment.

"Maybe we can remove Idrian as a threat without launching a full-scale attack," Lucan suggested. "If we move quickly with the right crew, we could have this rebellion wiped out before it has a chance to grow legs."

"It's a shame the other territories would never risk sending forces into Silvergard," Nox said, smiling faintly at his niece. "Now would be an excellent time to have friends."

Callan considered Nox's words for a moment before making a low grunt of agreement and heading for the door.

"You may be onto something," he said to the Noble Lord. "Give me a few hours to see what I can do."

Several hours later, Callan paced back and forth in the sitting area of the library, his eyes flicking to the door roughly once every minute. Two letters had traveled south on the wings of messenger owls, soaring on strong tailwinds. He hadn't told the others who he'd summoned in case they didn't show.

Nova sat on the sofa, a book balanced in her hands, though he hadn't seen her turn a page in some time. Lucan lounged beside her—asleep, judging from the occasional wheezing coming from his general direction. Nox's hand skimmed over a piece of white parchment, a stub of charcoal scratching softly as he sketched the sleeping commander. Despite his nerves, Callan smiled at the domestic scene.

Abandoning the path he was slowly wearing through the rug, he stood beside Nova and laid his hand on her shoulder, squeezing gently. She tilted her head, briefly laying her cheek against his fingers, before looking up at him with a distracted smile. He knew her apprehension rivaled his own; she was simply accustomed to doing her pacing in her mind.

The heavy door to the library suddenly swung open, the noise startling them all. Lucan woke with a snarl and sprang to his feet. They all turned sharply to face the entryway, and Callan grinned at the familiar faces of his cousins.

Nova's mouth fell open as Fawn entered the library with her brown eyes wide and trained on the enormous shelves reaching all the way to the ceiling. Evander stopped just inside the doorway, suspiciously scanning the great room.

"My gods, this place is incredible." Fawn's gaze found Nova, who wasted no time racing over and pulling her friend into an embrace.

Nova took a step back and gave Fawn a once-over, her eyes catching on the razor-sharp throwing knives strapped to her friend, five on each thigh.

"Close your mouth, Nova," Fawn scolded playfully. "I'm two hundred and fifty years old. Surely, you didn't think I'd spent *every* day of my life with my nose buried in a book."

Beaming, Nova introduced Fawn to Nox and Lucan. Before the introductions were even finished, Fawn pushed past the males to stand before Nova's portrait, which leaned against the wall waiting to be hung.

"This piece is stunning."

"It's my most recent work," Nox said proudly.

"*You* painted it?" Fawn asked. "Did you paint all of these, or are you a curator? I saw several sculptures on the way in. Are you a sculptor as well?"

Nox shot a sideways look at Nova, eyes seemingly saying, *Help me.* She shrugged in apology and returned to Callan's side. Evander sauntered over to where she and Callan stood together, hands shoved in his pockets. He carried a quiver of arrows across his back and his longbow hooked over one shoulder.

"I didn't expect you so soon," Callan said, clapping his cousin on the back.

"Someone owed Fawn a favor. She bullied the poor bastard into conjuring a portal."

"Why did no one tell me Fawn has weapons training?" Nova asked.

"Don't be fooled. The knives are more of a parlor trick," Callan said, his hand roaming from the base of her neck to her lower back. "Fawn is the most powerful fire wielder I've ever known."

Nova glanced at Evander, expecting him to refute Callan's assessment of his sister's skills, but he was busy studying them.

"So . . . the two of you are fu—"

"Yes," Callan interrupted before his cousin could say something crass. He wrapped his arm around Nova's waist. "We're together."

Her heart fluttered at the word.

"About time," Lucan chimed in. Inserting himself into the conversation, he fixed Evander with an appraising stare. "You'd have to be a complete idiot to miss the way these two have been pining for one another."

Evander smirked and clasped his hands behind his back.

"And how did you know?" Nova asked Lucan.

"Wolves have a nose for these things." He shrugged, shooting Callan a sly look.

Nova raised an eyebrow at Callan, but he only shook his head.

Just then, a servant entered the library, announcing the arrival of additional visitors. As the servant stepped aside, Arik strode through the door. A dozen Nivalian warriors, a mix of males and females, filed in behind him. Each one stood as tall and solid as a stone column. All were outfitted with thick brown leather armor, some carrying swords, others with axes hanging from their belts. Callan embraced his oldest friend.

Nova would never understand how Callan could doubt his own valor and the devotion his folk felt toward him. These warriors had crossed into what was considered enemy territory without hesitation, simply because he'd called for their aid.

Introductions were made all around, the usually silent library alive with voices.

"Excuse me!" Fawn called out, clapping her hands loudly. "I believe time is of the essence. Perhaps Cal should explain why he's summoned us all here with such urgency."

The room quieted with everyone listening intently and occasionally asking questions as Callan explained their predicament. Lucan, Nox, and Nova interjected from time to time with additional information. Once everyone had been briefed on the growing threat to not only Silvergard but all the territories of Aemoria, Callan laid out the strategy the four of them had devised earlier.

With only fifty or so soldiers encamped along the Gloaming Sea, a small group of well-trained warriors could conceivably take the enemy by surprise and corner them with their backs against the water.

Evander would lead a small group of Silvergardian archers to higher ground and mount an attack from above with Schadwen Mountain providing a suitable vantage point. The Nivalian warriors, led by Arik and Lucan, would surround the encampment and engage in hand-to-hand combat with the enemy soldiers on the ground. Fawn would incinerate any stockpiled weapons and supplies stored at the camp, while Nova and Callan located and dealt with General Idrian.

"I realize this isn't your fight," Nox said. "The Lunar Court has likely given you all far more reason to abandon it than to risk your lives in defense of it. But the simple fact is, we need your help."

"We can't do this alone," Nova added.

"I wish we had more time to prepare, but every passing hour is an opportunity for the general to gather more support for his cause." Callan paused to look over the faces of those gathered. "Are you with us?"

It was Arik who spoke first. "Until my last breath, my friend." He placed his fist over his heart in salute. The rest of the warriors did the same.

"Anything for the Realm," Fawn said, wrapping an arm around Nova's neck.

Guilt churned in the pit of Nova's stomach. They had decided to omit the detail about her being Omen's daughter, only sharing that she had been abducted by Idrian to be used as leverage against Nox, leaving the others to draw their own conclusions.

All eyes wandered to Evander lounging casually on the sofa, one ankle resting atop his opposite knee.

"I can hardly stay behind since my little sister has agreed to fight," he sighed. "Besides, I'd never let the rest of you have all the fun."

Cheers erupted, and everyone rose to their feet as Callan and Lucan rattled off instructions for last-minute preparations before their swift departure. Nox took Nova by the hand and led her away from the others and into his study, closing the door behind them.

"I mean no disrespect by what I'm about to say," he began, and she steeled herself. "But I would prefer that you stay behind."

"You know I can't."

"Nova, I can't bear the thought of you putting yourself in harm's way. Not when we just got you back. You could go somewhere safe until the threat has been dealt with," he said, laying his hands on her shoulders. "The Temple of Illora, perhaps."

Her mother had said Omen would never find her hidden behind the powerful magic that guarded the temple. But Nova had told her mother she was through hiding, and she meant it.

"These are my people, too. Every one of them under threat of death or being pressed into an existence they would never choose. I have to fight for them."

"If I can't persuade you to remain here, will you at least promise me you'll stay out of the fight?"

"I'm sorry. I can't," she said, fists clenched at her sides. "Idrian deceived me. I trusted him, and he betrayed that trust. He deserves to pay for what he did to me. For what he plans to do to our people. I intend to be the one to make him pay."

Perhaps her uncle sensed the rage crackling just beneath the surface of her calm exterior, because he relented without further discussion.

"I understand," he said, gathering her in a firm embrace and planting a kiss on her temple. "Just promise you'll come back to us."

"I promise," Nova said, believing with every fiber of her being that she would.

It was midday by the time their party reconvened in the black stone courtyard in front of the Estate. The unforgiving sun beat down from directly above. Horses snorted and pawed idly at the ground as their riders tightened saddle straps and readied themselves for the journey ahead. Nova surveyed the assortment of steeds spread out around the courtyard: snowy-white coats from Nivali and silvery-gray from Silvergard. Her eyes settled on one horse, seemingly out of place. A familiar mare with a charcoal-gray coat. Nova jogged over to Shade and ran a hand along her horse's neck as the animal snorted a greeting.

Arik's voice came from behind her. "I thought you might like to have your own horse with you."

"It was very kind of you to bring her," Nova said, dipping her head in a quick bow of appreciation.

"It's the least I could do after you saved Callan's life. I'm in your debt." He laid his hand over his heart and tipped his head to her before heading off into the crowd.

Several of the others began mounting up around her; it was nearly time to leave.

Nova took a quick inventory. Isla had braided her hair for her, coiling it into a bun and pinning it at the back of her head. She wore full Silvergardian fighting attire of black leather: fitted breeches and a jacket, a thick chest plate, and pauldrons dotted with metal studs. The bracers strapped to her wrists extended to just below her elbows.

She flexed her fingers inside her black leather gloves and patted each of her weapons—her Nivalian sword at her hip and her curved Silvergardian dagger at her thigh. Lowering herself to one knee on the hot black stone, she tightened the straps of her boots that hit midway up her calf.

The pommel of the dagger she'd brought from the Human Realm barely peeked above the top of the boot that concealed it. The blade seemed to have lost its luster, as any human-made item might when held up against even the most mundane Fae-made objects, all of which were seemingly imbued with otherworldly power. She'd nearly left it behind, but something compelled her to pick it up when she'd finished dressing.

She recalled how Anson had once found her playing with the weapon, having taken it from the decorative box in his chamber.

Careful with that blade, girl.

He had chuckled, scolding her playfully as he took it from her and showed her how to hold it properly.

Unless you're eager to see your insides on the outside.

A large pair of boots appeared before her, and she squinted up to see Callan silhouetted against the bright sky. He extended a hand to her. Taking it, she hoisted herself to her feet.

"Are you ready?" he asked, fiddling with the buckle of her sword belt.

"As ready as I'll ever be," she said, wrapping her arms around his neck and kissing him deeply. "I love you," she whispered, when she finally managed to pull herself away.

It was impossible to know what might come to pass, and she intended to never miss an opportunity to tell Callan how she felt.

"I'll love you always."

A few moments later, the entire party stood ready to depart. Nova nudged Shade into a canter, riding out of the courtyard with the others heading north, little more than half a day of hard riding between her and her vengeance.

FORTY-THREE

THE ARID AIR TURNED misty and cool as they reached the northern coast, the sun hanging low in the sky like a ripe fruit. Callan and Lucan led the patchwork band of riders, as varied in appearance as their horses, behind the large rocky outcrop that had shielded their position only days before.

The archers had ridden two to a horse. Even so, more than two dozen weary animals needed to be fed and watered. Nova slid down from the saddle and guided Shade by the bridle to a spring bubbling out of the ground a short distance away, its peaceful murmuring leading her to it. She crouched at the edge of the reflective pool as her horse drank greedily beside her.

Nova lowered the kerchief covering the bottom half of her face and eyed her reflection on the mirrorlike surface of the water. The face peering out at her was at once familiar and unrecognizable: pale eyes shadowed with the rage it took all her energy to mask. She dipped her hands into the pool, bringing the cool liquid to her lips and swallowing several mouthfuls before rubbing the excess over her sweat-covered forehead smudged with dust. Tiny waves rippled through her reflection, warping her features.

She rejoined the others moments later, everyone spread out, sitting on rocks and sharpening weapons or leaning back against the leafless desert trees. Scanning the area for Callan, her eyes met the golden amber of Lucan's instead. An almost imperceptible lift of his brows told her Callan was on top of the rock. In the late-afternoon light, she climbed to the slanted summit, carefully choosing where to step, and crawled silently to crouch at his side. He lay flat, peering through a spyglass.

For an instant, he glanced away from the viewfinder, acknowledging her with a friendly, albeit distracted, grunt. With her naked eye, she could barely make out the mouth of the cave that had been her prison and nearly her tomb. Callan's spyglass was pointed to an area farther east, beyond the foot of the mountain, where the land sloped gradually out of view toward the sea.

"We've sent two of the Silvergardian archers as scouts to assess the situation," he said quietly, returning to the viewfinder. "They should return within the hour with a report."

Nova smiled at this Callan and his gruff demeanor, so different from the gentleness he had always shown her. It appeared she wasn't the only one who wore a mask from time to time. Callan retracted the spyglass and slid it back into the folds of his cloak.

He looked at her briefly, catching her smile before she could tuck it away.

"What?" he asked, a bit bashful. "Sorry. I have to stay focused when I'm on a mission like this. Cut myself off from my emotions. Avoid distractions."

"I understand," she said, nodding. "Sometimes setting emotions aside is the surest way to survive."

Nova stretched out flat on her stomach, arms crossed in front of her with her chin resting on the back of her hand.

"You should rest," he whispered, tucking a loose strand of hair behind her ear. "I'll be right here keeping watch."

Nova breathed deeply and tilted her head to rest in the crook of her elbow. Callan's lips brushed against her cheek, and she soon drifted off to sleep.

A short while later, Nova awoke to Callan's firm hand on her shoulder. She dashed the sleep from her eyes and followed him down the rock face. The archers had returned from their scouting mission, and everyone formed a circle around them.

"Much has changed since the last scouts' report," the female archer called Zara began, her dark curls blowing in the breeze. "Three ships sit anchored offshore. We estimate the vessels carried an additional two hundred soldiers, which are now encamped just beyond the mountain's edge."

"Well, fuck," Lucan said matter-of-factly, scratching his scalp above his ear and looking at Callan. In fact, Nova realized, everyone was looking at Callan.

"What'll it be, Your Grace?" Arik asked. "Would you have us return to the capital and wait for reinforcements?"

Callan took a few slow steps in one direction before turning and pacing back in the other. Nova knew his mind was whirring, evaluating the potential risks posed by continuing with their original plan in light of this new information. He stopped pacing after a moment and turned to face the group gathered before him.

"No." He shook his head, his mouth a grim line. "There isn't time. I believe we can still make our original plan work . . . more or less."

Callan looked to Lucan, who silently made his own evaluation before nodding his agreement.

"Callan's right," Lucan said. "If we don't settle this now, those soldiers will be on those ships, sailing down the coast toward the Estate within a day. The risk to the throne and the civilians in the capital is too great. We have to end this."

"So, what's the plan, Cal?" Fawn asked.

Callan cleared his throat. He seemed to have only just registered the weight of everyone's eyes on him.

"The entire camp will be waking soon. Though they'll be awake, we can still catch them off guard, using the darkness to our advantage while they eat and prepare for their duties.

"Evander will lead the archers onto the ridge where Zara surveyed the encampment, setting up a covert line. Arik, you'll lead your team to surround the camp on foot. Between the archers and your blades, we'll dispatch as many sentries posted around the perimeter as we can. Quickly. Quietly. Efficiently.

"Lucan and Fawn will head for the shoreline. Once we've removed the sentries guarding the camp, we'll need a diversion." Callan turned to Fawn. "Do you think you can manage something?"

She snapped her fingers, a ball of flame igniting in the palm of her hand for an instant before she made a fist, snuffing it out.

"Oh, I can manage."

"Good. Once Fawn creates a distraction, the camp will likely fall into disorder. We'll use the confusion to our advantage as well, taking soldiers by surprise as we sweep through the camp toward the general's tent. As for the general . . ." Callan glanced around at the group, avoiding Nova's eyes. "Leave him to me. We move out once we hear the horns rousing the soldiers."

Callan turned and strode off toward the spring without a word to Nova. The others jumped into action, rushing to prepare for the orders they'd been given. Nova's cheeks burned as she pursued Callan. Lucan tried to intercept her but stepped out of her path, holding his hands up submissively, when he registered the fury written plainly on her face.

It was quiet in the fading light. The only noise was the babbling of the spring and Callan splashing water over his face. He looked up from where he crouched at the water's edge when Nova's boots halted beside him.

"What was that?" she asked, trying, and mostly failing, to keep her voice level.

Callan rose to his feet. He raked his damp fingers through the length of his dark hair and secured it at the back of his head.

"What was what?"

"Don't be coy, Callan," she said, her anger an animal tugging at its tether. "Surely you realize you gave everyone a part to play in this mission except me."

His mouth was drawn, the lines and hollows of his face accentuated by shadow in the low light. The muscles in his cheeks fluttered as he clenched and unclenched his jaw.

"I can't risk it," he said finally. "I can't risk you."

"So, I'm expected to do what, exactly? Mind the horses?" She scoffed. "You included me in the plan before."

"When I thought fifty soldiers stood between us and General Idrian—not two hundred and fifty." He, too, was struggling to keep his voice even.

"What's the difference? If our plan works, the archers and Arik's warriors will take out the sentries, Fawn's diversion will send the rest of the soldiers scrambling, and we'll be picking them off, one by one, on our way to Idrian."

He didn't respond, turning his face away from her. She took a step closer. Their bodies were practically touching.

"You don't think I can do it," she murmured, the realization striking her like a slap in the face. "Look at me, Callan."

His eyes were apologetic when he finally faced her.

"That's not true." His fingers closed gently around her biceps. "But these are trained killers, Nova. Their only aim in life is the complete destruction of their enemies. A couple of months ago, you'd never even held a sword, let alone killed anyone."

Nova stepped out of his loose grip, flexing her hands and bringing her arms to rest at her sides. She blinked once, banishing the tears gathering behind her eyes, her features melting into a blank expression.

"I'm not the fragile female you found in Timberfell."

"I know. I know you're not." Callan's words spilled out of him as he tried to take her hands in his. "But I cannot bear it. What if I can't protect you like I couldn't protect my parents?"

"You must stop blaming yourself, Callan. You would have been no match for Omen's dark magic."

"Then at least I could have died beside them!" His voice broke, the agony in it cutting through her rage.

He was quiet for a moment before he spoke again.

"Somehow, I've managed to live this long without them. I used to think it was a cruel punishment from the gods, forcing me to go on, forever carrying the burden of my shame. Now, I believe every year—every godsdamned second—I spent living in pain was so I could find you. I wasn't truly living until I met you. If anything were to happen . . ." He paused and shook his head ruefully, throat bobbing. "I don't think I could survive it."

Nova froze, caught up in the wake of his declaration, momentarily losing sight of her anger.

"Nothing is going to happen to me," she said, finding a shred of indignation to latch onto.

"Why are you fighting me?" he asked, his voice desperate. "Why won't you let me protect you?"

"I don't need your protection. I've taken two lives in as many days—one practically with my bare hands—protecting myself. You have no idea what I'm capable of."

Nova turned away from him, walking back to where the others were gathered, waiting.

"I'm only trying to help you," he called out after her, sounding defeated.

"I don't want your help, Callan," she said flatly, throwing him a look over her shoulder. "I want your respect."

Callan tilted his head back, lifted his eyes to the sky, and ran his hands roughly over his face.

"Fuck." The curse left his lips so quietly, only the first stars winking against the deepening purple backdrop heard him.

He *knew* Nova. Knew she'd spent her life convincing herself and everyone else that she didn't need anyone. Now he'd acted as if he saw her not as an equal but as a charge, defenseless without him to shield her. It wasn't how he saw her. She was a fighter. A warrior. He'd seen it when she defeated the lycane. He'd told her as much when they were standing on the rampart overlooking the autumn forest in Pyralis and he offered to train her.

But he couldn't ease the sinking feeling in his gut. Couldn't silence the bond telling him he would die without her. Couldn't allow himself to contemplate a world without her in it. Callan had never realized how much love and fear went hand in hand. And now the fear of acknowledging his love for her had been replaced by the all-consuming fear of losing what was most precious to him.

Callan tugged on his gloves once again and flexed his hands, breathing deeply before striding back across the sand. There was no time to waste. Once the deed was done, once Idrian was dead, he would do everything in his power to earn Nova's forgiveness. But first, he needed to focus on leading the others into battle.

When he reached the base of the massive rock, Nova was nowhere in sight. Their connection, passing between them like an invisible thread on a loom, had only intensified since their bodies had joined. Through it, he sensed her presence on the summit above.

The archers stood at the ready behind Evander, outfitted with longbows and full quivers. Arik's force of warriors waited in formation behind him, their hair braided or tied back, cloaks removed for ease of movement. Fawn stood nearby, shifting from foot to foot, practically humming with eager energy, while Lucan leaned casually against a boulder beside her.

Callan threw off his own cloak and rolled his neck and shoulders, joints popping faintly as they loosened in preparation for the fight to come. He looked around and nodded once, the motion a silent order to move out. Lucan caught up to him as they passed swiftly over the sand toward the foot of the mountain.

"Looks like you stepped in shit," the commander teased, keeping pace with Callan's determined strides.

Callan said nothing but shot his new friend a look that plainly said, *Back off.*

"If you live, perhaps she'll be so relieved she'll forget whatever you did to piss her off so badly." Lucan slapped him on the back and jogged ahead to join up with Fawn.

Callan focused on his breathing, setting aside his emotions and shifting his attention to the hundreds of soldiers rising from their cots in the enemy encampment ahead.

FORTY-FOUR

Nova seethed as she watched the others slipping silently across the sand. Understanding Callan's instinct to protect her did little to ease the sting of knowing he'd been partially right. True, she was no warrior. But she was no defenseless maiden, either. Callan hadn't witnessed the hours she'd spent in the sparring ring, improving with each passing day. He didn't know how quick she had become, how comfortable with a blade.

Roughly half an hour had passed when Nova saw a flicker of movement high on the mountain, there and gone in a blink. She only saw it because she knew Evander and the archers would be reaching the ridge overlooking the encampment. They'd be settling into position soon, arrows trained on the sentries patrolling the perimeter.

The Nivalian warriors would be spreading out to surround the camp as well, silently slitting the throats of anyone they encountered. Fawn's diversion would signal the true start of the fight, when the visceral rush of fear and confusion would send swarms of enemy soldiers scrambling for their weapons and hunting for intruders.

Nova recalled the hateful gleam in Idrian's eyes when he spoke of her uncle. His delighted grin as he spoke of his promise to kill her. Another male in a long line, spanning the years of her life, intent on taking something from her for his own benefit. Nova's hands tingled, thirsting for the feel of a hilt pressed tight against them. Pulling her dagger from its sheath at her thigh, she spun the weapon on her palm as she stared into the darkness.

A moment later, she rose to her feet atop the stone summit, the sky far too dark for anyone to spot her in her black leathers at such a distance. She'd scaled the rock earlier in search of seclusion. Suddenly, it occurred to her: She'd made no promise to avoid the fight. No vow to stay put. She loved Callan deeply, but he didn't control her. No one did. The others were risking their lives to protect the Lunar Court. *Her* Court. Clearing a path to Idrian. *Her path* to Idrian. Nova sheathed her dagger and turned to descend the pitted rock face.

She unclasped her cloak once her boots hit the sand, discarding it in a puddle of black on the ground. Free of it, she took off running across the wide expanse toward the base of the mountain, its jagged peak jutting up against the boundless, star-filled sky.

The shiny breastplate of a fallen Silvergardian sentry glinted under the light of Illora as Nova crept closer to the encampment. An arrow had pierced the soldier's throat, his death mercifully quick. She glanced over her shoulder at the high ridge where a dozen archers lay hidden.

Pressing on, she slipped through a grove of twisted juniper trees, rough needles scratching against her leather armor. The faint whine of an arrow slicing through the air nearby ended abruptly with a muted grunt and a thud. Nova took comfort knowing the archers wouldn't see her in the dark with nothing on her to reflect the starlight and reveal her position.

Pausing behind the trunk of a crooked tree, she peeked around it at the massive camp of white cloth tents dotted with the warm glow of dozens of cook fires. The encampment rolling out before her was set upon a slight decline, providing a direct line of sight all the way to the glimmering sea beyond. Three Silvergardian ships sat anchored offshore, each one boasting tiered decks and two masts.

Nova drew her sword, gripping the hilt as she hunched her shoulders and prepared to make entry, when a deep rumble vibrated her chest, like the roar of a great beast. It stopped her in her tracks. Before her eyes, a jet of fiery orange burst forth from the shoreline, drenching the nearest ship with liquid flames.

The towering masts and rolled black sails ignited immediately, creating an instant inferno on the ship's deck. The flaming material sloshed over the sides, dripping down the exposed hull and into the sea where it continued to burn as it floated on the surface of the water. Nova's breath caught as she traced the stream of flames back to the tiny figure of Fawn, illuminated by the light of her unbelievable power. Rooted to the spot, Nova could scarcely believe her sweet friend was capable of such profound destruction. From so far away, she couldn't be sure if it was Fawn's auburn hair fanning out behind her or flames. She looked like Embra in the flesh.

The sudden clamor of the camp springing into action pulled Nova from her trance. She wasn't the only one who had felt the ground tremble as a result of Fawn's magic. Frightened shouts and barked orders rose above the unceasing roar of the flames. As Callan predicted, soldiers ran down the slope and toward the sea in droves to investigate. Nova seized the opportunity to enter the camp unseen, slinking from shadow to shadow between the tents. Idrian's lodging was easy to spot, much larger than the others and erected at the center of the encampment. A small flag with the insignia of Silvergard flew from a short pole atop its domed roof.

The air grew thick with arrows raining down from the ridge, eliminating distracted soldiers as they ran along the narrow laneways. She hadn't yet spotted Callan or any of the Nivalian warriors, but several sharp cries ringing out in the distance suggested they had infiltrated the camp as well.

The stealth portion of the operation had reached its end.

Nova slowed, her back pressed against the support pole of a tent as she neared Idrian's shelter. Chancing a glance around the corner, she noted two hulking guards posted outside the entrance; Idrian was still inside, then. She pulled back out of view and tilted her face up to the sky, taking several deep breaths.

Just then, one of Idrian's soldiers skidded around the corner, stopping short in front of her. The female hadn't had time to don her armor, but she wielded a long, curved sword. Her eyes went wide when she registered Nova's shape, nearly indistinguishable from the surrounding shadows. Nova didn't give her a chance to raise her blade, slashing her across the throat and bringing the female to her knees in a heartbeat. The soldier sputtered for air before falling dead at Nova's feet.

All sound faded as Nova looked down at her shaking hands and the body lying still on the ground before her. She clenched her fists and closed her eyes, inhaling deeply through her nose and exhaling through her mouth.

Remember your training. Imagine you're sparring with Lucan.

Only Lucan was never actually trying to kill her. Well, almost never.

Releasing a shaky breath, Nova peered around the corner at the entrance to Idrian's tent once again. Although the guards remained at their posts, their eyes were fixed on the flame-drenched chaos unfolding along the shoreline. Their hands rested on their hilts as they shifted uneasily from foot to foot, eager to join the fray.

Keeping to the shadows, sword in hand, Nova doubled back to approach one of the guards from the rear. She eyed a weak point in his standard-issue Silvergardian armor, a crease between two sections of hammered metal at the waist. His partner would undoubtedly notice when she killed him, but she preferred her odds against fighting one of them over fighting both at once.

The shadows seemed to cling to her, gathering around her like a dark cloak and shielding her as she crept along the edge of the canvas wall. Like a reassuring hand pressed firmly between her shoulder blades, urging her on. She crouched low as she reached the guard, thrusting her sword into his back through the gap in his armor. The guard fell to his knees with a groan, gripping his side as a rush of blood spilled from the wound. The second guard hurried to his aid, initially confused but swiftly drawing his own weapon when Nova emerged from the darkness.

He charged her at once, bringing the curved blade of his sword down over her head. Nova beat against the cut, deflecting the blade and stepping to the right. His momentum carried his body forward, and she brought her blade back, slashing the top of his thigh. He spun on her, swinging his sword through the air horizontally. The guard was large but slow, and Nova ducked underneath the arc of the blade, rising swiftly a second later and bringing her own blade down on the elbow of his sword arm. His weapon fell to the ground, and he hunched forward, clutching his injured arm with his opposite hand. Without hesitation, Nova came down with her sword, gripped in both hands and angled at the point where his neck met his shoulder, cleaving the juncture with a fatal blow.

Heart pounding, she rushed to the entrance of the general's tent, parting the canvas flaps with the tip of her blade. No movement inside. She slipped out of the night and into Idrian's quarters. The space was cramped, taken up by a full-size bed and a large table, and lit by moonstone globes strung up on the corner posts. The surface of the table was cluttered with maps and sheets of correspondence. A changing screen stood beside a large trunk with clothing draped over the sides.

Nova panted raggedly as she scanned the interior of the tent, swiping her free hand over her brow. Her parched throat fought her attempt to swallow. A rustle came from the far corner, and she slipped behind the changing screen. As she peeked through a crack in the screen, Idrian burst through a curtain opposite her position.

He rushed about, dressed only in breeches and a baggy shirt, the hem hanging loose from his waistband. Droplets cast off from his hair as he hurried past her hiding place, presumably to investigate the noise. He must have been bathing when the roar of Fawn's diversion first thundered through the camp.

"What the fuck is going on?" he muttered as he came back into view, crossing to the bed. Nova crept out from behind the screen, slinking up behind him. Idrian's broad back was to her as he bent forward to pull on a boot. Nova stood a sword's length away, her arm outstretched, when she noticed a sheath leaning against the side of the bed, just out of his reach. Idrian rose to his full height and went for his weapon.

"Don't move," Nova commanded calmly as she pressed the tip of her blade to the back of his neck.

"Mouse?" he asked casually, though a hint of surprise clung to the edge of his voice. "Is that you?"

He turned his head slightly, trying to get a glimpse of her. She pressed her weapon forward, the bite of steel halting him immediately. He splayed his fingers wide at his sides, the gesture betraying the fear behind his mask.

"I said, don't move."

She should have struck already. She wanted him dead. Yet, she'd never killed someone she knew before. The lives she had taken were those of nameless soldiers standing between her and her survival or her revenge. In the moment, the idea of killing someone she had once considered a friend, even someone like Idrian, made her hesitate. Without warning, a Realm-shaking rumble reverberated through the camp, and the walls of the tent shuddered.

Fawn was calling upon her magic again. The noise coupled with the sensation took Nova by surprise. For an instant, her head snapped in the direction of the shore.

Unlike her, Idrian didn't hesitate.

Spinning to face her, he gripped the wrist of her sword arm and tugged her close to him. Nova barely had time to register the attack before his opposite fist collided with her jaw. Her hearing cut out, all sound around her deadening, as the impact sent her staggering backward into the table. She braced herself on the edge with her free arm, barely able to hold herself up as stars danced across her field of vision, a high-pitched whine ringing in her ears.

She shook her head sharply, bringing Idrian into focus where he stood several steps away from her, his blade now in hand. He didn't move to attack her, assuming an arrogant pose instead, one hand resting on his hip as he shot her a smug grin.

"Playing dress up, are we?" he mocked, raking his eyes over her sleek leather armor. "I must say, I prefer *this* over any of your fancy gowns." He gestured up and down, his tongue flicking over his bottom lip as he leered at her.

Nova regained some of her balance, letting go of the table. She bent her knees slightly and raised her sword, readying herself to strike.

"What do you plan to do with that, Mouse?" Idrian shook his head and chuckled.

Rage surged through her at his dismissal. She charged him with a downward strike. He blocked it easily with the flat edge of his sword, shoving his weight against hers and pushing her backward. He threw his fist into her side, just below her ribs, and all the air rushed out of her. Clutching her side, she took a staggering step toward him, trying to pin him with a thrust to his abdomen. He was much faster than the guard she'd fought outside, and he quickly sidestepped the strike. The momentum of her attack carried her forward, and she fell onto her stomach on the bed. She rolled onto her back immediately. Idrian wasn't advancing on her with any urgency, and she realized the fight was nothing more than a game to him.

He was enjoying it.

Enraged, she growled and came up onto her feet again, thrusting at him once more. He hit her blade with his own, sending her arm flying out to her right, and quickly brought his blade back, slashing a straight line along her abdomen just below her navel. She shot a glance down at the split leather. The wound was superficial, but she felt the hot rush of blood.

Idrian laughed as he leaned his sword against the edge of the bed again. Before Nova could react, he delivered another blow to her face with his fist, striking her cheekbone. She fell back onto the bed, only vaguely aware of him removing her sword from her hand and tossing it aside.

Her vision blurred, and she battled the overwhelming urge to black out. Idrian's face hovered above hers. He spoke, his voice muffled and faraway, as his fingers closed roughly around her neck.

"I told your father I would kill you in front of him, but I don't know if I can help myself." A cruel sneer split his jaw as he tightened his grip around her throat, cutting off her breath.

Nova bucked weakly underneath his weight. One hand gripped his forearm while the other lashed out at his face, a blinding white light beginning to form at the edges of her vision. All at once, Idrian removed his hand from her neck. Lifting her off the bed, he crushed her against his chest with an elbow hooked tightly under her chin. Still struggling for air, Nova almost didn't hear the familiar voice ordering Idrian to unhand her.

"Release her, General, or I'll split you open where you stand."

Callan stood in the entryway, unmoving, his sword held out before him. His eyes, dark like the roiling sea under a stormy sky, were trained on the general, daring Idrian to make even the smallest of movements. Idrian sighed, and his posture relaxed.

"Drop your weapons." Idrian's voice was calm and even as he issued the command.

Nova nearly scoffed at his arrogance, but she stared in disbelief as Callan's sword arm began to tremble, the veins in his neck bulging as he bit down forcefully. Slowly, Callan lowered the blade and held it out at his side before dropping it with a thud at his feet.

FORTY-FIVE

There was nothing he could do.

Callan clenched his jaw so tightly he thought his teeth would surely crack. But no matter how hard he fought, he remained powerless to disobey Idrian's command. Against his will, Callan reached down and removed his dagger from its sheath, dropping it beside his sword.

The general released Nova from his grasp, and she fell to the carpet, coughing and gasping for air.

"Very good," Idrian crooned, coming to Callan's side and kicking both of his weapons across the rug and under the bed.

Idrian took a seat at the table, lounging casually in his chair, a smug smirk playing on his lips.

"Kneel," he ordered, his smile vanishing as his eyes darkened with his display of power.

Callan willed himself to rebel, to pick up his sword and strike the general down, but it was useless. He fell to one knee.

"You too, Mouse," Idrian said, turning his attention to Nova. "Remove your dagger and get on your knees."

Callan couldn't turn his head. He could only watch from the corner of his eye as Nova rose unsteadily to her feet, drawing her own blade and discarding it on the bed. Her movements were irregular as she walked fitfully to where Callan knelt and mirrored his pose, lowering herself to one knee.

Callan heard her rapid breaths beside him. His heart stuttered as the scent of her surrounded him. Even the strength of their bond, his primal urge to protect what was his, wasn't enough to break Idrian's hold.

"Much better. The last of the Elsever bloodline kneeling at my feet," Idrian sneered as he looked down on both of them. "You seem surprised, Mouse. But I did tell you I have noble blood running through my veins. Look at me—both of you."

The general shut his eyes and pinched the bridge of his nose before shaking his head roughly. He raked a hand through his hair, calling attention to a streak of silver, standing out like a shooting star against the night-black strands.

"I haven't always been this capable. What you're experiencing now has taken decades of painstaking struggle, training myself to tap into the power lying dormant within me. A coiled serpent waiting to strike. As you can see, if you take full bodily control of someone, they tend to notice. But, if you merely influence their behavior, slip in a little suggestion here and there, they do as you command and are none the wiser."

Idrian stood and circled to the front of the table, leaning against the edge so he loomed over them. Callan couldn't even lift his head to look the bastard in the face.

"Of course, I prefer no one know about this little secret of mine. I find victory tastes sweeter when your opponent has underestimated you. The look in their eyes the moment they realize your power is . . . indescribable."

Idrian's hand shot out, grabbing a fistful of Callan's hair and forcing his head back. The general examined his face.

"Is this the same Nivalian scum who slaughtered my soldiers and stole

355

you away from me, Mouse?" Not waiting for a response, Idrian drew back his fist and punched Callan squarely in the jaw. Callan's mouth flooded with the metallic tang of iron. "He must have quite a strong connection to you to risk himself a second time on your account." Leaning closer to Callan's face, Idrian asked, "What is she to you? A friend? A lover?"

He gripped Callan's face between his hands, forcing him to meet his gaze. An unsettling laugh rumbled forth from deep in Idrian's chest.

"No doubt you'll be rather disappointed when I end her life," he tutted.

Idrian released Callan from his grasp, setting his sights on Nova once again. Burying both his hands in her hair, he forced her head back, tilting her face toward the ceiling as he stood before her.

"It's a shame, really. A waste. She'd have made an exquisite broodmare. She's certainly got the hips for it," Idrian said, gripping her by the chin with one hand. He turned her face harshly from side to side, as if inspecting a horse at auction. When he released her, she slumped forward again, her eyes trained on the floor at the general's feet.

Callan tried to yell, but choked on the sound as it caught in his throat.

"A bargain is a bargain, and I promised you would die by my hand." Idrian rose to his full height, towering over Nova's wilted form. "But I never said I wouldn't enjoy you a bit first. Stand up, Mouse."

Nova rose with great effort, her limbs trembling as she stood directly in front of the general.

"You—" Idrian snapped his fingers at Callan. "Eyes up here. I want you to see this."

Callan's head lifted. Nova stood chest to chest with the general, arms at her sides, her hand balled into a tight fist.

"Kiss me," Idrian drawled, one side of his mouth curling in a lustful grin as his eyes flicked briefly to Callan.

Nova raised her hands, her left coming to rest on Idrian's shoulder. She tilted her face and brought her mouth close to his, pausing just as her lips brushed against the general's. Idrian was so focused on ensuring Callan bore witness to the act that he failed to see the glint of metal in Nova's right hand.

Despite taking several hits to the face and being deprived of air, Nova had immediately recognized Callan's stilted movements as those of someone under mind control. She froze at first in fear and disbelief. When Idrian gave her a command and her body didn't immediately comply, she made the split-second decision to play along.

Mirroring Callan's movements, she dropped her curved dagger atop the bed and came to kneel beside him. Her rapid breaths and trembling limbs were not part of her performance. How long before Idrian discovered she was pretending? How long before he killed them both?

She took advantage of the general's tendency to ramble—he was clearly enamored with the sound of his own voice—using the time to calm her mind and formulate a plan. Kneeling on the floor, she had ready access to the human-made dagger concealed within her boot.

While Idrian was distracted, taunting Callan and striking him in the jaw, Nova swiftly drew the weapon, gripping the hilt and holding the blade flat against the underside of her forearm as she slumped forward. From the corner of her eye, she watched a drop of blood trickle from Callan's mouth. It required every sliver of will she possessed to keep from revealing herself and striking out at the general right then.

But Idrian sealed his own fate when he ordered her to kiss him. She'd spun the dagger in her right hand as she placed the other on his shoulder to brace him. Lucan's voice echoed in her mind.

You cannot hesitate *when the opportunity presents itself.*

The instant their lips touched, Nova thrust the weapon upward into the side of Idrian's neck, severing the primary vein pulsing at his throat. Blood spattered across her face as she twisted the blade and wrenched it free.

Idrian's hand flew to his throat, pressing uselessly against the wound, blood gushing rhythmically around his trembling fingers. His wide eyes stared into hers, his mouth opening and closing silently, like a fish washed up on the shore. It dawned on her: This must be the look Idrian described. The shock of having underestimated one's opponent. She savored the moment and Idrian's stunned realization. She stepped to the side as he fell to his knees and tipped forward onto the rug, expelling a final raspy wheeze.

Released from Idrian's control, Callan leapt to his feet and wrapped Nova in his arms. She sagged against him, gripping his shoulders as her legs buckled beneath her.

"I-I'm sorry," she stammered, pressing her face against his chest, registering the sting of a split lip and a cut on the inside of her cheek from when Idrian struck her. Shame drenched her like a soaking rain, seeping into her bones and distracting her from the pain. She'd allowed her anger to cloud her judgment, and it led to chaos, just as Lucan warned it would.

"Everything is all right, love," Callan murmured, breathing heavily as he stroked her hair. "You did it. He's gone. He can never harm you again."

A chorus of frightened shouts rang out in the distance, startling them both, and they abandoned their embrace. Callan crouched, reaching an arm under the bed to reclaim his sword. Nova still gripped her dagger, the blade wet with Idrian's blood. Together, they rushed out of the tent and into the misty night air, barreling down the slope to the sea's edge where Fawn's flames continued to burn bright, lighting up the night and illuminating the scene along the shore.

The vast majority of the Silvergardian forces still lived, caged behind a wall of flames as tall as Callan. Two ships remained anchored offshore. The third had been reduced to ash and chunks of charred planks scattered on the surface of the sea. Pools of Fawn's liquid flame continued to blaze, floating like seafoam atop the black waves.

Nova and Callan reached the shore where Fawn and Lucan stood. The waves lapped calmly at the toes of Nova's boots, the sea remarkably tranquil despite the destruction Fawn had wrought upon its surface. Nova scanned the faces of the captured soldiers, fear and uncertainty painted plainly across their features in the glow of the flames.

These were Lunar folk. Her folk.

The rage Nova harbored toward Idrian faded as she looked upon them, the raw emotion withering until it was eclipsed by compassion. These soldiers had been poisoned. Manipulated as Callan had been. She empathized with them, as she knew her uncle would. Nova raised a hand, signaling for Fawn to reduce the intensity of the flames, which shrunk to half their size in the blink of an eye.

She gripped Callan's hand, using him to steady herself as she climbed onto a small boulder on the beach. Her dagger remained in her right hand, her right forearm pressed to the wound on her abdomen.

"I am Nova of Silvergard," she shouted above the clamor of the crowd. "I've come as an emissary of your Noble Lord. General Idrian is dead."

A hush fell over the beach until the only sounds were the soft crash of the waves against the shore and the low, droning hum of the flames.

"The general has been controlling you. Training you all to accept conquest and destruction as your only options. Convincing you there is no other way to live. But Lord Nox fervently believes there is another way—that a better life is possible for all the folk of Silvergard. I beg you: Lay down your weapons in favor of another path. Do this and your Lord will grant you mercy." She paused, breathing deeply and pressing her arm against her wound. "Will you choose another future? Will you choose another way?"

The night was overwhelmingly quiet as the soldiers seemingly weighed her words. Nova began to succumb to the exhaustion she'd barely held at bay, her consciousness ebbing with every drop of blood that fell from the slash across her abdomen. Her lids fluttered, and her eyes rolled back.

The muted thud of steel on sand hauled her back from the brink, eyes snapping open. The sound repeated itself over and over and over as nearly two hundred soldiers dropped their weapons at their feet. When they knelt on the shore before her, it looked like a shimmering silver wave rolling forth from the sea.

FORTY-SIX

NOVA DRIFTED ABOUT IN a haze, her senses and affect dulled by weariness, oppressive and bone-deep. While their small band of warriors emerged from the skirmish with only two casualties, both from Arik's squadron, the rebel Silvergardian forces had fared far worse. She insisted upon honoring all of the fallen, working alongside the survivors to gather the dead, and commemorating them with a funeral pyre along the shore.

All but Idrian.

"What would you have us do with his body?" Callan asked soberly.

Nova's rage flared anew, and she forced her response through clenched teeth. "Leave him out for the crows."

Callan made no attempt to dissuade her, squeezing her forearm reassuringly before turning to Lucan and jerking his chin in the direction of Idrian's tent.

Nova limped through the somber crowd to a quiet spot at the water's edge. Thick gray smoke billowed up from the pyre, joining with the mist rising off the surface of the sea and carrying the souls of the dead to the After Realm. She pressed a palm to her abdomen. The wound had clotted, but the sting remained. She held her hands out before her, fingers trembling slightly and covered in dried blood. A mixture of Idrian's and her own. She spied Lucan and Callan emerging from Idrian's tent, carrying the general's corpse between them.

Had she smiled when she twisted the blade? Her legs began to shake beneath her. Nova conjured the moment in her mind, pictured her lips first curling into a faint smile, then splitting in a wide grin, like that of a madwoman. The same wild expression her father wore as he hovered over her in her nightmare. She spun to face the sea, eyes shut tight, inhaling through her nose and exhaling through her mouth. After several minutes, she opened her eyes again and looked out over the Gloaming Sea toward Raven's Isle, the Shadow Court lurking in the distance, invisible through the fog.

Nova flinched at the weight of a hand on her shoulder, twisting to find Fawn and Evander behind her.

"I'm afraid we must be leaving," Fawn said, tilting her head apologetically. "With any luck, no one in Pyralis will have noticed we were gone."

Nova scanned her friend's face. The weak smile and drawn features. The faint, dark circles hanging like crescent moons beneath her large brown eyes. Fawn pulled her into an embrace, and Nova registered how loosely her friend's slender arms wrapped around her shoulders. Fawn had overexerted herself; she needed to return home to recover. Fresh shame sent heat creeping along Nova's limbs. An apology caught in her throat. But she was certain that if she tried to give it voice, the full volume of her emotions would rush out alongside it like a raging flood. So she swallowed it down instead.

Fawn released her and produced a small glass bottle from within her corset top. Removing the cork stopper, she poured a substance resembling ash into her hand. Nova watched as Fawn blew a breath along her palm. The sea breeze caught the fine gray powder, and it swirled and gathered, revealing a portal where nothing had been an instant before. On the other side, a sea of vibrant sunset-colored leaves danced in the wind, the Autumn Court suddenly as close as an adjoining room.

"We'll speak soon," Fawn said, taking hold of Nova's hand. She squeezed once and arched a fine brow. "Perhaps then you'll tell me what's *really* been going on."

Nova nodded and squeezed Fawn's hand once in response.

Uncharacteristically quiet, Evander made no farewell of his own apart from a casual lift of his brows in Nova's direction. With the utmost care, he took Fawn by the elbow and supported his sister as the two of them crossed the threshold into Pyralis. The portal twisted and collapsed in on itself once they passed through.

Nova slumped down to sit in the sand, forearms resting on her bent knees. She stared out at the sea, listening to the rhythmic crash of the surf and pressing her tongue repeatedly to her split lip, determined to make herself feel the pain for as long as it lasted. Her wounds were superficial and would heal quickly, likely leaving no trace of a scar. Her sense of self would be another story entirely. She'd lost track of how long she'd been sitting there, the waves tallying the passage of time, when Callan crouched beside her and murmured that it was time to depart.

Lucan divided the Silvergardian archers equally, tasking each group with boarding the two remaining ships and accompanying the reformed rebel forces back to the Estate by sea. Nova mounted Shade, the horse anxious and jumpy beneath her, perhaps feeding off of her own unease. She twisted the reins in her hands as their party galloped south, clinging to the sting along the slash on her abdomen before it faded completely.

Despite the warm welcome that greeted Nova upon her return to the Estate, the cheers and deferential bows as she passed through the courtyard and dismounted, shame continued to weigh her down like a sodden cloak.

Shame sent her to her chamber, where she remained hidden away for several days. She lay in bed with the sheets thrown over her head, unable to face anyone, especially Nox. He had warned her of the dangers. Blinded by her desire for vengeance, she'd refused to listen. Eventually, her uncle sought her out, the mattress dipping as he sat on the edge of the bed beside her. Reluctantly, she tugged the sheet down to meet Nox's eyes.

"Lucan showed me how you spoke to the soldiers. How they responded to you." He fished for her hand, grasping it tightly. "I'm so proud of you."

Her weak smile didn't fool him.

"What's the matter?"

Nova spun her ring on her finger, rubbing her thumb over the milky white stone.

"I feel bad—no. Wrong. Not for ending his life." Nova knew she would never be able to muster a shred of regret for what she'd done, though, admittedly her complete lack of remorse was disconcerting. "For not burning him. Denying him passage to the After Realm. It feels cruel. Like something my father might have done."

Nox sighed, nudging her with his knee. She shifted to the center of the bed, making room for him to lie beside her, their eyes fixed on the ceiling.

"Lunar folk don't view darkness as something inherently wrong. Orika is neither good nor evil. She's a complex deity who enjoys mischief and upheaval. A dash of chaos now and again." Nox turned his face to her, but she kept looking straight ahead. "It's within *your* power to decide who you become—not your father's, not mine, not anyone else's."

Nox curled his fingers under her chin, gently guiding her to look at him.

"You shine so brilliantly," he said, his pride evident in his charcoal eyes. "But remember, my dear niece, even when the moon is at her brightest, there remains a side of her forever cloaked in shadow."

Nox remained with her for a time, speaking softly about his dreams for the future of the Lunar Court, seemingly intuiting that she wasn't interested in speaking much herself. When he left a short while later, she felt lighter somehow and opted to keep her head out from under the covers.

It wasn't long before her thoughts drifted to Callan, who occupied his own chamber down the hall. Nova had apologized to him, but her words felt deficient. Hollow. Pure luck had prevented her from being affected by Idrian's ability. True, her quick thinking had kept her and Callan alive and ended the immediate threat Idrian posed to them, to Silvergard, and to the Realm at large. Still, she couldn't escape the feeling that it was a sham when her recklessness had placed them in the situation to begin with.

A swell of emotion filled her chest at the thought of Callan. He had respected her desire to be alone, but she sensed his heart's desperate call to her own, beckoning her to his side. Unable to withstand it any longer, Nova threw back the sheets and slid out of bed, hurrying out the door and down the hall to Callan's chamber before she could convince herself to stop.

The Estate was hushed, with the majority of the residents having retired to their chambers for sleep. But she knew she would find Callan awake. That his mind, like hers, had not known rest since they'd returned. She knocked softly on the door and held her breath when he invited her in.

Barefoot and clad only in a pair of black breeches, he sat slouched on the low sofa, his dark hair loose, the ends grazing his shoulders. The sight of his large, solid form seated on the elegant furniture was almost comical, and a smile crept unexpectedly across her face. Relief flooded Callan's features, his brow relaxing and the tension in his upper body easing in a heartbeat. His mouth quirked up in a smile, a faint dimple flashing on his cheek as he held out a hand to her.

Nova rushed to where he sat, climbing into his lap and tugging at her nightgown to make room for her knees on either side of his long thighs.

Wrapping his arms tightly around her torso, he pressed his face against her chest and breathed her in before resting his cheek flat against the space between her breasts. She buried her fingers in his hair and rested her chin on top of his head, exhaling as she melted into him. He was the only answer to a question her soul would never cease asking.

"Your heart's racing," he murmured, skimming his hands over her lower back.

Nova hooked a finger under his chin and tilted his face up to hers. He hadn't shaved since their return. Perhaps he'd been wallowing a bit, too, she thought. The notion was oddly comforting.

"You've been hiding from me," he said, brows pinched once again.

"I'm sorry," she whispered, running the pad of her thumb over the hollow below his bottom lip. "It was foolish to challenge Idrian alone. You tried to warn me—"

"You have nothing to apologize for. I'm sorry, love. I had no right to cut you out of the plan. I was wrong, and I vow never to stand in your way again. I will always stand beside you."

Callan shook his head, curling his fingers around her wrist and kissing her softly on her palm before gazing up at her solemnly.

"But please promise me the next time you charge headfirst into danger, it won't be because you think your life doesn't matter, or the loss of you won't be felt. Because you mean everything—you are *everything*—to me, Nova. I need you to understand that. I cannot fathom a world without you in it."

Nova lifted his hand to her cheek, leaning into his touch. "You were right to worry," she said. "I wasn't ready. Idrian could have killed me easily."

"We should have faced him together, like we'd planned. Don't you see? If you hadn't been there . . . if I'd faced him alone, I would have been another body on the pyre. All my training and ability was useless against the power he wielded. You protected me, Nova. You saved me."

She let out a dry laugh, lifting one shoulder in a shrug. "You've saved me once or twice."

Callan's fingers ghosted up her spine, gently tracing the raised lines of her scars as a low chuckle rumbled in his chest. The sound vibrated deliciously against her stomach.

"You've physically saved my life at least three times by my count." The humor quickly faded from his eyes. "Truly, I've never felt more alive than when I'm with you."

A quiet moment passed, their bodies relaxing into one another as the last remnants of fear and anxiety waned, leaving a growing warmth between them.

"You told me I never have to hide from you," Callan said. "The same is true for you. If you feel you can't exist in this world without your walls, then brick me up inside them with you. Because there is nothing for me out here without you. All of you. Not just the smooth, shiny pieces you're growing to like, or the ones you feel comfortable holding up to the light. The raw, jagged bits, too."

He stared up at her, his gaze a dark mirror reflecting how he saw her: an uncut gem, imperfect and yet infinitely precious.

"With you, I feel safe enough to let those walls down. I know I can fall apart, and you'll still be there to help me put myself back together."

Callan tucked a lock of her hair behind her ear, before letting his hand fall to her throat. He brushed his thumb over the thrum of her pulse. Nova inhaled sharply as desire bloomed between her legs, pooling where their bodies joined in his lap. Callan pulled her face toward his, claiming her mouth with a kiss that was at first tender but quickly turned demanding and possessive. Nova moaned against his mouth and pressed her body into his as the need between them intensified.

Suddenly desperate, Nova rose onto her knees, hiking up the bothersome fabric bunching around her hips. Reaching down between them, Callan nimbly untied the laces of his breeches and lifted his hips off the sofa to shove the waistband down to his mid-thigh. He gripped her by the hips and guided her down on top of him, his cock filling her completely. Nova's muscles melted like warm honey at the satisfying fullness. The return of something she forgot she lacked.

Both ceased to breathe for an instant, eyes locked as she ground her hips in a slow circle around the hard length of him. Nova rose slowly before crashing back down, relishing the feeling of him, her mate, deep inside her. This male who saw her. Who knew her darkness, her pain, and still chose her.

"Gods, you were made for me," Callan groaned, dark eyes flashing as he drank in the sight of her. "So wet and sweet. And mine." His claim skittered like a lightning bolt along her limbs, tingling in the tips of her fingers and toes.

Callan slipped the thin straps of her nightdress from her shoulders, exposing her breasts. She gasped when he laid his hands on her, his palms coated with frost. He dipped his head, drawing a nipple into the heat of his mouth. Nova dug her fingertips into his muscled back as he took one breast, then the other, teasing her with his icy touch and warm tongue and driving her mad with want.

Callan leaned back, kneading her ass as she rode him. His gaze fell to where they came together, and he tipped his head back, his throat bobbing as he stifled a moan. Bringing his thumb to his mouth, he licked it languidly before skimming it along the softness of her stomach and swirling it in slow circles around her clit. Nova bent forward, pressing her forehead against his, their ragged breaths mixing together as she rocked her hips in his lap.

"Must you go home?" she panted against his mouth.

Callan gripped her hips and stopped her before she could take him fully again. She whimpered at the absence of him.

"Nova, *this* is home," he ground out as he drove his cock inside her, making her cry out. "Wherever I am. Wherever I go. In this Realm. And whatever comes after. This—*you*—will always be my home."

His words, punctuated by a steady cadence of deep thrusts, left her breathless and carried her to climax. Nova came intensely with heavy, shuddering breaths. She wrapped her arms around Callan's shoulders and pulled him close, clinging to him with every fiber of her being. Callan twined his arms around her back, holding her firmly in place and thrusting into her twice more before she felt his release pulsing inside her, his hushed moan muffled against the curve of her neck. They remained that way for a time, hearts beating in tandem.

The odd impulse to laugh rose within her. She had thought she'd made a life for herself in the Human Realm, but she hadn't been living. She'd been waiting to die. And what a long, slow, lonely death it would have been. Here, with Callan, even plagued by the lingering threat of death, Nova knew she was truly alive.

Laughter greeted Callan when he entered the library. He proceeded stealthily toward the sitting area, not wishing to impose. Lucan lounged on the sofa, his long legs sprawled across the cushions, purposefully poking Nova's thigh with the toe of his boot. Sighing dramatically, Nova shoved his foot off the sofa, nearly overturning a decanter of wine sitting on the low glass table.

Lucan sprang forward, steadying the vessel of red liquid with both hands as Nova sputtered, breaking into a fit of laughter. Callan's chest swelled at the sound, so lovely and still so foreign to him.

"Honestly," Nox chided. "The two of you behave like a pair of younglings."

Callan smiled to himself. The thought of leaving Nova pained him like an open wound, but it reassured him to know he wouldn't be leaving her alone.

Nova had a family.

He made his presence known then, lowering himself onto the sofa beside her. Their hands found each other's immediately, fingers lacing together on top of his knee.

"It seems I'm in your debt, Callan," the Noble Lord said, taking a seat in a nearby armchair. "Lucan told me how faithfully you led the charge against General Idrian's forces."

Callan shook his head dismissively.

"I was only one of many with a part to play." He brushed his thumb over the back of Nova's hand, hoping she understood the silent apology.

"Don't be so modest," Lucan said. "If not for you, we wouldn't have had those towering Nivalian warriors or the fire wielder on our side."

"What will happen to Idrian's forces now?" Callan asked, eager to deflect the attention.

"They have been given something they never had before: a choice. Most were conscripted into service at a young age without any alternative. Some will choose to remain soldiers while others will pursue education or another profession. Some may choose to do something else most of their days but will answer if Silvergard calls for aid."

"Could someone with a view similar to Idrian's take hold again in Stargrave?" Callan asked.

"You remember Zara and Oren—two of the archers who came with us?" Lucan asked. "They've agreed to return to Stargrave with those who choose to remain soldiers. They'll oversee operations there and keep us informed of the overall sentiment as things change."

"We're expanding the martial academy there to include trades and the arts," Nova explained, a genuine smile sitting above her pointed chin.

"One more question," Callan said, tucking away his own grin brought on by her happiness. "What happened with Idrian? I was powerless to defy his commands. Why wasn't Nova affected?"

Nox relaxed a bit, settling into his seat and resting one ankle on his opposite knee.

"It appears Nova is resistant to such abilities," he said, his charcoal eyes meeting his niece's silvery ones. "Perhaps one positive effect of those walls you've built up around yourself over the years. I had my suspicions. When we first met, I reached out with my mind to see if I could get a sense of you, but I felt nothing. It's why I resorted to entering your dream. Your defenses were slightly lowered as you slept. Even then, I needed you to invite me in."

Nova stared wordlessly at her uncle, who only chuckled quietly.

"I told you she was difficult to read," he added as an aside to Callan.

"As if he needed you to tell him that," Lucan said dryly.

"And Omen?" Callan asked, suddenly remembering the threat of the Shadowbringer.

"When I was Idrian's prisoner, I overheard him say Omen was too weak or too paranoid to leave his Estate," Nova said. "Idrian claimed my father promised him the support he needed to take the territory, but, as far as we know, Raven's Isle has no army. Perhaps Omen deceived him. For now, I suppose all we can do is wait."

"You can do more than wait," Lucan said. "Tomorrow, you begin training with the rest of the guard. You'll be ready to hand Callan's ass to him in the sparring ring by his next visit."

"I look forward to it," Callan said. "But I'm afraid the time has come for me to depart for Nivali."

Callan rose from his seat and bowed to the Noble Lord before turning to Lucan.

"I couldn't have gotten her back without you," Callan muttered as they clasped forearms. When Callan released him, Lucan gave a nod and laid his hand over his heart.

"Come with me." Nova slid her warm hand into Callan's. "I have a gift for you."

Nox and Lucan retired to the study, giving them a moment alone. Callan recalled fondly how he and Nova had already shared an intimate goodbye upon waking. Twice. He adjusted himself discreetly as he followed behind her.

It was going to be a long five months.

Nova handed him a small book bound in black leather, slightly larger than his outstretched hand. He lifted the cover and flipped through the pages, the edges gilded with silver foil. All of the pages were blank.

"It's a linking book," she explained, pointing to an identical book on the table. "I found the set when I was searching through the high stacks a couple of weeks ago. Anything you write on the pages of your book will appear in mine, and my messages will show up in your book as well."

"Much more convenient than messenger owls." He grinned, turning the magical book over in his hands.

Nova brought her arms up over his shoulders, her fingers combing through the hair at the nape of his neck. He set the book down and wrapped his arms around her waist, pulling her tightly against him.

"I'll write to you often," he said. "I promise."

"Five months isn't so long." Nova's tone was hopeful, but he could tell she was trying to convince herself of the fact.

He dipped his head and brushed his lips against hers. "Five months is nothing when I know I get to love you every second for the rest of my life. Though, you could come with me now, you know," he murmured, his mouth hovering close to hers. "Eternal winter isn't as terrible as you might

think, and I can come up with endless creative ways to keep you warm."
He pressed his hips against her, wondering if his all-consuming desire, his
desperate need for her, would ever diminish.

Nova laughed quietly and ran her fingertips along his clean-shaven jaw.

"It's tempting," she sighed. "But we both have responsibilities now."

"I suppose you're right." His smile faded as he glimpsed the unshed tears
shimmering in her pale gray eyes. "I choose you."

"I choose you," she replied, a tear escaping from the corner of her eye and
running down her cheek.

Their lips joined in a kiss teeming with desire, uncertainty, and hope.
Callan wanted to lose himself in her but tried instead to memorize every
sensation—the pillowy softness of her lips on his. The sweetness of her
tongue as it caressed his. The feeling of her body, both firm and soft, pressed
against his.

Forty-Seven

Nova paced across the ebony floor of the antechamber leading to Nox's council room. Sweat gathered on her chest, a single drop trickling down between her breasts. She slowed her steps and tried to remember why she had insisted on wearing this particular gown. Thank the gods she'd asked Isla to style her hair up and off her neck.

Since her arrival in Silvergard, she had been leading a double life of sorts: training in swordplay and hand-to-hand combat for several hours upon waking and socializing at court for several hours afterward. She'd kept the two areas of her life separate, and it had benefited her to a degree. Idrian had only ever seen her in her fine gowns, chatting idly and dining with the gentry. Not believing her capable of holding a sword, let alone wielding one, he had underestimated her. It had given her an advantage in the end.

Nova's decision to deny Idrian passage to the After Realm continued to haunt her. More than once, she'd awoken from a fitful sleep, the startling image of the general's decaying body burned into her mind's eye. She always saw him laid out in the black sand beneath an unforgiving sky, skin stark white and eyes cloudy. With every breath, she fought to heed her uncle's advice. To forgive herself and accept the darker side of her nature. The killer she had asked Lucan to make her. The killer she had become to save herself, Callan, and all those she held dear.

At times, it was a battle she waged moment to moment.

Nova inhaled deeply, smoothing her hands over the black satin skirt of her gown, light and airy, emphasizing the softness within her. Exhaling, her hands traveled to the waist of the black leather bodice with studded leather pauldrons, matching pocket-sized daggers sheathed conveniently at her hipbones: a clear warning of her growing lethality.

Lucan strode into the antechamber, his nose wrinkling immediately.

"Gods, it reeks in here," he said, waving a gloved hand before his face.

Nova sniffed at the air before trying discreetly to smell herself.

"Not you," Lucan said, a lock of his dark hair falling over his eyes as he shook his head. "Your fear. Have you tried breathing?"

"My gods, Lucan," she said, words dripping with sarcasm. "Are you certain you're not a sage?"

"You've no need to be so tense. It's nothing but a few dusty, old lesser Lords and Ladies in there. You don't need their approval."

"Perhaps I don't need it, but it certainly couldn't hurt." She winced, fanning herself with both hands.

"Just do as I do: Simply walk in there with a manner that says you're not to be fucked with, and pay them no mind." He punched her lightly on the shoulder and strode confidently through the council room doors.

A moment later, the posted guard informed her that she'd been summoned.

Inhaling a final steadying breath, Nova entered the room with her shoulders thrown back and her chin level, projecting an air of authority. While she might not match Lucan's level of confidence in her, she would do her best to pretend until she did.

Nova circled the round table of black stone, the glossy surface reflecting the light of the moon, nearly full and poised in the sky beyond the glass ceiling. Stopping behind the empty chair between Nox and his commander, she endeavored to act as if she was perfectly at ease with so many sets of eyes focused intently on her.

Nox rose from his seat and held a hand out at his side, palm up. Nova took it, and his fingers closed gently around hers. Her uncle shot her a quick sideways glance, and she nodded almost imperceptibly before he addressed the council. They had agreed it was no use hiding what many likely already suspected. Even so, Nova's stomach twisted anxiously.

"I would like to formally introduce you all to my niece, Nova Elsever."

Coolly, she scanned the faces of the nobles gathered around the table, gauging their reactions. If any were surprised by the revelation, they certainly hid it well.

"As my most trusted advisors, I expect you to closely guard the truth about Nova's paternity when you are outside these walls. I welcome her to the Lunar Council as the official Emissary of Silvergard, responsible for cultivating and maintaining relations with the other territories of Aemoria."

The district representatives seated around the table clapped politely, a few going so far as to nod approvingly. Nova dipped her head in a slight bow and took her seat, quietly releasing a sigh of relief.

"Now then," Nox continued, bracing his arms on the smooth slab of onyx before him. "Let's begin. As you all know, there is much to be done."

Nova focused her attention on her uncle as he laid out plans for the future of the Lunar Court.

Their Court.

Several hours later, Nova returned to her chamber, grateful to be out from under the watchful eyes of her uncle's council. Shutting the door behind her, she leaned her forehead against its wooden surface, closed her eyes, and drew in a deep breath. A faint scraping sound came from behind her, and her eyes flew open, her intuition flaring. Someone was in the room with her.

Slowly palming one of her daggers in her right hand, she rotated the small weapon until she pinched the tip of the blade between her thumb and forefinger. Another scrape cut through the quiet, and Nova spun, flinging the dagger toward the source of the noise. The blade landed with a thud, embedding itself in the frame of the terrace door and narrowly missing a mass of black as it escaped into the night.

Nova rushed across the room and peered out to see a raven ascending in the sky, past the glimmer of the shield Nox had recently woven around the Estate. She'd seen the raven several times since returning from the Gloaming Sea. *Thought* she'd seen it. Soaring above the training field as she ran drills alongside her uncle's elite guards. Perched atop one of the black stone spires that crowned the Estate when she returned from visiting the shops. Always there and gone before she could turn her head for a second glance. She'd begun to question whether it was real or a trick of her eyes.

Lowering her chin once the bird disappeared into the darkness, Nova caught sight of a bit of folded parchment lying at her feet. Its seal of blood-red wax was stamped with the insignia of a raven. Nova opened the letter to find nothing but a single black feather inside. Picking it up, she twirled the quill between her fingers as she spied a flash of inky wings against the moon's pale face. Though nothing was written within, the message from her father was clear.

Omen knew she still lived.

He knew where to find her.

And he certainly wasn't through with her yet.

ACKNOWLEDGMENTS

It is a wild exercise to be sitting down to thank the many people who made *Sun, Moon & Shadow* possible. My eternal gratitude to:

My beta readers Kristine, Kiki, David, Jaimee J., Vera, Christin, Krysten, Kara, Linda, and Michel, for your thoughtful insights and kind words.

My friends and peers in the Bookstagram/Writergram community (especially the Coven) for your support, your willingness to answer silly questions, and for sharing your own experiences with the rest of us.

My editor Briana Ozor for your expertise, your thoughtful suggestions, and your excitement about my characters and the world they live in. You are a gem!

My cover designer Rena Violet for taking my random ideas and turning them into truly gorgeous covers. You are so very talented.

All my friends and family who have asked me about this project and let me yap about it.

My friend Kara for your unwavering support of me and my writing, from beta reading to creating the most epic character art. You are a true girl's girl and writer's writer, and I am so thankful to have met you on this journey. I'm sorry the rest of the world now has access to Callan.

My darling Vera – I'm so thankful for you and our shared love of reading everything from sweet romantasy to unhinged smut. Thank you for loving Nova, Callan, and the whole gang as much as I do from the very beginning. Thank you for being my #1 cheerleader since forever, but especially while I wrote this book. Honestly, I may have given up several times if not for you talking me off that ledge. I probably owe you for marketing since you hype me up to every one of your book clubs. I heart you forever and ever amen.

My dad for introducing me to epic fantasy works like *The Hobbit* and *LOTR* when I was little, and for raising me to believe that magic is real. I love you!

My mom for setting an example as a voracious reader, paying out $10 per book report during the summers, and introducing me to *Outlander*. Thank you for reading (and then re-reading) my manuscript. You are the best—I love you.

My children who have been sweetly supportive of me ever since they saw the "Chapter One" heading on my laptop screen and exclaimed, "OMG, our mom is an author!" Please, my darlings, never read this book.

My husband for supporting me and this crazy idea from the moment I confessed I was thinking of writing a book. I know it has consumed me more than you probably thought it would. You are my best friend. Eu te amo para sempre.

Finally, to every single person who has picked up this book and has read it, reviewed it, or recommended it. Without you, this little indie author would be nothing. From the bottom of my heart, thank you!

ABOUT THE AUTHOR

Lorin Coffler has been telling stories with immersive settings and memorable characters since she was little. She is happiest when feverishly plotting future writing projects, losing herself in a good book, or scaring herself silly watching horror movies. She runs on perfectionism and iced coffee, and lives in the woods with her husband and two children.

Follow Lorin on social media to stay up to date of the release of the rest of the *Fate of Aemoria* series. She can be found @lorincofflerauthor on Instagram, Threads, and YouTube. To access book updates, exclusive sneak peeks, and bonus content, subscribe to her mailing list via her author site at the QR code below.

www.lorincofflerauthor.com

www.ingramcontent.com/pod-product-compliance
Lightning Source LLC
Chambersburg PA
CBHW020015120726
47903CB00004B/1293